The Age Of Aspiration

(Story of Indian Entrepreneurship)

Devinder Sharma

Invincible Publishers

First published in India in 2017 by Invincible Publishers

ISBN: 978-93-86148-86-5

Invincible Publishers
G-120, Sushant Lok III, Sector 57, Gurgaon-122001

Opposite Kasturba Ashram, Radaur Distt Yamuna Nagar, Haryana- 135133

Digitally Printed at Replika Press Pvt. Ltd.

Disclaimer

This is a work of fiction. Names, characters, places and incidents either are products of the author's imagination or if used then factiously. Any resemblance to actual events or locales or persons living or dead is entirely coincidental.

Dedication

In a sense, "Ajay Makes His Destiny" is not only the intellectual and spiritual journey of Ajay, but also a commentary on the of the Indian Software industry during the years 1998 to 2004. The book therefore consists of stories of hundreds of people engaged in software during those times –the engineers and managers, the entrepreneurs and investors, the teachers and colleges that taught software engineering and its management, the government officials and their contributions to the development of the industry. With their efforts, the industry became the fat cow, that made many milk it, the industry, and its caretakers prospered.

Officials of foreign companies who came looking for collaborations, the associations that ran huge programs in many countries, the capitalists and private equity investment firms, the quality certifying companies, the colleges and its outgoing professors, the officials in many government organizations both as buyers and regulators contributed. In the end all came for the skills and outfits that offered them and many other services and most importantly the humble programmer who mattered but often forgotten. Ajay could be me, you or anyone else. if there were scandals then not only were the Indians to be blamed as also the foreign who came for a variety of purposes equally culpable. He/she need not be in the software industry but any other successful and competitive industry, essentially driven where the purpose, the goal and efforts merge and became inseparable.

Covering a wide canvas is not possible without contributions from many. I have had the fortune of coming across many perceptive and opinionated people in the software industry in India and overseas and benefited from discussions with them. I met many lower level staff, their supervisors and all sorts of managers good, bad and indifferent, struggling to keep the body and soul together with a rare Ajay amongst them. Only the chosen ones become Ajay(s).

I met software people and their customers in the companies I worked for, at airports, railway stations and bus stops; in seminars, workshops and tutorials; during journeys, public discourses and private meetings with software evangelists and entrepreneurs; study of published works and lastly my personal experiences. Therefore, this work rests on the shoulders of many, whose names and faces have become a dim memory yet I remain indebted to them and my dues rest heavily on me.

Above all, I dedicate it to my wife who had the tough job of keeping everyone in our family happy and together.

I believe it is the soul in the books that connects with the readers'. Author's dedicate their work to known ones in their lives but I wish to delve into your mind through my book. Thus the most important dedication has to be you. I hope you have a joyride till the last word of last chapter.

I hope your agreements and disagreements pave a way to a beautiful journey here.

ACKNOWLEDGMENT

India is under a metamorphosis and so is the publishing industry. With 2,500 publishers handling 7,000 fiction titles in Indian English annually, the write-publish-distribute-read is a risky venture. Finding a good publisher to handle your manuscript is a challenge. Serendipity brought me to Invincible Publishers and I enjoyed working with Ajay Setia and his talented young team, who made what you are holding in your hands. I am happy to acknowledge. From our end, we have done the best and own shortcomings if any but the final test is the response of the buying readers.

Above all, I dedicate this book to my wife Kokila for her patience, keeping our family happy and together and filing in as the man of the house sometimes. She made the nine month drafting period a never to be forgotten experience.

Many a time you pick up a book and read the dedication, sure that your name will not figure there. This time it is though, I do not know your name or we have ever met. This book is for you reader. May you have many happy and joyful hours reading! If there are shortcomings and errors, I own up to them. Moreover, lastly you have every right to disagree.

TABLE OF CONTENTS

Prologue

It is time to look at the tumultuous years between 1998 and 2004 when the software and the call center industries were seeded. Once the roots deepened, its wake unleashed the entrepreneurial instincts of the nation. Today we see it flowering and its contribution to the country's role on the table of international relations that is undeniable and neither glossed over. It is indeed massive. Maybe, it is early to evaluate its contribution to the country's overall growth. Nevertheless, it is time to look at those years and certainly many more titles will follow. "Ajay Makes His Destiny" is different that software is incidental, no doubt very important and the making of Ajay is central.

This fictionalized journey of Ajay begins as a typical aspiring Indian of his time with the aspirations of young urban Indians of that time and still are. They were different from their older siblings. It would be appropriate to refer to this as the beginning of the"age of aspiration". The difference between aspirations and dreams is paper-thin. There comes a time when aspirations leads to a search for meaning of life and the reason to live no matter how successful one has been.

Is this all fiction? Is this all imagination? Is Ajay a convenient peg to hang the story? It is neither but a story made up of many true incidents with a literary license. There has been little effort to examine the history of the software world and that would be a gigantic task. Of course there have been numerous articles and news that kept appearing regularly and a few books that strove to explain the Indian software juggernaut and its inexorable march.

Today as the world notices the growth of the Indian software industry that some nations admire, few examine it to replicate it, others fear, and few try to stop its march. Some books have tried to analyze the reasons from hard and obvious to outlandish. "The Age of Aspiration" is in a sense fresher; there are no intellectual pretensions, no analysis, chronologies or debates here. It is the story of the software industry through the eyes of a simple lad who makes a success of his life. Many incidents presented relate to the story without getting deep into it but suffice to say they are true with a certain literary license. It is not how they came about or the caretakers who examined them but their simple portrayal. Indeed, there are reasons why they happened and the analytic thinking that followed the book does not delve into them. It is neither the right vehicle and detracts from the story of protagonist. The reader has the freedom to choose or provide them him or herself. There will be time when scholarly works undertaken to explain the phenomena, for it was definitely that.

The events of that time fit into the story of Ajay's evolution that should resonate with the dreams of the best and the brightest.

Many may question if there can ever be a Ajay. I think Ajay is very believable. There is an Ajay in every Indian or in fact in every person. Your Ajay lies bottled up in you. He resides in you. Ajay is crying to come out. Once you hear Ajay knocking inside you, as this book hopes to, you will experience a greater drive to bring your Ajay out. That story and journey will be entirely yours. You will do it all by yourself, happily.

Were there companies like the one Ajay worked for? Plenty and owned by big marquee names of Indian business and industry. Many of them could notsurvive. Software companies could spin wealth, prestige and recognition. It was an industry fiercely competitive and required hard work and great attention to detail, a genuine concern for people and little bit in the absence of a more precise word luck. Those who succeeded did so beyond imagination. Therefore, there is another purpose and that is to inspire you.

The horrible truth is that no matter how much we try to assume a role or a persona,it is not easy to carry it credibly for long. Everyone has his or her worldview and he or she is entitled to it. We cannot see ourselves objectively and reorganize others' feedback for us to merge withour sense of reality. Everyone knows this and we pretend it is not to be so. Yet it keeps happening.

If we focus on the Ajay(s) within us we will find there are some, which are so familiar, you know them intimately and it would be a shame to notlet them out. As they come out and you live them and live it under all circumstances, you become your own hero. Living autonomously in pursuit of your dreams, persevering them you will find the meaning of your life.

25th. September 2016

Dramatis Personae

In order of appearance

Ajay Khanavkar - The protagonist, born as Ajay Kamboj in 1969 changed surname to Khanavkar; referred to as Ajay throughout the book. Ajay means ever victorious and is a common name across India.

Seth Dhanwantrai - Proprietor of a pesticides manufacturing company where Ajay worked, who believes purpose of business is to take money where ethics or mercy is weakness.

Yeshayahu Kamboj - Ajay's father also called Yesha. He enlists in the army.During anti insurgency operations in Kashmir,he hadhis legs blown off and later commits suicide.

Nijjer Kamboj - Yeshayahu's younger brother who takes over as the head of the clan after his suicide and treats Ajay as his own son.

Madhab Bhuvan - An Assamese, Ajay's roommate in Delhi, worked in a company dealing with packaged foods and later sets up his own business.

Mythri Ramachandran –A Brahmin born in Tamil Nadu, spent her life in Delhi. Her father is a senior bureaucrat. She and Ajay were classmates. Ajay is attracted to her but shy to tell her. Her death was a phoenix moment in Ajay's life. She had a twin sister.

Mythili Ramachandran –Twin sister of Mythri pursuing medical course in Bangalore. After completing her graduation she enrolls for a master's course in pediatrics. Captivated by him and becomes her dream professional.

Pandit Badri Dutt Pandey - The priest of the family temple motivates the family to build a school. Tutored Ajay and his insight into life inspired him.

Ashutosh Sarkar - A software engineer from Bengal with entrepreneurial ambitions. He becomes Ajay's friend, helps him to get employed, inspires him to venture and becomes a manpower subcontractor to his company. Has a secret life.

Nigam - The renegade Indian software employee while on work in US jumps ship, becomes illegal faceless Indian immigrantand marries an American girl to become a legal citizen. He sets up a software company with a branch in Bangalore.

Kaveri Chengappa - A Coorgi lady who looked after Nigam's office in Bangalore where Sarkar was employed.

Mahesh Dagariya - Marwari accountant with accountancy and auditing practice and promoter of a software Company where Ajay worked. A perceptive businessman, many of his business bets turned good. Has an illegal business, aided and abetted by his wife Sushma.

Sharad Zende – A knowledgeable person employed as an HR Manager in a European MNC, minority shareholder in Dagariya's Company.

Kaanishk Venkataraman – The CEO and alternate director to Mahesh Dagariya. A Tamilian brought up in Bangalore worked with American and Canadian companies, ran the company's day to day operations.

Narasimhalu - An INFOSYS renegade helped the Company win their first Y2K project in the US. In his short time with Ajay leaves a deep impression on him.

Asha Ketkar - PRO of the company in her early forties, beautiful, stuck in an unhappy marriage with a past she was running away from. Comes close to Ajay and teaches him the

ways of the world and has a stabilizing effect on him. After seducing him, she finds the real Ajay and hero-worships him.
Ajit Ubhayankar - The MD of a Cooperative bank where Asha Ketkar's husband worked. The mastermind behind the scam in the bank aided and abetted by the powerful political wheeler dealers in Maharashtra. Helps Asha rebuild her life after her tragedy.
Sushma – Devoted wife of Mahesh Dagariya.
Alice Edward Smith - Member of the Committee of United States Postal Service charged to decide on the vendor for solving USPS's year 2000 bug problem. Impressed with Ajay's spiritual outlook, introduces him to her brother Ethan.
Mr. Ram Goopalam - The Chief Secretary of the Government of Mauritius who has the ear of the Prime Minister of that country.
Samir Arora –A second generation Indian in the US; ex IBM Sales Manager with a distinguished record who becomes Company's Sales and Marketing Director (US).
Andrew Barnaby - An Englishman, retired CSC Sales Manager becomes Sales and Marketing Chief based out of London and looking after continental Europe.
Alok Marathe - Ex TCS employee recruited to sell Company's services in the US and Canada. After an uneasy acceptance of Ajay, he was beholden to him later. His sudden disappearance effected company's business.
Agnes Barnes –An American lady who helped Ajay in handling Alok's car accident. She had worked with New York Times and became a meditation practitioner and a spiritualist.
Teja - The only child of Asha studying in an exclusive boarding school for girls; she is drawn to a Scottish nun learning strange mystical rites with overtones of lesbianism which her mother disapproved.
Sister Isobel - The Scottish nun who teaches in Teja's school. A mystic, becomes Teja's friend, teaches her how to read human

vibrations, and communicate and modify vibrations of others.
Kashung Kengoo -A Manipuri waiter at Asha's hotel; oldest and her trusted employee;an observant young man with a strong memory and uses gestures to make himself understood.
Vijay Bahula - Director of raids in the IT Department of Karnataka region. An IIM, Ahmedabad graduate with impeccable credentials and incorruptible.
Devin Hayden - American votary of Elegant programming eager to see Ajay start his company and made significant contributions in the start-up phase.
Stephanie - American of Italian descent and friend of Devin Hayden who built the website for Elegant Automation Software.
Lalit Jaiswal - The owner of a legal, auditing and management consultancy who took up the brief of setting up Elegant Automation Software.

Use of Ji - In the Indian culture, sometimes the word Ji is added at the end of the name to convey respect. Ji is an honorific used as a suffix in Hindi to give it a more polite tone and sometimes recognition. Ji is pronounced identically to the letter G.For example, if someone's name is Maya and we want to convey warmth and respect, we call her Maya Ji. However, in the Indian culture, no one will ask or demand that we add Ji when addressing them to show respect. It is up to us when we want to add the Ji after the name of the person. There is no compulsion that we have to add Ji to the name of everyone we meet and greet. Sometimes, speakers will simply reply with Ji as an affirmation of something someone says.

Chapter I
The Making of a Maven

A maven is someone who is dazzlingly skilled in his field or specialty.

Ajay trudged to the bus stop. Depressed, shoulders drooping he braved his way through the cold winds. Delhi had not seen the sun for a week and when by accident it peeped out, it was weak and without warmth. He knew intuitively that his chances of selection were zero irrespective of how he performed at the tests. He sardonically thought if he did the testsagain, the result would not change. He had set his heart on this job from the day he knew about the opening. He had done his best. Being cynical was against his upbringing. He rarely was. In challenging situations, he would chant *Hanuman Chalisa*[1]. This was one way to break

[1] *The Hanuman Chalisais a devotional hymn sung in praise of Lord Hanumanhas 40 verses (the words Chalisa means 40). Hanuman is a monkey and the foremost devotee of Ram (Ram is a major deity in Hinduism and the seventh avatar of God Vishnu and considered the Supreme Being). By reciting Hanuman Chalisa, the devotee invokes his strength, courage, wisdom, celibacy, devotion to Rama and the many other qualities. The Hindus believe that by reciting Hanuman Chalisa Remove sins we may have committed, remove obstacles in our undertakings, seek forgiveness of the sins we may have committed knowingly or unknowingly, get rid of evil spirits out to harm us and get the divine protection of Lord Hanuman and move about in the world fearlessly*

out of cynicism. He emerged hopeful after that.

The reality of influence pedaling and fixing was real and so pervasive that people took it for granted.

It was not rush hour. He found a seat near the window and gracefully slid into it, stretching his long legs, resting his cheek on the glass window he dozed. Yes, he was tired! He dreamt alighting out of a classy foreign car and picturing a fleet of cars lined up in front of an imposing building. Chauffeurs in their starched uniforms enhanced the prestige of their employers. Some leaned against their cars others trying to catch up on lost sleep sprawled on front or rear seats. A small group were smoking and chatting about their hard and unpredictable timings, lonely life, pain and distress of being away from families or the rising cost of living. Most of the chauffeurs were worldly people, thirty percent potential criminals.

He recalled the experience, which left a temporary impression in his mind, and for some time a cherished goal until he realized that this was a game of the idle rich living moment to moment and in comfort. It was in his phoenix moment that he looked at his experiences anew. A phoenix moment offered appraisal of what was hindering his growth and contours of renewal and rebirth.

The proprietor's right hand man had called him that afternoon. He requested him to stay back to deliver a package to proprietor's son. It must have been important to have him wait until everyone left and then collect the package. Advised about the delivery at the last minute, Ajay had no option but to wait. There was nothing in his life pressing enough that could not wait after office hours. When everyone left the office, the sentry called him from the reception. He gave him a package, instructing him to walk towards the traffic lights where a car would pick him. The driver would give him further instructions.

Ajay was excited but worried. Was it lawful? Was he doing someone's dirty work? Ajay had seen the proprietor's son a few times and even talked to him. As he walked past the traffic lights, a foreign car stopped in front of him and as he reached the car the driver softly queried, "Mr. Ajay? Seth Dhanwantrai *Sahib*[2] has sent me. I will drive you to the place where you have work to do. After you finish your work I will drive you home".

"Right,Sir", he replied politely, opening the rear door and stepped in clutching the package. Ajay felt it was some sort of film roll but knew that the 3 inch long and 1 inch thick cylinder was definitely something else.

After an hour's drive they reached a big three storied house silhouetted in light from inside. There were other houses along the street and suddenly the line of houses ended. Beyondit was empty, silent, and dark now. All houses stood in large plots of land. This house was a different one. Recently built, it was a massive structure of stone and steel with a geometric facade, which he likened to a jewel shining in the night. He stopped at the entrance and the guard after hearing him, asked him to wait and then disappeared. Returning, he ushered Ajay to a flight of stairs and climbing them he halted and waited in a long narrow verandah.

The door opened and a tall thin man with a bobbing adam's apple over a half-buttoned shirt stood in front of him. Ajay recognized him. He was Dhanwantrai's son. He patted him on the shoulder in a friendly patronizing way and Ajay handed him the packet. Everybody in the factory had seen him and rumor had that he had studied in America, married an American woman and only on the insistence of his father had returned to India to take over the family business. He was a headstrong person with his own ideas of running a business and lived separately and in hushed tones to guard his secret

[2]*A form of address or title placed after a man's name or designation, used as a mark of respect.*

life, which had something to do with money dealings with a firm in Mauritius.

Ajay could never explain how he mustered the strength to plead for a peek inside. The man put his arm over Ajay's shoulder and guided him in. As he entered the hall, blaring music drowned all other sounds. The music caught his attention while standing at the door and that fascinated and emboldened him to look in. Stepping in, Ajay disoriented for a moment wondered if he was in another country.

It was a scene he did not expect and likened it from the movies. It was neither a home nor an office but something like a banquet hall in a five star hotel, just like the ones he had seen in the magazines. . Inside a large room, was a 60 feet long and more than half in width circular stage about a foot high in the center. Over the stage, spotlights focused from the sides of the room.

The dancers' undulating outlines changed and looked different moment to moment. Visible now and lost the next moment as if frozen in time. The colours of psychedelic lights made the stage shimmer in new reality. On the stage, they were in a world of their own, frozen in dreamlike movements. The space outside the stage was in semi darkness where men and women were eating, drinking or just shaking to the music. His pulse quickened and his heart beat faster.

It would be difficult to converse in these settings. It looked weird. He could not pass judgement, as his experience of the new aspiring urban India was limited. That and his recent experiences of temporary jobs had made his determination to be someone important and to belong to the new resurgent India, firmer.

At one end of the room where food counters illuminated by the spotlights from the ceiling and warmed by wick lamps below the food containers. The party had just begun and most of these were empty. At extreme corners were two wicker trays filled with fritters and other snacks. The food being warmed but cooked in the kitchen inside and then dumped into the containers. When he familiarized himself, he saw about 40 men and women in small groups. Some talking, others dancing on the stage and the rest plopped on the few small narrow sofas. There was no other furniture and a few people standing against the wall as if not a part of this artificial setting.

The place smelt of perfume, tobacco and alcohol, and other smells of which he recognized hashish. Ajay was no stranger to it as most village folks in North Indian plains recognize the smells of ganja, marijuana and hashish. Consuming them was a part of the culture of these lands. He confirmed it through the smell. High on the walls were an array of concealed silent exhaust fans that expelled these smells. He wondered that the clothes and jewellery that the people there wore jewellery must be expensive.

People had to speak loud and lean into each other's ears for them to have a conversation over the blaring music. Ajay was unable to understand why the music was so loud that the people had to shout. It was a social gathering and with the accoutrements, a scene he had never seen before that captivated him. He imagined that when the food was on the serving tables it would resemble the variety like in extravagant weddings. His host guided him to a counter where only snacks were loaded and asked Ajay if he had eaten. Without waiting for an answer, he shoved a plate in his hands ordering him to eat. Others had snacks plates on their hands along with glasses. His host leaned towards him and shouted, "Never be shy in eating and sex. Those who are, remain hungry and unsatisfied," and taking a leave of him joined a group where he displayed his package.

At one end of the food table was a bar loaded with wine and alcohol bottles alongside several glasses. A bored waiter was cleaning and shining the glasses with a cloth and other paraphernalia associated with high-class bars. The waiters floated in and out in white liveried uniforms. They served snacks and alcohol shots in glasses arranged on plates with white gloved hands. Ajay worried that in the faint darkness he might pick non-vegetarian food. He then filled his plate with fritters and disappeared timidly to the corner of the room. He ate them convinced by their vegetarian flavor as he enjoyed the panorama before him. Indeed, here was something in reality that he could otherwise only imagine.

Then he saw a couple come out of a passage and joined the party. 'Probably there were rooms adjoining the party hall', thought Ajay. The couple seemed jaded. The man with salt and pepper hair looked the rich types and a girl much younger, tagged along. Looking at her clothes, yellow-brown hair and smudged make-up, it was tough to say that she indeed was an Indian girl.

He scanned the room and felt that everything there was exclusive. At least it looked like that. He could not fathom their price or utility but designed for ease of use and aesthetics. Their unusual shapes and colours, which he could just see in the dim lighting, screamed exclusiveness. They must be collector's pieces for he had not seen them in usual shops before.

Undoubtedly, these people spoke of wealth, power, authority and taste. Something he ached for and wanted, but in his limited life, he had not seen enough but with a belief that they were beyond him. He could not even dream of these riches to compare or articulate. A witness to this spectacle and the ten minutes he was there left a strong, albeit temporary impression on his mind. He could just blink and the pictures of that evening would flow past him. He would love to be rich and powerful like them.

This was his Green Park aspiration. He shared his

experience with his close friends. In the new aspirational India, was it an achievable reality? Making money, huge money and very quickly. Perhaps possible with a little bit of luck and right moves, believed some. Determination added some and others said it came by working with passion. Amongst his friends, no one had ever met even one super achiever. Newspapers and magazines spoke of young people making unbelievable successes. If it figured often and from all parts of the country then it might just be possible. The streak of individualistic ambition must have been very strong in the super achievers he thought.

Ajay broke out of his reverie. Dreaming was an acceptable way to come out and forget the cold hard world. Nevertheless, how often and how long could you live in a dream world like that? He could just not forget the hard cold reality of poverty that followed him like a shadow. 'Acknowledging what goes under the category of exclusiveness should not make it unattainable', thought Ajay.

Ajay worked as a Liaison Officer but hated the appellation 'Liaison Officer'. The designation of Liaison Officer grated him. An Engineer no matter what prefix or suffix would have made him happier. His job required him to deal with the Central Insecticides Board. He had to deal with the Board for payments, submitting of returns and arranging for inspections. All this was to ensure compliance to Insecticides rules, a set of archaic conventions. Officials of the Board could interpret these the way they felt like. Their rulings were the law and could make life miserable for the factory owners.

There were times when he longed for his village in Uttar Pradesh, the remembrances of which sometimes frayed at the edges, but he would snap out and his ancestral sensibilities would haunt him. Whatever happened or could happen, he was unable to forget his people and childhood that he spent growing up in his tribe. These memories gave him strength and centered his life.

He got his first science degree from Agra College and enrolled for a bachelor's course in Science. Before he could finish his degree, he found admission to the Institute of Engineering and Technology in Lucknow. This was a new college without much of a record of accomplishment. Admission still was not easy. His *Chacha* had to generate the right sort of contacts and raise the money.

Ajay graduated in Electrical Engineering with a first class. He could never explain what went wrong with his job interview with Bhabha Atomic Research Centre. It was a written test followed by an interview. Only one fifth of the candidates could qualify for the interview. Whereas he could not even answer simple questions on series and parallel connections of calling bells . Apart from that absurdity, he felt that he had done pretty well but the interviewer held that against him. He could not fathom how he could have made such a mistake. Ajay never forgot that episode. This sort of faulty understanding was not limited to Ajay. Engineering colleges set up during the 1990's and students who graduated from there were not comparable in quality from the older and stronger colleges.

There was a lecturer in his college who had been a brilliant student and hero-worshipped by his students. The tutor had joined the college after completing his graduate and postgraduate degrees. He obtained his degrees from the Indian Institute of Technology, Bombay a top notch engineering institute in the country and difficult to get admitted to. Circumstances forced him to take a teaching job in Lucknow. He was a down to earth person.

Living in Bombay, people refer to it as a city of dreams but mostly a city of slums where life is tough and forces people to be realistic.. As a faculty member, he told his students that the education imparted in the college would not fetch them great jobs. He advised them to move to bigger industrial towns and take whatever job they could get. Afterwards they should keep trying until they landed what they had set their heart on. Heeding his advice Ajay reached Delhi.

It was middle of January, the year was 1994 and Ajay was 23 years old. He had graduated in 1993, which was quite a usual age for engineers to graduate in those days. The biggest take away from his graduation apart from the basics of electrical engineering was the love for learning and the boldness to experiment that became a part of his sensitivities.

Ajay came from a village bordering Hamirpur town, the headquarters of the Hamirpur district. Derapur was his ancestral village where his family owned large tracts of land at the edge of the town. Ajay had heard about his ancestors who had something to do with Indian Mutiny or The First War of Independence. The nomenclature depended upon your political sympathies. No one knew what these worthy ancestors had done during the uprising and over the years, they had become heroes and a pride for the family.

There was a Hanuman temple owned by the family. Many years ago, when it was rebuilt rifles dating back to the times of the mutiny recovered from the temple. That was in the year 1940. The temple, half a mile from their house was in their agricultural fields and it had become powerful, meaning it had become famous and attracted worshippers from miles around. The family employed a full time priest. The monthly collections from the temple were enough to maintain the temple, for the priest's monthly salary and to earn a small surplus.

The family constructed a dwelling place for the priest and his family. The complex cordoned off from the agricultural fields. The position of the priest had become hereditary and no other priest was allowed to step in. The current priest was from the same family who had ensconced themselves in 1940. The priest was the third generation. He was wise and calculating and motivated the family to build an elementary school for the education of children in the neighbourhood. These arrangements gave strength and currency to the family's history, which in due course became preeminent for the area..

Not far from where they lived was the river Yamuna. Over the years the pollution levels kept rising due to discharge of effluents.. The pollution was proportional to the growing factories along the river. Industrial units set up rapidly in many parts of the state. Along the river and in the surrounding district, industries were sprouting. Ajay's district now called Ramabai Nagar, 150 kilometres from Lucknow the capital of Uttar Pradesh. Hamirpur, Jalaun, Etawah and Kannauj around Ramabai Nagar were all industrializing.

At some point, development works ceased. It was as if the ground beneath had begun to shrink. It affected everyone and everything including Ajay's family. Life became tougher and unpredictable. There were frequent conflicts. They were simple as well as complex due to unexplainable reasons. Tensions were between people, families and communities. Most were short lived but some simmered under normal life for long. They were simple people and forgot small injuries and arbitrariness quickly. Those that let them simmer inside often had horrible consequences.

Life and living was going through normal positive and negative events but their were big changes which few could grasp or its reasons. People were trying to adapt to the modification. The more they tried to come to terms with the changes the more they lost faith in sign posts that had given sanity to life - religion, community bonding, relationships, education, labour, concepts of service etc.

Hamirpur was no exception, similarily was also going through a subtle creeping change and Ajay was a product of this transformation. He could take it in his stride but the elders in the tribe were perplexed by this change. His father first and then a few other male members from his family trailed him into the Indian army. This was unheard in his larger family. Men began leaving their hereditary agricultural profession and taking up other livelihoods. He avoided joining the military in spite of persuasions. Derapur had expanded and their unindustrialized land was now a part of the town.

Agriculture was no longer straightforward. Expenses were mounting, labour became unreliable and expensive. Newer inputs like chemical fertilizers and shortage of river waters made use of irrigation pumps necessary. Electric supply was erratic. Intermediaries were ubiquitous and managing them had become complex. Ajay's father realized that old ways of agriculture would not be adequate and it would impoverish them further.

Ajay's family name was Kamboj and his name until high school was Ajay Kamboj and later changed to Ajay Khanavkar. Kamboj means a conch shell and amongst Hindus represents an elephant. The Kamboj family claimed to have come through Punjab during the time Sher Shah Suri was building the Grand Trunk Road. Ajay's great, great grandfather claimed that they were descendants of tribes in Iran. They had migrated to Punjab in the nineteenth century. Their migration continued with branches settling in western Uttar Pradesh, Madhya Pradesh and Maharashtra. They plied the trade of agriculturists or joined the military. No matter where they settled, the Kambojs were handsome fair and well-built people and retained their physical attraction and strength and Ajay was a true inheritor.

In 1940, the forty odd families set up their community living in their own houses with their fields within walking distance. Their communal way of living, emoting amongst themselves with common purposes and following the same set of unwritten familial rules transformed them into a clan or a tribe alike. Most of the houses were mud built and over the years some rebuilt in brick and mortar. Some had courtyards at the rear and a few had a clear space in the front and the largest ones, had both. There was a central place with a cluster of trees and some wooden cots and cane chairs, which was the community's meeting place. This was Kamboj Dhani, the stronghold of the clan.

Ajay's great grandfather was the *Pradhan* or the head of the clan. This was hereditary. The headship passed from Ajay's family to his *Chacha* under painful circumstances. This was destiny. The event had nothing to do with the change happening around.

His grandfather named Ajay's father Yeshayahu. His grandfather boasted that their clan originated from what is Iran and Iraq today. His ancestors worked with King Darius's armies. He was a man with a vision, industrious and hard working. A trait Yeshayahu imbibed from his father. He learnt that men whose lives were subject to moods were weak and by their moodiness frittered away the strength to win life's battles. His father heaped scorn on children of the community who were victims of temperament blaming their parents. Yeshayahu would remind the clan that good agriculturalists and military men were never moody. Those subject to moods succumbed to negativity and could not keep their minds positive. This shaped Ajay's thinking.

Ajay finished school at 17. He was a strapping lad. Fair, strong, sinewy with a prominent angular nose, long arms ending in big strong hands he stood just a little bit short of six feet in height. His mother, a beautiful woman doted on him. She would wake him up early in the morning and his father pushed him to their *akhada* [gym and a wrestling pit] to sweat for an hour. Exercising with weights made him strong and muscular and free hand exercises made him flexible. Ajay was the apple of the joint family.

Yeshayahu consulted his father and sought his advice on an alternate vocation and was advised to join the army. Entry to the army required a battery of physical and mental ability tests which he passed. He became the first in the clan to join the military. Due to a clerical error his name became Yesha Kamboj and the family name became Kamboj. Honour came to Yeshayahu Kamboj from his exploits in the army which was an inspiration for his clansmen. He inspired the younger ones to join the forces.

When Ajay was ten, Yesha's leg blew away in a counter insurgency operations in Kashmir and he had to manage with the pension. Medical interventions failed and he lived in pain. To escape his troubles, he started taking morphine. It became difficult to get through the government outlets. He started consuming opium because he could get it without any hassles. Seeing his condition worsening day by day and his helplessness, he committed suicide. In those days opium takers if they wanted to leave the world they brought it upon themselves through a deliberate overdose. After the passing away of Yesha, the headship of the clan passed on to his brother Nijjer.

Yesha realised the frailty of man and of life itself. He was witness to a mighty fall from a hero to the one who was ashamed of his presence itself. His awareness of his father was more from the tales he had heard than his own memories. Yesha after his misfortune, spent his waking hours on big *charpoy* (bed knitted of jute) alone. As the sun moved, he would shout and someone would come and change the direction of his bed. Ajay now wished that he had spent some more time with his father and his remembrance at times became so acute that his father's loneliness in his last days haunted him.

Nijjer, his *Chacha* had no children of his own thuslooked upon Ajay as his own son and perhaps even more. Ajay loved Nijjer whom he called *Bapu* but somewhere in some recesses of his mind was his father's face and his voice that would not leave him.

Depressed, tired and downcast he reached his bus depot an hour later. A bus depot was a large parking lot where Delhi state public busses parked.

As he stepped out, shivering in the bone chilling cold, he pulled his jacket closer to his body. The bus stop was full of young men and women like him from all parts of the country standing in queues, alighting from buses and walking around the bus stop. Most had come to Delhi to find jobs, study for competitive entrance examinations or to attend courses.

Every boy or girl desired to make money and tons of it. In some, the will was strong and their dreams bigger but most wanted to achieve at least what their parents had. Those who were qualified looked forward to a good life after their studies, which they believed to be their birthright. Who does not want to make his or her fortune?

This was not his ambition alone but of thousands of young men and women in big cities who had degrees. There were many with similar backgrounds if not educational attainments. Some in their 30's had four wheelers, booked flats, married and with bank balances and job security. This seemed to be the Eldorado of the millions of young Indians. It was a progression and as you began, *"Yeh dil mange more,"* [This heart wants more]

They lived in small dingy lodges and the more affluent stayed in *barsatis* [a one or two-roomedbed-sitter with a kitchen]. One hired a bed, that was that, and it may or may not have a bathroom and or a kitchen. What you did not have you shared with the others in the ever-changing temporary community.

There was certain camaraderie between job hunters and first time jobholders. If one was alert, he could always find out who was hiring. At the first level, an automatic grouping resulted. Like Bengalis, Punjabis, North East folks, Maharashtrians, South Indians etc. The next level presumed that there were regional specialties. South Indians made good accountants, Punjabis good salesperson, North Eastern girls' good sales women, Malayali Christians were suited for health related jobs and so on. This was no rule. Just that the youngsters from different parts of India gravitated to professions where their people were more in number. Apart from this, the number of aspirants exceeded far more than the jobs available. Engineers and doctors were not type cast though they were favorites. Clearing tests and one's background determined hiring. That was the thumb rule.

Ajay had spent two years from 1994 to 1996 in Delhi. After the first few months he was able to manage by himself and stopped asking money from home. A pushy youngster could always find a job. There was always some work available for sales representatives, supervisors, accountants, machinists etc.

If you were street smart, informed and a good conversationalist there were opportunities like smuggling gold and drugs or moving them for one city to another. There were requirements to front for corrupt government officials, transportation of illegal money, gigolos or a high-class call girls and many other job on the other side of the law. These jobs usually went through references and only those who fit could qualify. Once you expressed your interest or were referred or an employer found you, you were watched for some time and if found fit, invited.

Ajay reached his two-seater room, which had a small bathroom and a common landing with six rooms side by side and boarders shared two common lavatories. He walked up the staircase to his room wishing that his roommate Bhuvan was in. Ajay just wanted to talk with Bhuvan and let off steam. Bhuvan was three years older and an Assamese and street smart. Reaching the room, he saw the light coming through the window glass, meaning Bhuvan was in. Since the winters had kicked in, the sky was dark at five in the evening. An hour later, however the streetlights would be on. Before Ajay could knock, Bhuvan heard d the familiar sound of footsteps and opened the door. Ajay fell into the arms of Bhuvan.

They had known each other for more than a year and their camaraderie admired and secretly coveted. Bhuvan had rarely seen Ajay like this. Of course, something must have gone wrong. Bhuvan looked at Ajay's face. He guessed what happened but held himself back for Ajay to say it.

Ajay shared his experiences and thoughts with Bhuvan, even after knowing that he would not be comfortable with many of his ideas. . Such reliability and ease as Bhuvan was a sounding board and a shock absorber on which he could empty his angst.

"Now tell me what happened?", Bhuvan asked with curiosity.

Ajay removed his shoes and then sat cross-legged on his bed facing Bhuvan who was sitting on his own bed with back resting on the wall. In the 12 feet by 12 feet room, there were two cupboards, two small steel tables with steel chairs each against the wall in opposite sides. There was a small door to the kitchen. This was their digs and they paid Rs. 4,000 monthly.

"No, the results have yet to be made public. I know I will not be selected. I could read that Bengali interviewer's mind. He was leering and making fun of my pronunciation of English words, repeating them absurdly with a sneer. I was unlucky to get into the group discussion round with him again as observer," blurted Ajay.

"May be he had to select this Bengali fellow."

"May be, he was under orders," added Ajay.

This was a British electrical goods manufacturing company from Calcutta. It had set up a plant a few months ago in Faridabad, the industrial suburb of Delhi. For which the company wanted to hire two Trainee Production Engineers. Working for an old established Indian company with English collaboration was prized. It meant stability, possibilities of training and even a stint overseas. The company had the reputation of helping young men and women to earn good bonuses. The biggest plus was that the company was professional in its structure. The focus was on the job rather than pleasing the *Seth* [owner or high official in a company].

Ajay had begun his working life from the lowest level. He wanted to become financially independent as early as possible. He wanted to return the loan of three lac rupees that he had taken for his engineering degree from a public sector bank. The installments of which had to begin after a two-year grace period but he wanted to repay them at earliest.

His first job, where he stuck on for 6 months selling chinese and lookalike consumer products at traffic junctions, followed by selling books and encyclopedias in Dehra Dun for a month. He could not sell selling a single encyclopedia. Returning to Delhi, he joined his present company. His work was liaising with excise and sales tax departments of the Delhi Government. He did not like the job but the salary was not bad and the company was making money hand over fist. No matter how many times he represented to the management for a proper engineering job, "Yes, just please wait" was the stock answer. It was a tightly run ship and profit was the only reason it existed.

Ajay felt that his was a thankless job. Pushed by his management to get the best deal from greedy crooked government officials, he slogged at the unfulfilling job but soon got bored. He was cold and good, too good at that but the thought that he wasn't working as an engineer, rankled him. He was patient and listened to sad stories of his colleagues. They were domestic, hurt or stung by office politics, their children's problems and so on. In the end, he would get what he wanted from them due to his empathy towards them.

His people in the village called him engineer *sahib* and that made it worse as he considered his job as that of a fixer. It is a unique position, because it is very Indian and many businesses began to have one full or part time fixer. "The gradual and pervasive breakdown of integrity and honesty has added to the overheads of our businesses," was the common grouse. Ajay's company valued his hard work and impeccable honesty. He would receive cash rewards for his sense of duty, industriousness and tolerance It was high time that he wanted to change his job that would take him in the direction of a real engineer's work.

"I am so unhappy and wretched,"Ajay said. "I hate the false personal enquiries of government *babus* about my welfare. I have to keep bribing these bastards. Their selfishness is perhaps hereditary. They are shameless. At the surface they ingratiate themselves on you. The impression they want to give me is of being nice and caring but within they are rotten and stinking. For money they'll do anything. When I don't meet their expectations, they grin, offer false sympathies, but are willing to wait for their pound of flesh. I can smell their degenerated souls. Being shameless, they demand more next time."

"Yes that's a bloody fact. I know you too well," added Bhuvan. Bhuvan had completed a management course from

Dibrugarh University. He worked with a trading company, which dealt with a variety of products, most sourced locally and the rest imported. His company dealt in tea and other food materials like essences, spices, food preservatives etc. It was a conglomerate of many small entrepreneurial firmsor rather operations. Tea business was one of the largest and most profitable at the time. They procured tea from the gardens of Assam. After mixing different varieties they packaged them for others with their brand names. Many well-known companies dealt with them and had their export offerings customized.

Bhuvan had obtained this job due to the gratefulness of an old English tea planter in Assam whom his family knew for long. Bhuvan was a good worker and liked by the people in his company. As a purchasing assistant, he dealt with many sellers and because of his friendly nature, liked. "We also face same problems with government *babus*. I have learnt not to worry. How often have I told you that it is *kalyug?* Do not get too worked up with these thoughts. Be like the swan. You are in a cesspool and be like that swan who does not get wet or scarred."

"This culture of graft is pervasive. It is everywhere. Graft and corruption has not spared any place in the country. It started with the businessman demanding something outside the rule book, and he was ready to pay for that advantage. The intensity of illegality determines the size of the bribe," added Bhuvan.

Bhuvan went into the kitchen and returned with two mugs of tea and looking at each other, they enjoyed their tea. "Take your time. Refresh yourself. It will drive away your hurt and depression."

Bhuvan would get chests of high grown exotic teas from Assam and make smaller packages from the tea chest. He had been selling them for two years and had a loyal clientele most of whom would come to their room to collect. It helped him make good money, almost the same as his salary.

Ambitious and capable youngsters were always ready to shine. It was just a matter of opportunity. Whenever and wherever they could, they were ready to earn an extra rupee. There were ways of making some additional money made by selling goods, which were peculiar to a geographical area, guest faculties and private tutors, keeping accounts, giving performances using their skills as singing, magic, mimicking, or painting etc. Some even took on part-time jobs. Having multiple sources of income was becoming a dominant theme for the young urban Indians.

This was the beginning of a new aspirational India in the mid 1990's. There had been other such periods in the country's history where one felt that things would change but they rarely did. There was something magical about this one. The hard working urban youth consumed by the feeling that with a bit of luck they could reach the rarefied abode of "having arrived." It was all about material comforts.

As the two friends sat facing each other, they were aware of the shared bond and it comforted them. This bond had sustained them. It gave them strength to share and generate solutions to problems they faced. Being self-employed was a part of the great Indian dream. Bhuvan had achieved early.

"Don't you think Indians are the most colour conscious people?"Bhuvan asked abruptly.

Ajay wondered why Bhuvan should say this now. "Yes, Indians never learnt to accept and live with differences. When an Indian sees differences, he feels that he has the license to tag things as inferior or superior. We cannot live without making comparisons. No, it is what is. Nothing more, nothing less and that is how it is. This sensibility expresses itself in skin colour, place of origin, age, profession or trade or anything," Ajay explicated.

"Yes," said Bhuvan.

Ajay philosophized, "Differences add to life and not detract."

Chapter II
Ajay Begins his Career

Acknowledging his failure to find a job that recognizes and compliments his education, he could not come to terms with the existential vacuum gnawing within him. It comes from being helpless and the feeling of betrayal by unnamed adversaries. Not obtaining justice for which he had spent years of preparation and hardship made it unbearable. People learn street smartness facing discrimination or neglector not finding their métier, but Ajay became more perceptive. He also believed that being perceptive without actions is a wasted skill.

Amongst youngsters everybody was talking about software, call centres and programming. Only an obtuse youngster would fail to acknowledge where jobs lay and grew. Without understanding these narratives, one would fail to catch the new game. If you were in it, you had a future and if not, you were nowhere and consigned to ordinariness. This urgency gnawed his brain and tormented him like a leaking tap dripping drop by drop in the dead of the night. He decided to enroll for a part time software course.

Ajay consulted his *Chacha* in Derapur who was as progressive and forward looking like his father. Not to belie his elder brother's memory and his love for Ajay agreed to fund his computer course. His clansmen looked up to Ajay as one of their most educated living in a faraway city and destined for big success. The elders saw in his success the motivation that could spur youngsters in the family to fly out from their narrow confined lives. This overgrown village had nothing to offer them.

Nijjer Kamboj as head of the clan was conscious of his responsibilities. He was proud that his nephew consulted him on major decisions of his life. He looked upon Ajay as he would on his own son and Ajay reciprocated with love and reverence for this childless couple. Nijjer his *Chacha* believed that Ajay was born for big success, which was just around the corner. He never forgot to mention this to his family members whenever the situation seemed appropriate.

Whenever Ajay returned to his home, he always carried gifts for everyone. There would be a special gift for his mother and *Chacha* even if it meant spending half a month's salary.

The world was changing and Ajay acknowledged it more intuitively than hard analysis. He wanted to equip himself in belief, thought and skills to seize the world. It dawned on him that the dynamic forces sweeping across the country impacted the big cities more. Staying in his village was a losing proposition.

Ajay wanted to let go of the obsolete ways of thinking which was not in line with the emerging world. His *Chacha* remarked, "The village used to be full of matrimonial posters of brokers with their promises of perfect alliances *s*"and various medicines for common ailments including the ones that make you a sexual athlete. Now a new category of advertisements sprung up, companies offering vocational training- computer, television repairing, insurance, motor mechanics etc. We have to ensure that our people are informed and move with the times."

"I am happy, son. You think about the emerging world and new jobs. You are preparing yourself to move in that direction. Our children seeing your success will be inspired by your initiative and will follow you." said his *Chacha* admiringly

In the evening after supper, the entire group collected to listen to Ajay. Goaded by his mother and *Chacha* to inspire the youngsters and impress upon them the importance of education, he was keen to share information on newer opportunities that education was creating. Now and then, when someone went to Delhi for work, Ajay would take him around and show himthe sites. . They backed Ajay's explanation sharing again what they had seen.

Ajay explained about the course he wanted to enroll for. His Chacha in his down to earth wisdom suggested,"Choose the best institute, and do not worry about the fees. See it has a pan Indian presence and foreign collaboration. What do Indians know about computers and their teaching?"

He did just that, enrolling into a high profile and expensive computer institute. He opted for the system design course choosing C the hot programming language of that time. C was in vogue, most programming teachers knew, and taught the language. C is a general purpose, high-level language with strong programming features. It is popular and was loved by employers in 1998. In India C programing language provided a dependable entry into the professional programing world.

He cut an imposing figure in his class. He was the only engineer in the class who held a job, stately in his physique and looks, serious and hard working. Most of his colleagues were from science streams and middle class urban families.

Many, after constant job hunting with its attendant failures had come there. In some cases, families made financial sacrifices to have them study in these institutes as it was in Ajay's case.

The last learning class that Ajay had attended was over two years ago but he got into the groove soon and became an ideal student. He confided in his employers about his course and found some recognition with the caveat, "Fine, go ahead as long as you do justice to your job here," wishing that he might not leave in course of time.

Such courses were ubiquitous in big cities and their growth and popularity suggested that there was an undercurrent for software training shops to expand across the country and there were jobs that demanded this skill. He found a new respect from his proprietor when he began propagating the introduction of computers in the company. Seth Dhanwantrai, the proprietor listened to him, acknowledged his understanding and praised his exhortations.

Seth's son heard about Ajay and his advocacy for use of computers and sent a word that he would introduce computers after receiving a buy in from his father's loyal managers, which would take some time. His senior managers soon recognized Ajay. He was the only employee doing a part-time course. His proprietor knew that if he did not reward Ajay soon then he would leave. His son had warned him already.

Trying to understand and use a language without practicing was like learning to drive a car while looking at its picture and reading the manuals and therefore of no practical use. A programmer did not become skilled without extensive usage of language features outside classes and books. His tutors, after not being able to find suitable jobs ended up becoming teachers at the institute. The common wisdom was, if after studying in such teaching institutions you did not find a job you would gradually forget what you had learnt. It took two years to learn but being a tutor you were in touch with the language and still in the programmer's job market. If you idled for a year, you were unemployable as a programmer. Few of the tutors found jobs in companies while carrying on their training responsibilities.

He tried writing small programs but had no means to test them except at the Institute, where there was a clamour for computer access. Writing programs and not being able to prove them did not provide insight into the nuances of programming. Ajay was different. He would write two and even three different programs for the same problem. Success as a programmer required other skills than writing codes.

Ajay knew how the simple rural folks thought and lived. He imagined the rich and the money and wondered how they became what they were. He read about the powerful city autocrats and the hues in between. Ajay recognized that personal language skills and especially English language skills made noticeable differences to one's career. The very poor and the rich rogue's best know the harsh reality of life. Experience taught that the poor and uneducated could be exploited and driven while the rich were to exploit and thrive. The rich were invariably articulate.

The middle class educated, learned and possessing fine analytical sensibilities was still stupid and blathering. They refused to see the reality outside their job or vocation, spending their free time on bollywood movies, which were escapist song and dance dramas. Their free time pursuits apart from bringing up children were clothes, shopping, eating, TV and socializing. They were tragic sentimentalists. To be something, one must move away from these vignettes. To be able to do that one should try to pierce through the babble of familiarity, false standards and mediocrity. A good part of the Indian working class was mediocre. Sad but true!

He reasoned language conveyed thoughts, ideas and feelings influenced and wins people. Quality and conviction was a different matter. Writers like Rabindranath Tagore, Kalidas, Bankim Chandra Chatterjee, Premchand, or Sumitranandan Pant still read. Their works arrest you and are often awe-inspiring. Their work read even today, long after they have passed away. All had hundreds of contemporaries but no one cares about them. Any youngster who has studied for 16 years would encounter their names or would have read something by them.

They had a way with words and could draw or paint arresting incidents, pictures and create unforgettable dialogues with the felicity of words. It seemed natural that there could be many ways to write a program but there had to be one way that was elegant, purposeful and brief. Yes, he would love to become an 'Elegant programmer'. He had read about elegant programming in a book on styles of programing that he bought from the footpath. He was ready to do all that would make him one. One heard of a cat programmer, hot programmer, intuitive programming etc. and even sexy programmer but never an elegant programmer. These programmer classifications were common amongst computer people. He had never heard of an "Elegant programmer". Ajay determined to become one and it would take a few years for him to become one.

Students, he tried to befriend and discuss programming nuances disappointed him. They did not seem inspired and were afraid of stepping out of their comfort zones. Programming was programing and they preferred to live like automatons. His tutors could not satisfy his hungry mind and avoided discussions with him. They were afraid of their shortcomings or ignorance of being exposed. Without experimenting, practicing and analysing he realized he would be a bookworm like others. He wanted to go far, much beyond anyone he had known or read about. He concluded they could not help him as they lacked intellectual depth. It is not easy to delve deep in arcane subjects like program optimization, using fewest call expressions, replaceable software blobs without intellectual curiosity.

He recalled Jonathan Livingston Seagull, bored with the daily exertions of foraging for food choose to fly where none of his family had and when in spite of his elders' exhortations continued to perfect flying. He did not listen to his fellow seagulls and continued experimenting to be the best and experience the joys of ethereal flying. When he did not conform, they made him an out caste. He was happy being an out caste where he learnt to soar and felt the indescribable exhilaration of daring aerobic feats. He reached his limits and interpreted the advent of two teachers who appeared to take Johnathan to another world where gulls enjoyed flying and each was engaged in reaching and surpassing their own limitations, which he called sacred levels. He determined that waiting for the acceptance of his fellowmen was limiting him and the need to carry on alone in spite of all for his set goals was what meant the most. The life and learning of Johnathan seared his memory as much as his Lord Hanuman resides deep in him. It would become his talisman.

It was a strange that youngsters believed that the road to being someone was through education but without application, their education was worthless making them clerks or sales people selling toothpastes.

He was too shy to approach the girls who formed a third of the class. His life had so far been hard, never a moment to relax and think of the opposite sex. At 26 he was still a virgin.

There was this girl Mythri Ramachandran in his class. She amazed him with her impetuosity and intelligence. She could make the tutors look foolish and squirm if she wanted to. She could be accommodating and friendly when she wanted something. She always came well prepared for the class and everybody thought she was brilliant. She came from a South Indian bureaucrat family who had been in Delhi for long. She also had a twin sister Mythili.

Mythri had large expressive eyes, which seemed to be always moving, making her look busy. Her wide flaring nose over irregular lips did not make her a beauty in any way but she had an arresting presence. Her thick long hair gave her the south Indian look and her full plump crooked lips exuded sexuality. Her beauty lay in her asymmetrical facial contours that most Indians would not speak of as beauty but many would say arresting. She was tall for an average Indian girl, that made her delicate built with a small sized chest look like a waif.

She was dusky, not a desirable skin colour in the colour conscious north India. She had come to terms with that. Instead of finding anything wrong with that, she believed God-given personality traits she had inherited made her different and was not as worrying as most would have felt. She reasoned people covet what they do not have. She had learned to be proud of what she had and that was what gave her confidence bordering on arrogance.

It was serendipity that brought them together. They looked at each other in the class and acknowledged their presence and he admired her for her brilliance. There was an assignment tobe completed in groups. Receiving the task handed out, Ajay looked at Mythri, her smile beckoned him and soon he was in deep discussion with her. They shared work, assignments, and creating opportunities to be together. On one Sunday, she suggested that they have lunch together. Taken aback by her directness, he apologized that he should be asking her. She looked up at him and whispered, "Oh leave the formality and let's go!"

They went to a nearby restaurant that young people in that area frequented. Though crowded, they soon found a table near the entrance. It was a noisy place and you had to talk loud to converse. They finished their meal and made a quick exit. A few days later Ajay took her to a high-end restaurant. Alone, he would not have the courage to step in but with her, he gained a strange sort of confidence as if by association to take her in.

There was no hurry and soon they began to talk about their personal lives and she volunteered to get him homemade food someday. She cooked often and claimed to be an excellent cook. His taste and experience of south Indian food was limited to 3 popular dishes. After eating her well cooked south Indian fare, he could not help but agree that she was really good at it. It was tasty, spicy and though smelt different from what he was used to.

He shared his version of 'Elegant programing' with her. Being a compulsive knowledge gatherer, she admired and wondered what 'Elegant programming' could be. Encouraging him, she said that he was onto something grand and she would look up in her college library. This one narrative brought them closer and she felt that he was an insightful person and different from others. He had struck the right chord to deepen their friendship.

Whenever they met for the class, they found time to chat. Soon others began to wonder. Not only was Ajay a silent person but at least six years elder to her. What was going on between them? Quite often women find elder males more fascinating and worthy of their affections than younger men? What more could there be between them? Ajay and Mythri tried to unravel what 'Elegant programing' could be. Mythri would exhort Ajay, "Our assignment must be the best in class."

This was the first time when somebody would egg him

towards excellence. “Yes, Ajay we can do it,” she pushed him further. Ajay found that goaded like that was an exhilarating, which sent his self-confidence, soaring. Then one day she brought a book, which was making headlines, called, “In Search of Excellence.” Both read it and had something to say or comment on excellence. It was companies, their systems to encourage excellence and the few personalities they read about fired their imagination. This made a profound impression on Ajay. He began to seek excellence in everything he did and was grateful to her for creating this urge in him.

This was an incubation period in his life as his friendship with her brought many new ideas, feelings and confidence into his life.

Bhuvan returned from home and had a lot to speak about mountain climbing which he learnt from a Nepalese official. He had encountered him in the tea plantation near his house. They met a few times and the official told him tales about mountain climbing and about Nepalese porters carrying equipments and foods for professional white mountaineers, courses for young Nepalese on mountain climbing sponsored by the government and films on mountains, butterfly catchers and wildlife photographers.

What fascinated Bhuvan was listening about special tea grown in gardens over 20,000 feet and the life in those lands. They were across the border and knowing wine made from these tealeaves was fascinating. Bhuvan had bought a video tape and they watched the documentary together about Sir Edmund Hillary and Tenzing climbing to the peak of Mount Everest. To round it up they obtained a copy of Ernest Shackleton's discovery of Antarctica. They were up to their chins about adventure. Reinforcing Ajay's belief that a man could achieve anything provided he worked for it.

There was momentary excitement in their daily routines.

The three gathered one day to celebrate. It was a double celebration. Rejoice on Bhuvan's confirmation after 5 years of slogging. It was exploitation but one could do little about that. However, it gave him an added dose of security. The completion of Ajay and Mythili's computer course was the other reason to party. Their conversation veered around the new sunshine industry of computers and programing. The dream of a programmer was to find themselves body shipped to US or any other English speaking country. The purpose was to make money quick and return or if they could adjust, somehow stay back. Delhi for all its entrepreneurial culture and pushy people was not the happening place for computers in 1998.

Ajay dropped a bomb by saying, "I am determined to find a programmer's job and will not become a programmer tutor. I will try in Delhi for the next few months and if I do not succeed then I am determined to leave Delhi. I will go to some other city where there are real programing jobs."

Bhuvan asked, "Where will you go, Ajay?"

Mythri felt a twinge of remorse. She had begun to like him. She enjoyed his company and there was something original and warm about him. The more she spent time with him the more intellectual depth she found in him.

"I am determined to make my presence felt in the programing world," said Ajay.

"I want to go to Bangalore or Hyderabad".

"Yes, recently the papers had covered in a big article on Hyderabad as programmer's destination. People who reached there eventually found a job. A real programmer's job and I mean that. I think it depends on the person to go where he wants to for his or her first job", added Mythri.

"Oh! My sister is in Bangalore doing medicine," she said impulsively.

For Ajay and Bhuvan starting life in a new place was no big sweat. They had done it once and watched many friends doing it. Mythili felt that such a move was challenging for her. She remembered the preparations, contacting friends, acquaintances, and the many phone calls for her sister's admission to a medical college. Mythili was smart and scored well in the All India Entrance Test for the Christian Medical College where the seats for non-christians miniscule. The uncertainty was stressful when they landed in a new city without any job or a relative or friend to help..

Ajay felt the conversation float over them from far away and recalled Pandit Badri Dutt Pandey. He was the priest in charge of the family temple and had helped him in his studies in the evening. It was late winter evening and he sat opposite to Panditji who had come to review his school performance.

Ajay opened the difficult lesson. Panditji after explaining and simplifying it said, "Son, see how simple it is? Place the problem in your mind and think hard on it. Forget everything else, except the problem. Think tepidly and try to solve it. It is easy. Reduce all problems into its components, which are easy to understand. Anything easy is solvable. All have a solution"

Ajay had seen this happen to him from a tender age of twelve and remembering Panditji, "Determine. Determine with conviction". He grew up with a confidence and an ingrained belief that if he was determined enough then he could do anything. A great quality to pick before one is out of teens

Newspapers and magazines spoke of new India, changing with emergence of software companies and some spoke of a golden age at the threshold. It remained that - a mirage.

Competition in India is everywhere. It is tight and intense. Admission to colleges, getting jobs, starting and sustaining businesses, sports etc. are competitive. Everything else in our lives is competitive but there could be regulations to make it less severe and self-damaging. Severe competition need not promote excellence. Except in rare instances when the award is high while the claimants few. At times it brings in its wake influence pedaling or graft which are the seeds of corruption.

The vast majority eked out a bare sustenance existence. From the poor tradesmen and small entrepreneurs to varieties of middle class it was living hand to mouth. If you were a bit better off than your neighbour was, you have to spend a little more to maintain yourself. In the end, it was just endless running to remain in the same place and not to feel left behind.

Ajay remarked, "Stress and the consequent pain is a man's response to the unexpected. Agreed, change is a way of life. But, when unexpected vagaries confront us, we succumb to its suspense which brings anxiety."

"No, it is not the change but our response to change that causes tension. If we are confident that we can understand what the change can do then we can generate the confidence to manage it and there is no stress. But when we can't then it sweeps us and we succumb to the anxieties which we are not able to understand."

"We don't know what a particular change could be? Whether we invite it or become a victim of things happening around us we are afraid how it will affect our lives?" added Mythri.

Bhuvan shrugged his shoulders and admitted, "This is out of my depth".

"I think interpreting change is an important factor that determines attitude. If we accept the change or in other words accept life as it plays out in front of us, then anxiety disappears," hastened Ajay.

Mythri was in her elements, and no one except

Ajay knew what that meant and what it could lead to. She was impetuous. Ajay felt it was creating and responding to intellectual challenges. “If you think too much about the change then you create your own trap. Take life as it comes, stop philosophizing,”added Mythri.

Bhuvan added, “You will be in a trap when you allow yourself to wallow in despair and hopelessness! “

“Exactly,” said Mythri.

“Try to listen to the voices within you. We are so used to our own stories and our games and our secret conversations that we don’t give rest to our mind. We overwork our mind. If we learn to rest our mind like we rest our bodies, we will become superior. Superior in thought, feelings and actions in a way that’s difficult to imagine,” said Ajay coming out of his reverie.

“Yeah, there is strength in the argument. One could then be more successful. It would strengthen our mental and emotional capacities. Understanding of problems will improve and thus we can devise effective solutions,” seconded Bhuvan. “I know my mind is always thinking and running like an engine because it so agitated all the time. I become oblivious to what people are saying. I fail to interpret what the environmental cues are telling me and my responses become feeble only to douse the fire. There is no attempt to master my circumstances. I succumb to it”

“Elegant”, said Mythri. “I have heard that the power of now is the most powerful and sure shot success formula for business and personal success”.

“What are all these spiritual things?” Bhuvan asked.

Ajay joined in, “About being present in the here and now is definitely a powerful idea. Applying it is difficult task. I do not think there are any rules for doing it. One has to devise a way of living by this idea. Talking to wiser people will help”.

Mythri wondered, “These yoga and meditation teachers

and spiritual leaders will have knowledge of these conditions. If they have the insight then some will have techniques to handle these matters. Why don't we contact them?"

"Yes probably we should meet these people" Bhuvan said.

"This is not a yoga asana that if you do this once a day and its effect stays with you for the next twenty-four hours. This is a way of thinking and acting. Yes, meaning twenty-four by seven that is all the time. This is not a switch, which you can put on and off, as you like".

Ajay went on, "The first thing is to know your mood on continual basis. It is difficult but you can learn it. How can you do it? Often in the day, at any place or anytime put your hand on your heart. Decipher if your mood is positive or negative. Whenever you sense that, your mood is not good and negative it's time for action. A negative mood could be building or could be impending or it is on you."

"Brilliant! Well said?" Bhuvan and Mythri added in unison.

"Yes, it has to be all time, all places and an all weather sensitive thing", concluded Mythri.

Taking a deep breath Ajay added, "When you realize the negativity in you and allow it to persist, you are under an attack. It is not a simple assault; it affects us at a biological, emotional and spiritual level. It has serious repercussions on your health, confidence and on your relationships. To prevent that from damaging you, you have two options. You either throw it out of your mind, flush it out or replace it with the opposite set of feelings, ideas and thoughts. Your purpose is to replace negativity by a positive mentality. It is important that you don't allow the dark mood to grow bigger or get worse, harden which can be with you for days or more. Any problem that gets bigger becomes more difficult to handle later on."

Mythri concurred, "Yes. We seem to be saying the

same thing. Yes, I feel we all know our problem but have become ostrich like. We think that by ignoring the reality the troubles will disappear

Mythri added, "Yes, you all know this, the Gita says, 'Be even minded. An even mind is cheerful. An even mind can change our attitudes to our circumstances. Being positive is a state of being. Don't dwell on the past and neither think of the future'?"

"True Mythri Ji, you are absolutely correct" Bhuvan added.

Mythri protested, "Since when have you people starting addressing me with all this respect reserved for elders. You are building a wall between you and me. I do not like all this cultural substitutions"

Bhuvan had been following the discourse and was waiting for an opportunity. Bhuvan began, "In my Management classes, we learnt the Johari Window. Let me tell you about this concept. This is a tool using which we can know ourselves, increase our understanding of ourselves and become more sensitive. We can engage with others with intelligence. This way we can stop small complications from becoming bigger problems. It helps being in the present".

Mythri and Ajay looked towards Bhuvan indicating their interest.

Bhuvan launched into what he could think of as a lucid explanation, "Consider a house having four rooms. The first room is where we keep what we and others know about us and is completely open and called the free area. The second room is where those facets of our personality that others know lie but we are not aware of them and called our blind spot. The third room is our own private space about which nobody else knows. We do not share what is there with others and this is our facade. The last room is a mysterious one because here are the components of our subconscious parts. Neither we nor others know what lies there."

"We need to increase our free area so that it begins to enter into our blind spots and enlarge it. It is possible that some potential of our lives is in this mysterious room. It may be our calling in life and we might not be aware of it at all. If we knew that and made our career using this potential then we could be runaway success. By opening ourselves to these potentials, we can shrink and utilize the mysterious area and make our lives richer. As long as our private spaces are acceptable, there is no reason to let them remain private. By reducing them, we could adjust better to the demands of life. The idea is to increase the space of the free area and reduce that of others."

Bhuvan thought for a moment and continued, "You may wonder how this has a connection with the living in the moment? When you are aware of the thoughts and sensations arising in your mind then you are ready to determine how things really are rather than what they appear to be."

"Yes and being sensitive makes you integral to your environment," replied Ajay.

Mythri and Bhuvan silently acknowledged Ajay's extraordinary mental powers.

Chapter III
Becoming a Champion

Bangalore lies 3000 feet above the sea level. Given its altitude and the surroundings, it enjoys a moderate climate with distinct wet and dry seasons. It has more or less the same weather for three fourths of the year except the rains that increase or reduce humidity. An occasional heatwave can make the summer uncomfortable. Dry heat makes you miserable, though in Bangalore it is short lived. Of late, the weather is undergoing a systemic change with temperatures inching up. The city is paying for its unplanned development.

Ajay alighted at the City Railway Station and walked out to the street to face the full blast of summer heat. He had familiarized himself from his fellow passengers about Bangalore. If anyone was willing, he asked how to start his life in a city of seven and a half million, touted as the fastest growing city in the world.

May is the warmest month in Bangalore. It becomes hot and the locals look skywards for them to burst. When temperatures rise, sometimes it could go up to 38/39 degree Centigrade. If it remains hot for a few days' people expect rains to cool the atmosphere, giving the city the sobriquet air-conditioned city. Ajay was a practical man and not the one to trifle with these disadvantages. He alighted with one large and a smaller suitcase with a sling bag. After enquiring from a policeman he decided to take an auto rickshaw to the place teaming with lodges. Surrounded by touts he found a lodge that he felt was more cosmopolitan and took a room there.

In the evening, he walked around striking a conversation with a local person in the lobby of the lodge, people took kindly to his almost naïve and open trait, the stranger was forthcoming and sharing his knowledge of the IT industry in Bangalore in his response to Ajay's queries. He ran a canteen at INFOSYS, one of Bangalore's most beloved IT companies. He cooked meals for thousands of INFOSYS employees. He would transport the meals to the campus. Yes, he was making good money but the work had become tedious and he was committing more errors now.

Managing his inventory and logistics had become a nightmare; he explained how he was planning to computerize his operations. He seemed to be a good soul and promised Ajay to introduce him to someone who could help him find his way in the city. That would eventually help him to settle down and perhaps his newfound friend could even help him land a job as well. This well-wisher had come to meet a friend who was arriving from Bombay. The lodge owner was his brother and that bought him to the lodge.

He described Bangalore as going through a period of breakneck growth created by the IT and call center business. Growth brought with it consequent problems of unplanned urbanisation. Of course, the government was creating capital in the wake of MNCs. . Problem of overcrowding, rising cost of living, proliferating slums were putting tremendous strain on the city and its infrastructure. Pressure was on governance, law and order, transport, utilities, education etc. The infrastructure and civic services had reached a breaking point. Bureaucratic and political corruption had spread their tentacles across all government citizen interfaces and taken novel shapes.

The city had grown as much in ten years than it did in the last fifty years. The local government did its best to keep pace but after some time threw their hands up. . To move government bodies to work now required money under the table. It was like cancer that spread widely and largely. Local leaders caught in sleaze had neither the time nor the motivation to improve the city conditions.

The magnitude of slums in Bangalore was far less than the other growing cities in India like Bombay. Criminal but controlled alienation of land and displacement of people, epidemic and health crises, severe water shortages and sewage problems were impinging on the quality of life. The newer urban areas, which sprang around IT clusters, were relatively modern and better provisioned. There were water shortages here as well but people had learned to cope with water supplied by the tankers when the tube wells failed. Tube wells were dying regularly as the water level was falling with more and more concrete covering the land. The government filled their coffers from these companies but did little to make the city livable.

With a fifty billion rupee economy, Bangalore is and remains a major economic centre of the country. Karnataka had the misfortune of never having a good, strong development oriented government. People in the know speak of Karnataka government as *kar nataka* [do dance], a government that promises a lot and does little. Governance politicized schemes were seen through the prism of politics. There were three major and two small political parties and half the time of civil servants and their political masters spent in pulling the tails of their political rivals within and outside their parties. Where was the time for governance?

Ajay listened with rapt attention and volunteered, "Sir, that maybe the case but people in my profession from all the big cities want to come to Bangalore for work."

Writing the telephone number behind his name card, he passed it to Ajay saying, "Contact him, give him my reference he will surely help you." Wishing him, well they shook hands and parted.

Before settling for the night, he bought a local paper in English and was surprised to find a local newspaper in Hindi.

His new acquaintance introduced him to Ashutosh Sarkar, a Bengali engineer over the phone.. Following Ashutosh Sarkar's directions, Ajay reached his room in Koramangala the next evening. Soon they were talking like they had known each other for years. The Bengali expatriate community and especially the software engineers were thriving in Bangalore. There were no jobs for them in Bengal and the economy of home state inching downhill and all public matters acquired political hues quickly.

It was a strange sort of politics. At one level, it was the left versus right but overriding it was the real politics. It was any narration that brought votes or created pocket boroughs for the politicians. Though meant for the cause of the common man this competitive politics actually impoverished them. Droves of good educated ambitious Bengalis left Bengal for greener pastures like Bangalore.

Bengalis are proud of their culture. The current set of cultural and political leaders were unable to comprehend the stalwarts of yester years. Bengali intelligentsia seventy-five years ago thundered, "What Bengal thinks today India thinks tomorrow." The new commissars of Bengal failed to provide the inspiration and leadership the youth needed. Along with their migration, they carried their little Bengals in their heart.

They set up cultural associations, stuck together and made annual visits to their hometowns. Marrying amongst themselves and the sounds of Bangla added to their comfort. The older ones who had been here for twenty years or more set their roots deep in their adopted city. Their children loved to call Bangalore their own and their Bengali sensibility replaced by the new pan Indian aspirations.

Sarkar was in Bangalore for the past four years and knew the job scene well. He had bought into the new emerging India and his Bengaliness was notional. He had succeeded well after his engineering degree from Jalpaiguri Government Engineering College where he gained entry after clearing a tough entrance exam. The college in spite of its reputation had many jobless alumni. Advised by his father, a retired bureaucrat who had spent most of his life in Delhi and Bombay, Ashutosh landed in Bangalore with a letter of introduction to his father's friend.

Ashutosh a good footballer with strong life skills and a combative approach to life quickly found his feet. He was now earning Rs. 30,000 a month, a handsome salary at that time. To reach at that level he had changed two jobs. His local guardian and his parents, who came every year to visit, kept pressurizing him to marry. He was sure that amazing success was around the corner and marriage after that would be the right decision. His value in the so called arranged marriage market would go up certainly by then.

Ashutosh entertained entrepreneurial dreams. Which successful software engineer did not? The stupendous success of IT companies spawned in the last four years fired the imagination of many a software engineers. It was an old dream that had begun forming in his mind while he was still a student.

In 1998, the software industry in Bangalore was concentrated in Cunningham Road, Banashankari, Koramangala,

Jayanagar and the upcoming areas were like the Electronic City and the Software Technology Park. There were some small pockets in other areas but not important. Each pocket could be providing employment to a few thousands. Entry into big established companies like TCS, WIPRO, Texas Instrument, Blue Star and others was tough. However, it was fair. One had to go through number of competence tests. *Sifarish* [influence mongering] did not work here, explained Sarkar.

Yes, these jobs were prized. They provided chance at foreign travel, opportunity to save after living well, professional development and confidence. Working in these companies, the engineer's became articulate and prized catches in the matrimonial market. In short, it was the doorway to join the new class of ambitious and successful Indians – the aspirated Indian.

"As an outsider, without a degree from an esteemed college and small town mentality one takes whatever job comes one's way. Use that as a base and maneuver through the thickets of the job market for entry into top-notch companies. It is very possible and hundreds follow this route. Earning is a matter of destiny. If willing to work hard one would make lots of money anywhere," advised Sarkar.

Ajay realized that this was the only route for him. One does not look at the teeth of a gifted horse. Yes earning well in spite of being blessed and desirable qualities was never certain. Competition was intense.

"One never stopped trying and aspiring. I know a few fellows from my college working in big companies and I earn more than most of them. Their jobs are nothing more challenging than mine. The exposure in my present job gives me stronger and better experience."

"There are plenty of computer and tech jobs. From manipulation of old programs and databases to regular software maintenance and development. Most jobs with big companies are about moving data from one to another environment or writing small programs to work with data from databases or reengineering existing softwares. Majority of them are foreign clients. Sharp experienced computer people with the gift of gab can access these jobs. From the source of the job to the eventual worker there are many levels," explained Sarkar.

"Quite often it happened that a middleman holding the baby with time running out was happy and relieved to dump the job to an articulate Indian's promise." The Indian entrepreneur would receive a third or a little more of the outsourced price the larger part eaten by the middlemen."

"Oh, this situation must be creating many opportunities for different people," said an astonished Ajay.

Sarkar was equally astonished that a rookie could think like that. Sarkar nodded, "Yes, for the employee, the employer and the entrepreneurs. Everyone gains".

"It creates Sattva[3]."

"Getting employed by the top notch companies is

[3] *In the phenomenal world, there are three gunas, energies, or qualities, which are in constant struggle, opposed yet complimentary. In the process of evolution sattva is the essence of the form, which needs realization, tamas is the inherent obstacle in its realization and rajas is the power by which the obstacle removed and essential form created. Sattva, tamas and rajas are the three energies responsible for all manifestation in the phenomenal world. Illustrated as: A sculptor decides to make a mud sculpture of a horse;the idea or the inspiration to sculpt inspired by sattva;he gets a lump of clay which represents tamas; its formlessness is an obstacle which he has to overcome. There may be some tamas in his mind when he thinks - This is going to be lot of trouble. It is going to be difficult. Why should I make the effort? The force of rajas comes to his aid in the form of the sculptor's will to conquer his lethargy and the difficulties inherent in his medium. By generating sufficient rajas the obstacles presented by tamas will be overcome and ideal form of sattva will be embodied in the tangible clay figure. From this example, it should be obvious that all three gunas are necessary for any act of creation.*

Sattva/Sattavic/Sattva Guna: Sattva guna is characterized by qualities such as - confidence, joy and happiness, satisfaction, modesty, nobility, enlightenment, forgiving, contentment, disposition for faith, forgiveness, courage, renunciation, purity, compassion, exultation, satisfaction, rapture, humility, purity in all acts having for their object the attainment of tranquility, righteous understanding, indifference, brahmacharya, freedom from expectations, equability, truth, righteous, purity and the like and whose conduct is marked by these virtues are said to be wise and possess correct vision merit based. While in others it is basedon your knowledge and networking and the rest on matters like your origin, referrals, personality and salary. The number of jobs in the other companies is many times the top companies," enlightened Sarkar.

"Others, means not the top companies."

"You mean what the programmers do in these companies are different from the jobs that programmers do in top companies?" queried Ajay. He, not yet had the finer nuances of conversing in English.

"No they are not; as a matter of fact half the programming jobs in the top companies are similar to the ones in other smaller exporting companies. Just, that the number of middlemen involved in securing these jobs is less and jobs can be bigger and sometimes call for skills which are a bit rare to find in the candidates that apply," clarified Sarkar.

"These jobs are in companies with a long tradition of creating and managing software that may have come from many sources. There are integration issues. The good thing is that these software jobs come with supporting documents. Documentation makes it easier to understand the code and its design, logic and algorithms. Also, you interact with knowledgeable people."

Sarkar meant all those companies with revenues greater than Rs. 25,00,000. In the year 2000, only 50 companies fell in that range out of two thousand. Over the next decade the picture would change beyond imagination with 4,000 companies out of twenty thousand.

"Are these jobs complex?", asked Ajay.

Ignoring Ajay, Sarkar added, "Look my friend, the first thing is to sell your skills and get opportunities to learn at the same time. Without a job how will you test your skills and add to them?"

"In the end how fast and error free code you can

produce is what matters. Speed and avoiding rework is the hallmark of a good company and company productivity is sum total skills of its engineers. This determines your strength as a programmer. If your code is often, more than good and you have excellent public relation skills you are a marked person. You will be known in your company and perhaps outside as well," added Sarkar.

"Of course only one fifth of the programmers reaches there and become known. Once you are there, then it opens doors to many opportunities. Opportunities come to those who look for them and these opportunities could be huge and exciting. They could do wonders to your life that you can't yet imagine."

"You do not find opportunities strewn on the roads. You have to look for them, you have to seek them out and even create them. Those who are seeking employment opportunities have to be part of employment networks. Those who are business minded have to become members of business networks. You have to be a member of appropriate network. Networking means being in regular touch with people well informed about developments in their networks. These people tell you what is of interest to you without any fuss"

"Yes, Sarkar my friend I realized early that getting anything requires you to be good in many things. Being truly successful and becoming, somebody of importance, requires apart from programming skills, knowledge of English language and being articulate. Without this you can only go so far", confessed Ajay, opening his hands six inches apart.

Sarkar ridiculed those political and self-styled nationalist opposed to the English language. They had no world view and articulated pre-independence values that had little relevance today. They were sort of luddites taking the country back to poverty and superstition. "All important positions in government, business and industry and are with

English knowing people. They are eloquent and aware of what is happening in the world. Can you imagine a lecturer teaching engineering without knowing English? How can a secretary in the government converse with foreigners in an Indian language? Highly esteemed and respected, they are the ones who run the country. They are today's elites," concluded Sarkar.

"My father thought like this and drilled this reality into my sister and me. He never wanted me to remain in Bengal. Which was becoming impoverished and losing its soul. The malaise begins when the state ceases to listen to its intellectuals. Then it spreads to the common people who forget that there is a government and they try to settle disputes amongst themselves or through vigilante groups, which ally with a political party. In today's world it makes people sharper but spiritual out castes."

Ajay nodded in agreement. He was not able to put his feelings in words but warmed to this thinking.

Sarkar gave directions on how to return to his room and assured him that within a week he would be able to get him into his network. Of course, that is the basic requirement but it also depended upon his luck and the way he played his cards. Sarkar's kindliness was inspiring. Ajay needed that as he had just weighed the anchor. Leaving home far behind, he had burned all his boats and now challenged. In his supreme confidence, he knew there were no effort, no sacrifice and no hardship he could not bear for the success he had set out to achieve.

As he rode the bus, he could not forget Ashustosh's words, "The software industry is a great leveler. Educated, experience and imbued with a strong venturing spirit was all that was needed to become an entrepreneur."

Was it possible? Ashustosh had offered examples of some of his friends who were thriving software entrepreneurs.

Of course, there were failures but unlike in other industries a failed software entrepreneur still had increased marketability and was preferred in job interviews.

~~~

Sarkar had another life unknown to all and he zealously guarded it. Now in his moment of soul searching he was letting go of this life and assuming a new honorable persona of altruism. Sarkar was employee in a small company owned by a person called Nigam, an American of Indian origin. Nigam had gone to the US for an on-site assignment with Tata Burroughs, an Indian computer company. He like many other Indians in the US on work visa believed that life would not be complete unless he found permanent residency in US. That was difficult if not impossible. He did what thousands of Indians in the US do. Abscond!

That one night Nigame slept in his house like he always did and early morning he had cleaned out every shred of his existence. Putting the key, the rent cheque and other dues in an envelope for the lessor, he deposited it with USPS and vanished. There were thousands like him. They came from all parts of the world that did this. Once the period of visa expired, he became an illegal alien. It was no big risk and most found ways to live safely as illegal expatriates until they obtained citizenship.

During his stay in the US, he came across a struggling American entrepreneur who was glad to hire him at less than half the wages. It was a temporary arrangement and both knew it. Nigam was happy to get lost until he found a legal way for permanent stay and his employer, a good engineer.

Six months later, he appeared as the spouse of an American girl and became a regular citizen. This was his dream. A desire that became stronger and deeper with time. After a few years of working in the US, he set up a software company of his own like any other enterprising Indian
~~~

American and was in business. Unlike many other non-Indian software entrepreneurs, he had a support system in India. There were his colleagues from Tata Burroughs who considered him a smart operator. He forged ahead setting up a software development company in Bangalore. They were willing to work a deal, which involved money, partnership or move to the US. When they found he was unable to or would not yield the promised, they started avoiding him.

He was unable to find a loyal and a committed manager who was professionally sound and could control from 14,000 kilometres away to look after his operations. He had set up his company in Bangalore as he felt it would be cheaper than Bombay where he had worked for Tata Burroughs. He tried working with two managers. He was not pleased with any of the two.

Having Indian operations enabled Nigam to compete on price, which his American competitors could not. His competitors could not match his prices, delivery schedules and quality. In spite of low prices, his margins were better than any one of them. His ambitions were modest like most employees turning businesspersons.

Nothing succeeds like success.

He had tried everything to attract the right manager for his Indian operations. He tried search agents and recruitment firms. They not only short listed expensive and demanding candidates but the search firms were torturously slow. He made trips to interview them but unable to find a dependable and an efficient manager, his incessant search and frequent calls brought in Kaveri Chengappa.

Kaveri was a rich corgi woman with an engineering and management degrees and four years of experience with a big company. It was through a referral system of Tata Burroughs he found her. He called her to London for an interview with all expenses paid. For her it was an out of the ordinary, a big thing. Nigam hired her as the manager and offered her a minor partnership and she agreed to invest an amount that was equal to her year's salary. She felt happy, as this was a sort of investment, which she could retrieve after two years at agreed formula.

Kaveri was efficient, effective, and dominating. Nigam soon realized that she did what she felt was right and brooked no interference from him. She refused his offer to open and manage a marketing office in England. It was still the best arrangement he ever had. She brought the staff strength to forty. Whatever projects entrusted to her, she had them done well and delivered in time.

Nigam suggested her to send Indian engineers to non-English speaking countries and she was game for it. To sweeten the extra duties he agreed to profit sharing. It was not the money that motivated Kaveri but the adventure in doing so. She agreed to support him by shipping young software engineers to places other than US. Once she agreed, she started looking for engineers to ship to other countries. Most were unwilling to go to places like Norway, Denmark, and Brazil etc.

It was then she came across Ashutosh Sarkar. Sarkar had reached a dead end in his job and looking for a change. They met a few times and she felt he came across as a trustworthy person, experienced with hiring talent for on-site assignments and she was eager to develop an on-site business. An on-site business was easy money. Sarkar convinced her to look for cerebral types and those challenged with adventure. They would be more likely to take up such assignments.

Sarkar became her employee and did his best to recruit engineers who were willing to go to exotic places. First, it was two engineers to re-engineer databases of an electric supply company in Turkey. Once it began the requirement of engineers by the Turkish company kept increasing. In 6 months, they had a dozen engineers moved to Turkey. The next labor assignment was shipping engineers for offshore drilling in North Sea for the Norwegian government. Then it was Chile and later Brazil. Business was flourishing.

Smooth talking Sarkar became Kaveri's lover. She had an apartment of her own and an imported car and their trysts moved from hotels to her flat. There was pressure from her parents who were coffee planters in Coorg to marry and settle down soon. Her father was the owner of a coffee plantation. He had spent his life working with Life Corporation of India moving from city to city, until he finally retired.

Repossessing this estate from relatives and hired managers was a tough and daunting exercise. Hr father was successful not because of his efforts but circumstances. To reclaim his property he had to part with a third to his relatives who had managed it for 35 years. He knew the pain and anguish of losing a property so large that it took an average person to walk for an hour to traverse it around and return.

The corgis marry amongst themselves and especially estate owners encouraged alliances within their circle only. Her marriage into a coffee plantation family would be the best thing and if not he was ready to sell the estate. He could after selling, move to Bangalore and live the life of a rich retired man of many interests. He was an outstanding manager and awarded as such by the corporation three times. Apart from this recognition he was meticulous and a handson manager who tolerated no nonsense.

At this point in life, he had no appetite left to take care of the property which after his death none of his children would look after. Corgis boasted that Coorg was the of Scotland. Their evening drinking sessions in Coorg would be about politics and personal lives. During these conversations, the Coorgis compare their district to Scotland, assert about their physical prowess and army, whisky and estates. They were proud of their warring race an epithet given by the British. Along with this military honours, hunting and love of sports would find an outlet. He would miss these evenings in Bangalore.

Kaveri knew that well. She was beginning to get restless. Amongst her friends and classmates, she was a super achiever. She needed to think and sort her life lest she get stuck. There was much to look forward. She was 33, just crossing the Indian suitable marriage age for girls. Messed up, her private life in tatters and she realized Sarkar who was uncomfortably deep in her life unreliable and selfish and she had to jettison him to become whole again. Sarkar was still no marriage material. She could not do what she wanted until she got rid of him.

She made up her mind and told him that love and romance was over. He could stay in the company and run his enterprise as long it did not conflict with his duties at the company. Sarkar had no choice. In real terms, it was a win-win for both. He had learnt many things about domestic and foreign software business. He could work for her and earn a good package and could set up his own business clandestinely while she was free to lead her life the way she wanted.

There was the ever Damocles' sword hanging over him. If she left or another manager replaced her or if the company closed down then the arrangement may not continue. He had to find a way to get out of this problem and that required growing his business or creating another arrangement. This story no one knew about and for the world, he was just a Manpower Sourcing Manager.

Locating the bus stop Sarkar had told him about, he caught the bus going towards his lodge. Riding in buses came to Ajay naturally. Bus travels sharpens one's instincts as well and you get to know your terrain quickly. He could quickly find out who could be helpful and who would not in a crowd. As he alighted from the bus, he watched a couple of his age hailing an auto rickshaw.

He thought of Mythri. He had felt for her, liked her combative spirit and sensed her desire to escape from the small insignificant life she was leading. She was far feistier than many women were her age, well informed and adventurous. Ajay remembering her said to himself "If she moved out of her comfort zone she would be a big success and discover herself. She was twenty-one and imagine what she would be like five years later. Working, she would be a thorough professional, smarter, more confident with new ambitions. If she married, she would be a demanding wife and a strict mother". How he built such a picture of her he could not explain. Perhaps it had shades of what he wanted her to be.

Being two thousand and five hundred kilometres away from her in a new city retiring for the night, the silence nudged his loneliness to think of her. He began to ask himself did Mythri attract him. "Certainly", his heart and mind said. He walked to the public coin operated phone outside the lodge office. He found the right coins, he was never out of them due to his bus journeys, and dialed her number. As per their protocol, he disconnected after two rings, and rang again. She picked it up. He told her about Ashutosh Sarkar and their conversations. He wound up expressing how he missed her and she responded that so did she. Was he all right, yes he was? In four minutes, the conversation was over. They wanted to keep it that way, for amongst the middle class India, mixing of sexes was unwritten but regulated and propriety had strict rules.

He lay down on the frayed bed sheet in his cubbyhole. He was happy. He was optimistic. Dreaming of peacocks mating in his village he fell asleep.

It was the rainy season. There was a lull in the weather.

The rains had ceased and children came out of their homes to play. In the thick shrubs, sprouting from a water puddle was a flock of peacocks and hens. The male opened its plumage spreading its shimmering tail as it swayed the shades of blue and green took on indescribable brilliant hues. A big male peacock was strutting amongst a flock of peahens vigorously shaking his tail and howling to attract a female. The females must be selective, thought Ajay that he had to go through this ritual with great eagerness and energy. Perhaps the shape, colour and the richness of the plume was the core of attraction for her. Maybe it indicated its ability to produce healthy offspring.

Things were beginning to fall in place.

Chapter IV
Ajay's Angst

Employment into the top software companies especially the larger ones were through tests and interviews, which were fair and unbiased. The lesser-known and smaller companies relied on informal networks,word of mouth and depending upon urgency of need on normal channels. Competition for good engineers was intense. The main source for throwing the net and identifying potential employees were advertising, personal contacts and staffing companies who never had it as good. Most companies whether big or small used informal networks for recruitment. Few admitted that. Companies rewarded employees for referring good candidates.

Some well-meaning computer professionals created networks that broadcast opportunities. Many IT workers, freshers and the unemployed followed these networks. Employment networks operated by kindly souls from major cities and computerized. There were weekly tabloids listing job opportunities in all areas. The government had a weekly paper providing employment opportunities. The computerized network offered tutorials on computer related matters and hints on tests and interviews.

Members and supporters of the IT jobs networks released employment opportunities as soon as they came across one. Not all were 100% good. In the fast changing world of openings accuracy and timeliness was of utmost importance. The system had a way of filtering the real from the bogus. It could also receive corrections and updated them where possible. It served a purpose and contributed to the IT culture of the city. The network provided information that would be helpful like selection procedures, interview panels, expectation and the reason for the vacancy etc.

Companies that encouraged referrals found out that as soon as a need arose it was in the network. An award awaited an employee for getting known person to apply if selected. Those who referred acknowledged and awarded on the outcome. At times people who were leaving, referring another candidate eased their departures. Ajay was happy that he had gained entry into a network in quick time. Oral networks supported the job networks. There were many.

Within a week, Ajay attended two interviews and joined a sweatshop, which Sarkar thought as a company with future. Located in a part of the city that was not within the IT belt, with a continual churn and neither the place and nature of work exciting. The company had two large halls one above the other in a by lane near the city's best known gardens, Lalbagh. When the top floor fell vacant, the company leased that and when Ajay joined it was getting organized.

What others may like to call a sweatshop and avoid if there were options did not deter Ajay. Such descriptions were of no concern and he remained unperturbed. He thought it was destiny. Sweatshops also made money and paid salaries. Some made much more for the number of employees it employed vis a vis the bigger and better known companies. Sarkar assured Ajay that salary was regular and timely. Ajay wanted to be a good worker and win the confidence of his employers, as he had always done. Apart from the culture and power structure, the place had few rules. It was laissez faire unlike the big process oriented and professionalized companies.

Ajay was ready to work beyond normal hours including off days. He had those traits that come naturally to people from small towns. He would seek and wish his supervisor before leaving. He was easy going and willing to share efficiency and productivity ideas and being helpful to anyone came instinctively to him. At times, he would put them as a mail that he marked to everyone in the Company. Resented first by the senior managers and spoken of as toadying by others but in course of times many people looked forward to them and a few congratulated him. It was never beneath his dignity to learn from anyone. He felt nice extending support to others.

Ajay was always positive and careful about personal qualities. His attire was neat if not flashy or in tune with the times. Where engineers avoided documentation, he liked documenting. These are small matters but when followed consistently they create an image. Ajay did not follow these prescriptions for political reasons. He believed that such behavior creates *Sattva*. Creation of *Sattva* made *prakriti* supportive of him. In a few months, he was beginning to get noticed and known.

Amongst spiritualists, not only in India but in many other countries there is a belief that *prakriti*[4](nature) ordered

---

[4] *The word prakriti means 'nature' or natural form of any material or its constitution including the human body, while pra means the 'beginning', or 'the source or origin' and kruthi means 'to perform' or 'to form'. Put together, prakriti means natural form or original form or original source. Everything material in the universe is composed of five basic elements called pancha mahabhoothas. These are Akasha or space, is omnipresent and all pervading, Vayu or air, is responsible for the movement of all types and is vital for the existence of all creatures, Teja or Agni is the element of energy or heat, Jala or aapa in water is the element of water essential for sustenance of life, Prithvi or earth is responsible for structure and bulk of the material and Akasha is the substratum to the other four elements and due to its presence one can separate or differentiate material.*

men, matter and affairs such that *prakriti's* interests advanced. What the higher powers decree must happen so believed the ancients of most religious persuasion. Nevertheless, what a man does and makes for himself he can modify, alter or undo. The first is fate, the second destiny. The former comes from outside his personal ego and the latter from his own faults. The evolutionary will of his soul is a part of the nature of things but the consequences of his own actions remain even though slightly, within his own control.

The number one goal of nature was preservation followed by the "Law of Natural Recompense"[5]. Thus, nature was unfolded by a set of rules. Rules like gravity, attraction, thermodynamics etc. were pervasive and supported Sattva wherever it was trying to sprout.

A contraption or a machine which conserved energy made less noise, occupied less space, had fewer parts, was more likely to succeed than a similar one over designed. Getting that right balance was a challenge. To rise to the occasion was acquiring insights into software engineering. All may sell but genuine users preferred that what was straightforward and easy to use. The Gods, Indians believed were likely to support and help those who allied with nature. Being an

---

5 *The law of recompense also called the law of reflection. This is because every act finds its reflection back to its doer and every thought reflected back to its source, as if by a vast cosmic mirror. According to Paul*

Brunton, the idea of recompense carries too strong a moral implication. Hence 'recompense' is too limited a meaning to be the correct equivalent for the word "karma." In karma, we find a key to many puzzles of contemporary history. It is a doctrine, which warns us that we have prepared the cocoon of our present lot largely by the thoughts and deeds spun out of ourselves, during bygone earth-lives and the present re-embodiment. Now the doctrine is as applicable to the history of whole peoples as to the history of single individuals. There is another modern explanation that says that the sum total of good or bad, growth and decline, prosperity and stagnation, success and failure or opulence or poverty and the like in given interests, or amongst people or in a country or a large geographic area etc. does not alter much year on year. A section enriches itself at the expense of some other section, blooming vegetation in one part offset by drought in the neighboring area and thereby the total remains unaltered.

ally and a friend than being antagonistic with nature made people and their efforts successful. This applied in the same measure to human relationships. He had seen this happen repeatedly in his village life from his education and now he was observing in the professional world.

The Company management learnt to cope with regular departure of employees. In spite of this malaise in software, company managements had met time and quality deadlines most often. The company's prized customers were Karnataka State Police, New York Police Department and the Nepal Industrial Development Corporation. All government customers and their contracts were excellent ground for developing ambitious software engineers.

Ajay learnt his work fast. He had to pick records from large databases one by one and then manipulate them. Ajay would laboriously go through the files and extract marked data connected at first and often second level and conduct consistency checks adding them to his working file. As per logic and instructions, he removed those that were unnecessary. Later he ran computerized testing, sometimes-creating data manually and at other times generating data using computer routines. This required creating test data a laborious repetitive job following a set of rules. There were issues of completeness and comprehensiveness that required swapping work. It was repetitive, tiring and boring.

Apart from using tools, where possible there were always manual tasks that still needed. It was the manual, time consuming and boring jobs. He began to see patterns and suggested development of tools for handling manual tasks, which foreign clients avoided and contracted to Indian companies. Ajay was quite happy doing that, and some of his ideas implemented that increased productivity and quality.

~~~

There was a new India in the making. This India comprised of young men and women who had no connection with the freedom struggle. They did not know of the begging bowl that India's leaders carried or the socialist dreams of Nehru. India at independence or a century ago was something in history books. The students bemoaned that they had to study historical facts for a few marks and wondered how it would help them in their career. They could not understand the reasons why the current leaders were reluctant to let go of these legacies. They complained that Gandhi's India became corrupt due to the unnecessary need and power of the wayward. They were everywhere. Over the last fifty years, the perverse were found in all spheres and walks of life.

The small corrupt seedling found fertile ground and grew to a gigantic banyan tree. This spread its branches covering everything that was vile and distasteful. Ajay believed that the freedom struggle, the satyagrahas of Gandhi and the flights of idealism of Nehru, the large industries created and owned by the government laid the foundation for the new India. Most of the people he met at his work or outside were only worried about their present lives, their needs and their environment. Past was of no practical use to them.

The decade beginning with 2000 was of the new generation born in the late 1970's and 1980's. They were more aware, informed and of independent thinking than their parents. This generation had read and heard about the materialistic societies of China, Singapore, Thailand and Malaysia. They felt it was their birthright to expect more and the government should deliver. Soon their parents began to feel the same way. Fed on false promises of a better tomorrow that never arrived, they joined their children in castigating the government. They spoke of the government in jest or snidely.

"What was the government if not the politicians,
~~~

bureaucrats and public servants?" queried Sarkar once. The new generation had seen them become rapacious, rent seekers and venal by the day. Seeing everything purchasable, they found idealism as a weakness. Sarkar justified, "Today what matters is I, me and myself. What is in it for me?"

The youngsters of this generation believed hard work and education would itself lead them to opportunities and from there to a definite better tomorrow. If the government could not supply let the private enterprise do, if religion or false morals became obstructions throw them out, if culture erects constraints loosen them and if we have shortcomings lets work around them. This was the new generation looking for jobs in factories, offices, malls, in transport, tourism, hotels and the new jobs that modernizing economy creates.

If jobs and opportunities are only in newspapers and magazines and not on the ground, the social transformation that a developing country needs will not happen and progressive forces pulled back by wrenches of obscurantism and superstitions. Both Ajay and Sarkar belonged to this generation that wanted success. Sarkar was typically of this generation. Ajay subscribed to the values of his conservative parents also.

Corruption is deep rooted and pervasive in the country and only shows signs of exacerbating. This scourge is spreading like insidious cancer and at one end shaking the roots of the country and at the other ushering a jungle raj where each man gets away with anything as long as he can. Corruption was steadily eroding personal, moral and legal foundations set up painstakingly by the earlier creators of India.

Everyone knew that the atmosphere was corrupt and forgiving. The majorities don't even know when they had been corrupt and the environment pushes them deeper into the quagmire. There are few men and women with the moral fiber and ethical backbone to see through the charade of pragmatism. The country needs many more people with a broad vision.

If ordinary citizens lie in court and police fabricates evidences for any reason, it is corruption not for private gain but out of misplaced sense of justice. A public official channels money into his private account or gets favors for his kith and kin in the form of jobs or assisted education; a political party secures a majority by stuffing ballot boxes with false votes; a police officer fabricates evidence to secure convictions; doctors and hospitals connive and refuse to testify against a colleague who is negligent in an unsuccessful surgical operation that led to loss of life; a judge delays a case at the behest of the weaker party or favors it for some gratification in the name of misplaced justice; a sports trainer provides his athletes with banned substances to enhance their performance; the list goes on. We are not seeing the woods for the trees.

Ajay was doing fabulously well. Dagariya sized Ajay and marked him out. He planned to bring him into his inner circle. Reflecting, "It was a good selection. He would make strong contributions to the Company's growth," he confided to his wife Sushma.

The Company had three partners. Mahesh Dagariya, a Marwari Chartered Accountant who owned sixty percent, Sharad Zende, a Maharashtrian who was the HR Manager in a European MNC and bought his experience of staffing and then Kaanishk Venkataraman, a Kannadiga who ran the operations on day to day basis and was also the CEO of the Company.

The Company was getting regular business, solvent to pay salaries within the first week of the following month and known in good light the city. The directors and senior managers knew how brittle their company was. Actually, the owners were staring at a revolving door company but had no idea to ensure longer tenures and erred by promoting supervisors and managers who had proven themselves extraordinarily loyal. There were months when the corporation took overdraft to pay salaries. Generally, settled quickly, but there was an occasional sticky period. The Company purchased real estate in the form of flats, commercial spaces and land whenever it had a surplus. Independent thinking employees and smart professionals rarely entered the inner circle where power lay and affect the working of the firm. Ajay was given Rs. 4,000 raise after three months. He was unmindful that his proprietor groomed him for a responsible position quietly.

Ajay was not dumb and he knew that that there could be a catch with all the quick appraisals. What it could possibly be it was that he could not deduce. He dismissed these dark thoughts and interpreted it as Hanuman ji telling him to be grateful and work harder.

Bhuvan and Mythri were happy that Ajay was doing well. Ajay thought Sarkar too would be happy at his modest success that the first break immediately landing in Bangalore had him. Gradually Ajay become confident of himself and once during a conversation, "Mythri dear if you want I can get you a job in my Enterprise," he raved. Meanwhile she had resigned herself to taking up a tutor's job. She was getting more uptight. Confined to her home, she felt her love interest fading away and Ajay far away could not understand that. For the last dozen calls Ajay kept popping the suggestion: come to Bangalore, come to Bangalore, and come to Bangalore.

Ajay, a virgin at 26 as many middle class urban Indians are at the time of marriage, there were islands where morals and mores were changing and no different than in the prosperous countries in the west, which commentators liked to label as 'the new India'. The old India and the new India were in conflict and created fault lines. There were Indians who were virgins beyond this age but to be so in a land that gave the world Kama Sutra and Ananda Ranga was anachronistic. It was unfair.

Thrown amongst girls who were half the workforce at his company, Ajay was a witness to amorous games. When they came, became noticeable and could not be able to hide their sexual dramas told in not so hushed tones. The management tacitly encouraged such behavior. The management perceived these games as an involuntary barrier against employees leaving the firm. No one could prove or disprove this theory. Dagariya's wife did not discourage, rather liked such conduct and she had a strong influence over the Chairman, her husband.

Well built, fair, good looking and sympathetic listener Ajay was a centre of attraction for girls. Because he was oblivious of their interests, it increased his attractiveness and the management's trust in him. He became all the more exciting and attractive.

The first girl in his life was Mythri and he wanted her to be his last. He admitted that it was not that his feelings for her were not romantic. The reality was that he just did not have the courage to express them and he felt that neither had she encouraged him. This was not true because he failed to catch her tentative suggestions. Once he talked about her to Bhuvan who in his worldliness said, "She is an Indian girl, she will take time to open up to such feelings"

It was during their telephone calls when they discovered the love for each other. Their love was natural and pure because both had few opportunities and its manifestation soft and understated. For Mythri it was reflecting the mores of their parents. There were suggestions and invitations from office girls. He found ways of keeping distance from them and rumored that he had a sweetheart tucked away in Delhi. The word went out that he was committed to her, and true to his nature, he could not be but faithful.

Ajay and Mythri developed a new protocol of talking.

Her parents, especially her father was protective and suspicious. If he was to know about their frequent telephoning, he might get livid with rage and spew his anger on her. They feared that he might go to the extent of cutting them off. This was her belief but she did not know that her parents knew all about their hushed conversations. Mythri once had mentioned that her parent's marriage was a love marriage.

Her father and mother distantly related, met the first time at a wedding and nobody noticed their natural interest in each other. They began to come across each other more often at community functions and got familiar. As soon as Mythri's mother became of age, her parents began to search for a groom. Mythri's mother maneuvered so that matrimonial talks between their parents began. When her father's parents came with a marriage proposal, she agreed instantly. Coming from a conservative and tradition seeped Madras to a progressive and corrupt Delhi was a cultural shock for her mother.

Ajay would call Mythri every alternate day.

He was with the company for six months now, Diwali was approaching and he looked forward to meeting her and his family in Hamirpur. He had met Mythili her twin sister a few times at Bangalore Christian Medical College. He told her about his impending visit to his village. Of course, he would be meeting Mythri and he would love to carry any message or anything from her for her sister. Over the next few days before he left for home, Mythri avoided Ajay.

From their conversations, it appeared to Ajay that Mythri never indicated that Mythili had shared her feelings about him though the sisters were supposedly close. He wondered!

Whereas Mythri was thin, reserved and protocol oriented, Mythili was plump, bubbly and laid back. Perhaps being away from her parental scrutiny and living independently made her that way.

He could have bought a second hand motorcycle or his company would have given him a loan but he was happier in sending money back home and used the city's notorious bus services. He was always on the move and never had the time to think or plan.

His worth in the eyes of the people who mattered to him soared high. There were many office girls ready to share their breakfasts and lunch with him for anything. He was not interested. He splurged a month's salary buying gifts for his mother, Chacha and few kids of the family and then of course for Mythri and Bhuvan.

In November, he boarded the train for Delhi.

Within a few hours of reaching, they met. She was waiting for him outside the restaurant they had previously frequented as classmates. She was standing alone with a scarf covering her head. She looked thinner and tired. Seeing her, Ajay sprinted across the road and caught her hands and led her inside the restaurant. They found a table with two seats and quickly took it. Smiling at each other and small talk punctuated with oh's and aha's though there was a lot to talk but they could not establish the flow. After their order came and they finished, she began talking.

Ajay was dumbfounded when Mythri informed him that she was very sick and fighting for her life. With a storm raging in his heart he goaded her, "why did you not share with me?", "what made you silent about your problem when we talked so often?", "hiding from me, why?", "failed to trust me?"or "you thought you would be ok in a few days?", and with many unarticulated barbs his voice trailed away into helplessness and disbelief. Mythri listened to his diatribe with swollen eyes and holding her tears, she burst into torrents of sobs that shook her shoulders and chest. He got up, walked behind her chair, and held her shoulders shaking her until she turned her face to look into his eyes.

They just forgot they were in a public place and that people were staring at them.

He gestured the waiter for the bill. Cutting the silence that had long followed, Mythri spoke about what she had been dreading to get it off her chest finally. "Ajay my love, I may not live for long," she said in sobs.

"I am suffering from third stage of cancer."

Ajay felt his warm sweat oozing out of his body. It was the beginning of winter. His body heated up and then his knees began shaking and hitting each other. Holding a chair adjacent to her, he steadied himself and sat down. Seeing him swoon , a waiter rushed carrying a tumbler of water.

"Really, things are bad. I have gone through hell. Our conversations were all I lived for. I was so happy to hear of your successes. Your voice spoke of your feelings for me. Nothing can take that away from me. Not even death!" She paused and continued, "We talked about very common things but your way of sharing with me and speaking of hope and of our future was a world I made for myself. With time this world became as real as you are sitting in front of me. Your phone calls were the highlights of my day," confided Mythri.

Her talk was so simple, straight forward and piercing. Knowing that the worst could happen and learning to live moment to moment with the inevitable as if nothing had happened was no ordinary strength. This was not carelessness but making a pact with the Gods to let her live as if nothing had happened. "There was nobody else except Mythili to share my problem with. We made a pact to keep this away from you," cried Mythri.

"Later my parents came to know about our conversations but they never came in between. Rather my mother wanted to know about you." She confessed that these matters though trivial receded in her mind and she would have loved to dwell upon in happier times. They were important for a few hours but a day later, they became small inconsequential things. Her cancer was eating her.

"Mythili knew of our love and how many times she would tell me, 'Baby you are very lucky. What a fine man you have found for yourself, I am jealous of you.'"

"It soon became a dream for us and Mythili was always afraid when she met you lest she gave their pact away. She liked you tremendously and teased me why I do not share you with her. Mythili did not have the courage to meet you, as often she would have liked, in case she said something that would break the dream. This is in short my story."

It was some time before Ajay could return from his emotion-scorched reality. They left the restaurant and took an auto rickshaw to Buddha gardens. This was a place where romantic couples found privacy. There were garden formations, which served this purpose, and if there were other amorous couples, it added and brought on a sense of security. No one cared or bothered what occupied others.

They found a lonely place where they spent the next two hours. These moments would be a part of Ajay's forever when he returned to Bangalore. He could only recall them as a dream. Their first kisses lying in each other's arms and cuddling was natural and spontaneous. It seemed they were just finding themselves having met a year ago. Emboldened she said, "Let's forget the world for what it is." His sensibilities were aflame. His hands sought her flesh wherever his hands could stray and she cooperated. After a long bout of petting and necking, they left and took an auto rickshaw to her home.

A day later as he tried to reminiscence he realized that his desire to come closer to her and holding her was not sexual in anyway.

On the way she described her medical treatment

and how she feared and hated the repeated chemotherapy sessions every twenty days. She had to undergo six. Nearing the ward the smell of chemotherapy was nauseous. Each session tired her and nausea would continue with vomiting for the next two days. Once these were over, she underwent another six rounds of radiation. She spoke of how she had lost her long tresses that was the sure give away of her south Indian features and questioned her will and determination.

Born and brought up in Delhi she spoke Hindi as any *Delhiwala*, same fondness of street food and mannerisms. She described how her father became busy coming late from work and her mother cared for her. Her mother was not a strong woman in physical sense and timid in her emotions. The treatment had continued for six months and she had looked after her in the hospital and at home. Mythri could not comprehend from where her mother drew the strength to be by her and become her 24 by 7 companion. It was her mother's affection that she would remember and carry to her till the end knowing that she never could give that to her child. When he shared her condition with Bhuvan, he replied laconically, "Destiny."

She felt the strain of Going to the hospital and returning after many hours Mythri was lucky in a sense that she had the attention of the best cancer specialists. Her sister Mythili would get letters of reference from her professors for expert opinions. God was kind to her for she received favored attention in an overflowing sea of patients. Her father's government health insurance scheme covered her entire treatment. There was never any concern for the expenses. Her mother allowed her to talk to her friends and especially Ajay. Bhuvan knew about her problems and got her a telephone handset that she could carry to her room. Talking to him was what she lived for. She pressed his hand brought it to her lips and waved him goodbye and ran into her building.

~~~

Next day Ajay took a bus and reached Hamirpur in the evening. His mother overjoyed to see him kissed him on the side of his neck as she always did. Her kissing was the expression of love mothers gave their sons in their tribe. She kissed him many times until he felt embarrassed. His Chacha came and fussed over him. In the evening, he and his mother were at his Chacha's house and other important members of the group were there. Chacha had hosted a big dinner. He carried the gifts for giving away and his mother and Chacha did the honours. As the evening wore on, it became cooler and answering questions was tiring him. He could not stop until his mother summoned him and his Chacha called an end to the evening.

A week passed and he enjoyed the love and attention from his people and a day before his departure told his mother about Mythri. As tears welled in his eyes her mother hugged him and said, "Son, this is the will of God. In this matter, what can you do? What can her father and mother even do? Neither can her doctors do much."

"This is the gift of God and only he can take it back. If God decides, then nothing will happen to the girl. When God takes it upon himself then whether you give or do not give treatment is beyond the point"

"All that you can do is to make your girlfriend have full faith in the almighty and be happy whatever happens"

"Yes my dear son if possible you too pray and seek his blessings for her."

On his last day in Hamirpur, another function organized where he talked about his new city, Bangalore that he had come to love. He promised to host people of his community visiting Bangalore. He told them that there were as many engineering and medical colleges in Bangalore as in the whole of their state. The numbers of educational and
~~~

vocational institutes were outstanding and people from all parts of the country came there for learning. Prodded he added, "Even from far away countries."He would be happy to help them get admission in those colleges.

In the end he was subject to the same old counsel, the refrain was his marriage. After all had spoken, her mother said that she would start looking for a bride for him in a few months' time and by then he would have entrenched himself in Bangalore. After she would get him married, she would go to Bangalore to settle them up. Ajay told her looking at his Chacha that her coming to Bangalore and his getting married were not connected events.

He was in Delhi for two days, which he spent mostly with Mythri and Bhuvan. They tried not to think about the worst and those were some of their happiest days. Their close and warm camaraderie brought out the best. In their togetherness, they instilled in each other vague religious beliefs. They believed in strange notion that when God accepted your prayers you could get away with anything. If the Gods decreed, nothing was inauspicious even dreadful medical reports. Only Mythri knew that her end could be any day.

He returned to Bangalore on a sunday afternoon and talked about Mythri and her disease. Sarkar, shocked at the sudden turn in Ajay's life sympathized with him. Then he met Mythili and they wept in each other's arms. At night when he lay down to sleep and unable to control his emotions the sound of the hoofs of wild horses running in his brain were dreadful. He did not want to think and surrendered to the deafening sound of horses galloping and seeking exhaustion and fall asleep. When he woke up, he realized he had overslept and rushed to the office.

He was unable to get restful sleep. Sleeping had become troublesome. He would often wake up in the night and tried many stratagems but sleep evaded him. He had forgotten what it was like to face the day after a restful night. Mythri's conversations tinged with sadness that sought no sympathy but her pain were haunting. He longed to hear her voice and waited for it for hours. It affected him in a way that he could not comprehend normal things, which began to tell on his physical health. Her efforts at levity were not natural but forced and both knew she was hiding her anguish. There were times he wished to reach out and help her and other times he wished to run away from her and avoid listening to her voice. Waking often in the night and oversleeping became a worrying pattern. He sometimes reached office late unlike being the first one in earlier.

People began to notice his changed behavior. Those in his team felt that something awful had happened and his silence did not help rumors flying. One day Ajay entered the conference room, surprised that it was silent and no one was there. He believed there was a meeting scheduled and he had come to attend but that happened yesterday. A programmer saw him seeing the notice board outside and shaking his head. He had selected him and the programmer looked up to him. Then he told him the invitation was on his table and he may not have seen it. Ajay kept quiet. He reminded him that his and other team member's progress reports were on his table for review.

This lapse of memory happened again and when his colleague pointed it out, he kept quiet. Then it happened again and this time he put up a weak and almost a ridiculous defense insisting he was sure of time and place. Of course, he remembered the memo but the contents. His teammates did not want to create unpleasant situations with the fear his his angst burst forth. They wanted to help him to open up and share his problem and were willing to help him steer out of his crisis.

At work, he became reserved. Sometimes he would become unresponsive and often found it difficult to focus his attention. Where he was once alert and energetic ready to take part in any technical or personal conversation, he had now become aloof but still respectful. This personality flaw affected his metabolism. He became careless about food becoming a frugal eater.

At times he would become restless and forcing himself into repetitive actions. He would sit up or lie down forgetting what he was doing, stop midway and look down or behind while climbing stairs. He would scribble repeating symbols on paper, repeating lines while coding or drafting. It had happened a few times that he would have visions of people, situations and events, which were imaginary. When Mythili came to know, she feared that these visions were of an overworked brain. They were dangerous and likely due to decreased oxygen intake that could lead to sleep apnea.

Sarkar empathized with Ajay's spiritual needs and sized the problem. He justified, "Mythri would not live for long and a month later Ajay would not only be the same old self but a supercharged person."

The rumors concerning Ajay's behavior reached Dagariya, the Chairman of the Company. Dagariya hearing it felt that he should do something to understand him. He told his wife about this young lad whom they were trying to promote. She counseled him to wait and watch how things turn out.

When his brother in New York became insistent on opening a new line of business, he could not ignore it. It was a short window of opportunity, but it would provide good returns plus foreign customers and contacts he reasoned. The Company would neglect it at its own peril if it did not grasp this opportunity warned Dagariya's brother. Venkataraman argued that it would be foolhardy not to enter this market. If the top companies were gearing up to enter this market there were solid reasons behind it. By relinquishing this market, it would be doing injustice to the promoters and the Company. Here was a big opportunity for quick and high revenues and the opportunity to become visible on the radar of many foreign customers. It was a strategic opportunity that comes rarely. The Company would do well to run after the opportunity that was there for its taking.

It required within a short time frame reengineering of millions of lines of code. The converted programs could absorb and account for the day one of January 2000. This was the software opportunity of the century and called Y2K. Dagariya agreed with the reasoning and told his management to build Y2K business around Ajay as a leader.

Hearing about Ajay's melancholia, Dagariya described Ajay's condition as an outcome from a drastic shock. He talked with his partner Sharad and they decided to draw him out and understand the cause of his behavior. There were many rumors and explanations. His co-workers who had known him felt that at times his behavior was not as it normally was. The Personnel Department stated that when he returned after Diwali Ajay had changed. The rumor was that something painful had happened. There were many versions but none of them true. The Personnel Manager had met Sarkar earlier and knew that they were thick friends. After he heard Sarkar's version he confirmed the same with Mythili and then took the matter to Dagariya.

Dagariya was a calculating shrewd Marwari as they come. An old Marwari saying is, when *a* Marwari steps out of his house with an empty mug,he returns filled with gold. Public credit their financial acumen as the reason behind their successes but what they forget is their uncanny hereditary instinct of sizing people. Once you know motivations and drive of a person, and using his strengths coax them for favorable outcomes.

Sushma heard Dagariya and with her feminine instincts suggested, "I think that this guy is not stable at the moment. He has tied himself in knots. It is a temporary phase for him. I think he is a moralistic and a religious person. He is emotional. I think he is a virgin."

After some time she added, "Poor guy! He is oblivious of the sense of time". "Just be kind and approach him with good intention he will become a grateful employee"

"So what I should I do?", demanded Dagariya.

"What do you want to do? Do nothing! Talk to him. Give him hope. Assure him that we are with him. Sit quiet and when the girl is no more then we will get close to him", she advised.

Ajay's telephonic conversations with Mythri were becoming listless. Unknown to him, she was going through another round of chemotheraphy because her cancer had relapsed. It was stronger this time and after her injection drip she could not talk for two days. His voice was a source of strength for her. This voice whispered and he prayed that she draw from her reserves and the will to live. Mythri did not say anything one day after his repeated statements and enquiries. Finally, after a long wait she said the end was near and put the phone down. How fast the cancer had spread? What was once a bubbly girl yesterday today she lay wasted. When Mythili told him, she would be leaving for Delhi, he lost no time in getting her the air tickets. He dropped her at airport. They hugged for a brief moment and went they separate ways. It became uncomfortable to share their emotions.

Ajay had heard about the Year Two Thousand problem. Called the millennial problem amongst the computer people and if its impact was as serious and far reaching as knowledgeable said and then there would be many opportunities. Alas, these did not fire his imagination. Everyone connected with the software industry was theorizing about it. The company directors were networking. The Company was a member the country's apex software body called NASSCOM[6]. This provided opportunities to network and informed about what the top companies were thinking.

One day Dagariya sent for Ajay. He reasoned with Ajay that being in a trauma for long imbalances even the strongest. He impressed upon Ajay that he owed to himself and his family and not forgetting the company to come out of his melancholia. Ajay had to balance himself and his well-wishers in the Company including him were with Ajay but he had to take the first step. Dagariya reminding him the trap he was in him. He knew counselling would not work. Time for counselling was over.

Dagariya looked at Ajay benevolently. He felt that his message was sinking in.

Dagariya stood and came behind Ajay's chair and holding his shoulders said, "Son, never ever forget that the Company and especially I am with you. I understand your pain. I have instructed the Personnel Manager and Mr. Joshi, the accountant to assist you whether it is leave or money to help you. You are free to call me for any problem or any need".

Ajay was touched and moved. His eyes welled and tears fell from his eyes. Before he could recover Dagariya's secretary tiptoed in and asked him to step out to sign some papers. He returned in a few minutes and said, "I have

---

[6]NASSCOM is the National Association of Software and Services Companies, a not-for-profit Indian consortium created to promote the development of the country's IT and BPO industries. It was set up in 1988 and today has become global trade body with over 2000 members in the business of software development, software services, software products, IT-enabled/BPO services and E-Commerce with 15 % of them from china, US, UK, and other countries. When formed it provided yeoman services to its members and played an important role in making the world know about Indian companies and their capabilities.

learnt that the best way to deal with threatening emotional situations is to forget yourself in your work. Time heals, time sorts everything."

He added, "There is a lot of talk about Y2K and I want to build a Y2K division around you." Time heals everything. Would you like to go to your seat or to your room?", helpfully questioned Dagariya.

Ajay got up saying he would leave at the closing time. A plan was forming in Dagariya's mind.

The Y2K also called the millennium problem or simply Y2K. This problem arose because of the way data of years leading to the year 2000 was stored. Computers during the 1980/1990's were completely different. The cost of storing data was expensive. Computer manufacturers were few. The leading companies were IBM, ICL, Bull, NEC etc. In 1980's companies like DG, Digital and Compaq etc. began manufacturing computers. They manufactured another breed of computers, which were more powerful, smaller, cheaper and smarter. No matter what vintage the computer, the predominant programming languages were COBOL, FORTRAN, ALGOL, and PL/1 etc.

Programmers abbreviated the year's four digits into the last two digits. What it did was that the way years were stacked. The century beginning 1900 was indistinguishable from the century beginning 2000. The year following 1900 was 1901, 1902 etc. but at the end of the year 2000 the computer was clueless what it was to do.

Thus, representing a year by its last two numbers created a logical problem when 2000 end becomes 2001. This would create date related data processing errors. Whenever the computer had any calculation to make from this point for day, date, time it could be erroneous. In some cases, these errors could be catastrophic. Without corrective measures, perfectly running systems would malfunction on this date.

People said planes would fall from the sky, trains would crash, bank accounts would become zero or piddling accounts could become overfilled to the envy of billionaires and so on.

Computer world people began calculating as their wont. With millions of lines of code the fixing of the Y2K bug required thousands of programmers. Scanning millions of lines of code to find the hidden bugs and correct them represented huge money. Doing it on the scale that experts spoke of presented a massive challenge. The window was short; programmers must be good using old computer languages and programs with no or little corroborative descriptions. Added to this was absence of standards with far less programmers with requisite skills.

Over the last few years many Indian software companies had provided services to American and British companies. Working with Indian programmers, Americans and British managers had come to know and appreciate Indian skills. They could work with Indian programmers for they were friendly, communicable, hardworking and disciplined. They could deliver gracefully otherwise they would with brute force. Deliver they would.

Bhuvan was trying to reach Ajay in office for the last two hours and as soon as he did, Ajay sensed it was all over. Later in the evening Mythili told him about the end. With God's grace it was a good painless end. She slept in the afternoon and never woke up. When they tried to wake her she did not stir. Her face was peaceful. Her expressive eyes were open and staring far away where she had to traverse. Bhuvan attended her cremation and suggested Ajay to take up the threads of life again after a vacation. "Friend there must be some learning in this also", added Bhuvan.

"Think about the past and see what new insights into life you witnessed. Go to the hills or the sea. Relax, think, rebuild and come back fighting. She would have liked you to do that." Ajay was inconsolable. He cried and cried so much as he had never before.

Loss of focus, preoccupation with trivial things and failing interest in office were worrying him. Mythri's passing away hurt as if he had never felt such intense suffering.

The ferment in the software industry frightened him making him think he was incapable. Massive changes are a usual feature in any industry especially with the software industry. When you take your eyes of the ball you can get indecisive. Loss of motivation and inability to order priorities saps strength. He confessed to Sarkar. Sarkar read the confusion on his face. He knew Ajay was distressed and he learnt from his colleagues that on some days he would be stressed beyond belief and behave like a man too preoccupied and depressed.

Mythri's last rites were over. Now he felt in a perverse way happy that it was all over. He was waiting for his phoenix moment. It was building up in him and could erupt anytime.

Anxiety means you have extra worry, you cannot relax, you feel tense and you could have panic attacks. That was the reality. Tiredness and stress puts you on the edge because your feelings get hurt or warped for no or trivial reasons. It was seductive. Now was the time to leave that behind and pick up life again. Sure, the future often arrives before you are ready. It comes with no calling card.

Dagariya had gone to New York to confer with his brother about actualizing Y2K opportunities. Without a strong sales team, the Company would not be able to generate business. His brother would be the point man for marketing set up that in the US. They agreed to start building a contact list. He was not sure if Ajay could become a salesperson for his division and lead it. In software companies, one does not get to head a vertical until the incumbent had demonstrated high-level managerial abilities and salesmanship qualities. In Ajay's case, things were tailor made just for him, unlike established company practices. This was what Dagariya did. A practice he had noticed amongst his successful clients.

He would be back on the coming Monday. He had created a strong and inspiring professional opening for Ajay. In a few days, Ajay was his normal self and ready. He had created a vision of a Y2K software division with him as its Chief.

As he pondered over the possibility, his mind travelled back to the last few days he had spent with Mythri and Madhab Bhuvan in Delhi. Before leaving for Bangalore as an unemployed engineer, the power of the film on Sir Edmund Hillary and Norgay Tenzing ran through his mind. He visualized climbers making their way systematically in the blinding icy winds. The frightening sounds, the blizzards with their heavy sweeping atmosphere weighing the climbers down was a tough environment that could become more forbidding any moment. They would have to live with until they reached the peak. There was no road, no marker or a guidepost to steer. A hostile land where nothing grows and every labored step left them breathless. In moments, new paths appeared and disappeared. There was no one to confer or seek advice from except them. They were lonely but there was a definite picture imprinted in their mind of what they had set out to reach. Driven by one and only one single purpose they had to reach the peak. Thinking of it inspired him.

He smiled to himself remembering when someone asked Hillary why he took all the troubles facing extreme danger including possibility of death to climb mountains. His simple but powerful answer, "Because they were there," was cryptic and few would understand it. If a problem was there, someone had to solve it. Consider yourself to be fortunate and a chosen one to solve other's problem.

When a man finds singleness of purpose in life, he is blessed. Few get the opportunity and these lucky souls have to make that lonely, hard trek to what had inspired them.

The degree of single mindedness in any work differentiates the extraordinary from the ordinary. The extraordinary worker has the highest probability of catching the worm. Having chosen a path the aspirant sets the key parameters based on a vision. A choice can only be within one's physical and intellectual capabilities. As a dedicated leader progresses nature fills him with extraordinary strength and intellect. Even a spiritualist's success is within the seeker's limitations. It reduces to enlightened self-interest and the seeker's spiritual intent.

For the aspirant enlightened self-interest ingresses each act of his or her life. Never for a moment can he or she ignore altruism or the larger good. It is a choice that will be with you always. It is in the eating habits, the physical exercises you do, your favorite readings, pursuits during leisure times and sleeping. Times, places, directions, comfort and intensity are a part of it. With regularity, awareness, and wakefulness the seeker begins his journey. As the seeker passes milestones, he takes stock of where he is and the distance he still needs to travel.

He learns that there are tests on the path. Beginning with simple and small ones and as he successfully passes them, he traverses further there are tests that are more difficult. If he slips,falls or stumbles he will have to surrender some of the gains he made. The tests continue. Dealt more tests he has to win them one after the other. The efforts required of him after each failure will be more than what he gave in the test before he stumbled. The aspirant cannot afford to slip even once.

Each test that the aspirant passes he evolves. Each milestone brings with it bliss. In the beginning, each success is a short-lived bliss. As he passes bigger tests, periods of bliss becomes longer. A true seeker knows that the end of his evolution is perpetual bliss. The aspirant learns the reasons for his failures. There are innumerable temptations and inducements on the path. From simple follies to indiscretions, from minor and to major sins and he has to learn to manage them. A wise and a steadfast seeker learn and creates a regular tune within him. As he gets deeper, he refines the many variables and the preoccupations of his life.

Refinement requires removal of the unnecessary and unwanted and it removes imperfections. Some of these are as just that – worthless. Others appear to be good or prized virtues, but now unwanted as the seeker has mastered them. A true seeker realizes that progress on the path beyond a point depends upon being as light as the rarefied atmosphere demands. You have to free yourself from needless relationships, commitments, social agreements, and pretensions. They have no meaning or utility. In rarefied heights, the aspirant needs a clearer vision that sets new priorities and requirements. He has to do these in face of ridicule, censorship and hostility. He has to live with only that which is necessary and nothing else. This makes the vision a stirring reality.

Ajay saw his goal as Arjun beheld the eye of the fish.

Chapter V
The Sorcerer's Way

Unknown to many, a position of a Public Relations Officer (PRO) was created in the Company and a new office set up. Its occupant was an attractive middle-aged woman Asha Ketkar. An unused room now spruced up for the new occupant Asha. Situated in the middle of landing on the second floor hidden behind the wooden railing of the staircase, the office was quite inconspicuous.

Reticent and shy, Asha Ketkar confined herself to her work spending most of her time in the office. She would attend Company meetings when necessary or invited. Her office well furnished with a conference room adjacent to it and high-level meetings with prospects and customers scheduled here. It had two entrances a separate entrance via a staircase from the ground floor and another one from her office.

She had a PC, which she used carelessly storing all sort of personal and professional data. Unlike new joinees, her welcome notice not displayed nor was she introduced publicly. She received instructions directly from Dagariya. She organized meetings and presentations for foreign buyers and delegates. Asha found challenge and enjoyed putting together slides, preparing documents and reports for publicizing the firm that had now grown substantially. She shared the services of a secretary, a young girl who did her typing work.

Asha was a Bombayite with a scandal, which she wanted to hide and forget. Her husband was a manager in a Cooperative Bank at the Head Office in Bombay. He was also a part of a gang that helped politicians and white-collar crooks to defraud the bank. He earned a small cut of the money the gang arrogated. The gang was powerful and led by the Managing Director who had a few chosen managers and a handful of clerical staff totaling about twenty. The net spread across a third of the fifty branches across Maharashtra. The fraud had been going on for years without any visible effect on the bank, except it getting impoverished. The last audit was a decade old and with government's largesse and the help of powerful bureaucrats and politicians, the fraud well hidden.

How could the bank carry on without audit for ten years is not difficult to comprehend? The minister under whose jurisdiction the bank fell was powerful enough to let the bank function and signed on papers that testified that nothing was amiss. Since the last ten years, there had been three ministers. There was never an embarrassing question raised in the *Vidhan Sabha* (the state parliament). Any enterprising journalist who dug dirt and wrote something unflattering or an expose he or she was bought and silenced.

For a junior manager, Ketkar had a flat in Andheri and three bank accounts with a locker. His daughter attended an exclusive school. His wife wore costly clothes and jewels and she was a regular at the ladies' social circuit. It was too good to last. He liked to bend his elbow and well stocked with the best spirits money could buy. The Ketkars never purchased a car because it would be visible and easier to get around in taxis.

The CBI was keeping an eye on the bank for a year. The Bombay head office and its biggest branch in Bombay received CBI's added attention. One day they raided the bank head office and few selected branches and homes of some employees perceived as part of the gang including that of the Managing Director. Three officers landed at the Ketkar family house. During the raid, a scuffle ensued and a CBI official hit his temple on the edge of the table and died. The CBI official was responsible for the scuffle. It hit the headlines and became a cause célèbre.

Her husband's trial began in the session court, which awarded him 10 years in the jail, and proceedings began for assessing bank's loss and its recovery. The case went to high Court on appeal and the gang arranged for Asha's husband a sharp legal luminary. He not only got the sentence reduced and convinced the MD to create a trust for his daughter. The trust mandated a considerable sum in her daughter's name managed by Asha until she attained the age of 21. The trust would look after her education, boarding, and lodging. Ketkar's flat leased to Asha's sister who refused to part with it after the lease period. She was an ungrateful greedy woman but Asha could do nothing about it.

A hotel purchased in Ooty, a favorite honeymoon and tourist destination in the name of Asha Ketkar. It was a perfect place to hide. Amongst the many lodges, hotels, restaurants, and cottages this was another transit accommodation for honeymooners and revelers. Seventy percent of the population was migrants who came here to work and stayed for a season. The other migrators were merry makers rarely staying a week. The owners of many boarding, lodging and guest houses did not live in the town. A hotel here could be a good source of income, keep her busy, and remain hidden from the prying eyes and away from her socialite friends and those who would like to trouble her. Maybe she could continue her clubbing lifestyle if she wanted that. There were many rich idle people here and had their own diversions.

The man behind rehabilitating and creating new identities was the Managing Director, Ajit Ubhayankar. He realised that he could not have carried on with his racket and intrigues without these accomplices for 10 years and this was his parting gift. His political masters had given him three months to clean as much of the stink before they let their dogs on the gang.

Ubhayankar was a quick thinking and foresightful man.

Over the years,he had built a syndicate of loyal unquestioning thugs and fraudulent financers who would do anything for him. It was essential to rehabilitate and create new identities for his men. Everything ends, even life philosophized Ubhayankar. There would be a time for the second innings.

Asha's husband was a simpleton, a small cog in the wheel. He ended up from a temple going, God-fearing man to one sunk so low in his own esteem that he was not fit to be a human being. He could not opt out. Weak as he was and under constant fear and took to drinking. He would go out of the bank when depressed, frightened, or guilty and find his way to a bar. He drank the choicest alcohol. He did not remain out for long but returned stinking. This became a problem and he could have been dismissed but for his gang.

As his alcoholism became serious, he became a wife beater. Asha had her own life, and he had become impotent and her husband only in name. She found wings with the money he lavished on her and she had time to spend in kitty parties, beauticians, restaurants etc. She was way smarter and discreet than her husband.

Settling in the hotel Asha had her daughter, Teja admitted to a Christian Ebenezer Higher Secondary School. An exclusive boarding school for girls in a place called Elagiri in the district of Vellore. It was a scenic hilly place, four hours bus drive from Bangalore and Ooty. Asha was a free bird without a care or responsibility in the world. She wanted her past to remain secret and therefore avoided the rich who could wise up to her. Soon she got bored. There was nothing much for her to do at the hotel. Confined to her hotel full time, she spent most of her hours in her suite and tried to run the hotel. In spite of her best efforts, her staff swindled her.

One day Dagariya happened to come to her hotel with some business associates. He had a roving eye and soon got to know Asha. He made another trip with his wife and she opened and narrated the highlights of her life. Neither Dagariya nor his wifetry to dig deeper than what she was willing to narrate and quickly won her confidence. She just could not manage her hotel and left defrauded by her staff. She would have liked but could not move to a bigger city where she could find outlets for her interests. Her hotel held her back. She could not trust any of her staff.

Though an owner of a hotel with an organization to run for profit, she had become a prisoner of her employees. She was alone. She knew that if this continued for an extended period her money would not last long. At times, she thought of selling out. If she did, where would she go and what would she do. It was a frightening spectera and threatening.

She had never worked before but smart, worldly wise and an engaging conversationalist she tried to do her best. She was confident of doing any job that called for such skills. She had played hockey for Maharashtra and was a sports woman to the core. When situation demanded she could handle situations and take care of herself well, so she thought. She had done that and well before. Her manager who was a crook with a tight leash on the staff who would obey him than listen to her out maneuvered her. She found herself out of depth.

In the evening as it began to get cold, she found herself with the new guest of the hotel. Quickly they established rapport. Asha during the very normal and wandering sort of conversation shared with her conversationalist guest her unhappiness. She tried her best but she could not turn the hotel into a financially successful unit. On the guest's prodding, Asha briefly explained how she came to buy this hotel and the developments in her small family. Her husband wrongly jailed and she had a young school-going daughter and they had no one else in the world. Asha had learnt that being truthful carried the day more often than not. How much and how one stated the truth was a personal choice and dictated by circumstances. It might sound trite and commonplace but it was hard as nails. Most people rarely understood that.

Next day during breakfast Asha joined their table. Dagariya's wife Sushma suggested, "Ashaji, please have full trust on us. We will make you the PRO of our Company. We will get an honest and sharp hotel management professional and place him here. He will run your hotel. We will have our efficient and sharp accountant, Joshi ji look after your accounts. He will come and check your accounts every three months"

"Will you manage my hotel? Will you make it profitable? Finally, why do you want to do it?", asked Asha

Sushma chose to reply, We are happy Asha ji that you asked these questions. When you told us about your unhappy life, itmoved us. Please do not mind my being blunt, because being truthful creates opportunities. It is good for all. Our culture and upbringing demands that when our friends fall in bad times to support them and help them to the best of our ability. Why are we helping you? Because you made us your friend and by helping you we stand to gain also. We want 20% of your profits for this help."

Continued Sushma,"Is this acceptable to you?"

"If you need time to think please do so and tell us

later", added Sushma.

Asha could not estimate what the hotel could earn if run in a professional manner. She neither had the remotest idea that if the 20 % fee the Dagariya couple asking was fair. She knew that the hotel was making about Rs 20 Lakhs per month. At the end of the month, she was just about breaking even or making a small loss. Loss meant she had to bring in money and if it continued that way, she would lose that as well.

As Mahesh and Sushma walked to their room, Mahesh turning the key of their room said, "That was a masterly speech dear. We need a secret and quiet place away from inquisitive eyes."

"Of course Mahesh we do. It is important to give our guests the best of hospitality."

Parts of her old days flashed past her in images. They were colorful and bright and not like old sepia prints. Asha Ketkar thrilled and recalled the fortnight that led to this hotel. She was meeting Ajit Ubhayankar the first time in Park Hotel in Belapur, away from the busy area in a quieter neighborhood. Her husband's trial and sentencing was over. She had been a beneficiary of Ubhayankar's munificence. She had no reason to be apprehensive. She arrived at the hotel and found her way to the Bamboo, a Chinese specialty restaurant in the Park.

As she entered, the Manager ever deferential bowed and asked her if she was Mrs. Asha Ketkar and then guided her where Ubhayankar was sitting. The restaurant was classy, the ambience warm and with private spaces. Ubhayankar was a gracious host and an excellent raconteur. There was no hurry and Ubhayankar was all concern for her and her daughter. Over delicious food, his conversation and stories attracted Asha like a magnet. Ubhayankar was going to South Africa for a week and he would be pleased to have Asha's company.

He wanted her to accompany him where he would explain to her the plans he had for setting her up in business. She would have not to worry about money for the rest of her life as long as she ran the business seriously. This way she would protect herself and her daughter. She would be able to look after the future of her daughter as well. Importantly she would be away from the reach of undesirable people from Bombay. There were many who knew her story and there were people who prey on defenseless and unfortunate women like her. If she agreed, he would have all arrangements made. He said it with suaveness and feeling.

Asha excused herself and repaired to the restroom. There was nothing that she could do but accept his offer. She realized it was nothing much that he wanted from her against what he promised. Leaving the restroom after freshening herself, she walked out wondering if the cunning and crooked persona or the suave person was the real Ubhayankar. She agreed good naturedly to go with him to South Africa.

Ubhayankar had seen her during the trial at the high court when the case moved from the session's court. He found her bewitching, true Marathi features and he figured her to be in sexual matters, mature and experienced. He went about planning to set her up and save her and her daughter from shame, ignominy and destitution. In situation like these, anything was possible in the big bad glamourous city of Bombay. Bombay was all commerce with a thin veneer of culture. Scratch a little and you will meet its thin underbelly of corruption, vice and amorality. He had decided that he would do something more for her than his other partners in crime.

His minions arranged for her travel. Her passport, visa, and clothes to arrangements for her daughter to stay until they returned, made discretely. She did not have to stir out of her house and everything arranged. When necessary, someone called her on her cell and quietly conveyed what she had to know or do. All formalities were done post haste.

They travelled individually to the Bombay airport. Sitting and waiting for their flight away from each other, without as much as glancing they passed off as strangers. Disembarking at Cape Town, they took different taxis to Knysna.

They motored on the Garden Route one of the most scenic drives in the world. The white sandstone cliffs enchantingly separated it from its coke colored lagoon. The taxi sped through thick green covers of trees and she could hear the pounding surf of the Indian Ocean. Asha was astonished and forgot her trauma. She felt as if travelling through some enchanted land in the heavens. It was an inspiring and joyful beginning.

As the road went flying past she surrendered herself to what the future would bring. Her heart beat faster. She had never been so cheerful and rested since the beginning of that which changed her life forever. They checked in Azure House, a classy boutique hotel as two individual people. Once they checked in, they were discretely together most of the time and in a few hours established a routine. In spite of the most horrifying period that had laid her low, she felt the stirrings of happy times ahead.

When he was not with her, he was either in his room or in the business center of the hotel. He would be talking on the phone or sending mails. He carried a small notebook in his blazer, which he always wore. He would scribble in this dark blue notebook after he made a telephone call. He would be staring and shuffling the pages of 4 inch by 3-inch book. What he did and what he was planning did not concern her in the least. He had been good to her and Asha did not want her relationship with him extended unless fate willed it otherwise. She never asked anything about his personal life. However, she was intrigued looking at him with this notebook and being extra protective about it.

He outlined his plan at the first instance. He was going to buy her a hotel and transfer it in her name in a tourist destination far away from Bombay. If she ran it cleverly, she would have a steady income for the rest of her life. There were exclusive schools within 80 kilometres radius where her daughter could study. He could have arrangements made for her admission.

Ubhayankar found Asha fascinating. He had no complaints. She willingly cooperated and enthusiastically in his complicity, avoiding asking anything that could be his private life. She coquettishly avoided his questions about her personal life. She was fascinated with his notebook but never asked anything about it. One day she found the occasion to leaf through it and found that many entries coded. Somewere in Marathi and long list of numbers, which she assumed were telephone numbers, and below it were numbers, which must have been monies with the currencies written. There were diagonal arrows against the currencies some arrowheads flowing out and the others flowing in.

Being with him, she heard a few of his conversations. She would move out when these telephone calls arrived. She concluded it was not a holiday to de-stress as he had told her. It was work. It must be so demanding that it required painstaking planning, clarity, and confidentiality. Perhaps he could not do it in India and that was why he had come here. Asha knew he was a thug but quite refined at that. She was an object that he could buy and play with. She had agreed to that.

He treated her as his woman and she gave him what he wanted gracefully. She considered it as the risk of being a woman and her payment for a business deal. Before leaving for Bombay a week later, he assured her that he would not come in her life again. It was a sex-drenched day that flowed into the next until they were exhausted and the holiday ended.

She followed him to Bombay a day later.

Asha loved her stay at Azure. If she was not with Ubhayankar she would lose herself overlooking blue water lakes interspersed with greenery as far as the eye could see and break out of her melancholia. Azure made an impact on her and she would carry the design and layout of the hotel in her mind for years.

Everywhere, whether in the rooms or open spaces the beauty of furnishing was eye catching and exquisite. Everything positioned and built for comfort, elegance and service. Each room was like a functioning apartment. The apartment spoke its language of privacy, warmth and purity in white. She dreamed and prayed to Ganapati to make her the mistress of such a hotel that Ubhayankar was promising.

After she took over the hotel, she spent time planning the renovation of the hotel. It had a hideous commonplace name typical of hotels in tourist places in India. The hotel named Pinewood that spoke of no class. In her mind, it was Azure and she wished to make it in that tradition. It could never be like the Azure but it could be as close to what she had seen. She wanted to rename it, Azure. The word Azure conjures images of bluish and greenish white colours of water bodies. There was no lake nearby except one used by honeymooners for boating which could be seen through binoculars. The hotel was on a hill that made it private nestled amongst a coniferous forest. Perhaps that gives it the name Pinewood.

Snapping out of her reverie Asha replied "This is your greatness and my good fortune. You good people met me and helped me inmy difficulties. You have showed me a way. I accept your offer. I will do what you ask me to", replied Asha.

Dagariya rubbing his hands looked at Sushma and said, "Let us reduce the management fees to 15%. It will be a win a win situation for both." Smiling at Asha he added,

“Let’s drink to our friendship and new arrangement.”

Whether it was 15 % of revenues or profit was not stated. Dagariya said he would have a formal written agreement couriered to her for her approval and signature.

In the evening Dagariya and Sushma invited Asha to their room for a glass of wine and give final shape to their agreement. Sushma told her about their business interests other than the software company. They had minor interests in many other businesses and they had helped many smart people set up businesses. They never acquired the companies where they invested. Their interests were in building industry, trading and Kannada entertainment businesses. They had many friends who were well connected. Because of the building boom due to the software and call center businesses, they knew many builders. They counted film personalities and builders as their friends. They had the money to splash. Surely, some of it was illegal which business did not create black money for a rainy day.

Asha would be the Public Relations Officer of their software company.

Asha was stunned. Never in her wildest dreams did she imagine she would get such a secure lifeline. It came visiting her. Thanking Ganapati, she did what any smart person would.

She went to Bombay and through her friend; a manager in a construction company helped sell her flat in Bombay and enrolled her for a course in PRO. It was easy and she was convinced she could do justice to the position. Immediately she bought a computer and learnt how to use it. There were her old friends and eager beavers she avoided lest they asked about her present life. She wanted to hide her new life much more than her older one. Hardly had she finished, she left Bombay and landed in Bangalore.

Describing the genesis of her friendship with the

Dagariya family to Ajay, she said it was immaterial if it was 15 or 20%. She considered this as the salary of a new manager who would make her hotel profitable.

Asha joined the company and Dagariya went about professionalizing her hotel. She was quite clear what she could do and soon became confident of delivering more and better. Anyone who worked with her spoke glowingly of her creative energies. Since she reported to him, he was impressed with her freshness and novel way of thinking. In spite of being 45 or more, she was bubbly and voluble. She correctly imagined Dagariya as a worldly man. Life had taught her that nothing comes free.

Indian software exports are a misnomer but a term ingrained in the popular collective psyche of the country. It was in 1992/93 when Indian software companies sent their smart engineers overseas to look for business. They traveled to software cities like London, Paris, Chicago, New York, Brussels, Ottawa, Michigan and Seattle etc. This was how the exports of Indian apparel and knitted products began 50 years before that. The so-called software exports business took the same route.

The intentions of the software marketers were simple. Meet and interest buyers for software development and services. Apart from low cost, promise to meet their schedules and sincerity they had little else to offer. They talked of expertise, which was simply a promise. Unlike apparel buyers, the buyers of software services were clever and educated. The new clients for software services from a faraway country were adventurous, because they were pioneers and willing to risk. They began with small contracts. The Indian companies worked their arse and meet expectations and slowly but surely contracts became bigger with time and excellent customer support.

Some had prior appointments and those who did not,

waited for a few days. The sales people would daily trudge to the prospect's offices and seek for appointment with the engineering or purchase staff. They parked themselves until they felt they had exhausted their ingenuity and welcome which could be a few days to a week. Pitching for any work and even willing to do it free quite often moved the host organizations. The aim was to get in and do good piece of work in shortest possible time. Once in, it was possible to get repeat business.

Companies like TCS, Wipro, Blue Star, Patni etc. had their own foreign sales organizations. It made sense for them to use their existing networks to sell their software services. Their foreign offices helped identify potential customers for their software engineering expertise. It was common to motivate Indian sales and business people on their overseas beat to point out opportunities. They even contacted friends and relatives in these countries. In all cases, the sweetener was finder's fees paid on success. What they sought was leads, contacts and even newspaper reports that might lead to an opportunity.

There were other Indian companies that sold hardware for European and American companies. These hardware manufacturers sought software works contracts for their customers who bought their hardware. Indian companies stray successes at providing software services to their principles led them to believe and acknowledge their skills. The proof lay in the fact that the Indian works were for their customers and they had no complaints. Soon these arrangements motivated Indian companies to seek overseas works through their principals. Their Indian affiliates were willing and capable enough to create softwares or sell it back to their parent firms.

When you have belief in yourself you can do almost anything is the folklore.

Sensing money agents and intermediaries set

themselves as consultants. They promised leads and jobs few of which materialized. IT outsourcing or offshoring had entered the consciousness of astute executives. The real world users were still to be fully convinced of its practicality. Their shortsightedness was their inability to see beyond the attractiveness of the price differential. Indian companies now knew how to break through. Could the Indian professors in American colleges left behind when they saw easy money? They straddled the Indian end as well as their American business contacts. For some extra bucks, they could arrange introductions and let on the requirements of prospects. They facilitated business, which was the reason Indian software companies courted them.

To have created a massive global business from these nonprofessional forays was amazing. Portions of manufacturing had been subcontracted or outsourced since the end of the world war. Outsourcing manufacturing was initiated by the automotive industry. Over the next 50 years, outsourced manufacturing had become stable, predictable and quality assured. Since then outsourced manufacturing has become as reliable as manufacturing in one's own backyards.

Outsourcing and overseas software contracting or such intellectual works not tried before. Amongst opinion makers and software intelligentsia, it was difficult if not impossible. Technical protocols created for software services for clients thousands of miles away. It was a joint operation by the supplier and buyer, which required common, cogent and acceptable protocols so, went the thinking. Bringing standards in brain work, which is by nature complex, was a tough challenge. It needed adventurous and astute management to discover and establish this link.

Tata Burroughs's India center doing software work for its parent company was an inspiration for Indian entrepreneurs. For some perceptive business houses, this was a new business opportunity, small in terms of revenues but the market in numbers sky high. There were a few more such instances. Indian software companies began canvassing with American and British customers for software work. They offered to build application systems or re-engineer existing systems or undertake maintenance work. For the buyers, it began as a gamble and the Indian prices tantalizing. It cut both ways - cheap and images of a con job. Persistence and good work laid the foundation of many an Indian company for later success. These companies could justifiably boast of experience in exporting software works for overseas customers.

The word spread that Indian programmers were good. They were inexpensive, fast learners with good English language skills. You could trust them with completion ofa job. On on-site work[7], they were willing to work beyond office hours or on holidays if required. They were compliant and non-demanding.

Programmers going to customer sites called body shops, land at customer place for software work on their computers. They lived there until the work was completed. A decade later, the labor business continued as it does even today the word body shop used in a pejorative sense. The foreign buyers were comfortable with this nomenclature and called it labor business.

With small successes and winning confidence of American customers, Indian companies after studying customer requirements brought work home. With a judicious placement of onsite and offshore work and engineers, Indian companies delivered to customer's delight. Experience increased their competence and bandwidth to undertake more complex and

[7] *Software work of almost any type or a part of the software development life cycle done by Indian engineers in the client's establishment in another country. Engineers working on the site were managed sometimes by the Indian company and other times by the client company as the contract was drawn. The engineers so deputed called "body shops".*

bigger work contracts. They were handling business from a few thousand to hundreds of thousands of dollars.

Good and responsive backend procedures resulted in quality and timely deliveries that constantly improved. Techniques of understanding and capturing requirements, development of technical solutions and estimating work became essential. When many Indian companies bid for the same contract it increased the confidence of buyers.

Highlighting these skills became inescapable for overseas contracts. Companies refined their methods for pricing, project management, documentation and quality assurance. Training and processes for managing quality intellectual product became a company's intellectual property. Once in place with constant engineering, the systems and procedures evolved to a higher degree of finesse.

These non-direct software activities constituted as much time and effort as actual engineering. They ensured the delivery and installation of quality work. It took ingenuity, considerable thought, experimentation, and communication to convince foreign clients. In a few years, it made outsourcing and offshoring a solid work and business. In one decade Indian software companies were years ahead of companies from other countries trying to emulate them. Many tried but had little success to show.

Much work performed in the host company under the supervision of the hiring company managers. Soon there were tens of Indian engineers in a company and they began to have their own managers supervising them. It was not out of ordinary to have 100 engineers in Paris or 200 in London and many more in New York and still more in Boston.

Charts of presentations became a necessary and powerful method to assure customers of what they were getting into. This was overstated and that was how the company engaged with clients. There were lists of foreign customers and the services provided. These charts were used to make presentations to prospects when foreign companies or consultants who had come looking for Indian companies. Used by their sales team posted overseas whenever they could inveigle an opportunity. Even senior managers and software company owners delivered such presentations. They hoped to get business through these presentations. They actually did!

Making these charts had become unavoidable. Hours spent on tuning work and performance statistics. Descriptions of successful projects and displaying them in a variety of ways were standard. Companies competed amongst themselves in outdoing each other. Each company created documents for discussions and submission to foreign visitors.

Asha Ketkar became adept at preparing such charts. She learnt to visualize and articulate graphically. Her assistant created them on the computer. Her work was as good as any that floated in the market. Her graphs were as good as any in the software exports business and noticed by competitors. She loved doing that.

In the early 1990's documents of larger companies floated around and freely copied. The best were by Tata software companies and were hot property and other Indian companies vied to lay their hands on them. With her ingenuity and networking skills, she began collecting specimens from other companies. The quality of her company presentation materials improved. The senior managers felt it was comparable to the best. Asha was proud of them. Nevertheless, in terms of billable and shipped engineers the company was still small. Dagariya saw the opportunity to expand in the wake of Y2K opportunity. The yardstick for company performance was number of billable resources and their utilization. The firm's utilization was less than half of TCS, WIPRO and PATNI etc.

As the Industry matured, buyers developed confidence and well informed in contracting charts became non-issues. Experienced foreign buyers examined technical competence and had staff who could probe. They wanted to know the depth of understanding of the business areas the company had worked in. The Indian software industry was now visible in advanced countries. The number of Indian companies ready to offer software services to overseas clients increased many folds. Large enterprises were always poaching smaller companies for programmers. Resume making became a skill. Companies employed bio data makers who could tweak bio data on the fly to match requirements. Large companies like TCS, WIPRO, INFOSYS, PATNI and SATYAM etc. had not hundreds but thousands of bio data's in their data banks.

The image of successful software companies were comfortable facilities, fanciful canteens, good employee satisfaction provisions, quality certifications and high salaries. Behind this popular picture was the solid structure and systems. Built on experience and good sense by managers from the best colleges they sowed the seeds of excellence. When it flowered ten years later, it made safe the position of Indian software engineering. It contributed to the halo of the engineering capabilities ensuring a seat in the global business table.

In 1990, Videsh Sanchar Nigam set up satellite based data communication facilities. Using them, Indian companies could communicate with customers in different parts of the world instantaneously which is taken as a given today. A year later, the government created the software technology parks. This was a scheme to provide facilities to new companies and units of existing companies. This led to the growth and stimulated software exports. Nothing spurred the growth and entrepreneurship of Indian software more than these two developments.

The government bet on the Indian software industry bringing the Government of India and the software companies closer. Many a time the government and other industries would be quarreling over intricate issues and sometimes it led to an adversorial relationship. However, in the case of software, the government encouraged the industry and opted for the path of collaboration. Fortunately, there were capable and wise people from both the sides. Leaders from large software companies maintained close touch with the leaders within the government. For the next decade, the industry was the government's blue-eyed favorite industry. The sops it received became a cause of disagreement with other industries. At times, the government's foreign policy makers elicited the software industry's views.

A highpoint was the research and development centre by Texas Instrument in Bangalore in 1985. This resulted again from the active collaboration between the government and the industry. Both supported the cause of Texas Instrument, which led to a record of sorts in quick completion of Texas Instrument center. The Texas Instrument research center was first of its kind in the world and fired the imagination of many front ranking companies.

Many began to investigate the feasibility of setting up their centers in India. Other collaborations followed where foreign companies established their centres in India. Companies like Silicon Graphics, Sun, Burroughs, Digital Computers etc. aggressively sought Indian partners. These relationships enlarged from Indian companies selling their products to software collaborations.

It was a shock for India's largest software company when twelve people out of its complement of fifteen walked out of its Australian office one day. Another Bombay company lost almost half its staff in a North European country where it was executing four projects. To have engineers sent to work at customer sites vanish was no longer an event. It happened with depressing regularity.

At a meet organized by the Department of Defense with a clutch of big software companies, the sad reality came home. It was an unusual but a sad reflection when Murthy, the CEO of the top company complained of reneging by four engineers lured by competition a day before they were to leave for customer site. An engineer sent to a Japanese company to understand requirements never returned to his company. While in Japan, he was in regular touch with labor agents and on returning to India, he vanished.

An invited article from Indian software stalwart appeared in a special issue of Spectrum. Spectrum is a respected journal and what it writes settles many a debate and sacrosanct. The article spoke about the opportunities and strengths of the Indian software industry. It dwelt on the extreme competition amongst companies. The author the Director in Charge of TCS ended the article comparing the industry as a pail without a bottom full of crabs. When one started moving up the others clawed it back. The back biting, pulling your competitor down, speaking ill of other companies, appropriating work not done by the company was a part of the software landscape.

The worthy failed to recognize that competition is inevitable in a progressive profit oriented industry. With experienced people switching from one to other company and some moving in the direction to start their own venture, the industry grew and so did the country. It was Sattva. The arts of war and competition were quite similar. Ten years later the software industry changed beyond recognition.

The growing number of customers and their unceasing appetites fired many entrepreneurial dreams. The ability to understand increasing technical complexity and sophistication in creating solutions fostered and shaped these dreams. If you had strong English language skills, it made it easier. Sure, there were opportunities as the industry grew and unleashed the Indian's animal spirits. Nehru's socialist hubris had suppressed the entrepreneurial instincts of Indians for long. Now this 2000's generation was staking its claim to repossess it.

ഗ്ഗ

The Indian software companies attracted the best and the brightest from the very best educational institutions. They were practical people. These engineer managers knew what how to make things work in spite of massive imponderables, constraints and restrictions.

Sarkar began visiting Ajay often in the company in the evenings. He had many a tales to tell. He was keen to become a software labor intermediary. He had the influential contacts, the knowledge and required expertise he often boasted. He would talk about software works characterized by big numbers – revenues, locations, engineers, durations etc. Ajay felt elated if for no reason that he was finally in the right industry.

One day he thrilled Ajay, "When the country's largest software company signed for a massive reengineering program for one of the largest insurance companies it was stuck with many constraints. Winning the contract was itself a singular achievement and not without severe competition but executing it was a massive challenge not attempted before."

Sarkar continued, "Imagine training over a thousand users?"

Ajay nodded wide-eyed, "It must have been a challenge to train this number and surely they were not in one location."

TCS was operating from many campuses in different cities. Sarkar continued, "The company finally choose Madras."

"Perhaps it was a political decision," ventured Ajay and Sarkar nodding replied, "All big companies have their favorite states and your mother tongue sometimes influence decisions though everyone pretends it is not so."

Sarkar continued, "The peak operating was of the order of 600 software engineers. Seating them, inter and intra communications, ensuring standards, documentation uniformity and a whole lot of problem solving methods involving six hundred people when modern communications like teleconferencing, even emails were rudimentary, exchanging huge files over distances unreliable and chancy the company handled it with aplomb."

"Space being limited as also computing resources the company ran three shifts. Programmers in the first shift left the office with a note for the engineers in the next shift who took over from where his colleague had left. It worked and the company delivered in almost the allotted time."

"What did the departing engineer leave for his replacement?" asked Ajay.

Laughing, Sarkar volunteered it began with hand written notes and evolved to a shift report made on the computer which became standard. The Company took innovation a step ahead. "By developing a computer assisted learning module that the user could learn whenever he wanted and where he wanted."

Ajay asked, "There would be competition to be posted on the project?"

"Yes initially. After sometime, the novelty wore off. Engineers were not overtly enthusiastic for a posting to the project. I guess it was boring. Coming in and writing codes with no one to talk and at the end of day report the lines of code you created," replied Sarkar.

Indian ingenuity had won the day. There were many other works, which put Indian software on the global map firmly.

It has never been easy to do business in India. There

were certain castes and communities who were excellent business minds. They knew exactly how to set up, and conduct business and be profitable under all situations. These communities spread across the country. They were often concentrated around a district from which they derived their identity. They bonded tight and like clans stretched to help each other. Their experience and thinking handed down from father to son. They did not believe in writing anything except their accounts. Bankers knew when such people sought finance for their business. The enterprise may or may not prosper. The loan may become sticky but the borrower would always prosper.

Software changed that. Any bright person with the strong desire, knowledge and skills could become an entrepreneur. Focus and single-minded pursuit made some new companies as big as many big old time companies. Hundreds of software firms were set up and many failed but it changed the climate for venturing in the country. Apart from a stray mention in print and visual media, this churn was a topic of conversation amongst aspiring people.

Ajay was comfortable with what he was doing.

At the bus stop he heard two young school children trying to memorize the poem:

How many miles to Babylon?
Can I get there by candle light?
Yes, there and back.
Yes there and back again,
If your heels are nimble and light,
You will get there by candle light.

It sounded so simple and melodious. As he heard the girl recite to her friend, he could not help but be moved by the poem's subtlety and lyricism.

He learnt that still waters run deep.

Being unperturbed in face of provocations was the road to success.

Chapter VI
Becoming Professional

After Dagariya returned from New York, there were many meetings to understand the Y2K gorilla. Charging his management team to keep their ears on the ground, Dagariya began cultivating agents, brokers, professors and consultants for Y2K information opportunities. Asha became the fulcrum because she collected and maintained information perceived to be helpful in launching Y2K business. She would prepare notes for circulation and followup. They would talk or mail or message seeking Y2K business opportunities. Dagariya would talk to his foreign contacts at night and update Asha the next day of the developments.

Asha contacted engineers and managers from Indian companies who had ventured into Y2K business. The Company was on the lookout for employees with Y2K experience and they were difficult to entice. Companies took good care of its Y2K stars. There was market information to share, short-term staff requirements, invitations to bid and a variety of consultants and advisers willing to share information that they claimed was hot. The word went out that anyone who could share hard information about Y2K was very much welcome. The contacts informed about their finder's fees, employee references and technology updates. Those who provided information perceived to useful dined in Bangalore. Foreign and out of city informants sent gifts with notes of thanks from Dagariya and the Company.

The more he talked with people the more it convinced him of the Y2K business potential. The urgings of his brother tilted the balance. As he gained confidence, he had to find a leader to create and run the Y2K business. His Marwari mind searched fora leader looked up by employees, loyal, hardworking and without distractions. He had already decided to cast his lot with Ajay. He had hinted as much to him. In return, Ajay could not help but be grateful to Dagariya.

Securing a buy in from his partners Sharad Zende and Venkataraman, Dagariya sought Asha's sense. Could Ajay fit the role? She concurred. She felt Ajay was the right choice.

Asha being the PRO would have to prepare charts and presentations for marketing the Company's Y2K services. Sushma suggested that in addition to providing those services for the new business Asha would keep a leash on Ajay. Being a part of Y2K network, she was helpful in identifying people who would be of use in this business. For some time Dagariya was planning organizational changes in the company. Since the last two years, Sushma began playing the role of PRO from her home. She was a good conversationalist and initially she was not only the PRO she was the Company's impresario as well and liked doing it. Document preparation and correspondence done at the office based on her directions. The clerk assigned to her tasks would regularly go to her house for understanding her requirements. In the two years that she handled these tasks,three clerks resigned.

With time, Sushma was overloaded and began blaming

others for her shortcomings. She was at sea with technical jargon, which she believed she would be able to imbibe with time and little effort.

A time came when she had to admit that she was finding it difficult to turn in the assignments at the pace it was required. On the advices of his close Marwari friend Dagariya decided to keep her at an arm's length from the actual workings inside the company.

Asha Ketkar happened to be available to replace Sushma . New responsibilities added to Joshi ji, the company accountant and Dagariya's confidant. The reason given was to make the management committee focused and empowered. The fulcrum of the committee was Venkataraman. By empowering Joshi, Dagariya was in effect taking out some responsibilities from Venkataraman. Venkataraman was too busy managing projects that he loved doing. The real purpose was to discourage Venkataraman's interference in accounting matters. A distant relative of Dagariya's brother a professor in the US appointed as the new Chief of Marketing. The incumbent made to quit on flimsy reasons.

Dagariya was clever to stage them bit by bit. Asha's induction completed the new organizational structure.

The new Y2K business line consisted of a half dozen engineers and cross-functional support from other groups. The new division was to be lean and mean. Venkatraman's role was overseeing than managing which was Ajay's domain now. Since this arrangement was for 12 to 18 months before closing, it was in line with Company policy to groom leaders.

The division dissolved or merged into another division after the Y2K business dried. This made admirable sense for it did not need senior management's attention. Dagariya would run it the way he wanted without anybody's intervention and scrutiny. It was a risk so why let this add to the company's total risk. Should it fail Dagariya could cut the cancer from the main company? If it succeeded, reorganize and enter a new area or strengthen an existing one. It made eminent sense and there was no dissent.

True to his style, no one except the directors, including Ajay knew of the organizational changes through the grapevine. Engineers interested in the Y2K opportunity were not pleased when the announcement came. They wondered how could a new employee with insufficient experience, be selected. Further, he was coming out of a personal crisis. Was it an error of judgement? Was it an act of bravado? Was it not a big gamble? Of course only time would vindicate Chairman Dagariya's judgement or otherwise.

Dagariya known for his audacious decisions, many of which turned good fed into the informal network by his cohorts. Soon this became a part of company folklore. There was an element of the extraordinary, which a section of people put it as his prescience. Dagariya and Sushma encouraged the propagation of the folklore – a far thinking, decisive and risk taking entrepreneur. Organizational histories are replete with such characters.

Ajay and Asha were invitees at a dinner hosted by Dagariya in his house. His partners Sharad and Venkataraman and some other software company directors of other companies were present. Ajay felt out of place.

As he surveyed the gathering, his Green Park experience spilled over. From a mere spectator to a participant was a big jump. Ajay heard the same laughter, the clink of whiskey glasses, the awful tobacco smell and the waiters weaving their way through the easygoing cognoscenti balancing trays of foods and drinks. The difference from the Green Park setting was the fewer people and still lesser woman, most connected with the software business and formally dressed and the music, soft. Except the hosts, Asha and Venkataraman and Sharad he knew no one. It was natural that Ajay and Asha huddled together more out of compulsion than by design.

Sushma called Ajay and Asha gesturingthem to come into her kitchen. Most of the guests were busy chatting in groups. The bigger group was around Dagariya in the balcony and the smaller huddled in the living room. Dagariya owned a spacious and tastefully done flat in upmarket area just off Cunningham Road. Sushma would tell her first time guests that she had conceptualized it and done by Nandita Motwani the best-known designer in Bangalore.

Guests were busy with their drinks and eats while conversations centered on software exports. Dagariya was explaining the need to his partners to strengthen marketing. Venkataraman explained the need for more technical and soft skill training. Dagariya trying to convince everybody about the pot of gold in the Y2K business assuring his listeners that there would be no dearth of resources for creating a strong Y2K business. All knew that the window of opportunity was small and time still lesser. Venkataraman made it clear that Ajay, Asha and the new Marketing Head responsible for the success of the business. Recruitment would begin in a month's time. It was to be a short compact team.

The director in charge of the India's largest software company said that he could run the company with only freshers. It was a strong statement. He had said this admonishing his senior managers who had not met his expectations. It only showed the reliance of senior managers on their first line designers and programmers but who in reality were overworked and short charged. The message rippled through the software industry and commented upon and some even said the old man gone soft in the head. A small group at the party was discussing this very remark.

The exports component of the Indian software industry until 1998 was three fourths body shopping. That was how software offshoring began and even when the market developed for custom-built software, it was through works contracts that were extremely competitive. The foreign buyers for long could never figure the Indian companies costing. The Americans and the British began to play one Indian software company against the other because the Indian companies were competing against each other for same work.

The user companies employed consultants to help them select their Indian software vendors. Thus, the term "outsourcing consultants" came into usage, who were professors from universities, retired software professionals and enterprising consultants from established consulting companies and anyone who knew Indian companies, personalities, and access to using companies in the US.

Having warm bodies with a modicum of skill was all what it took to enter the game. A company may not have a skill on its rolls but having access to one the company could stake a claim. Any number of companies from a single engineer operator to thousand-man companies could enter the game. All you needed to be a player in the body shopping market was access to a warm body who had the skill and experience required for the job.

Most of the early players were from Bombay, the leading software city. Quickly companies from Bangalore, Hyderabad, Delhi, Bhubaneswar and Madras entered the fray. There would be a body shop opportunity in the morning and by lunchtime or worst by teatime closed. The country was staking a global claim as a dependable source for skilled software labor. Companies like GE, BULL, Bell North, Silicon Graphics and others set up their own offices in India. Some set up office as a one or two man team operating from five star hotels. If many had a plan, others did not and hoped to find their way after planting their flag. They preferred software cities like Bombay, Bangalore, Bombay, Hyderabad and Delhi, which had a commercial outlook and entrepreneurship culture.

The Company decided to use labor arbitrage. They would access skills without having them as employees on their roster. They would recruit from other small companies and use mercenaries of which there were plenty. The idea was to maintain its inventory of grocery type skills and network with other companies for the rare or less used skills. The Company could not afford to keep a large diversified pool without a successful history of placements. This had been going on since the last year and the results were dismal.

Without wining labor assignments on your own than through second or third hand, your margins suffered. Only the big companies with a few thousands staff companies achieved balance and made handsome profits on shipped engineers quarter to quarter. Some small ones also made good money but the midsized companies were often stuck in their holes. The bench eroded some of the export earnings. A small bench balanced the exigencies of business but a bench greater than 10% was not affordable. They had to find productive work for their idling engineers lest they encountered cash flow problems.

Body Shops had not been a successful operation for the Company. Dagariya kept egging Venkataraman and his senior managers in face of dismal performances and other engineers kept dousing fires because of the inept way the labor business done.

The Company was stuck in the "bid without resource" syndrome. With a sense of bravado, the Resourcing managers convinced that they would find the resource when the time came. Half the time they failed. In some cases, the short time hire reneged. It was galling but the management brazened it out. All small companies had the same problem so there was little discomfort except the opportunity lost. Each day would bring with it its own problems. The lure of earning dollars was a huge a motivation and the rewards too good to miss.

The labor business had limped for the last two years and now needed steam to justify its existence. The promoters determined to drive software offshore labor business with aggression. They reasoned that so far it was reactive, listening to market gossip and running after elusive business that rarely materialized and affected egos negatively. Most often, the market news was stale or too late and the rest of the time, it was just nothing but rumor. It was not Ajay's Company but half of the companies worked this way. It was poor management and carried negative impression in the market place. Since, most of the company's competitors were in the same boat there was nothing to feel bad articulated Dagariya. It was time to take a checkpoint and power the business to respectable results thought Ajay and conveyed to Venkataraman.

Dagariya and his team talked about getting the right sales people and strengthening marketing function. The management team would provide enlightened leadership. The Company responded by creating new or tweaking sales and PR material, and motivating senior people to follow on telephonic sales calls on prospects unearthed by the regular sales people. Demanding more from their sales systems could not help for they were primitive and unsuitable. Everybody knew these initiatives were necessary therefore, they attempted and implemented but nothing much changed. Three years earlier, they had leased satellite communication links without reaping much benefit. The management team kept assuring Dagariya time was propitious and success was round the corner.

❧❧❧

As if on cue, Ajay and Asha walked into the kitchen. Sushma and the chef were busy conversing. Sushma motioned them to a corner out of the earshot of the head cook. Turning towards Ajay she questioned Ajay, "Ajay where is your glass?" Looking at Asha, she shrugged her shoulders and asked her,

"Your hand is also empty. What would you like to drink? What should I make for you? Would you like a whisky or a glass of wine?"

They looked at the ground underneath and then Ajay's eyes caught Asha's eyes. Ajay blushed making their host accuse Ajay, "Hey Ajay, you should not feel shy! It is showing on your face. If Asha feels, shy it is acceptable but I know she is not the one to feel shy"

Ajay's fair cheeks turned pale. He looked at Asha and an unspoken message passed between them and the hostess. It was basic primitive sexual instinct that expresses itself. Ajay had seen Asha as a fellow employee but suddenly Asha seemed different - a beautiful woman.

She at once pounced on them and coming closer, hushed in a conspirative tone, "Why don't you both go for a holiday! Ajay do you know that Asha ji has a hotel in Ooty and she is its sole owner?"

"Please do not reveal my secrets", chimed Asha.

Ajay turned towards Asha and asked cheekily, "Is this true Asha ji? Are you the owner of a hotel? You must be very rich."

Before anyone could turn the conversation into another direction, Sushma admonished, "Ajay, why are you addressing Asha as ji?? Surely, Asha does not like that and how can you address her that way. Is it not Asha?"

"What to do? Ajay is always serious and earnest," replied Asha.

"Ok then, I will get two tickets for friday for you both,go for a holiday and have some fun. I will explain and get Dagariya ji's approval. All talk ends here. I do not want to listen to anything. It is final."

She looked at Asha and winked secretly. It happened so fast and in good faith, that Ajay was speechless. Asha turned towards Ajay and in an amusing way mimicked, "No

Asha ji. That Asha ji!Cut these ji's."

Asha mimicking Sushma shook her index finger admonishing Ajay, "No more calling me with ji's henceforth."

Ajay holding his ears with his fingers said, "Yes teacher!" and all laughed.

She put her right hand on Ajay's shoulder and left on Asha's back and guided them to the balcony. The atmosphere here was one of joy and mirth. The spirits were flowing,tongues loosened, many loud voices, and much laughter. Before Ajay could offer excuses and change his mind, the hostess motioned the waiter who came running with a glass of whisky on a tray. He looked at Ajay and asked whether he would like soda or water. Ajay said, "Anything will do"

He cheered others and his mind drifted to the Green Park experience again. He had held a glass of alcohol the third or fourth time in his life of 27 years. Before dinner, Dagariya raised a toast in honor of Ajay. He announced that from Monday, Ajay would lead the company's Y2K business. Dagariya's wife remonstrated, "No sir not from Monday. Let him start from Tuesday, because Tuesday is a good and an auspicious day".

Asha seconded saying, "Tuesday is Lord Hanuman's day. Let Ajay take his new responsibility from Tuesday."

There was a general agreement and people clapped. A fresh round of drinks was on the way.

Ajay was in a daze. Life had changed so much and so fast in so few days. What was the catch? He wondered.

Reaching his room, he bathed, changed into clean clothes. Lighting essence sticks, he read Hanuman Chalisa 108 times and thanked Lord Hanuman. Without His Grace he reasoned with himself one cannot achieve his objectives. With Him, one is successful in spite of obstacles. He removes the constraints that might be there or crop up later and crowns one's efforts with success.

People pray to Gods to know and feel God's immense power and seek benevolence. Gods are all powerful and people pray to them with the hope that some of his powers may rub on the devotees. They seek his mercy and grace to meet their goals and lessen their miseries. Lord Hanuman has immense power, is immortal, paragon of extreme devotion and humility. His devotees believe that praying to him will help them achieve their goals under all circumstances. Ajay was a devout Hanuman devotee. Hanuman, the son of the God of Wind was an essential part of his upbringing

IBM had the largest number of its computers installed in the country. It had machines of various vintages like IBM 1400, IBM 7000, IBM 2090, S/360, 90 Series etc. In India and in most other countries their machines outnumbered others. IBM had differences with the Indian government and the minister in charge George Fernandez asked IBM to wind up and leave. They did, leaving behind their machines and software and an army of engineers who knew these machines inside out. Many of these machines installed in Government organizations located all over the country. The popular languages of that time were COBOL, FORTRAN, ALGOL, PL/1 etc. There were other machines like DG, Digital, NEC and BULL etc. using the same or similar programing languages.

To be in the Y2K business, a company had to have people with experience on these machines, compilers and other system utilities. Programmers become champions by extensive programing using popular languages of that era on different machines. They strengthened their experience by working on a variety of machines engaged in different works, from creating to maintaining code.

Once an application system is up and running, it needs maintenance. Conditions change from user end leading to development of newer services or modifications of existing versions of applications. The systems software is which that runs the computer and manages its operations, which needs update and optimize from time to time, forcing maintenance requirements on applications. Coding, debugging or quality assuring and re-engineering are the bread and butter of a programmer.

The software industry had powered many entrepreneurial dreams. There were money bags,skilled people and demand and connecting them made business. From a one-man show to a fifty man company funded by resourceful people were offering training German to the Y2K business. When the big companies saw the opportunity, they developed their own Y2K training programs. TCS, CMC, Tata Burroughs, Datamatics delivered better training edging out the smaller outfits. By 1998/99, many courses to learn Y2K works were available.

Sharad Zende suggested that Ajay attend the training given by CMC a Government of India Company. CMC was in the business of computer training and software development and delivered two courses on Y2K. CMC had strong experience and the market endorsed it. It maintained government computers of many vintages sourced from all parts of the world. Ajay enrolled for both the courses in CMC, Madras. The main course was on using tools, database redesign, creating and embedding tracers etc. The other course was on business development covering estimating, time and price, making proposals and presentations.

∽∽∽

On Monday, Asha inviting him to her office said, "Bus tickets are with me. Come and collect them." She continued, "Ajay we have four clear days. Back and forth journeys are night affairs and do not count. The buses are comfortable, and I usually travel with them". Ajay looked at her and before he could say anything, she continued, "Now stop with your ji, ji. The bus will leave at ten at night, and so you come a bit earlier. The bus stand is in Kalasipalyam. You could also board at Peenya."

Smiling with a new found confidence while sitting opposite to Asha he said, "Ok! Asha I will let you know on wednesday evening"

"About what?" asked Asha in exasperation?

"Where I will board the bus," said Ajay shyly.

They chatted for some time and then he got up and quickly squeezed Asha's hand on the table. She admired his confidence and making a circle with her middle finger and thumb waved at departing Ajay. It did not escape him that she was much older than he was, possibly a good fifteen years or more but she had maintained her body and therefore looked younger.

He did not know from where this surge of confidence had come. His exchange was not sexual but a simple statement of being happy having her befriended him.

Ajay informed Sarkar on phone about his elevation as a Business Head of the new Y2K business. They met for dinner. Ajay told him what was necessary. He was beginning to get worldly wise and more focused. He knew that he was reinventing himself.

Listening to Sarkar's do's and don'ts to succeed in his new position Ajay intuitively grasped that he should not expect his experience and environment to be too open and confide in everybody. He would be competing with other Head of departments. Sarkar cautioned to keep his personal data protected. Singularly focused was the unsaid message. They examined the software industry and its evolution as also the new India's aspirations.

The new Indian aspiration now stretched to entrepreneurship. Before 1954/55, jobs were with the government and later in the growing public sector. Twenty years later, it was the turn of the banking and financial services. The flood of jobs hit the banking and financial industry that spread across the country. Then it was the turn of the software sector in 1994/95. Entry level banking jobs did not require any special training while computer jobs required intensive specialized training. This period characterized by the changing business landscape.

This sort of upsurge in the economy leading to life improvements in a broad swathe of the population occurred every twenty years. Going by this rate the next big economic swing would be in 2018 onwards.

For an ambitious young man the preferred opportunity was to work for Tata's, Birla's, Ambani's or others of their ilk. Entrepreneurship opportunities were non-existent and rare. However, there was self-employment in the fields of accounting, law and consulting. The software industry opened entrepreneurship like nothing had done in the last hundred years. One-man companies to large companies employing a few hundreds of people sprang up. Entrepreneurs sensed the need of services like recruitment, training, legal services, research etc. and were busy creating these services and setting up companies to provide them. Most started as one or a few man outfits. Those that survived two years grew and prospered. As the software industry grew in numbers, it reproduced the secondary and tertiary services.

There were many success stories in varied services, from outsourced canteens to air conditioning to janitor services. These success stories motivated and fired the imagination of thousands. The simple logic went like this, if my friend or my friend's friend or my neighbour has done it, why can't I do it? Alternatively, why do I not try it?

It was a powerful idea for an ambitious young man or a woman. It unleashed the entrepreneurial instinct of Indians and we are seeing its first, flowering today. Not without reason pollsters and commentators with world knowledge, count Bangalore in one of the top ten entrepreneurial and creative cities in the world. Delhi or Bombay or Hyderabad is not far off.

~~~

Ajay was as narrowly moralistic as Sarkar was loosely pragmatic and practical. Ajay had strong opinions on corruption, nepotism, favoritism and discrimination. For Sarkar, life was all about winning and once you set out to win nothing is sacrosanct than your goal. More than half of India supported this idea and thought like Sarkar. However the left out are in dire straits and India is approaching the next decade at war with itself.

Ajay came closer to him even though he was an idealist and Sarkar was proud to call himself pragmatic. Both wanted to get ahead in life. "Why blame the government for every wrong thing? We all pay bribes to get things done. All this adds up to national character, which is the aggregate of individuals. It devolves on the individual," elaborated Ajay.

He wanted to set up his own firm for labor intermediation by hiring and placing engineers in companies and set up offices in cities with major software hubs. His conversations and dreams inspired Ajay. Never in the history of India in the last two hundred years, entrepreneurship flourished in this infectious way and created so many dreams and hopes for the youth.

One day Sarkar discussed with Ajay the possibility of him supplying engineers to his Company. He wanted to have his company listed along with other labor vendors. Ajay promised to work on this. Sarkar explained the nature of this business and its soft corrupt underbelly.

The number of engineering colleges that opened their doors through the 1995 decade was so enormous and simultaneously the number of engineering opportunities in
~~~

the software companies increased albeit disproportionately. The average age of a software employee in a company was twenty-seven. The average of an INFOSYS employee was between twenty-seven and twenty-eight and half the engineers in TCS were twenty-seven or less. The software industry was fullof youngsters unlike any other industry. However, the bugbear was that the percentage of quality engineers and managers out of the thousands produced was dismal.

The insatiable appetite of the industry for software engineers and managers with sound theoretical knowledge who could put this into practice, possess good English language skills, at least acceptable personal quality and logical thinking spawned varieties of training and recruitment companies. Both were closely connected. The pivot around which they revolved was the HR or Personnel or the HR managers in the hiring companies. He or she was the kingpin of the recruiting game.

People in the human resource and personnel streams was taught the necessity of being fair, honest and ethical in their professional courses, but in practice majority of them were all but that. It was a fraud-tainted profession. The number of recruiters was a legion at the turn of the century. Recruitment companies were concentrated mostly in software oriented cities of Delhi, Bombay, Hyderabad, Pune, Bangalore, Calcutta, Coimbatore, Cochin and maybe another two or three cities. The number of firms in Bangalore was 1,000 by conservative standards. They were from one-man shows operating from homes to large multi city professional firms employing scores of staff.

Sarkar continued, "Whosoever could get hold of resumes of engineers actively hunting for jobs was a player and could enter the game. The number of sources from where resumes sourced was limited and therefore the same resumes floated in the databases of many recruitment companies.

The response to a call for resume for a particular skill could result in the same submitted by more than one recruitment company. The resulting conditions were tailor built for fraudulent arrangement and schemes."

The guilty and unpardonable rascals were the chiefs of the recruitment function. They could be blatantly setting up companies in the names of their wives or known people, promote recruiters who were in league with them, release information selectively, manipulate the name of the submitting recruiter to the one they favored, mark a received resume from one to another recruiter he or she wished to favor and so on. Sometimes few staff members would get together and subverted the recruitment process. There could be one or more delinquent staff acting on their own and in some cases directed by their chiefs.

"Normally the fee paid to a recruiter for a selected candidate was his one month's salary and if difficult to source skills it could be as high as 20% of the candidate's annual salary. The number of engineers and managers recruited in 1999 from the open market less campus recruitments in 1998 estimated as hundred thousand. . You can estimate the value of the recruitment industry computed as one month salary of one hundred thousand engineers. That is a large amount," concluded Sarkar.

Ajay was astonished and skeptically asked, "You mean even the big MNC's and other top companies are guilty?"

"The Multinationals are very much guilty and I know of managers who demand their gratification as a birthright. They are ruthless and straightforward with their open palms twitching. Again, this is a network and if you are not a part of this network, you were out. No entry," said Sarkar painfully. "If I were to tell you the names of companies involved you'll be shocked."

"But why do the recruitment companies do so? It

beats me why do they part with their profits. You will say this is the cost of doing recruiting business!"

"Bribing to get business is a part of your costs. There is a jungle out there and in this cutthroat competition, maintaining your cash flow is vital. A few months of negative cash flow could throw you out of business," reasoned Sarkar.

Ajay countered, "You named some successful people and businesses that made phenomenal success and crazy money?"

Sarkar replied, "Yes there are such people and after making obscene money diversified into construction business and even became venture capitalists."

"Some became politicians by joining hands with the main political parties. Madras has quite a few," added Sarkar thoughtfully.

"But those must be rare kind of people. A dozen or two dozen people from a hundred thousand would be a very small percentage. Isn't it?" amazed Ajay.

"No Ajay. I would think there would be two or three dozens in each major city. If there were not so many successes, business and businessmen would not enter," clarified Sarkar.

"You will be surprised to know about the kind of people, I mean the quality of people in this business. You do not need any great skills, just good strong networking abilities. Theskills you might need to get hired, in which case you have to get an entry into a network be alive to the numbers game and keep everyone happy," added Sarkar.

"When you are willing to grease the palms of HR people, everything becomes easy."

"I remember you introduced to me a recruiter, if I recall his name Pamesh Singh Rana. I could not make out what he was saying. He sort of was mumbling his speech, eating words, really Sarkar; I could barely make out what he was saying. Yeah, the quality of people in this game is poor and personal qualities not critical to success," added Ajay.

"So you see any guy can be doing this play. The last time I talked to him, he was talking about buying a piece of land in Himachal, from where hehails," informed Sarkar.

"I remember you wanted to make some business arrangement with him. What happened finally?" queried Ajay.

"He was too money minded and self-centered. Such people are always planning a fast trick on someone. They do so because they are intellectually empty and would not think twice before selling their mothers for two bits of silver," concluded Sarkar in disgust.

Sarkar had fanciful business plans and when challenged he reverted to labor placements.

Sarkar had assiduously built a network comprising of fresh and experienced engineers from computer training institutes. It was a symbiotic relationship with these training insitutes. If they could place their students, their stock rose. It leads to more enrollments with consequent more candidates to choose from. Sarkar had cultivated the personnel managers of a few companies building commercial connections. They extracted fees for each placement. He was moving engineers from one company to another at Rs. 9/10 thousand and paying them 5/6 thousand, while pocketing the rest as profit.

When his business picked up, Sarkar employed a retired project manager. He operated from his home who took his cut for interviewing and forwarding them to prospective employers. A large number of managers of employing companies charged commissions, which were unavoidable. It was like an unwritten rule. It was a messy gravy train and once you knew the big companies and names involved, you would be shocked! Creating and manipulating this network looks simple but it was a dirty sweatshop and sometimes you stooped so low it was debasing oneself. Pamesh Singh is a prime example. He crawled and took it out on his staff that lived on tenterhooks about the security of their tenure. Most failed, few succeeded and still fewer succeeded amazingly. Sarkar always spoke as making it big. Big success was around the corner. It just did not come easy.

Ajay wondered how he could run his own business along with his employment with another company. Whenever he asked Sarkar, he was evasive. Did it not mean conflict of interest? Not really, as it was quite a common thing. Many did, few complained.

There were engineers moon shining in the market. Experienced, working with successful companies, technically sound engineers were ready to have second jobs clandestinely. Working on weekends and for rush jobs in. The moon shining culture championed by big newspapers. It was not a big deal, the newspapers propagated and how it was done in many countries, the highest racket was luring Japanese engineers and managers to Korea. The newspapers motivated moonshiners, to advertise their services on their papers, free of cost. They saw these jobs as extra income and for some it became a doorway to entrepreneurship leading to setting up their companies in course of time. The game was high on perceptions. Perception is reality and reality is perception. That was that and after a year or two of doing a second job on the sly for many dreams remained dreams and the urge faded away.

This was the stage of software companies during the closing of the last century. They worked in an environment of power shortages, undependable data circuits and not so reliable techies who could resign for a few rupees more at the most awkward time. In spite of all these the Indian software industry was flourishing. The industry grew further. The Indian software industry generated 15 billion dollars of exports in 1999. This was about 1.5% of the country's GDP and 10% of exports at the turn of the century. It employed almost one million people directly and three times in the secondary and tertiary sectors.

The dotcom era began and crashed two years later. In 1999, two firms opened each day in software cities and one closed shutters. This was undoubtedly fastest growing sectors in terms of employment and revenues. Importantly entrepreneurship was visible in every facet of the tech industry. This created the ground for innovation and dynamism.

Dagariya called up Sarkar and registered him as labor supplier. He completed the formalities and signed a standard contract running into eight sheets of paper. The contract detailed rates, payments, training, replacements of engineers reneging, duties, responsibilities etc. Since he did not have a registered company, he signed as a consultant promising Joshi ji to establish a company and replace this contract with a new one.

For Sarkar it was a big day. For all the thinking, planning and scheming and after some stray deals he was dreaming of his own company, which would become legal in a few days. He was now convinced that he was onto bigger things. He had to form a new company or partnership and if he did that, then he may have to find a new office in case Kaveri asked him to leave.

Ajay began his journey from his work stretching out into the industry.

He was expanding his horizon.

Chapter VII
Ajay's Seduction

Ajay boarded the bus at Peenya. Asha had got on earlier and looked out for him in Peenya. He saw her and leaned over her to place his bag on the overhead rack and while sitting down his elbow dug into her breast. Conscious, he felt goosebumps burst on his arms and before he could apologize, she offered her hand and shaking it he forgot what had just happened. In the soft diffused light, he looked at Asha and she smiled in return, her bright red lips opening and spreading sideways.

She was attractive beautiful for a woman in her late forties with a school-going daughter of 16. She was fair, with big eyes, well placed pointed nose, uplifted tight breasts that he discerned rather than see through her blue tee shirt in the faint light in the bus. She had shoulder length hair cut in the day's fashion which according to her signified youth. Her feminine hands with long straight slender fingers ending in red painted nails added to her beauty.

She smelled nice and Ajay wondered why splash a

perfume for a night's journey in the bus? They chatted and as the bus hit the highway, lights switched off and the bus picked up speed. After some time they fell silent. Relaxed, he stretched out his legs and his thigh touched her's. She pressed her thigh on his and eased.

Her shape and her behavior had lodged in his memory as he was seeing her often with his new responsibilities and now whenever he closed his eyes her image would not leave him. She with her firm buttocks under her flaring hips was an ingression in his memory and he wondered if he would be able to doze.

Soon it was pitching dark, and silent, the forest ceased to be visible through which the bus was speeding and the only sound was the whoosh of the tires. Most of the travelers were sleeping and even Asha seemed to be sleeping. She began falling on his shoulder. He moved away and she followed his movement. Again after some time, Asha began leaning and resting on Ajay. Her thigh and leg jammed against his and her head rested on his shoulders. Her breast was digging into his chest. It was a harmless and a common picture that could have occurred with any man and a woman friend traveling at night in a bus. However, it made Ajay uncomfortable. Ajay was not sure if she was sleeping! Maybe she was, maybe she was not!

Ajay shifted away from her seat and folding his arm over the aisle armrest,he put his head over it and dozed in fits. Having never faced such a situation,he was distracted. He thought the setting not ordinary in the night bus but sex crept into his thoughts. In one's daily life in the Indian metros,such experiences are not rare and one does not give thought to them and moves on. For Ajay, this was novel made more so by his imagination. As his imagination went overboard, he realized that his sexual reverie had given him an erection. Feeling guilty, he controlled his emotions. In her moments of sleep and wakefulness, Asha was aware of what was happening. What she could not see, she inferred.

She had known Ajay as shy, uptight and puritanical. Perhaps it was his inexperience or simple prudery and maybe the settings might have affected him. Asha in her younger days looked forward to strange and out of ordinary settings for sexual dalliances. Her husband was a God fearing man with a Victorian outlook. That was also her complaint in her marriage for she had a healthy sexual appetite with an experimental side. She was missing the touch of a male for quite some time and its absence made her long for it. She recalled her sex-drenched week with Ubhayankar and her unsuccessful attempt with Dagariya as the only encounters in the past four years. Dagariya's was a disaster as they agreed not to include sex in their relationship.

Of course, Ajay was puritanical. He had to be seduced. That was her challenge and she could deploy her best arts of seduction. When the need arose, she could transform herself into a wild stormy and a crafty coquette. Her life moved from her work in the company, to telephoning and short meetings with her daughter and monthly visit to her hotel. Everything was businesslike where there was no opportunity for man games or seduction.

Her hotel was doing well and after deduction of expenses, she was earning a good amount, subcontracting the hotel's operations to Dagariya seemed like a good move. She had been transferring her earnings into her bank account. The bank manager advised her to invest in safe government and other banking products, which she did. Then her manager introduced her to his brother who was a retired bank official and now investment adviser. Her money was there forewell invested and diversified. Asha's Income Tax records were straight and nobody knew about her net worth or her money arrangements. She handled inquiries about her financial dealings from Mahesh and Sushma cautiously. After her reluctance, they never tried to delve into her life.

She, at all times kept her eagerness of becoming a secret party, hidden. Forced to get Ajay to her hotel for a holiday before he took up his new job responsibilities, she concluded why not enjoy it whatever be the reason. She was a willing accomplice even though the situation forced on her. If there was one person who could twist Sushma and plant ideas into her mind then Asha could handle her life splendidly without scruples. Asha liked what was happening and believed that it giving Ajay the experience of his life would be a win win for both.. She could not understand that why it took her so long to realize that she had actually admired him since the day they first met. Slowly like a young virginal girl growing up and feeling the curiosity of sex, her admiration for Ajay turned to idolizing him. If she had a choice to create a perfect husband, then she would have always chosen Ajay.

They reached Ooty bus stop at six in the morning. It was chilly and Asha took out a shawl from her handbag and wrapped it around herself, and Ajay put on a sweater. It was late November. Early morning fog, low clouds and greenery with a picture postcard look was as good a welcome that ever could be. However, her visits were monthly and she always landed unannounced, and this kept her manager in suspense and the staff on alert.

They hired an auto rickshaw and reached Pine Woods. The manager came out to receive and courted them to their rooms. She stayed in a special suite reserved for her, on the third floor. Ajay's room was next to her. They were spacious rooms with their anti-chambers outside the bedroom and adjoining the bathrooms. There was a fireplace in sitting room from where a small passage opened into a pantry with a gas stove and a private balcony. Ajay was impressed. When he mentioned to her the beauty of the place, she said, "This is

God's play. God gives and God takes it all way. This has been the experience of my life."

By eight,Ajay had toured the property and was fascinated. It was picturesque, secluded green below and the low clouds meeting in the far away horizon. A romantic setting helped clean and uplifting of the spirits. Nevertheless, when you see this regularly then, after a couple of days you find that this is all that is there. There is nothing more to do here. There is nobody intelligent to talk with, no shopping arcades, food courts and only honeymooning couples lost into each other you are bound to get bored. Asha was proud that she bore it for more than two years without any excitement and listening to complaints, which upset her so much that she wanted to run away until Dagariya rescued her.

She had reconciled that her dream of converting Pine Woods into something close to Azure was far and impossible. She was a practical person so she moved on and soon gave up on all attempts to refurbish it, as she would have loved to. It spun money for her and that was all she wanted and was happy.

At ten, they had a breakfast. Asha chose her words carefully to suggest hers not too happy life, how she was a victim of circumstances and disguising her longing for him at the same time in odrder to not nudge him. Asha's story was simple. A poor sprightly girl, the heartthrob of her college wounded by her innocence and betrayed by her own.

She spun her tales around what Ajay would love to listen and with as many true incidents that embellished it. He was impressed that she had found a cause to live after everything crashed, and she had many lows in her life. In spite of misfortunes, she maintained a happy disposition and kept her pains and frustrations hidden. She felt honored to share parts of her life with a sensitive and honorable person like him. She did not expect sympathy but only understanding of the mystery called life. She had her own life to peer into and through it wove her world view.

Yes, she had kept herself in good shape. Having played hockey for the state, she exercised for an hour most of the days. She ran, walked and worked out at the gym, careful of what she ate. Yes, she looked much younger and often complimented as long as she could remember. She had her beautician who worked with her once a month, in Bombay. Since her tragedy, there were no beauticians in her life. She drank occasionally for the joie de vivre it brought but never to forget the past. She was the one quick to laugh whether on a joke or the stupidities of people or the frailties of humankind.

Ajay could not agree more and gushed, "No doubt! You have beautifully managed your life even after such traumatizing events, which would have shattered any other woman. In India, relatives are quick to enter a rich woman's life when she is down and fighting life. After winning her trust, she becomes an easy prey for manipulation. Manipulation leads to dependency and often leads to bad consequences."

"I admire your strength and fight for independence and self-preservation. There must have been relatives trying to inveigle in your life?"

"Don't ask me. Many tried to sweet talk to me," shot Asha. "When God marks you, he sends people who take care of you and creates situations that are just right for you."

It was cryptic. Ajay let it pass as another received insight into life.

She did not want their conversation to get more personal. At least not now, when they were trying to know each other and she thought let there be room for course correction if needed. The signs were there and Asha told Ajay, "I will check the operations of the past month. I have arranged a motorcycle and I am keen to show you the sights outside Ooty which few people got to visit unless they have a strong liking for that. I will be back in an hour."

He could rest or go about discovering the place.

An hour later Ajay stood under the hotel arch admiring a huge old 1961 modelF650, 652 cc dark blue BMW motorcycle. The motorcycle stood cleaned scrubbed, washed, and polished. Shiny chrome exhausts, wheels, brakes and handlebars looked just beautiful. It looked straight out of a magazine advertisement. The seat remodeled to accommodate 1 + 2 people. It had a history to it that an Englishman had driven the bike from Cardiff on an adventure trip with his girlfriend. She fell sick in Lahore and returned but he had carried on and reached Ooty. He later ran out of money and sold this to the owners of the hotel.

Asha was no motorcycle enthusiast and once given the keys as if by providence reached it before the manager could, was just about to sell it. Later when she learned about its ownership details, she had it kept safely in the small basement that served as a storehouse for all the garden tools and hoses, old kitchen utensils, and unserviceable hotel items marked for disposal.

Asha Ketkar inherited the motorcycle through purchase of the hotel and was its third owner in the last 15 years. She never knew that the previous owner of the hotel, a Tamilian businessperson owed money to Ubhayankar's bank and he agreed to sell the hotel to the bank against settlement against his dues. The bank buffeted by scandals, he quietly changed the names on the sale deeds into Asha Ketkar's name and she became the new owner. Ubhayankar never spent a single pie for acquiring the hotel.

Ajay was not much of a motorcycle enthusiast himself but he could drive well. The mechanic began kicking and soon the engine roared to life. The mechanic started and switched off a few times to ensure reliability. Ajay sat astride, made a short ride, and said, "I am quite comfortable with it. For this size and power it is almost noiseless."

Asha was watching from the reception. She was dressed in a white tee shirt and blue jeans. They greeted each other and Ajay missed a beat and whispered in her ear, "You are looking gorgeous"

"Let's get out fast." A bearer came running with their packed lunch and water bottle and as she sat astride he shouted, "Such scenes must be common with hundreds of honeymooning couples." His words trailed away lost to the winds. She might have not heard them. She shouted aloud that she was not afraid of speed in response to his query on fast driving. At a traffic light, he asked her cheekily to come closer to him and put her arms around him for more comfort and better driving. Her breasts flattened on his back, she put her hand around his waist and her thighs, and legs were brashing into his. As they crossed the city, she leaned and crouching up shouted in his ear,"Ajay take the right turn, it will take us to the highest point in Ooty." They were like any honeymooning couple going for a spin on hilly roads. She was thrilled and happy beyond imagination. Her past disappeared as she hummed a bollywood song until Ajay asked her, "What are you saying?" Are you singing? Sing louder. I also want to hear your song". She tried being louder and Ajay heard snaps of her hum which went like . . . .

"Bachpan ke din bhi kya din the

Udte phirte titli ban ke
Wahaan phir they ham phoolon mein pade;

Jahaan dhoondte sab hameen chote bade
Wahaan phir they the ham phoolon mein pade;

Jahaan dhoondte sab hain chhote bade
Thakh jaate they ham kaliyaan chunte
Kabhi roye to aap hi hans diye hamey
Choti, choti khushiyan chote chote wo gham."

[Ah for those days of our childhood,
When we use to flit about like butterflies,
Moving in and out amongst flowers in gardens,
And, our parents and the young ones would search for us
As we gamboled amongst bunches of flowers.

Our elders and our young friends,
Search for us amongst clusters of flowers.
And, sometimes we would cry and other times laugh merrily
At those, little joys and sorrows.]

The air was getting cooler as they climbed higher. When she shivered in her tee shirt, seeking warmth her tremors passed through Ajay.

"What is happening to you? I have never seen you so happy"

"It is nothing. Nothing, I do not know what is happening to me today"

"You seem to be very happy. Humming ever so softly, speaking from your heart. I can only hear a few words. Next time sing for me", said Ajay in the whooshing wind.

"Yes I am very happy today" and snuggled closer.

"Neither happiness or sadness can be grasped in your fist. Just as you wish, switch on and be happy or cry, Ajay", shouted Asha against the roaring sound of the wind whistling past them.

What could have happened to Ajay? He was moving

with the flow. Cold misty air flowing past him, and he was driving as fast as safety permitted. He was a programmer who by training does not take risks. The moisture in the air, clouds and the empty road was inviting the opening up of his suppressed feelings and lost sentiments. He would not have thought twice even if he made a fool of himself. Something new was creeping into his soul.

The future beckoned.

They enjoyed the ride on the snaking road cutting through thick forests with tall wide trees. Along the road a swathe of tea gardens, one after the other exuding aromas of native tea leaves and heaps of leaves lying in straw baskets. There were factories distilling aromatic oils and manufacturing medicines and unguents from herbs and could be smelt miles away. At last, they reached the parking lot. Parking the bike, they rubbed their hands together for warmth. The temperature was around 4 degrees centigrade.

After settling the bike on a flat ground they walked following a trail that cut through the forest taking them to the highest point in South India. High altitude, birds were chirping most of which they had never seen before. He asked her about the tourist spots and she said breathlessly that there were many. There was the zoo, botanical garden, nurseries, sundials. They reached the place called the Suicide Point that infamously a favorite spot for people to jump 600 feet down below to end their lives. It had been fenced now.

Ajay led her and after half an hour's walk, they found a place to east. The cool temperature and the aromatic air stoked their gastric fires. As they sat eating, Asha asked, "Now you hold an important position, and Sushma told me that no one gets a position like this at such a young age. What are your plans for the future?"

"You can trust me. Unburden yourself."

He did not know what to say. He continued chewing

and thought that it would give him respite from answering her. She guessed and persisted, "I know the Dagariya family well and visit them often. That I do, but I still maintain a certain degree of formality. I address Mahesh as Sir always, whether it is office or his house. Your friend Sarkar works and has his own business. There seem to be many opportunities for doing business in software today. Is that not so?"

"I don't know too much about that. Of course Sarkar keeps talking about that and he has been doing his stuff for the past four years but he has nothing much to show for his efforts. Moreover, I do not like labor business. Though body shopping is essential to keep IT export companies running," replied Ajay.

"But seems like you want to know if I would like to start my own business? Yes, I would definitely, someday but it is early yet." She put her hand on his and squeezing it added, "Yeah, it maybe early. Having a goal makes one conscious of the future he wants to create. Your goal in life is always in front of you. You cannot run away from your goal or ever forget it." Except Mythri, no one had talked like that, egging him and motivating him. She said with force and concern and it hit like a shot into his sensibilities, inspiring him.

"Ajay, I know you are cut out for greater things than simply being an employee. I see in you qualities of a successful businessperson. Be close to Dagariya Sir. He funds people who he feels can create new avenues. He has investments in many businesses, from a token amount to more than 50%. What I mean, he invests to help them start their business. Sushma told me that Dagariya thinks highly of you."

Ajay rolled his eyes heavenward and smiled. "So, how high will you take me?"

"When you start your company, don't forget to make me your employee," laughed Asha.

"Sure I'll make you my personal secretary", chirped

Ajay.

"Is that all you have for me? You will only make me your secretary. I will be your partner", retorted Asha.

"Stop cooking up so many dreams. You will get a bad stomach", responded Ajay.

As they guffawed, he stood up and offered his hand and taking it, she was on her feet. They walked through the forests and could see the sun setting down and feel the evening getting colder. In the undulating goat tracks they bumped, their waists rubbing and hitting each other. She slipped her hand in his to steady herself.

She felt happy and contented. When was it like this last time?" She asked herself. She steeled her mind and threw her self-questioning out of her system forcing herself to come into the present. There was no past for she had jettisoned that coming to Ooty and they were eight thousand and five hundred feet above the sea level. She was happy! Deliriously happy!

They started the ride back to the hotel, lost in the clouds and chilled to the bones. It was five when they reached the hotel. Tea was awaiting them. As they climbed to the room she said, "Ajay let's have a bottle of wine before dinner."

"I have bought this bottle of wine with great feeling, just for you. Do not disappoint me. Come to my suite between seven and seven thirty," she looked at him with shining eyes..

He shook his head in affirmative and walked into his suite.

Ajay walked to Asha's room and knocked. She had kept the door unlocked and invited him in a singsong voice, "It is open. Come in." She had been waiting for him and as he entered, she rose from the three-seater sofa she was sitting on. Spreading her arms wide welcoming him, Asha continued, "I have been waiting for you."

He sat on the sofa opposite her's. Asha was wearing

a dark blue nightie, which came below her ankles hiding her anklet and open-toe white strapless sandals. Her tomato red toenails peeping out sexily and the face fresh without make up except a hint of pink on her lips, made her look younger and sexy beyond her age. She must have just showered as water droplets stood glimmering on the ends of her hair tied in a bun. Ajay not prepared for this instinctively thought Asha definitely attractive and he felt goosebumps.. She had cast a spell on him. He gawked at her. To break the awkward silence Asha said, "After a shower, I feel fresh and clean. You also look fresh too."

The wine bottle was lying in the ice bucket on the table and two bowls of short eats. One contained assorted dry fruits like fried almonds and cashews and the other fried chicken pieces. Walking to the sideboard under the sky window, she returned with two glasses and a corkscrew and he helped her open the bottle. She filled their glasses, clinked and cheered. Thanking him for the wonderful morning. Her bun untangled and the hair cascaded down onto her shoulders.

She lifted her bare feet up and put them under her haunches. To put him at ease she asked him if he liked the morning ride, and other things like if he felt tired after the driving and walking. No, he was not and she had exerted the same as he had. Pointing to the wine cooler bowl with intricate carving and cute handles she told him that it was a rare white wine from Australia. It was difficult to acquire and she had to make many phone calls to get it. Ajay said, "Thanks. I am impressed by your choice and effort." He shrugged his shoulders, "I admire your knowledge and taste and know that I am in safe hands. This will be my first wine drinking experience. I know nothing about wines."

She pointed to the eatables on the table and added that eating them moderated the effect of the wine. Wine being acidic and drinking fast without eating could get your insides acidic and drunk.

"Ajay feel the slight tipsiness of alcohol! The carelessness and the tipsiness which wine brings is only experienced with one's own. Urdu poetry is full of wine and tipsiness", lisped Asha.

"Oh yes, without a doubt! A good part of Urdu Shayri is on alcohol and taverns." Ajay added,Definitely alcohol is an important part of Urdu poetry. I have no experience in these matters". "I do not know", Ajay tried to suppress his guilt and unworldliness. It was true. Ajay did not know what to say. He was excited. "Just stop me when you see me getting tipsy," implored Ajay.

She smiled and laughed. Her full throaty laugh rose from her chest, emerged on her face, and bathed her face naturally with a hint of coquettishness. As they chatted, they let their guards down. He had never met someone like her. She had a distinct personality and she was trying to be friendlier. He had found her to be caring and kind when she was not being funny. As a woman, she was worldly wise who knew the value of having fun and not taking life too seriously. Ajay was not that sophisticated to differentiate between the natural and the superficial.

Displaying a level of intimacy, tension and passion, she became philosophical and serious. She engaged Ajay, trying to allay his concern and also understanding his sensitivity. He was at peace and felt the chemistry between them warm, exciting and enticing. Ajay decided that Asha was a woman that he could trust.

Asha seriously, "There is a saying that God knows better than you do?"

"Yes, God is Omniscient, isn't it?"

"So whatever you get in life think of it as God's gift. He has chosen for you the best in his infinite wisdom. You may want whatever your heart or mind desires, but he knows better. If he gives you what you ask which may not be what you really need? You think you want that but you may not really need that. If that creates problems and make you unhappy, you will blame him. If he does not give you what you ask but something else, again you will get angry saying what sort of God is this who gives me what I have not asked for. Both ways, God is made responsible. So leave it to God," philosophized Asha.

Wine added to their loquacity. Asha, did not require anything to loosen her tongue when she wanted to.

Ajay nodded in agreement.

Asha continued, "You must be forever grateful to God. Believing, thinking and acting this way you will) come closer to God, get inner strength, and never be fearful."

Ajay found the logic compelling. He had grown up with this belief if not logic. He asked Asha, "How can we make this way of thinking and living a part of our lives?"

"Firstly don't fuss too much about yourself. Think more about others. Do not dwell on the past or think of the future".

"What you say is true. My grandfather use to exhort everyone to forget the past and neither think of the future and always live in the now and here," added Ajay.

They sipped through their first glass. She asked Ajay to pour another. Ajay hesitated and she said slowly, "Nothing will happen. Do not be scared. I am there to take care of you."

In their banter, they failed to sense they were getting tipsy. After he filled both their wine glasses the fourth time, the bottle was empty. He walked around the table and handed her glass. She took her glass and squeezed his hand. Her flirtatious chatter and the bonhomie made him at ease and he wanted to reach out and touch her. Feeling her amiability, he ventured and touched her cheek and swiped his finger on her lips, which she pretended to bite.

She let her legs fall on the ground slipping her feet off her sandals. Ajay's eyes took her in and his eyes fell on her low cut nightie. She leaned forward slightly and he could see her cleavage. In his drunken haze, he saw it as beautiful fair, firm with baby fat and poking out. He felt his mouth extraordinary clean and the morsels he munched tasted sharper. He carefully avoided the chicken pieces. She saw it but avoided mentioning it.

Asha despite her age had the features of a classic Indian beauty and made efforts to look and behave like a modern woman. He looked at her and his gaze traveling from her shoulders downwards as far down as he could see across the table. She slyly caught his stare and with a hint of a smile turned towards him and he looked in another direction avoiding her look.

Asha tried to read his mind and feel his sexual temperament. Having created a high level of comfort after chatting she forgot her tipsiness. She had to make an effort to keep her eyes open and, worried lest she dozed off. The next moment she bent down and stretched her arms to adjust her ankelt. Her cleavage was clearly visible. Was that deliberate or she found the jewellery uncomfortable? Was its imperfection disturbing her sense of aesthetics? Ajay stared at her cleavage until she straightened.

He was seeing her chest in detail with the textures and colours of her breasts. The blue veins crisscrossing her fair breasts, the large light brown areolas, and the big oval nipple in the center with the hint of pink. When he asked her if she was high, she blinked. He began to feel the effect of the wine. Their conversation signaled that their brains were working slowly. Their speech became a bit slurred.

"That stupid ankelt got stuck in the hem of my nightie. It is rubbing against my ankle and scratching it," said Asha.

"Yeah, that could be irritating. It disturbs one's sense

of balance and beauty," offered Ajay not aware from where he was able to find the guts and gumption to speak.

Bending again to adjust the other anklet, she said, "Right"! This time her cleavage was in full view. Ajay took this as flirtatious and seductive. He did not know what to do or say and but sexual sensations were welling up in him. She was enjoying his attentions. "Ajay can you remove it", she asked him to take off her anklet. Patting the vacant seat on the sofa, she invited him.

When he sat down, she turned and put her feet on his lap and said, "Come take it off. Is there anything else you want to take off?" she giggled.

Ajay could scarcely think in a dazed alcoholic haze. There was nothing to take off except her nightie for he was certain there was nothing inside. He was finding it difficult to unhook the anklet. His coordination and movements were unsteady. She leaned into him and their arms, hands entangled helping him get it payal off, and finally he succeeded. He did not know what to do next and began massaging her feet while she giggled.

Though his stomach was strong and it could tolerate all sorts of rubbish, both had visited the bathroom thrice in the last hour and more. Now when he got up to go to the toilet he found difficult to stand and walk. She realized his balance was not perfect and both their speeches slurred.

He returned walking with no control on his legs and fell on her. She helped him adjust himself on her. Lying on her, he kept murmuring in her ear sorry, sorry, and sorry. From somewhere within her she in a drunken speech pattern said, "Is it not the first time? Not to worry! It will be good next time."

They did not know how long they slept and lay there like that. Asha stretched out the lounger and when she called, he tried to help her stand up but she could not and fell back on the settee. He tried to walk to her bedroom but somewhere he tripped and fell on the ground. Later in the night, he woke. Standing, he recollected what had happened. He cleaned up the table. Picking her up from the sofa, he carried her in his arms to the bed. He laid her on the bed covering with a blanket and tip -toed to his suite.

It was cold, very cold.

Reaching his room and fighting his demons, he slept.

Chapter VIII
Coming of Age

In the morning, they met in the dining hall for a late breakfast. Feeling shy and miserable, Ajay was uncomfortable and the silence painful. He picked up courage and asked her if she had a slept well. She smiled and thanked him for carrying her to the bed and cleaning up the place. Again, he said, "Sorry Asha. The wine knocked me out."

She knew from experience that contrived encounters led to ludicrous ends. Knowing that people forget and continue dreaming and planning. When they happen on their own, the outcomes by the nature of suspense and novelty are happier and more satisfying.

Suddenly everything was normal as if nothing had happened.

It was late for breakfast and they were the only two people in the hall. She opened her hands and placed them on the table, palms up as if seeking strong hands to grip them or jettison the past. Both knew they had to look ahead than behind. She called for the waiter and ordered breakfast turning to him softly whispered with bowed head not ready to face him, "I told you that the first time is something like that. There is no need to repeat it. It will be very nice next time. Sure!"

"Tell me, what should we do today?" asked Asha.

"Shall we go for another motorcycle ride?. Do not say no," replied Ajay.

Why not? I'll never say no to you," replied Asha. "I do not have the guts to say no to you," Ajay clapped his hands and she smiled.

Soon they were off and after two hours of driving, first down and then uphill they reached a small settlement. This was on another thickly wooded breathtaking mountain range straight out of a picture post card. They cruised past habitation, found a goat trail, veered into it, and discovered a spot to stop.

Spreading a sheet on the grassy knoll, they were talking about the beauty of the green hills. Soon the conversation veered around their recent past. Ajay introspecting explained that after Mythri's death he lost faith in God. He felt cheated by Lord Hanuman. When he reasoned with himself, he realized that his attitude akin to a defeated man. Who should you blame?"This was God's wish." If he continued that way then it would be seeding his mind, body and soul with a negative attitude. Negativity can only breed negativity. He was living in a way that shut out happiness. It would be a negation of what his upbringing was; his own dreams and he would not live up to the expectation of his family and the tribe.

Within a week, he had set in motion what he called a virtuous cycle of becoming a phoenix. He had mentioned about phoenix earlier and to her query, he said it was another name for rebirth. It was about being reborn. The moment passed away leaving the word in her mind. Without a context, it was just that - a word. Now that he mentioned it in a situation that brought them close, her curiosity resurfaced.

"What is this phoenix? I thought this is something one buys in the market. I have seen advertisements with the word phoenix," asked asha.

After a pause she added, "What you are referring is not that."

Ajay explained,"The phoenix when it sees death approaching, it would consciously consume itself in flames. Out of these flames, another phoenix would emerge. Rising from its ashes as a new bird to live another cycle. The phoenix is the symbol of that transformation to create what we desire and throw away what is pulling us down. However, without effort we are unable to discern these cycles within our mind. This death and rebirth is essential for our creative endeavors to flourish. Our ego transformed in a conscious attempt. This transformation is an undeniable fact of human existence."

"In any case, there comes a time when our consciousness matures to an extent that we recognize this process. Through this recognition, we can know the time for our transformation and consciously attempt to move to a new cycle. Sometimes we become bound and blocked and have to force ourselves into transforming ourselves."

"I realized that the time had come when I had to be reborn. Therefore, I had to forget or dramatically renew my old knowledge, experiences, and outlook and even my world view which is an important component of how we perceive the world. I had to uproot and throw them out of me. I had to burn myself so that I am reborn again," affirmed Ajay.

She stretched her arms out and fell over his shoulders. Moved by Ajay's words, she was silently weeping. Asha intuitively understood the need and importance of rebirth. Too much had happened in the recent past. When Asha's was husband sentenced to jail, she was left shocked. She resolved to get out of the mess if not for herself at least for her daughter, Teja. Her husband's trial and conviction was over in such short time. He had lost the will to live and never appealed to the higher court. For her it was gradual, happening day after day creeping as it were and she responded by going private and internalizing it.

When it became market news, it was like a swift butcher's stroke. It was traumatic. There was no place to hide and her best friends started avoiding her. She became another person not by will but just by responding to her environment. After the devastation, she realized that she had to create another life. She had no idea how long she might live but she had a daughter to take care of. Her husband though provided her but was not a part of her new world..

With her mind and heart in turmoil, she asked herself if she had her phoenix moment during her recent painful period. Was her present life a manifestation of rebirth? Was her life undergoing a rebirth? She reminded herself she was lucky and blessed. New events happened by themselves with the medium of someone whom she had never met earlier. It must be God above. Her faith in almighty strengthened.

He looked at her crying eyes and clutched her into his strong arms, hugging her tighter until she could breathe calmly.

Silently they left for their journey ahead. In the silence, they had exchanged what they would not forget their entire lives and it was compassion.

They stopped on the way for a few moments and she asked him, "Who told you about the phoenix theory?"

"I heard about the phoenix bird in my social studies class during my engineering studies. Professor Hemlatha used to teach social science and she taught us about the literary allusion of the phoenix. The English writer D H Lawrence confronted his entangled and difficult situations of his life by sketching the phoenix whenever he came to a dead end. Sketching of the phoenix by D H Lawrence was Ajay's response and understanding of his failures and pain. He would sketch so laboriously and lovingly and the world is richer because of not only the innumerable sketches he left behind but also scholars rummaging into his mind, inspired me. Later I read more about the phoenix as a myth, motivational and inspirational tool," Ajay explained.

As they sipped their hard orange tea they felt the warmth and heaviness of the aromatic smells in the atmosphere. The orange pekoe tea from the Nilgiris tea gardens refers to a particular variety of tea bushes and is the celebrated black tea, which contains higher caffeine content. It has a hard taste that lingers on the tongue long after. Black tea is generally, drunk without sugar and milk.

On their way back, she clung to him as if her life depended on it. Her mind wandered back to that french tourist once staying in the hotel who talked of his remarriage to the woman he had drifted away from. He summed up his life and his relationship with her in his very french way, 'Bonds of Delicacy'.

She did not have to invite or tell him, Ajay read her thoughts and promised to be with her. Whatever had to happen would happen.

"It has happened. Over. Period. Let's walk ahead," Asha whispered as he slowed the motorcycle to negotiate a sharp bend in the road.

When they reached the hotel, she told him, "My new life is also like your phoenix."

"People entered my life and they gave or did what they had to and then disappeared. I called nobody, this kept continuing and changing myself as a person and I was reborn. Perhaps I must have done something good in my previous life."

Ajay knocked on her suite door and she opened it. She was planning to take a shower and when he saw her ready to step into her shower, he told her he would come later. To which she replied, "Beware you are not going anywhere from here. I will keep the door open and we will talk."

She kept a steady chatter and after some time came out with her hair tied in a towel. She was wearing a bathrobe, hurried to her room, and emerged in loose black pants up to her knees and a white tight tee. You had to give her the credit that she had the sense of dress and the demands of the situation. Soon they were flirting and she suggested, "Let's go to my bedroom. We can talk comfortably or watch a movie."

She switched the TV opposite to the bed they were sitting on and started surfing through the channels. Both knew what she was looking for. She started searching for movies and stopped at a Tamil movie called Doubles. It was a heroine based film with Raasi, the lead who was a Malayalam actress known for baring skin and her raunchy dances while shedding clothes. None of them knew Malayalam but had a notion that Malayalam cinema was either highbrow art films or middle class sleaze cinema. Asha was searching for erotica.

As soon as Raasi began shedding her clothes the music became louder and she swayed to the music with slow languor. As the music picked up the actress kept in tune and her body rocked vigorously. Ajay was excited. He placed a cushion on his lap to hide his arousal. They were sitting side by side leaning on their pillows with Asha to his right. Asha had a naughty and flirtatious ; she hugged his right hand and rested her head on his shoulder. Whenever something pleased her, she would adjust her position and when she did that, her hugging would get bolder.

The sun had set and it was dark, the only light in the room was that coming off the television screen. Ajay was feeling her left breast digging into his shoulder. He was sexually aroused. When there was a dance scene with explicit sexual overtones, she put her hand on his thigh. She guessed what he was going through and removed the pillow making Ajay restless. Asha grabbed his shoulder and pulled him closer.

Ajay put his arm around her shoulders, let his hand fall over her chest, and cupped Asha's breast. She responded by taking his other hand and putting it on her other breast. He was playing with her breasts over her tee. This game continued until Ajay put his lips on her's. He closed his eyes and after sometime, she opened her lips and invited his tongue. She was sucking his tongue as he squeezed her breasts. She slithered down and motioned him to come on top of her. As he did so, Asha wrapped her legs around him gripping his waist. Ajay not knowing what was expected started rubbing his penis through his trousers on her vagina under her pants. It was instinctive.

Soon he came and his trousers were wet and got up and Asha admonished him, "Where do you think you are going? Nothing has happened yet."]

She switched off the televion. The sudden silence was deafening and only being broken by their breathing.

She realised his plight. He was too excited and could not control himself. Laughing would be rude. He needed her to coach him. She did not let go and kneeled facing him, crouching on her knees and toes. He was standing on the floor and his face leveled to hers. They began necking and their mouths found each other's. He put his hands under her shoulders and his hands like a thief found their way through her tee to her bare breasts. He yanked her tee off surrendering himself to their warmth and allure. She arranged herself sitting on the edge of the bed facing him.

He buried his head on her chest and she cradled his head and began to rock on her toes. He felt her softness and the heady aroma of her armpits and closed his eyes. She put her palms onhis cheeks and his hands exploring her made her hunger stronger. He did not know whether it was due to shyness or guilt that made his eyes to shut repetitively. Asha rocked him and the earth underneath him moved as a wave in sea. Lost, he did not want it to end.

Then he heard her patting the bed signaling him to come on the bed. He obeyed like a good horse listens to its master.

Slowly she released him and he stumbled to the reality of the moment. It was dark and he wanted to see her. He untied the cord of her pants and his hand slipped inside. He gingerly moved the tip of his finger on her vaginal walls and then his hands began caressing her back. His hands slipping down to her buttocks, caressing them and he cupped them. He squeezed her buttocks. Asha moaned. His penis made him feel uncomfortable – hot, stiff, wet and pushing against his trousers.

He whispered in her ear, "Wait."

As they unclenched, he removed his trousers, and then his drawers. He sat on the bed and removed his shirt. She removed her pants and stretching her hand turned on the bed light. Ajay felt more confident and reassured seeing her in soft diffused light. She was real! Her smooth, glossy skin was hairless with almost no hair except between her thighs. He worshipped her in his mind as a dedicated painter or a sculptor would idolize his subject. Her skin in the soft light highlighted her undulating skin as she stretched and moved her body. For someone who had never seen a nude woman in real life, she was beautiful and an arresting view.

Her body smelt of roses with the heather frame emanated. She lay down and pulled him on her. He lay on her, her hands moving and she began caressing his back. He kept kissing and licking her face, and then his lips and tongue could find its way. After some time, he turned and lay by her side. Her hardened breasts with her oval nipples were stiff and standing. He leaned over her, sucking her one nipple and tweaking the other between his thumb and fingers. He started to bite her nipples and Asha was moaning with pleasure while her hands clutching his hair and pushing his face into her chest.

They must have been at their foreplay for more than half an hour and whenever he shuddered, she knew that he had climaxed. She taught him that a man and woman's fluids during lovemaking were sacred and it was natural to let it flow. You could play with it, smear it, taste it and even drink it. This was against his upbringing and sensibilities. According to him, body fluids were not clean.

Asha rose and turning around, she pushed his legs apart and sat on her haunches between his thighs. She took his penis in her hand and started stroking his wet member on her crack. Ajay could not evade the sexy look in her eyes. It was palpable but not acknowledging it was lust.

She slithered down his body resting on her haunches over his knees. Her mouth was on top of his penis while her fingers held it in position. She sat up and said, "Ajay dear shall I take it into my mouth?" He looked at her dumbfounded and shocked for a moment. Few moments later, he managed to smile in return. He was learning and was a fast learner too!

She sank on her haunches lowering her head and took his penis in her mouth. Sucking the tip, she covered it with her saliva. She began licking his entire member from front to its head. Adding novelty she began licking and sucking his balls. This game went on. She would lick the length of his member and then releasing it would cup his balls and put them in her mouth licking and applying suction.

He tried to lift his waist under her and she read his intention taking it fully in her mouth. He could feel his penis touching her throat. Her hair came in his view and her gorged mouth while she sucked him. He moved her hair back with his hands. It was extremely erotic for both though the impact and intensity was rising by the minute. He could not have dreamt it! After a short rest with her straddling him, they looked at each other with glazed eyes. In the silence, there were no words except their breathing. His penis was again in her mouth and her hands were caressing his balls. Ajay was aflame. He was going wild.

He felt that he would spurt his semen and by instinct started pushing his penis in and outside her mouth. She guessed it and soon he released his hot semen in her mouth. His outpouring was prodigious and she swallowed it and let it leak onto her face and her breasts and on his thighs. She then smeared his semen all over his penis, balls and thighs. As the breeze dried it, he felt a different sort of titillation partly sexual and partly love.

She got up over him, swung off the bed, and walked barefoot to the bathroom with her arse swaying. She gargled, poured water over her thighs, splashed water on her face, threw a mug of water on her feet, and started wiping herself dry. Ajay followed her and after dry cleaning himself was seeing her naked. He was aroused again.

She was at the washbasin as he saw her; he was enamored of her buttocks. Standing behind, he started caressing her buttocks and rubbed his penis between her cleft. His pulse rose. She felt his stirring and her mind recharged her. She saw him in the mirror and moved her buttocks facilitating his efforts. He turned her around and lifted her in his arms, carrying her and lay her on the bed.

This was a first in her life. Women dream of being transported by their lovers in their strong arms and laid onto the bed and loved savagely. Very few ever get to experience this in their lifetime.

He jumped on her and started kissing her and she

joined him. After a long bout of kissing, she pushed him off and clutching his hair indicating what she wanted him to do. Licking her, he moved from her breasts down and stopping at her vagina. He opened her vaginal lips, inserted his middle finger, and began to push it in and out. Ashamoaned and stretched out her legs and spread her thighs.

"Mmmmmm aaaaaa hhhhhh, mmmmm ahahahaha ... her sounds lost in her throat she kept moaning, "Yyyyeeeeaaaahhhh, more, more, aaaaaaaaahhhhhhhhhh; oh my god, faster Ajay."

They lay for a few minutes breathing heavily. He was by her side and slithered down. He found her clitoris, which had swollen like her excited nipples and began manipulating her wetness there. She went sex mad! Spreading her thighs wide she invited him. Lying between them he saw her body fluids, the warmth of the flesh from her thighs and their assorted smells.

She pushed his head down with her fingers. He began tongue kissing and then shifted to put his head at the end of her vagina lip and sucked it. He felt that she would like his tongue inside her, so he separated her labia with his fingers and shoved his tongue inside, driving his head down. In his homage, he let his tongue penetrate her. All he thought about was to shove it as far as it could go while she was enjoying the waves of pleasure as the sea hits the shore.

Asha put her hand on the back of his head and pressed. His tongue started moving inside, feeling her vaginal walls. After some time he got tired and lay on her stomach with his face covered with her juices.

She could not help and instinctively lifted herself and pushed her clitoris towards his mouth. He could only lick which he did with gusto. That slippery, wet inch of her very intimate part would just now stay in his mouth and kept slipping out. He tried to pull her clitoris in his mouth and sucked it in a motion of swallowing it. She lay spread eagled with her arms stretched out and lifted her legs. He returned between her thighs. She spurted on his face, over her thighs and his fingers that had spread her vagina and now extravagantly wet.

'Phew! What an orgasm', her mind resonated! She had not had one like that for a long, long time. In her gratitude, she took his fingers in her mouth.

She went to the bathroom and Ajay sat up waiting for her. He could hear the sound of the water faucet and then she stepped into the room standing against the wall bathed in soft reading light. Of course, she looked like a middle-aged woman.

Anything old has texture and so with her body. To see the details of the textures requires good strong focused light. Nevertheless, he felt that her body was exuding a personality that he had never associated with her and her womanly fat inviting to touch,feel and roll his tongue over. The folds of her skin arrested his attention. Her body shape was different in her nakedness from when she was clothed. His mind was in a daze and could not care for the beauty and shape of the human body. What mattered at this moment was that she was real, absolutely real. The soft light added to her solidity.

In the lassitude of his mind, he could only imagine Asha as a beautiful girl. Asha was sexy. For the brief moment, she stood naked against the wall and water glistening around her washed crotch, Ajay felt her body had taken a sexual personality. Her body, its movements, its smells and her spoken and unspoken words were drenched in desire and longing. She lay down and they snuggled in a loose embrace.

When she tightened her embrace, he felt the new surge of energy carousing through her. He half climbed on her and began to play with her breasts and kissing her lips. She asked him to pinch her nipples tightly and that aroused her again. He wanted to fuck her. He wanted to enter her vagina. He moved over her and crouching between her thighs ready to enter her. Asha parted her legs taking the cue and put a pillow under her buttocks. He bent over her and whispered, "Asha, I am a virgin and you are the first female whom I have seen fully naked. You are my first kiss, my first taste of female juices and the aroma of a woman in heat."

"I can't believe this is happening. This is a part of my rebirth. My phoenix moment!"

Asha raised her arms, put them around his neck pulling him down over her,and hugged him. Kissing his lower lip, she took his penis in her fingers and guided it into her cavern. Her vagina was wet. He was completely inside her and stretched out full length. She pulled her legs up even wider and her soles planted firmly on the bed. He began to move inside her in measured strokes. She facilitated his stroking by moving her waist to answer his thrusts.

The room reeked of semen, their moans, and entwined limbs. What mattered at this moment was that he was on a new adventure. It was no imagination but real. He was no longer a virgin.

In the last few months, he thought of his virginity as a torment. He would hear snatches of conversations of his younger engineers, who were patently sexual. Hearing them rather challenged him and his virginity. Their sexual innuen does whether implied or overt, disturbed him. He had heard such conversations two or three years ago but they never impinged on his consciousness as they did now. As a teenager and the society he inhabited was rigid with a Victorian outlook. It was more so amongst the older middle class and for the teenagers of today sex was the least to talk or worry about.

He pushed his hands under her back and gripping her shoulders he began moving inside her. He stopped as she signaled him with her hands pressing on the small of his back. He breathed deeply as she tried to still herself. They lay like this for some time and then she hoarsely said, "Ajay, fuck me, yeah fuck me. Fuck me hard. Fuck me, fuck me."

He could feel her muscles contract and open on his moving penis. His thrusts became vigorous, he emptied his load into her, and she climaxed. She clung to him and squeezed him with a ferocity that shocked him. He rolled off her and they lay holding hands and slept.

~~~

When they woke up it was 3:00 in the morning. They were hungry and Ajay started dressing up, she implored him, "Sure, get dressed but do not leave me and go. Nobody will know. No one comes here until called.".

"Please!"

Draping a shawl on her nightie she said,"Ajay, I will organize something for you to eat. You must be hungry. After eating, tell me more about the phoenix. Yes, also about the phoenix moment. I saw a big bird flying in the sky in my dreams."

He went to the bathroom and splashed cold water on his face and returning dressed in hurry. It was cold and he went to the fireplace and lit the few wooden pieces that lay there. Soon there was a fire giving warmth and a soft glow to the room. She went to the pantry and returned with buttered buns, cake and steaming coffee.

"I repeat, the phoenix is a mythical bird. When it saw death approaching, or when it chose, it would consume itself in flames to be reborn. Rising new from its ashes as young and beautiful bird to live another cycle. Our creative endeavors or shocks whether we set upon a new journey or a life project or understand the enormity of a tragedy or the reason for awesome happiness can be the cause for a phoenix moment. This moment transforms our egos."
~~~

"It becomes essential to understand them for our growth and evolution. I would add that we should let the understanding that comes from this phoenix moment unsettle and tear our smug mindset. Creation must come from the stillness of death. The phoenix has become a symbol of that transformation of human consciousness and our creative spirit. Every human being has to confront this reality many times in his or her life. Trusting the outcome of the phoenix reality brings elements that help us to join the dots. This is a prelude, the beginning and from this starting point, we can create situations we desire. The method that we use is of our own but it has a process."

"Have you not seen or read of nature turning wild and unruly, unexpectedly or suddenly. These massive cycles of change are a part of the universe itself. There are cycles inherent in nature which pervades the universe. Although, it is not obvious to most individuals, there is evidence that transformation is an undeniable fact of human existence. Yet we do not see and often overlook the breakages in our lives crying for transformation. People are afraid of accepting their phoenix moment."

"There comes a time when our consciousness matures. We intuitively recognize this process and we can freely let go as we move through our cycles. Sometimes we become so obligated and blocked that transformation is the only alternative to get out of the rut. If we don't we sink deeper into the quagmire with frightful consequences. In the end, it is death that allows us to escape becoming trapped in any one given pattern."

"There are those who will be forced to experience a painful death. These are those people who never cared to stop, and give benefit of doubt to voices within, remaining insensitive to those slices in time that were their phoenix moments. Failing, they let their world shrink and become smaller and smaller. Some types and kinds of death can be so intense that we experience a dark night of the soul. It more often leads to a slow lingering death. This is most hurtful and violent death that can happen to a man. When it comes to people who turn their back, on their phoenix moments, it is too late and then all that is left is the slow senseless death. Death in those cases ends our pain."

"Death must have a purpose as much as living has."

"Who would like to die without fighting for life," responded Asha.

She leaned over him and stretched herself. Tired, sharp and alive Asha tried to reach in her memories, instances of her phoenix moment. Travelling back in time she stopped at her traumatic period. In hindsight, she imagined her world crashing. As her world crashed and she fended for herself, her daughter, and that night it rained without let up. All through the night, Teja lay clutching her. She had to do whatever was necessary for Teja. That was her phoenix moment.

She steeled herself and though haunted she decided that she would secure herself and her daughter's future come what may. She was willing to do anything. She sweated in the stillness of the moment and the gales of rain outside. Then the storm ceased as suddenly as it had started. Ganapati must have heard her. She felt secure. Becoming owner of the hotel and Teja settled, she thought her phoenix moment consummated.

That happiness is within the realm of anyone. It is a choice you make. Released from all constraints, Asha began to believe one could be happy with the worst of possible situations and be wretched with the best of circumstances. Happiness was a state of existence that the mind created. If you were serene and calm,you are automatically happy. Pictures of her hockey playing days flitted through her mind. At the start of play, she could run, trap the ball, assess her fellow players and the opponent's moves with ease and it came naturally, but when she tired her reflexes, her play making and thereby her performance flagged and dropped. She then experienced a feeling of inadequacy.

If, she reasoned one was happy with what one had instead of fretting and planning to acquire what one did not have then what one did not have would cease to bother. Yes, that was her phoenix moment. Simple! Who does not know it? Imagine if everyone believed and lived, being sensitive to their phoenix moments, it would be a different world.

She conveniently forgot that without Ubhayankar her life would have been impoverished and tough. Her phoenix moment had come upon her without her knowing and best explaine das serendipity. She was honest for that slice of time and it left her as innocently and quickly as it crossed her mind.

Ajay added, "Similarly when one thinks of unfulfilled desires the mind becomes restless. There was always the possibility that these unfilled desires could cause havoc and become a source of sorrow. Perhaps, God in his infinite wisdom never arranged to let you fulfil these desires."

"I think this is being spiritual. Spirituality in practice is reducing your needs, desires and your dependence on the world. You could thus make the best use of your talents, strengths and energies. Your focus is total and unwavering. Surely, this will lead you to success and richness."

He did not know in the darkness when she had fallen sleep. Her head lay on his shoulder. He was so meticulous and expansive in explaining that he forgot to hear or acknowledge her verbal and nonverbal responses as he kept talking. As he raised himself on his elbow, only see her fast asleep.

Just before dawn, he disengaged from her. Lying by his side, he freed and gently unwound her head and arm from his shoulders. He covered her in the blanket and tiptoed out.

Ajay was happy losing his virginity to Asha.

Chapter IX
The Leader's Apprenticeship

Sharad Zende found that CMC's Y2K courses in its Madras center highly regarded, effective,one of the best and recommended it. Venkataraman after a telephonic call with its Madras Center chief heard that their course were a good mixture of theory and practice and Sharad concurred. Many top companies venturing into the Y2K business patronized CMC. Some CMC tutors moonshined and extended technical consultancy. Someone must learn solving Y2K problems if the company was venturing into this business. CMC beset with huge potential Y2K issues. This was where their Chief, Gupta decided offering courses professionally and dominating the Y2K training market. Company enrolled Ajay for the course with CMC.

Returning after his Y2K training, Ajay enthusiastic and confident knew he had to prove himself and do justice to his learning. Waiting for the first assignment, he at times doubted his experience in handling a project as a leader. He had made a note on his training and sent it up marking a copy to Asha. She was an active member of Dagariya's Y2K network. Through the participant's list, Asha started identifying good Y2K engineers in Bangalore. Without projects, it was not possible to offer employment.

It was difficult to get a realistic picture of the actual Y2K business. Going forward the window was just 18 months. The company invested little except funding Dagariya's visits to the US. This was more social and less professional. These indiscretions were inherent in Indian private companies. Small group owned public owned companies were no better. The owners of Bhoruka Steel and Dagariya's friend ran his large household on company's account and purchases meant for personal and household use passed onto company account. It was pervasive.

Until he got his teeth into an actual Y2K related work, he launched himself into a learning plan that included sitting with star programmers and project leaders and listening to their experiences. They need not be Y2K related. Since he was not on any project, he had the time and what better than be acquainted firsthand about managing real life problems.

Because of his friendly and caring nature, most project managers were ready to sit with him. Sometimes they were baffled at the unusual questions he had for them. Soon, a few project managers began sharing their current problems with him. Trying to jointly sit and find solutions was learning for thems too. He believed that learning and then the experience would be the best training for his new position. The more he listened, the more buddha like he became. Listen without commenting, never statements but questions.

The hot emerging business was the BPO (Business Process Outsourcing) business. The Indian BPO industry had begun six years ago. They had pioneered the business leaving other countries way behind. Indian companies worked hard and by their innovative ways, moved up the value chain.

They added or extended services over voice.. NASSCOM (the Indian Software Industry Association) renamed it as BPM (Business Process Management).

BPO work involved transfer and execution of certain category of business processes from offshore locations. Companies from high cost geographies contracted their work to low labour cost destinations like India. It became possible because of cheaper computing power and communication technologies. The vital part was the Indian English speaking youth who worked in these BPO's. These youngsters were willing to tweak their pronunciation that was understandable to foreign customers. Indians mastered this and captured one third of the world market. The business was growing rapidly.

This was at the shirtsleeve level but the lure of money drove American consultants and intermediaries as an excellent opportunity to feather their pockets. Many cared only for that and least about the end customers and sometimes did not even know them in details.

Linking BPO skills with computing, Indians began configuring larger total solutions. These had to be high in concept to deliver productivity improvements and yet affordable. They stitched solutions with many components from within their company. When these companies offered complex solutions linked to business outcomes, their sales pitch was compelling. They could be any of the many areas from accounting to statistical analysis to shipments. There were requirements of manipulation of data for research purposes. New requirements came like developing cost effective routings for worldwide dispatches, loading containers on ships to maximize space and so on. Indians set up companies in Southeast Asia, Eastern Europe and South America. This transformation from voice BPO's to complex skill driven services made Indian companies stand out. This was a transformational move from correctness and efficiency to effectiveness and business impact.

BPO created a job market where any person with twelve years of education at school could fit in. In India's BPO factories, it was not essential to have an engineering or other degree; any high school pass student with good English language skills would open doors to his career advancement. The opportunity for making youngsters BPO ready emerged suddenly and it was sky high. The Indian entrepreneurial instinct went about creating hundreds of training shops. . Success led the entrepreneurs to spread to second tier cities. Training, willingness to work hard at odd hours and the lure of higher earnings fired youngsters. Quality of work was important but in performance it was not uniformly high quality but the companies were still on the path of learning.

The average age of engineers delivering value measured in US dollars was getting lesser and lesser. Indian software companies initially modeled on the hierarchical order in Indian traditional companies. The declining age of engineers delivering substantial values shook the organization structures and the Indian software companies embraced the change. Software engineers were earning well. In some cases more than what their parents earned, which was a triumph of Indian entrepreneurship and created massive employment opportunities.

Not only the Indian BPO[8] companies reengineered

---

[8]BPO or Business Process Outsourcing is outsourcing like other outsourcing manufacturing or assembling or packaging etc. in a variety of businesses like auto etc., but BPO here specifically refers to outsourcing involving contracting of the operations and responsibilities of a specific business process to a third party located in another country. BPO is typically categorized into back office outsourcing that includes the contracting company's internal business functions such as human resources or finances or accounting or dispatching etc. and also includes customer related services from contact centers located in other countries to assist a customer on the trouble shooting and operations of products. BPO that is contracted to a company's neighboring (or nearby) country is called nearshoring and for countries far away the outsourcing is used and in practice both merged at the time under discussion here. Within BPO's are other segments like Legal Process Outsourcing, Product Trouble Shooting Outsourcing, Knowledge process Outsourcing etc. Indians had a finger in all these including medical related areas.

themselves but began offering these services to their clients as well. Combining computing skills and functional expertise corresponding to American, British, German and French functional standards they were creating customer delight and delivering excellence. Software companies had their own areas of functional expertise. This expertise extended to areas like finance or shipping or sales, manufacturing, insurance, or purchasing etc. Using their functional expertise the companies set up their own BPO centres. Specialization and working 24 by 7 they delivered impressive results and prospered. Smaller companies learning from the bigger ones could offer the same services and quality at cheaper costs. A new breed of BPO entrepreneurs and companies sprang up.

American management consultants started referring Indian companies to their American clients, they had worked with or whose experience they could vouch for. This reputation motivated UK consultants and business development professionals from other English speaking countries. Most of these consultants were prominent American politicians, retired diplomats,businesspersons and academicians and some offered board seats by the bigger Indian companies. This created a buzz and the perception of Indian expertise became stronger.

A new breed of BPA[9] entrepreneurs and companies sprang up.

Ajay's Company was in a dilemma. How should it

[9]*Business Process Automation (BPA) is the strategy a business uses to automate processes in order to contain costs. BPA solutions are therefore transaction and work flow focused. It consists of integrating applications, restructuring labor resources and using software applications throughout the organization. It began as low hanging fruits meaning those areas and operations of the contracting company amenable to BPA methodologies. Generally, BPA is most relevant for document and information on them or connected to information banks intensive processes. BPA offers quick implementation and sold by contractors as ROI after a study at the contracting parties sites. Automating processes provides the company the abilities to improve processes significantly in terms of time, cost and quality. The outsourcer still maintains overall control of their processes while maintaining agility.*

allocate their not too considerable resources? The Company was grappling which resources to be used as all-purpose and which for specific works to use, when and where to use them? Should the company position itself for Y2K, BPA, ITES, or all? Quality labor was the biggest constraint for all lines of business. This was in spite of large availability. The young workers were supposed to have working knowledge that their certificates testified. They could crack entrance tests but somewhere they failed to deliver as expected. It was not only competence but other social factors as well.

With money, jobs and economies of big IT cities prospering, no one cared about the psychological problems of youngsters in the software or BPO Industries. Occasionally mentioned in the media and those affected had to live and solve their emotional and physcohological problems as best as they could. Many of them had no idea and refused to acknowledge they had problems. Luckily, family support and involvement prevented the problems of maladjusted youth while similar problems in other foreign cities were replete with drugs, alcoholism, permissive lifestyles, vandalism etc. this was where the Indian family system supported the disturbed and such instances can be rarely found in other countries, least of all in the developed countries. It never becamc a national problem. With the gradual break up of joint family systems, family support become weak and will continue to become a less steadying force in times to come. What shape they would take in coming years only speculated.

The industry grew rapidly in Bombay, Delhi, Hyderabad, Madras and Bangalore and some second tier cities like Jaipur, Jodhpur, Coimbatore etc. creating hundreds of jobs in secondary and tertiary sectors. Many supporting entrepreneurial units mushroomed to provide transport, catering, security, cleaning services. The need for services directly related to business like recruitment, legal documentation,

documentation, making proposals etc. sorely felt and the only way for a company was to use its own experience. Industry watchers and commentators felt the need for these services offered on professional basis creating more entrepreneurial opportunities.

Training companies mushroomed and BPA companies invested in them for refresher courses. The Industry prospered. Smaller companies had to pay higher salaries, and did not have the practical understanding but carried lesser overheads. They were flexible in taking up jobs that helped them to keep their costs low. In the final analysis, they could provide near similar quality and reliability. Their major weakness was foreign marketing. Exporting companies came up with ingenious ways to market themselves. This made the industry very competitive and at times confused the buyers. Many small and first time foreign buyers hired consultants to help them strike what they considered a good deal. This symbiotic relationship between American and the Indians sometimes turned into rackets.

The company management debated the way forward. Ajay invited to sit during their deliberations, which were a measure of the confidence and trust they reposed in him. Hein turn, read and learnt as much as he could about the Y2K business and managing offshore projects.

There was a subcontract for a Y2K project by a leading company and it selected Ajay after grueling tests. He was looking for such an experience.. After working hard, staying back late, working on weekends over a three-month period learning as much as possible Ajay's confidence grew. He learnt the ways of approaching and methodologies for solving Y2K problems. It was also an free opportunity to get an insight into how how the big company worked and their processes. Dagariya had arranged for a stenographer to take down his observations on the phone. Through this one single project and Ajay's dedication, the Company was ready to enter the Y2K game.

The big moment for which the company was waiting for, arrived. United States Postal Service invited his Company to study their Y2K problem and bid for their project. Ajay was the obvious choice. He was the only one who had the confidence, training and experience in the company and the Chief of the Division. In the end, it was Dagariya's trust that weighed in his favor. He would go alone if an experienced engineer to accompany him not found.

Venkataraman pulled an engineer with a strong Y2K record of accomplishment from another bigger company. He agreed to accompany Ajay, knowing that his company was also in the fray. He was a victim of office politics. Narasimhalu was an employee of a top company in Bangalore. His passport stamped with visas of the countries he had traveled for his company's work.

The company pulled strings, Asha worked through the bureaucratic maze, and Narasimhalu obtained another passport. He reported sick at his company. With the new passport, he flew to Washington then to Baltimore with Ajay and returned through New York all within three weeks. He brought with him samples for process engineering, estimations, and making bids as well as any in the world. Narasimhalu's services were expensive. The Company had to pay a large sum for the value of his technical knowledge and experience.

Company management stood firm behind this opportunity. Working with Narasimhalu, Ajay absorbed all he could from him. .

When they started the requirement study, Ajay was dumbfounded at the sheer size and energy of United States Postal Services (USPS). The USPS established in 1775 during the Second Continental Congress and Benjamin Franklin was its first Postmaster General. The chief office was in New York City. USPS is an independent agency of the United States federal government. It provides postal services in the entire United States. The USPS by law charged to serve all Americans, regardless of geography, at uniform price and quality. USPS employed 600,000 workers and operated 210,000 vehicles in in 1999. The USPS is the operator of the largest civilian vehicle fleet in the world and their vehicles custom built. It had generated 60 billion dollars in revenues in the previous year and operated 31,000 post offices and locations in the U.S. delivering 170 billion pieces of mail. Private companies like FedEx and United Parcel Service (UPS) compete with USPS but USPS remained the favorite choice of Americans for sending their mail and parcels. Itis a striking example of how a government organization could match the efficiency of the best private companies in the market. It had become a case study for governments around the world.

They started the study in Washington, spending a week working on all days. The USPS had a long history of computerization and the workers were loyal and proud of their organization. They had access to many officials and computer teams that were helpful. Completing Washington assignment, they flew to Baltimore where they spent a week and then to New York. It was hectic. Narasimhalu and Ajay became good friends and were happy to be working together.

At New York, he purchased presents for his friends and managers in the company and especially for his mother, Chacha and others in the extended family. He even had to buy a collapsible suitcase to fit them all in. He liked American brands and his shopping experiences were amazing. People were friendly and they impressed him by their discipline and cleanliness. He marveled at the American malls policy of buy back or a return without question, which for an Indian was difficult to comprehend. He fell for their consumerism. A person whom he met during his stay explained that consumerism was the engine for America's growth and prosperity.

On returning, they got down to the writing of the proposal. Just as they finished Dagariya called Ajay to inform them that he had obtained the check sheet for evaluation of proposals. The bid was tweaked and better priced. He worked for 60 hours without a break, without sleep and rest. The proposal completed and shipped to their associatein New York. There was nothing else left to do but wait.

Dagariya's contacts were following. There were joyous moments when they learnt that they had made to the last three. A week later Dagariya, Venkataraman and Ajay left for Washington for discussions and negotiations. The USPS team hosted them and impressed by Ajay's sincerity and honesty. The woman member, Alice Edward Smith moved by his religious and spiritual outlook invited him to her house. They maintained touch and whenever he visited US, he would find time to spend with and presents for her.

During one of his meeting with her, Ajay met his brother Ethan. Ethan had built a big successful furniture empire. Asian furniture makers, especially the Chinese invaded America and he was one of the few to survive. After two-failed computerization attempts, Ethan discussed with him company wide computerization. Ethan shared his previous failures and learning. Ajay technically challenged, spent many hours thinking about building long life computer systems.

They reached Bangalore and the days that followed were full of suspense. It was a strange and complex feeling.

Dagariya was confident that the Company would crack the deal. The labor required to start the project was around 30 and peaking at 50. Ajay working with Venkataraman and Asha started looking at people to involve in the project. Dagariya called Sarkar and requested his help.. It was entrepreneurialism at its best. The engineers assembled, belonged to a new breed of the middle class aspirational Indians.

Ajay was restless and he would saunter into Asha's office. The fun, the laughter and the endearments were there but in a non-sexual way. What struck her were his unflappable manners. He had bought her a woman's vanity case with lots of beauty creams and lotions and an expensive perfume. Laughing she chimed, "Ajay I have not given you anything. You have given me so much." He smiled and reached out and tapped her cheek. There were no words to exchange.

Dagariya's confidence in Ajay paid off.

It should have been simple to find half a dozen people with the right sort of knowledge and experience on Y2K in the city. Bangalore boasted of three of the big five IT companies of the country. It had 17 engineering colleges in and around the city, 1,500 software companies and housed 150,000 software engineers but finding Y2K engineers with sound experience and willing to move to another country became a huge challenge. It brought Ajay and Asha together in search for engineers.

It was getting difficult to get good engineers with a potential to deliver. Records of accomplishment invented. Mediocre engineers were good at doing that. For a small company, getting a good engineer was chancy and uncertain. Once in and if he was a misfit the only remedy was to ask him or her to leave. If the word spread, getting others became doubly difficult.

Companies made investment in the development of their employees. Providing on the job training, smart deployment and resources for self-study created, yet there were rogues. The big companies believed that whatever an engineer had to deliver, he would in his first three years at work. It was the duty of the management to create opportunities for the smarter and ambitious ones. Smarter employees identified, given bigger assignments with bigger targets. If they delivered, they were valuable and hence suitably rewarded and promoted. They would become "one of us, "a jargon much used in the country's largest company.

The big companies in 2000 were mass recruiting. They would be recruiting at many cities simultaneously. There was a employment season which was twice a year with a 15 to 20 days window. Even the pre-final year students recruited in the same aggressive way. The final year students would be ready to join within 6 months and the pre-final year students joined a year and a half later. A big company could recruit 25, 000 to 40, 000 engineers in a year. The attrition rate was 15%. More important was to estimate the likely business over 18 months. The recruitment was matched to estimated time and Indian companies had borrowed techniques from the Americans and fine tuned staffing for each phase of the project. It had never been attempted before anywhere in the world.

Training the graduates and getting them to deliver was a massive managerial challenge. Indian companies had to arrange quarterly trainings, which was no mean feat. This was the years when two new engineering colleges were set up somewhere in the country within three days.

Venkataraman and Asha working overtime created a potential list of Y2K experienced engineers. After screening, initial interviewing began.

The USPS project had begun. It was December 1999 and within a week, Ajay would have to take his first team to Washington. Engineer allocations were under examination. Amongst the software engineers with three years of experience, there was excitement and expectations. Sarkar would be in the office every evening. If he could, Ajay would spend time with him. It was quite astonishing that within a month a team of 30 engineers assembled. He liked to believe they were engineers with proven skills or the potential to learn quickly on the job. Ajay left for Washington along with four engineers. Three of them were mercenaries organized by Sarkar and one from the Company, which became a sore point with employees.

He conceded to himself that he did not have the experience to lead them and worse, all belonged to the same age group. He feared that if they insisted on positions to take without exhausting options, the project would suffer. There would be endless technical debates. This was a crucial phase in the life of the project other than delivery and installation. Their commitment and loyalty was essential. He cultivated them, spent time with them, and explained the correctness of what he was doing taking a leaf out of Dagariya's book. He knew that this phase if thoroughly done with diligence would increase the probability of his success.

Ajay felt that the company should be indebted to Narasimhalu who had shared with him forms for analysis and problem statement. His sense of fair play led to the Company to hire him as a part time consultant. He would come once a week for two or three hours to review work. He brought with him forms, checklists and other materials that made the process reliable, personality independent and with measure quality. These were from one of the finest IT company in the country. Designed after considerable experience and used intuitively. Purloining was a depressing part of the software industry but a sad reality.

Software engineering has creative elements. When engineers use the word intuitive they refer to combining human perceptions with engineering. These helped the analyst to be of far thinking when interacting with users.

They started with the problem analysis and spent many hours with the computer staff of the Washington facility. They started studying the existing programs and identifying where and how the date field called for processing. It was important to understand under what circumstances and used directly or indirectly. To make sense of logic with none or unreliable in-program documentation written fifteen years ago was a challenge, tedious and backbreaking job. It provided scope for an enterprising programmer to create something extraordinary with tight deadlines. Sample programs scanned one by one and problems identified. Ajay explained to his team this was an excellent training in software engineering. His force of personality carried them through. By end of 1999, they were through. They had worked on those days also when the office was on skeleton staff during the Christmas vacation.

In the last week of December, they returned to Bangalore.

Ajay put ten engineers working on the paper listings and code on magnetic media that he bought with him. He gave detailed instructions and they would take a few weeks to complete the job. He took another five with him to Baltimore. He chose a senior engineer from his Washington team to be the deputy manager. Then for the next few weeks, he kept shuttling between Washington, Baltimore and New York. Another 5-member team was in New York.

Once his team had come to grips with the project, Ajay found opportunities to discuss programing styles with American computer specialists. With some, he struck immediate rapport and they found his questioning clarifying their thoughts. There were new insights for both.

Programming is creative work. Like any creative work, you cannot separate aesthetics from the final product. Aesthetics has to do how pieces joined, the message it conveys, its brevity and number of parts that make the whole. Great artists, musicians and aesthetes create masterpieces of everlasting value with the fewest of elements. Ajay was acutely conscious of this.

Surely, a program has to solve a problem and must deliver stated functions. Thus, there were two schools of thought. The software engineer majority and their managers swore on effective code and the smaller set for beautiful code. The beautiful code proponents had little support; they were individuals who stood out from the hordes. He was convinced that beautiful and effective code was mutually exclusive as advocated by its proponents. Maybe, he mused. The purposes though seemingly similar there were serious points of differences.

The proponents of beautiful code swore that this was concise, more maintainable, easy to adapt. It was also long life and reusable. The Pragmatic code is quicker to write. It may use more variables hiding bugs and these bugs may or may not show themselves in future. Nevertheless, this code designed to be only functional.

Indian companies swore and undertook large expensive initiatives to create maintainable and reusable code. They were monumental failures since Indian programming ethics and styles built upon functionality. Being functional and reasonably speedy was the shibboleth. Indian software companies measured their productivity on the number of lines of code a programmer delivered per day on a long-term basis. Programmers became long distance runners and did everything to create lengthy programs. To contain costs they used brute force methods instead of long life fast executing elegant algorithms.

The speed of execution is a function of how well the code optimized. Beautiful code is easier to optimize and faster. Beautiful code writers swore by this shibboleth.

Elegant Programming derived from the way the problem dimensioned and solved. However breaking the problem into subproblems provided greater insight into the big problem. The linkages between subprograms across the entire body of the system provided greater clarity.

No leading Indian company subscribed to beautiful programming concept and neither would Ajay's Company. If a company had to adopt this style, mulled Ajay it must perforce create. It was not there, not in India.

He exhorted his teams on running the extra mile in problem understanding. In the middle of February 2000, he along with his team returned to Bangalore. Within a week, he allocated work to thirty engineers reporting to four project leads.

The Company after winning the USPS project was more confident than ever. It planned a major initiative to secure foreign business. Dagariya's wife prodded her husband for foreign projects once she smelt the obscene profits with correctly dimensioned projects and executed within estimated effort. Dagariya did everything to drill the desirability of such projects and engaged the management cloud. It appointed two sales and marketing executives in the US and UK. In the US they found an Indian, an exIBM sales manager with a long record and a retired English CSC manager in London. Both had years of experience and had assiduously built their networks. This was the key requirement spelt by Dagariya to their consultant Gabriel & James. Their annual salaries and hiring costs were equivalent to a quarter of the USPS contract value.

Ajay promoted again and designated as a Delivery Manager. He had a dual role. Overseeing delivery of foreign projects and being the Division Manager of the Y2K operations was more than a full-time job. His salary doubled in a year and he never bothered to know what his bank balance was. Asha would take his travel details for claiming travel expenses. She never did this work for any other executive in the Company. She had almost become his personal secretary voluntarily.

Wherever he was, he would call her every few days. Whenever he found something she might like he had it shipped to her until she complained about his extravagance.

The company started winning overseas projects and not all were Y2K. His advocacy for Elegant Computer systems though appreciated by some prospects but most preferred the old tried and patented methodologies. This made him realize that there were hidden customers who appreciated Elegant Systems. They could be educated and unlocked. He asked himself if he would like to do that. Yes, he was. It did not matter if the whole industry was not for it. Somebody had to do it.

Venkataraman explained why the Company could not practice 'Elegant Programing'. The company recognized his talents and commitment. The management construed this as his concern for the Company but for him it was purely professional. He had now become a roving inspector for the Company. He went to inspect projects under negotiation, at other times check on quality. Project managers encouraged to seek his advice to solve tricky problems. He was sometimes invited to review deliveries before shipment.

Ajay spent most of his time flitting from one place to another from one to another country. He would be out of the country for 10 or 15 days returning to Bangalore for only a few days and then he would leave again. With those jet lags, his travels were tiring and energy sapping. It would be between days he could talk to Asha. It was during one of those rare meetings with Asha that she told him that she observed the visits of top ranking officials from the building industry calling on Dagariya. It also happened that at times a company official would ring and ask for a meeting with Dagariya in the next hour. At other times, the official would come announced and insist on meeting the chairman . These were difficult situations.

"I am no professional secretary. I have no knowledge about Dagariya Sir's professional contacts. He may have unofficial contacts and I have no interest in them. His regular personal secretary may know about these contacts and their relationships. Once he admonished me when I stopped someone from meeting him. The reality was that his next meeting was due in the next 5 minutes and that man had rung from the parking lot that he was on the way. I did not say anything."

Ajay asked her how often she filled for Dagariya's regular secretary. It was once or twice a month, she replied and only when she was on leave. Sometimes it could be 3 or 4 days which was rare. Asha then volunteered, "I analyzed these visitors and their antecedents and found that most of these visitors were from building companies."

Ajay concluded, "Looks like some of them were secret meetings.".

They could not fathom why should builders and their representatives come so often to meet Dagariya in his software Company. The representatives of the companies who would come to meet him had no software development contracts with the Company. If Dagariya had to meet these visitors, which had nothing to do with the business of the Company then why meet them here. He could have met them in his auditing firm office. Probably he did not meet them there because they had nothing to discuss about auditing. He had membership to well-known clubs where he could meet them. It must therefore be that these visitors wanted something from him than the other way round.

Asha recalled that Mahesh and Sushma during their first meeting spoke of their contacts and wide friends circle, which included others like builders, people from the film industry. Why should friends or their assignees come seeking meetings in the Company's office?

They left it that. Maybe that was a part of his life, which he did not want to share with anyone. "Why should we bother about his personal life," asked Ajay.

Asha smiled and nodded but every bit of information about Dagariya was important to her. She told herself that he had pulled her out of a ditch of her own making but after that, he made his hold on her. She was afraid of him and could not avoid him. He would remind her of that without saying it in her face.

Ajay began to taste small victories every few days. His confidence soared as the belief in his powers.

Chapter X
The Maven Soars

As he sat in Asha's office one warm day, she confided in him about meeting her husband every month. Ajay was stunned to hear that. It was another facet of her personality and a part of her value system, which he or anyone else did not know, and she had hid it. Leaving by the morning flight to Bombay, she would go straight to the jail. She would meet him, spend some time with him, and return by the evening flight.

A few times her daughter Teja accompanied her. "I would go on Sundays and nobody ever knew. There was little to talk. We spent maybe two hours looking away and some desultory conversations. He was falling, dying, and unable to think, driven by people around him. What he looked forward to was a bottle of expensive scotch whiskey, which I carried for him. I never tried to find out if he consumed it or if it was snatched by the guards or by any other prisoner. Everything is possible with money in Indian prisons. When you do it for someone you feel about, then you no longer harbor the guilt of bribing."

Asha invited Ajay for a drive expecting to continue their conversation on the phoenix moment. He had been so busy that it just would not happen and this was one time. If he returned to the US, she was fearful it might never happen. They drove out of the city to an amusement park and found a place where they were least likely to be recognized. Being early in the day, they sat in a large open-air self-service restaurant. They were the only people in the eatery. It was early for the crowds to come.

"Before my rebirth, I had no destination. This moment of realization, my phoenix moment was a journey and a destination together. My grandfather used to say a man with moods, is a weak man. My rebirth began with a conscious attempt not be influenced or become a victim of moods."

"Asha how even minded can you be if you are dictated by moods? Managing moods is managing emotional states."

"It is easy to say. Anyone can tell that. How do you do it? What is its formula?"

"It is very simple. Form a habit to put your hand on your heart. Do it many times a day. Stop everything for a moment. Feel what your mood is at this moment. Is your mood dictating your thoughts, speech or action? Take action. Manage your mood to create Satava," explained Ajay

"Sit comfortably. Listen carefully!"

This was vintage Ajay what she liked to remember him by - serious, easy going, respectful and intense. Smiling, she spread her arms and stretched her legs and the end of her saree settled lower on her shoulder. He saw her neck and the swell of her breasts. It failed to stir him if that was the purpose but he believed it was not.

"Look Asha, a mood is an emotional state but it is not emotion. Emotions are intense. Emotions may have a reason, triggered by a stimulus. Stimulus arises within us from our desires to give or receive or our response to the panorama of life as it plays itself out before us. Moods may have no specific reason. Certain personality traits like optimism, melancholia, hyperactive, morose etc. may trigger a mood. Unexpected events like happiness of seeing an old friend, excessive fall in stock market, betrayal by a partner, and bad news in the morning paper, a sudden tragedy may trigger a mood. We are in a mood or without one. Moods last longer than an emotional state. Also, moods affect the quality of your thoughts, ideas and actions."

"Sometimes a mood grips you so totally that it stays with you through the day. Sometimes it stays with you for days,", volunteered Asha.

"That's why moods are dangerous to your emotional and psychological wellbeing. They can also affect your health."

"Moods could be good, bad; positive, negative; open, close; aggressive, defensive; conquering, ceding; loving, hating; etc. There could be a long list. Look at these pair of moods not as opposites and neither are they meant to be. However, in human sensibility it has a range. These moods represent extreme ends. You can calibrate your mood anywhere in between and be at a point that is life giving and Satava producing. It requires persistent efforts. With that, you generate faculties within you to enable this calibration. It is Godly. You are rebirthing; you are being reborn. Do not look at this as a process or a destination but as a journey. This will happen many times in your life."

"Yes Ajay. If you are not alert, maybe that is not the right expression, you will miss your truth. Moreover, that treasure of your being will be will be lost. Nobody can help you or maybe one or two people who know you intimately and care for you can help you to some extent. You have lost your ability to sense this moment and your sense of sensing gets weaker and weaker with time," added Ajay.

"Yes, you said it accurately," said Ajay and continued,

"In a journey you may change direction or simply stop or wait. Then you can restart. You may get another phoenix moment after some time or after many years and you set into motion another rebirthing process."

"Do we keep doing this continuously throughout our lives?" asked Asha.

Ajay replied, "Yes. However, most people go through life driven by their moods, ruled by their emotions and succumb to their circumstances. Many do not even know the necessity of the phoenix moment. Being of equal temperament will help in sensing our phoenix moments. "

Ajay repeated, her face brightened and she asked, "How will you know that you have achieved or are at the verge of achieving equanimity. By equanimity, I mean centered. Not leaning on any emotion or infecting an unfolding situation with your mood. Just let things, situations and matters emerge and fade away. Is this not the most important realization from phoenix moments?"

"As you get to grips with your mood and don't allow them to dictate you. You find yourself unconcerned, calm and tune yourself to real listening. You are fast developing the ability to hear, listen and read the meaning without losing the context. You may also know the intent behind the statement. This intent may or may not be important but just knowing the meaning and its context helps you know what is value adding. "What is" is the real communication. You know exactly what the other person wants to say irrespective of the words he/she uses," answered Ajay.

~~~

Beginning March 2000, his tasks took him to Washington, New York, Chicago, London, Ottawa, Montreal, and Brussels, Mauritius. People in the company did not know what he did but the engineers he interacted with were full of praise for him. He had built a compact team of Y2K engineers
~~~

who could handle most matters amongst themselves.

There were stories circulating in the Company about how he inspired the Prime Minister of Mauritius. He would later describe his meetings with the government in Mauritius as mind-to-mind that transcended language. The government was keen to computerize the bureaucracy.

Because of special facilities provided by treaties with the European Union, Mauritius had become a bastion of free trade. Its geographic importance was not lost to businesspersons, midway between Asia and Europe and at the tip of Africa. Many businesses from other countries set up industries in Mauritius. Some had just offices and or just bank accounts for international business. Mauritius had become low cost manufacturing gateway to sell in Europe. Chinese, Indians, Russians, Saudi were present in Mauritius with their offices and factories or funded operations here.

A meeting set up with the chief secretary of Mauritius by Andrew Barnaby. He was the company's Sales and Marketing Manager based in London. Ajay met Mr. Ram Goopalam, the Chief Secretary to the Government of Mauritius. Andrew and Ajay had met before and Andrew had complained that Ajay was not aggressive. Dagariya liked aggression and asked Andrew to coach Ajay.

At the meeting, Ajay was a gracious salesperson. He was more like a reticent retired management consultant. He began asking Ram Goopalam about the government's desires, fears, dreams, and compulsions. He showed no interest in knowing the computing needs of the government. He wanted him or his assignee to share the government's perspective plan. He ignored the computerization plan made by a British consulting company, a copy of which Mr. Goopalam showed them. The meeting ended and Mr. Goopalam promised to have a briefing by the Planning Secretary. Later in the day, Mr. Goopalam called them to inform them that the Prime

Minister had shown interest in meeting them.

The met in the Prime Minister's conference room and Ajay listened to the Planning Minister's presentation intently. After the Prime Minister's vision, the floor thrown open for questions. The Prime Minister looked at Ajay and Andrew to take up the thread. Ajay talked about Ram Rajya, the rule of Lord Rama. All except Andrew were Hindus and hence conversant with Ramayana. Andrew had an inkling of the epic. After an hour's description of an ideal people sensitive government, he went on to outline what should be the computerization imperatives. They broke for lunch. The PM brought with him his lunch tiffin a simple lunch, which any middle-class family would eat. Ajay was impressed.

After lunch, Ajay suggested that the government should take up computerization on a non-political basis. All eyes were on the PM's response. He said, "After hearing such an illuminating lecture on an ideal government my government will not take now or later a partisan position." That single sentence set the tone for the country's computerization. A series of computer systems discussed. Ajay recommended an information system that would talk to every Mauritian citizen. It won the day.

Later Andrews would review the meeting as a masterpiece. Here the PM was present and Ajay touched the hearts of everyone and creating the flow. Dagariya called Mr. Goopalam who talked about starting the project soon. He had praise for Ajay whom he described as a wise person much beyond his age and valued his transparency and honesty. The Company sent a team of their best engineers to start assessing computer requirements.

Ajay's desk resembled confusion. It was a usual desk like others but he had a shelf fixed on the wall behind his desktop. Here all manner of papers, magazines, books, removable hard disks etc. were stored and stacked. Memos, faxes, newspaper and magazine cuttings were pinned to the soft board on the right. While his bills do lists, telephone numbers were pinned on the left side. His table cluttered with manuals, computer listings, notes, jottings etc. Everything seemed jumbled and chaotic. One would be tempted to call it disorganized for the litter would speak of itself of some months old junk with areas of dust. Perhaps, cleaned many months ago, however new memos etc. were in a white envelope and kept on the top shelf. No one dared touch anything. Surprisingly, Ajay knew each item or a document where it was, when last handled and where to look for it. He could locate anything he wanted by giving instructions on the phone.

His way of working was different. If someone went to him for advice, solution, inspection, reviews he would gesture him or her to sit down. He might continue doing what he was at and not look at you until he deemed it necessary to close what he was doing. He might order tea or coffee as you liked from the canteen. If you ever thought that you could rush him into something he would completely ignore you. You are coughing or clearing your throat to catch his attention would not work. If he knew something about you, he would ask you – your illness, your parents or your friends or your hobbies. You could not budge or force him into doing anything you wanted him to do. Impatience would get you nowhere.

When he finally decided to listen, he half closed his eyes and heard patiently, nodding his head from time to time. When he was hearing, time was not important. If he was going through your listing or a document he would read it as if you were not there, neither looking at you. He might go through it again. Then he would be asking you questions and sometimes he would be asking you about your state of wellbeing – what was your mood like, did you quarrel with someone, were you tired, rushed up etc. when you wrote the code. He was almost bonding with you and become an extension of you and your problem. He was like a philosopher or a musical conductor. There were many ways to do it but there was only one elegant way. Imperceptibly, he took you into the artistic way of computer programming. He would give you the solution in staccato commands. If he felt you were out of depth he would take a paper and write it for you. More often than not his solutions would work.

Certainly all work meant for his scrutiny not convertible into an artistic rendering because it came for his scrutiny after it had begun. However, his deliberate patience, bonding and thoroughness created solutions that defied answers. He was profoundly involved with you and your work. He was like a true yogi where the problem and he became one.

With all the travelling Ajay was dead tired. He needed rest and spoke about it to the management. The next day Dagariya's wife called him to suggest a holiday to rest and recuperate in Ooty. She had already spoken to Asha. He did not like her interference in his life and then Asha caught him and fixed the tour for coming friday. "It will be hot this time.. Yes, I am there to remove your tiredness.".

He guessed what the rest and recuperation to Asha's hotel in Ooty might be. The curiosity of sex was over. He was grateful to Asha for introducing him to man woman relations. He knew that in his gratitude he would be willing to what she wanted him to. It would be a duty and not a diversion.

~~~

The company had a secret that it tried to brush under the carpet. The CEO, Venkataraman used his ingenuity to keep the stink away from Dagariya because Dagariya did not want to hear about it and the management team could not hide it. It was the Company's first large project after competing with the best and biggest companies in the market. After winning the project, Dagariya never tired of boasting. The Company set
~~~

up in 1993 and the project happened three years later. It was no mean achievement. The Company had spent considerable time, effort and money to win this prestigious project.

The Government of India instructed the Reserve Bank of India to computerize the public sector banks. The Central Bank made an open invitation to companies to come forward to computerize public sector banks. Eight software companies finally selected after rigorous evaluation. Each company was to sign up with a different nationalized bank to develop a Total Banking Software (TBS). The TBS would computerize the front and back office operations of a bank. It would merge operational results of branches to make the trial balance sheet.

The initiative for computerizing banks initiated in 1996/97 by the Government of India. The apex body of banks in the country the Indian Bank Association endorsed the need and described the scope. Finally, the Reserve Bank of India blessed the initiative. This was a prestigious project to computerize the banking sector, which had resisted computerization. Meant for public sector banks the trade unions had opposed it tooth and nail for a decade. Through this program, selected banks were to experience the benefits of automation and computerization. Other public sector banks would follow later. The government wanted to end the stranglehold of the white-collar unions. The government organizations' white-collar unions had been blackmailing its owners for long.

The project was to develop a working prototype. After specification proving tests, it was to convert into a software product and installed at all or many branches of the selected bank. The Company had begun development of TBS in 1997 and kept adding labor, which at peak was 60, and on the average 20. It had been going on for three years. There were temporary peaks and troughs. It was never ending.

Engineers kept coming and leaving and allocation to the project was a punishment. The Company lacked prototyping and productionising skills. Reviews listed problems and along with it new or improved solutions and sought new deadlines. The next review was similar and so was the one after and continued depressingly for 2 years. Dagariya had the team moved to another floor.

The cost overrun was six times the price sold. This was as per the calculations of Joshi ji the Chief Accountant. The operations management contested that. The management was no longer interested in profit. The management realized that it had neither the skills nor the heart for productionising it. The company wanted to wiggle out of it but for the prestige it brought and escape the ignominy of failure.

Ajay had heard stories about it but acknowledged it by shrugging his shoulders. The project manager, he was the fourth in three years, promised to ship it in 2001. After three months, Dagariya received a letter from the Chief General Manager who was in charge for the computerization in the bank. It censured the company directly. The bank doubted the company's ability, experience and seriousness. It ended closing with a flourish how the company was awarded, indirectly questioning its ethics? The bank employed consultants for acceptance testing. After 3 months of testing, it forwarded a list of 3,450 bugs and the possibility of another 20 % that might be lurking.

Dagariya was in a rage. Dagariya would have blown his top if anybody suggested that his ostrich like attitude was the number one cause for the mess it was. Winning the contract was a feather in his cap but when the project began to stink, he never wanted to hear about it. He would blow his top hearing singular bad news from the TBS software and its leaders. These happened with regularity, once in every 3 or 4 months.

He asked Ajay after talking to the Project Manager and Venkataraman to see him. Dagariya invited Ajay to hear his top of the mind views and felt a bit disappointed at what Ajay had to say, which was little.

Dagariya talking to himself than to Ajay under his breath swore, "That lame bastard Dasgupta buggered up the project. He was the second Project Manager who lasted the longest. His strength was monumental ambition and disingenuous lying. He wanted to be the Deputy CEO."

After waiting for Dagariya to regain his composure Ajay began, "Sir, my suggestion would be to convert this ugly loss making monster into company's showpiece. Throw this out and redevelop using 'Elegant programming' principles. I am sure a strong project manager could complete it deploying half the number of engineers. You do not need trainees but good engineers and wise leadership. I think using appropriate program development tools it could be completed in 9 to 12 months", offered Ajay as the way forward.

Dagariya looked at Ajay as if he had committed sacrilege. He removed his spectacles, closed his eyes, and leaned back shaking his head. His demeanor indicated he had heard something unusual. That was the last thing he expected to hear. Ajay knew that a wise businessperson never puts good money into a hole that just sucked and never returned. Thus, his suggestion would be unacceptable. Dagariya articulated what Ajay thought, "Ajay, does anyone throw good coins after bad?"

The conversation dragged on for some time. During which Dagariya answered two phone calls. Then he said, "We need to find at least six engineers who have strong prototyping and product development experience. Each engineer should be able to fit at any leve."

"Surely there will be engineers like that. However, finding them and making a team will be tough and take time," answered Ajay.

"I sometimes get scared that this project might sink the Company," said Dagariya.

Good companies and perceptive leaders do not allow such situations to develop. They build early warning systems through people and review mechanisms to spot problems early. Nobody likes surprises and problems hitting when you least expect it, it is extremely demoralizing. Surprises kill the energy of a team. Solve them early. The company lacked that development maturity and its documentation was extremely poor.

It was about 9 months ago when Venkataraman and Asha found a process engineer to begin with a Development Handbook. This was ready two months ago. It was difficult to apply the procedures, processes and create quality records for projects that had gone far in their life cycle. Thankfully, the USPS project followed the guidelines. Possibly the Development Handbook played a role in winning this project. It was during the marketing of USPS that discussions on the Development Handbook took place. Ajay was present for each when he was in the country.

"Yes Ajay, we need to find experienced engineers. We can get them into the company in one or two instalments."

Then in a flash of brilliance Dagariya said, "Let's find a small company whose only business is building products. It should be faltering company. Such an outfit would have labor resources, strong processes and with management skills. This company would have a product under development and be seeking infusion of money to survive and finish its product. We can buy such a company and get them to help us finish our banking software and our purchase price will fund them to finish their product."

"Such companies are small, entrepreneurial with

strong engineering skills. Often the leaders of such companies are visionaries," replied Ajay.

Dagariya kept quiet. Chin jutting out in a 'come again' mood, he uttered, "Don't be negative."

"When effort is grossly underestimated making their products such situations arise. It takes great effort to build a team, which is working, and always-in flow. When people begin leaving the outfit it is near to closing and almost impossible to rebuild," added Ajay.

"I don't know if such a company will be available and for us to use it the way we want it to. In addition, it must be in Bangalore. A company somewhere in Bhubaneswar or Calcutta or Bombay would not work for the TBS project with the speed and quality we would like. Of course, if you do not buy but make an investment for a teaming arrangement that would be practical. We could get the right engineers to come to Bangalore and work on the project. Their stay etc. would be under the partnering arrangement," offered Ajay.

Dagariya grunted and said, "Yes, I have understood your suggestion and noted your solution. Ajay, there is a difference between a real life problem and theoretical solution."

"All right I will call Sarkar and talk to Sharad tonight," roared Dagariya.

Dagariya thought this was a brilliant piece of thinking. Ajay was not convinced.

A day later Ajay happened to bump into Asha who pulled him into her office. Ajay told her about the disaster with Total Banking Software. She knew there was something going on about banking and people were afraid to talk. The engineers working on it kept it to themselves. She confessed she knew nothing about it. She was not aware of searching a local product development company. When Ajay expressed his fears that it could make things worse, Asha was scared. Asha pumped him and suggested, "Ajay think of starting your own company. I am serious!". Ajay was tense with excitement and enthusiasm from a rush of adrenalin that Asha's suggestion brought about. He could not sleep that night. In his mind, he was building and closing companies.

Sarkar, Venkataraman and a consulting outfit were on the job. They had to find a product company seeking funding and available as a takeover candidate. Soon, they had a shortlist of three companies. Sarkar asked to investigate a company called Technologic. Sarkar believed that to begin investigation of a company talking to a few employees helped to get the big picture. Talking to a few employees of Technologic posing as a recruiter, what he learnt was not encouraging.

Established by four friends to provide software services to Indian customers, the company barely managed to survive. Companies providing software services locally were in cutthroat competition. Technologic decided to build a software product, which the directors hoped, would catapult the company into the big league. The company was a revolving door and could not retain its staff. Given its intellectual capital and the emotional quotient, it was a foolhardy venture. Nevertheless, that is how many great companies began, betting on one big idea. The precedents of the directors were neither inspiring for such an undertaking.

Sarkar learnt that the partners were unhappy. They had grouses against each other. They carefully hid these from outsiders but few employees knew this reality. Each wanted to opt out but stuck because no one was able to generate alternative or had the cojones to move out. In their hearts, they acknowledged they were unemployable and risk averse to create a new business. The directors were bound to each other not out of admiration or a great purpose but for sheer survival was the stark reality.

Sarkar met the directors and learnt that indeed they were in need of funds to keep the development tempo and finish the product. Banks and venture funding companies refused to entertain them. The four directors made it clear that Technologic was not for sale. Would they be willing to offer equity in their company against the infusion of funds? Sarkar concluded that they did not have the insight into product development and neither the experience. They were in no position to help in their Total Banking Software. Employees were disenchanted and half their time spent in scanning for opportunities outside. Any further talk would be waste of time.

Hearing Sarkar, Dagariya had a telephonic conversation with the Technologic Managing Director. The whole exercise had taken a month and the total banking software languished until the General Manager of the sponsoring bank asked Dagariya to come and see him. He warned him that failure on his part would lead to severe consequences. Before he reported to his Managing Director, he would like to dialogue with Dagariya.

Sharad Zende made discreet inquiries. He suggested, "Sir, take Venkataraman and the Project Manager with you when you go to Bombay to meet the host bank. Out of the eight companies engaged in developing their version of Total Banking Software, only four have delivered. I think that our General Manager is bluffing and acting in sheer bravado because he is also stuck."

"Maybe he could continue if we get him to see our view point and a couple of lakh rupees?"

Dagariya smiled and wondered if that could establish good relations and wait for the next official to take his place and that could be a win-win situation. Without batting an eyelid, "I am game for it and get the beast out of the door."

Venkataraman who knew him said it was unlikely.

He then continued, "The GM can't go shopping and buy one off the shelf because they are not available. Yes, foreign packages are available but had not attempted in Indian banks so far. They will not fit. For any other company to start from scratch would set the bank back by 2 years at least. Cashing the bank guarantee was no big deal, though it was not small. If we can have some sort of implementation within 4 to 6 months it would be a good deal for both."

Dagariya recalled what Ajay had advised him, "Sir the best policy is honesty. If you are honest, if nothing you will win customer's sympathy. That is a big thing."

Dagariya with Venkataraman and the Project Manager met the GM and made assurances about completing the project expeditiously and keeping the GM informed regularly. The project manager looked through Dagariya and Venkataraman and swore another hoax.

Ajay reading the memo from Asha[10]he runs into the

[10] *Asha had condensed the 180-page ITT (Invitation to Tender) document to two sheets to get the process of staking a claim started.*
Preamble:
As of 2001, over a 100 million people in India live where water severally polluted. The Ministry of Drinking Water and Sanitation examined 632 districts and found only 59 districts had water safe enough to drink. Pollutants such as chlorine, fluoride, iron, arsenic, and nitrates exceeded national safety limits. With increasing industrialization and urbanization, more than 40 % of India's available surface water used every year and that has been going on since 1995. In the northwestern region, this is our breadbasket about 70 % of the surface water used. Depending upon nature when the monsoons fail there is no replenishment and creates havoc in the countryside. Once the surface water is exhausted, people dig more to find water. Groundwater levels have fallen alarmingly in the last decade. Falling groundwater levels means water is further down the surface soil and difficult to access. Since 65 %, farmers depend on ground water levels and rains to grow crops and do not have irrigation facilities the agrarian social, economic and employment crises is becoming severe progressively and has to be arrested earliest. To make matters worse, the government subsidizes electrical pumps for farmers, which they use to pump water putting excessive strain on electrical grids in India, which is power-starved country. The Ministry has estimated 700 Million people who walk to collect their water, 60 % are women and 12 % children, which is a terrible waste of human power and utility. India is the second most populous country in the world with 1.35 billion people. Half of India's populations a staggering 570 million practice open defection. Diarrhea kills more young children than AIDS, malaria, and measles and remains one of the leading causes of infant mortality. Unsafe water and lack of hygienic practices are

conference room where the meeting is just about to begin chaired jointly by Dagariya and Venkataraman. Dagariya invites Ajay to take a seat next to him. Dagariya reminds the group, whichconsisted of his senior most executives the importance of the project and what it could do for the company if it won it. He says, "Winning it under the noses of TCS, WIPRO, HCL, INFOSYS, Oracle Financial, Datamatics, "Would pitch us smack in the center of the software industry and we will be grouped with the top 10 in the country."

Ajay had read it and flabbergasted. He had spent his life in a village, luckily that was near the Ganga and only lately began facing droughts and drinking water problems. That it should be so hurt, Ajay. He was all for the project.

There was no doubt about the importance and uniqueness of the project. Firstly,its size (29 states and 7 union territories and almost as large as Europe in terms of area and population). Secondly, the importance of the initiative as a space-faring nation with such high illiteracy, health and water deficiency was unacceptable. Third, the

creating untold suffering and devastation in the country's agrarian and rural areas.
Call for Tenders:
The most recent dipstick study concluded by the Ministry before the issue of this "Call for Tenders" found 70 % districts face water scarcity and afflicted with issues of water shortage, water stress or deficits and unsafe water and water crises. These combine making water stress difficult in obtaining sources of fresh water for use during a period and it may result in further depletion and deterioration of available water resources.

This threatens the food security and health of the country. More than half of India's total area is facing high to extremely high water stress. Almost 600 million people are at a higher risk of surface water disruptions. Shrinking supply might have serious ramifications for the country's agriculture sector, health, and growth of the infant, leading to serious social upheavals. While the current situation looks grim, there is a possibility it can get worse. The government of India has determined to computerize the entire water lifecycle covering identification, collection, storage, supply, usage and replacement. The Ministry charged with the responsibility and has taken the challenge, and will execute the program using best talent available in the country under Rajiv Gandhi Drinking Water Mission in mission mode.

need (threatening the very idea of India), four its impact (a minor increase in GDP of drought prone areas could jack up the GDP of the entire country); and finally the rural and agrarian governance (panchayat raj leading to justice and ending exploitation of the weaker sections of the people).

There was a general agreement that the Company should bid and put its best people on the bid as they had for the United States Postal Services. Soon the meeting lost the bearing. Ajay advocated dividing the country into three state clusters as developed, moderately developed and backward. He would like a pilot of four five districts in each cluster leading to one, two or the maximum of three models and take them into each state and working with the state government delineate requirements for each district. Venkataraman suggested a pilot in each state and development of one or two models for each state. There was also the idea that working on state capitals would create models specific state and modified for each district. Ajay and Venkataraman made the proposal and Dagariya took it to the Ministry and the evaluating Committee headed by Dr. Rai.[11] The company did not win the bid and the reason for failure was not lining Dr. Rai's pocket.

When Ajay discussed with Sarkar he realized that winning government contracts invariably was nepotism based and under the table gratifications often won the day.

11 *A project of this size created, bid and executed as far back in 2000/2001. Sadly, after the Requirement Study the project died and not followed. A few years later a similar effort for computerization of government services countrywide was taken by the island of Crete.*

Chapter XI
The Man of Healing

The furious pace of growth the software and call centre industry was doing wonders to the economy. Call center growth percentage surpassed the software industry. Other sectors like banks, consumer goods, ready to make and fast food industry, small format cinemas, nursery and middle standard schools, ready made garments, entertainment electronic goods, innumerable vocational and training programs for skills required in the new industries in the economy were growing and generating employment across the economy.

Educated and trained youngsters found jobs. Those who survived the first 3 years bought motorcycles and scooters. Those with industry experience of 6 plus years bought four wheelers. Within ten years, most married and had one or two children and prepared to invest in real estate. Foreign travel and even immigration to the US or other countries were part of this dream. These were the aspirations of youngsters.

Those born in the 70's saw these as necessities and the successful individual did their best to climb this ladder as quickly as possible. This was the dream of every young Indian. For the urban majority in their quest for success, morals and ethics were not necessarily important. Their parents began their lives believing that being honest and ethical behavior as necessities and the struggle for material success a lifetime pursuit. The desire of their children to better themselves than their parents and quickly without moral hang-ups became ideal targets of consumerism.

Those who had visited American and European cities had interesting stories to tell. The malls, the entertainment centres, tube railways, fast food outlets, fine dining etc. Listening to this life of ease and convenience whetted the appetite of those who had not visited El Dorado's of new age. The pent up demand stimulated entrepreneurial instincts of the go-getting class. Everyone knew someone or heard of someone who had set up a small business and prospered.

When you are jobless or do not like what is on offer, the escape could be becoming an entrepreneur. The other is what you aspire for and try to realize in spite of a regular paying job. Both are entrepreneurs but this was the first time after independence that the latter class of entrepreneurs became aspiring Indians. They came from ordinary families and entrepreneurship was a choice made for self-expression. It added to the gross domestic product of the nation and grew entrepreneurial culture.

When you have money and do not have to worry about tomorrow, consumerism is a fatal attraction. Fatal in terms of creating a cycle of ever-increasing wants most of which are useless. The lengths people go to alleviate their never-ending needs bordered on devil may care carelessness to planned creativity. Working hard during the week and for long hours, they reserved the weekends at the altars of consumerism.

The malls were becoming the new playgrounds and

for some people they were the temples. Very few engineers and even builders knew the depressing rate at which malls were closing. The government of the day had succumbed to foreign blandishments and the urgings of the capitalists to allow malls after a two-year long debate.

The acquisitive nature of Indians is as old as India itself. If it were not then the most revered saints, teachers and philosophers would not have argued against possessive behavior. They argued that negation of covetousness as an important component of enlightenment and salvation or moksha[12].

The lure for Indians going overseas for work or business has always been a part of the Indian dream. One ventured overseas chiefly for amassing money. Later many grappled with the idea of residency in their adopted countries. This became necessary if they and their families wanted to establish themselves in their adopted countries. It made the urge to create kinships with similar people because they had left their bloodrelativesback in their countries. They had no desire to remember what they had left behind. The new obliterated the old, and some forsake their Gods. In the last 50 years, this immigration assumed shocking ways and subterfuges. Slave trade to stowaways to illegal entries to selling themselves Indians did not leave any avenue that could take them overseas.

Indians have always been bewitched with the white skin. It was their love for the English before the Great War

12 *It is the process for the atman or soul to attain liberation from the clutches of samskaras and escape residing in another body after the death of the individual. Once the atman has attained a human body in the process of natural progression, from lower to higher forms of life, then in its subsequent incarnations it will inhabit a human body only regardless of the quality of its earlier karmas. The quality of an individual's life in a particular incarnation will depend upon the quality of its accumulated karmas.*

and later the Americans. They have rarely paused to ask themselves if those people returned their love. In spite of being, a one-sided love affair, millions who could not escape, looked upon those who did as successful. Those who made it were envied. Many who traded their country for a few pieces of silver insisted immigration as a way to escape mediocrity and akin to a business deal. Business has no sentiments.

Unless India grows in a big very rapidly, it will not be able to look after all its citizens. Citizens expect their governments to provide the means for achieving their life goals lawfully. Citizens have body, mind and spiritual needs. Until the government creates avenues for its citizens to achieve a modicum of personal growth in these directions, the urge for the west is unlikely to stop.

Arguing with Sarkar Ajay said, "I believe that with little common sense, a bit of sacrifice and the will of the government can wipe out its poverty in reasonable time."

Sarkar mocking Ajay asked, "What is that reasonable time? It will take many decades."

As Indians become prosperous, there were inevitable comparisons with the west. Conversations veer towards gadgets, equipment's, labour saving devices to conveniences to healthcare and lifestyles. Who will believe these lifestyles to be extravagant, wasteful and harmful of nature? These denizens feel that these new ways of living would integrate India into world economy and make India prosperous. They have forgotten the India they left behind. These thoughts and advocacy are in rarefied settings. If we did that, a profession, a skill or a tradition might be lost forever. A noticeable sensibility today is the pervasive selfishness in the society, especially in urban areas. The rural areas touched by some modernity are not so much tainted. This selfishness includes everything from individual demands to that which belongs to all and shared. Being a part of modern culture, the varieties of selfishness does not enable distinctions. It is in every thought, activity and relationship. It seems India and Indians have forgotten simple respectability.

❧❧❧

TCS after debate and discussion hired an American consultant and created its Development Handbook, the first in the industry. This was to guide the execution of their projects. The company made many copies and distributed it to hundreds of its engineers. This was the first practical attempt by any Indian company to systematize management of software. INFOSYS, WIPRO, SATYAM followed.

Academicians in the US first articulated the need for a Development Handbook. Then consulting companies made their own templates and software companies made Handbooks. The Handbooks created by software companies were practical and detailed. These documents provided frameworks and guidelines to develop maintainable software and brought in predictability to the process of creating and installing code. Along with these developments, time estimations of efforts became finer.

There was opposition to the use of Handbooks among the middle phalanx of top companies who actually saw projects through. Writing code given requirements suited their nature and they found excellence in this. Adding descriptions, annotations, later maintenance etc. to their code added more work that they found distasteful and performance standard unchanged there was resistance. The smaller companies faced many challenges. Each big company developed their own implementation plans. It was long uphill journey.

Later versions more detailed and process oriented and their utility appreciated by the senior managers, investors and customers. It reduced rework that could bleed a project to death like the Company's TBS. Many bleeding projects at the same time could hemorrhage a company. Smart management created a movement for its implementation in their companies.

Pioneering Indian companies stretched to include processes from first customer contact to delivery. The totality and expanse included foreign customers. This meant front-end processes finding a place in the document. These were before development. Though situational, it gave a semblance of orderliness and confidence to customers. As the Indian software business in 1990's was primarily application development, re-engineering, and maintenance all notoriously difficult to estimate. Now it became a much more accurate leading to competitive bidding. The top software services companies were leading the industry.

The Handbooks developed by Indian companies spanned all distinct areas from requirements studies, proposals making and bidding, pricing etc. to delivery and warranty. It was more comprehensive from companies in other parts of the world. In later versions, processes extended to include communications between teams at different locations and allocation of engineers. The Indian companies revised them every now and then based on their experiences. They thus created their unique Development Handbooks. The comprehensiveness put the Indian application software companies ahead of their counterparts elsewhere in the world.

The adherence to their handbooks covered the entire life cycle. Having operations follow a predictable manner gave firms the confidence to seek quality certification. In 2004 the greatest number of certified application software development firms were from India. Certifications were by American, British and German certifying companies.

Two years later Indians formed their own certifying companies. They first collaborated with foreign companies and later set up their own companies. This was an important factor in the maturation of Indian software industry. Process a byword in the software industry percolated to many other industries. Process Engineering became a subject taught in engineering and management colleges. It was not that it was not taught earlier but mostly in the prestigious colleges. Now it was available as a course in many engineering and management institutions and individual consultants sought process related assignments.

Ajay's Company unleashed a major initiative for the use of its Development Handbook. Itshand book based on the TCS document purloined by Asha. The management believed that with its involvement it would get all projects to follow the Handbook. They gave themselves 6 to 9 months. Later the company would seek ISO certification. Company management underestimated the enormity of effort required for projects to follow the handbook. The Company had no idea of implementation approaches and strategies followed by pioneers.

The front ranking companies had sensitized their engineers and supporting staff over long periods. Only after company wide appreciation, they released their Handbook for implementation. Some companies distributed hundreds of copies to employees to create the environment. Some created groups of pioneers and champions to seed culture across the company. Many employees in mature companies knew their Handbooks inside out. By managing development as per the handbook, company quality indices rocketed upwards indicated exceptional maturity. The average time a company took to enforce standards was 2 years.

It was not the case with Ajay's company. Sensitization across the company and pulling in engineers for a shared vision dispensed with. The management decided only certain prestigious and especially foreign projects follow the handbook. It was not a wise decision. There was pressure to finish projects in time with understaffed teams. Project Managers complained that following handbook incurred overheads and took away productive time. Venkataraman argued for employing consultants to help the Company become process mature. Dagariya was in no mood to commit funds. Soon it became a child that no one wanted.

Indian software engineers had always been documentation averse. Few leaders like Ajay forced engineers to follow the handbook. He drove his engineers, pointing out the positive impact on their career growth by managing software development deterministically than going by the seats of the pants as they did. The stretch for excellence took long for wide appreciation. Some followed many did not.

Eventually there were small companies within the company, few islands of excellence in a sea of mediocrity. In Ajay's world, 'Elegant programming' and process orientation could be a snug fit but there were forces that would not let it happen. He knew this. If not, then he would build a software company following Elegant Software making models. The rumblings of entrepreneurship began to reverberate in his mind.

Venkataraman noticed the difference in rework between projects executed with and without the Handbook. He had his findings presented to the Board. The Board forced Dagariya to outsource the implementation of the Development Handbook. It was a lost year and by the time consultants could begin another 6 months had passed. The Company was brittle and cracks had begun to show.

ISO or CMM certifications were the international gold standard of quality assurance for a software company. It was more than a year away from the Company. These certifications were becoming important differentiators for customers to award contracts. Venkataraman championed the cause supported by Ajay but one Ajay was insufficient and the Company needed many. The company was rift with divided opinions and Dagariya would not admit to the rumblings. The Company began to falter, pulled in many directions. All were for the progress and well-being of the Company but with too many opinions there was no strong and decisive leader to check the drift.

Ajay realized that there was no Alexander in the Company to cut the Gordian knot. After his best efforts he walked away wary of taking any position.

Developments on the TBS were not good. The Project Manager resigned and Dagariya shaken and feared promises made to the bank, which now seemed impossible to keep. He had returned after promising the bank fortnightly reports. The Company was overdue with two. Money was not the consideration but the inevitable bad reputation would be disastrous. For the past few months, he was under stress and Sushma feared for him.

Venkataraman had to find a solution. He did what any crises ridden CEO would do, he talked to every engineer in the office to get a sense of the malaise. He promoted the second in charge with a secret deal. He would later insist that he had no option. He did not try to identify the technically sound engineers who knew the project well. A group or committee leadership would have been a better choice. He was not for it because a shared project management would require his time. He believed that these people could see the project through. Of course, they had to have an inspiring leader. A deputy of the leaving leader could turn out to be a misfit. Within a week's time of departure of the Project Manager, his best technical man who knew the TBS also resigned. Offered a position in the same company, which the Project Manager had joined, he scooted. It was imperative to retain him, so he doubled his salary.

"Yes it is a bad practice but getting the project restarted after a month's lull was an imperative," reported Venkataraman to Dagariya.

When Ajay heard of this after a month, he predicted that the company would take more time to get the stalled project running again. He reasoned that TBS required strong personnel skills and an astute management to heal the TBS team. This would not happen with an unwanted child. He wondered what made Venkataraman take such decisions. They were wrong and compounded the problem. He doubted the management including Venkataraman to solve the TBS problems. Managerial success rests sometimes more on human relations than on technical brilliance. This was what TBS required.

Dagariya and Venkataraman reckoned that once the TBS software was tested, debugged and corrected the pressure would ease. Venkataraman argued that periodic status reports would ease the situation. Let implementation take long, the situation would have changed and there was no need to think about that now.

Reworking software umpteen times makes the entire software unwieldy. Big blobs of software become critical which ordinarily would have been routine commonplace processes. The reality was that it was poor work. Number of key or prestigious projects successfully delivered measures the success of a company. In the lifetime of the company's working existence, TBS was the most important and its failure would send a wrong message.

⁂

There was more of bad news. Alok Marathe, the Company's Sales and Marketing Manager in the US was getting restive. He was demanding more. The Company had two options. Call his bluff and find a replacement or succumb to his blackmail. Dagariya was a worldly man and knew that subtle blackmail if not defused now, he was at the mercy of the extortionist and pressurized repeatedly later. Having built the Company, he will not allow coercion to succeed.

He asked Ajay to go to USA, talk to him, and find out what Alok wanted. He had talked to Samir Arora and Ajay could rely on Samir's counsel and help. Ajay was perhaps the right person, guileless, ethical and high-minded. Dagariya believed his originality, problem solving abilities and accommodative human relations would defuse the problem.

Marathe's advent into the company a year ago was under shotgun conditions. When Samir Arora resigned and left suddenly with a week's notice, it created a panic situation. Samir was having family problems. Having his son arrested for juvenile delinquency was bad enough. His daughter marrying a Negro and absconding was a shocker for the Arora family. Dagariya let him go reluctantly. It was essential to replace him to keep Samir's contacts alive and follow his hot accounts. Creating new contacts could wait. Asha discovered three candidates and the company hired the one who could joinat the earliest.

Alok Marathe was from TCS, Bangalore and he was ready to go to US within a month if his salary for the notice period reimbursed. He had done two stints in US. He was a victim of regional problems with the local chief, Dr. Ravindranath. Overlooked for a foreign posting, which should have been the case, hurt him. Due to regional factional fights he was feeling left out and becoming a pawn in these tussles. Tamilian dominance in Bangalore and Madras had become noticeable. He joined the company for the foreign opportunity and the consequent capital accumulation. He was a bright lad with a management degree from one of the best Indian business school i.e. IIM, Ahmedabad. He could see his dreams crumbling before him on considerations that were unethical and not competence based.

Alok spent a day with Ajay and they did not get along. He felt Ajay did not have the skills and competence.

This was on specious grounds. Alok felt that he did not have postgraduate qualifications and graduated from a third rate college which was a negative. Alok came with a chip on his shoulder and Dagariya felt they had erred. Under such circumstances, his papers hurriedly got ready to send him to US as soon as possible. Until he left, he should acquaint himself with the company's current and past assignments. Knowing that the company's skills inventory was necessary to sell in the US, h also should interact with thought leaders and briefed on the leads that Samir had created in US. This brought him to spend a day with Ajay and he had heard Ajay's stories in the company.

As soon as he had accepted the offer, Asha began working on his travel documents. In 2001/02, the American visa rules began tightening up. Ten years later, the Americans would come down with vengeance to discourage Indians. Later it became a Presidential election issue. The plea was that Indians working in US stole American jobs.

A fact that US forget today American consultants, commentators, politicians and business analyst had willingly acquesied in the hiring of Indians engineers in the US and cared more for the greenbacks than the quality of the engineer. The pool of Non Resident Indians and illegal immigrants in the US from 1999 increased like never before. To blame Indian companies and Indians a decade later smacks of hypocrisy. The Americans were as culpable as the Indians were in the increasing illegal residents in the US. The Americans from all professionals contributed – consultants, companies, fake universities, legal counsels and others.

The American manufacturing sector had been losing jobs for the last three decades. First to the Japanese then to Koreans and now to the Chinese as they invited American multinationals to set up shop in their country with promises of cheap labour, power and land etc. Subsequently companies from these countries flooded American market with cheap and equally good if not better household goods displacing labour.

Facing resistance to their goods the Japanese responded by setting up companies in the US. Slowly they began buying distressed American companies, turning them around and making them successful. It was quicker, cheaper and administratively cleaner. Employing all sorts of American consultants, they found lobbyist for themselves without investment. In their wake, Koreans emulated the Japanese with success. The Chinese went about buying US treasury bonds in billions of dollars. This gave the Chinese a beachhead in America and being the largest creditor nation it acted from a position of strength.

By the time, the Chinese goods entered the USA the Americans found they could do little. China had all the legal, international trade and treaty rules and economic factors in its favor. In addition, the manufacturing sector employees were blue-collar workers and their influence in the American economy had been weakening since the last decade.

The American services sector was different. It was vocal, middle class, white Americans educated from top engineering and management schools and colleges. They could bring pressure on legislators and supported by the media. They would not allow Indians to take away their jobs. The crescendo peaked and it became US presidential election spiel. American jobs robbed by stinking Indians sitting thousands of miles away.

Samir Arora had settled in New Jersey 4 years before he quit IBM. He had planned his life carefully. After settling, he covered his territory from this location and IBM valued his 20 years' service and let him work from his hometown. When Dagariya asked him to come on board, he had no hesitation. He insisted that he would continue from New Jersey. This was his base from there he had maintained his links with IBM's customers. Samir's counsel would be available and the list of his contacts, prospects and customers would become that of the company.

New Jersey is quite Indian in a way that every fifth person there is an Indian. Arora hired a one-room apartment in New Jersey for Alok Marathe, who landed in New Jersey in September 2001.

To have graduated from IIM, Ahmedabad Alok had to be good. Samir liked the young, Alok whom he found to be smart, knowledgeable and well informed. Samir thought of Alok to be ambitious, a self-starter who wanted to make money fast. He was an excellent professional. Samir briefed Alok about the American companies that he was marketing. Many of his contacts in these companies were Indians and Pakistanis. Samir introduced Alok Marathe to them first over the phone.

Samir taught Alok the essential deskwork emphasizing it was an imperative for creating a strong funnel of prospects. You had to do that before contactingany company. He taught Alok to study those variables in the American market, which are important to size a company you want to sell. He taught him how to interpret purchased databases of companies. He learned to look behind company's web sites to make what Samir called the 'Qualified List'

Alok enjoyed making his own database. He had specialized in marketing in his business management course at IIM, Ahmedabad. Alok was ready to launch and start cold contacting prospects in his database by blind telephoning.

Ajay landed in New Jersey and reached Alok Marathe's apartment. Alok was resentful. He could not decide whether Ajay had come to smoke him out or negotiate for some sort of settlement or a prelude to show him the door. Alok was sure that he had not committed any impropriety. Rather Samir believed that he had worked heart and soul for the company.

Alok knew that Ajay was a management man. There was simmering hostility beneath their simple conversations. Ajay was sensitive. He tried his best not to respond to prejudices with careless remarks. He tried his best to be friendly with Alok. He sincerely admired his knowledge, praising his initiative and his desire to learn from him.

A few days later on a Sunday, they were returning from breakfast at an Indian eatery. Alok darted across the street against a red light and a speeding car hit him and fled away.

Ajay took charge. Helping him cross to the pavement, he began hailing every passing vehicle. An old woman saw them, suggested to go to an emergency nursing home a mile away, and called a taxi. Alok was in extreme pain and howling while waiting for the taxi to arrive. The kind woman listened to all that Ajay told her about them. She seriously and honestly commiserated with them and offered to loan them money if they were short. Finally, they stopped a taxi. She gave instructions to the Bangladeshi taxi driver and Ajay had Alok registered for treatment. He had a broken right arm, a concussion on the right shoulder and bruises.

When he was satisfied that he was under medical attention he called Samir Arora. He explained Alok's plight and he sought his advice. Samir asked Ajay to put him in touch with the doctor treating him. Samir arranged to have the bill paid on the net and Ajay took Alok in a taxi to their apartment. For the next few days, Ajay tended Alok like a brother.

A fortnight later when Alok was better and was able to walk with his plastered arm in a sling, he felt the sheer goodness of Ajay. Alok realized care, concern and dependability was a better ingredient for friendship than all the degrees in the world. They became friendly and shared their views on lifemanship. Alok's hostility vanished without a trace of rancor.

He stuck up a friendship with Agnes Barnes, the woman who helped them at the accident spot. Meeting her sometimes in the park where she went for her morning walks. Through her, he began to know the American life. Consumerism was the big trap that had beguiled and enslaved the Americans. It exercised its power through conformity and hence the phrase 'to be different is to be indecent'.

She related her life as a writer for 30 years with New York Times. She, like many of other Americans welcomed the Greening of America as a counter culture. It was about individualism, openness and quest for happiness. It was about tolerance and the right to be different. It spoke of an unstoppable revolution where individuals became leaders. This revolution would change the political structure of the country. She recollected that New York Times had never received the number of letters before in response to this book. She welcomed the brave new world.

Ruthlessly set upon by the big business, the movement collapsed a year later. Five years later, she believed that American business had obliterated it and the dream lay wasted. Seminal works never go waste and sprout up in other forms at another time. Therefore, it was with the Greening of America.

Working with Alok, Ajay found him to be a thorough person who enjoyed doing the backbreaking boring deskwork. Identifying prospects was the beginning of any sales process. Slowly they built a rapport. Samir liked this young person as much as he liked Alok. He would have loved to have him as a son-in-law, but it was too late. He was waiting for the right time to approach Dagariya for an Advisor's position, and decided to work through Ajay.

It had beenmonths since Alok was in the US and Dagariya wanted to see the strength of his prospect list. Alok had nothing to show, even though Samir Arora contended that he was in right direction and results would be visible soon. Alok had a tough job, but he was confident of making a success. Now he understood the American way of life at professional and cultural levels. This was one part of a quintessential salesperson and applied for selling in any country. In USA the usage of Americanisms were important to come closer to American buyers. Dress code, language, timing and degree of formality, professional approaches and deadlines as sacrosanct were very much a part of American professionalism. It was imperative to follow them. Deviation when they occurred must be informed.

Their day would begin making a list of phone calls to make in the day. For each call they made, they had in front half a sheet of facts about the company. After the call, Alok would add his notes which added value to the background information which could be used, when he or Ajay spoke next time, but mostly they would be speaking into a voicemail. Rarely would there be a response for the messages left.

Alok used the scripts given by Samir. It went about saying how their company could save big money if they sent their IT work to his company in India like many other American companies had done previously. The story had to be over in 30 seconds conveying why he was calling, how their company could benefit and ask for a meeting. Alok was used to having the door slammed in his face. A deep breath and he would be calling again. The pitch had to be in a balanced manner, and not overboard stressing a maximum of key points that whet the appetite of the listener. He must come to the point for the prospect to ask for more. As he made more calls, he perfected his delivery.

Ajay learnt that most Americans had little knowledge of India or Indians. The average vision of India was a land of snake charmers, elephants, rajas, houris and slaves. Who would like to send work to such a faraway country? The initial meeting was more to dispel these myths and learn the buying structure of the host company. Alok explained the risks the purchaser of software services took. Selling project works was different than body shopping.

The purchaser needed confidence on power supply, reliability of communication circuits, durability of the service provider, tax matters, failures, political stability, manpower, purchaser's/user's visits and their safety including safe place to stay in India and so on. Unless the contract was for big jobs, the engagement between the host company and his company was Alok. Alok was the company face until someone from his company visited India.

Samir noticed that Alok had new respect for Ajay and mentioned it to Dagariya during a telephonic conversation. Dagariya began to wonder about the rare quality of Ajay that made him such an amiable person. He could get along with anyone and convince the most negative or unwilling buyer.

Neither Samir nor Alok could help him in his search for 'Elegant Programming'. He began searching for people and companies who claimed to have opinions on 'Elegant Programing'. Only few individuals entertained communications. It was difficult. Some, when they learnt he was from India discouraged him or took him to be too theoretical or impractical. From his search, he found an 'Elegant Programing' evangelist. Devin, a third generation Knuth practitioner (Professor Donald Knuth remembered for his multi volume books on computer programming which have become rules and paradigms. His work considered as important in computer programming as Leonard Euler is in mathematics. Knuth considered even today as the largest contributor to logic and programming. He championed the cause of free software and evangelized that open programs were only as good as algorithms they are using; he shunned admirers and avoided public glare). Devin had collected around him a bunch of similar thinking people like a secret society. After a few personal mails to him, led to many contacts with whom Ajay spoke often. In a month's time, he created a document whose abstract was as under.

'Elegant Programming strives to create code that is simple in design and uses least amount of resources. Computer resources refers to memory, disk space etc. The programs compile and execute fast, easy to maintain and in a suite easy to replace. Thinking in language of Elegant Programing, complex algorithms created elegantly. These would be simple and readable expressions of ideas and therefore permits reuse. Elegant Programing is multi paradigm. It makes it easy to read and understand supporting logic. This thinking is able to handle the imperatives of functional programing by breaking the functions into simple repeatable ideas, meanings, thoughts as rules, search algorithms, logic trees etc. Such program carries least burden which compiles and executes faster'.

From his many discussions with proponents of Elegant Code, Ajay became a strong votary. He came to believe that bad code writers took great pains to defend their concept of practical coding. They emphasized that code should work and there is nothing called beauty in code. It was true at a basic level. Like everything in nature ages, matures and withers away, why spend precious time on a code that has an inherent life of few years these people reasoned. When new overtakes the old regularly why bother about code beyond 2 or 3 years. Such engineers vehemently said that beautiful code takes time. What takes more time? Thinking, analysing, writing beautiful code or code that works, and maybe carrying bugs? Correcting bugs and junking it at half its promised life turns out to be more costly. An Elegant Code is smaller than a functional code doing the same job. More lines of code mean more errors. Expressing ideas clearly and elegantly leads to better code quality and maintainability.

What is the use of code that might be fast, but contains bugs? An Elegant Code will be faster than the original because it is less complicated. Where performance is an issue which of two would be easier to optimize?

Evangelism is not about reading and discussing. Evangelism is preaching and about converting people. He vowed that he could best do it by setting up a company for 'Elegant coding'. It was through his work he would convert users, companies and developers.

Ajay was moving in a narrow tunnel but his vision was wide.

He had done no course or training on entrepreneurship. Let alone that he had never read a book on entrepreneurship. He was imbibing entrepreneurship intuitively. His boldness and childlike simplicity to reach out to people was turning into the most powerful learning and imperceptibly changed his thinking.

Chapter XII
Danger Rear its Head

Ajay received Mythili's invitation and three follow up calls asking him not to miss her graduation ceremony. Contacting was much easier now with cell phones becoming common usage. He was not present for his own graduation ceremony and had not even witnessed one. He sat in the rows meant for parents and visitors.

The procession of graduating students entered the auditorium led by ex-army men called Marshals. These retired army men were wearing big-waxed mustaches in smart green fatigues brought a sense of purpose and strength to the ceremony. The entry of students were followed by the faculty, heads of pharmacy, pre-clinical, para clinical and other non-medical staff looking after hostels, sports etc. The Marshals led the two rows of students entering from the two main opposite entrances. The girls were dressed in white sarees whereas the boys in white shirts, black trousers, black shoes with bow ties and black blazers.

They Marshals led the students to their seats facing the stage. The teaching staff sat in the first and last seat of each row and the seats between occupied by graduating students. Reaching their appointed seats they stood until all the dignitaries had assembled on the stage. When the chief guest escorted by the Principal and Director reached their seats and sat down, the others followed suit. The Chief Guest was a legal luminary, much in news and talked on the need of medical jurisprudence.

The ceremony began. The Chief Marshal asked the first three rows of students to stand and that they walked towards the edge of the stage. On a table were the graduating gowns and next to it was a gown attendant. He helped the student into the gown and put the hood on their heads making sure it was right. He looked for tight fit, buttoned and ensured that the hood at the rear remained unknotted. When the graduating student's name called the third time, he or she ascended the stairs. They stood facing the audience till an assistant knotted the student's hood at the rear. The student then walked towards the Chief Guest to receive his/her certificate after shaking his hand. Before leaving the stage, the student turned towards the audience and gave their best smile with the certificate roll held in both hands and the photographers at in the center on the ground photographed them. They had worked for this crowning glory for the past five and a half years. This new identity would serve them for their future. A Marshal escorted the student to his/her seat in the hall.

When Mythili's name announced, Ajay's was the loudest clap and he stood up for a moment. While sitting down he turned back to look and there was Mythili's mother. He greeted her and she smiled in recognition.

After all had received their certificates the students walked out in a file to the tune 'excelsior' played on the piano. It was a solemn occasion. There were many a moist eyes for they were doctors of medicine finally. Some would stay back in the college and continue with further studies. Other would join hospital duty. All would leave for the next phase of their lives.

Ajay sought Mythili's parents and soon he and her father were in deep conversation with sharing his career plans. He was thinking of starting his own company and Mythili's father encouraged him. He reminded him that he was there to help him in whatever way he could. He took an immediate liking to this young man and her wife thought what a fine son-in-law he would make. Then Ajay took out from his pocket a Rolex watch that he had purchased in London for her. Receiving it she hugged him tightly. Mythri was a bubbly girl, but today she was at her best and her eyes were shining.

Mythili explained that her application for MD in pediatrics was under consideration. Her mother assured her of her success. The head of pediatrics happened to walk past, caught Mythili's eye, and joined them. After a brief chat with her parents, he congratulated her. Everyone looked at him wondering about his decision to enroll her in his department. He could read their mind and cryptically told Mythili to come back after a refreshing holiday.

Ajay simply said, "You are in 100 %." She had always wanted to be a pediatrician, she disclosed. If she did not, she would carry the stain of rejection for a long time.

Simple engineering is more valuable to a new developing company and the using organization as well. Good engineering is about finding the most cost effective solutions. Measuring cost can be tricky and could be in terms of money, hours, morale or lost opportunities. Some costs transacted immediately others assumed as debt. Some costs are less obvious than others are.

Among the unconsidered costs, the most deadly one

is the complexity cost. Complexity cost is the debt accrued by complicating features or incorporating technology. Both are to solve problems.

Requirements studies are about user requirements. The designers in their zeal add more and increase complexity. Unless the company possesses an inbuilt discipline about keeping software simple this attitude is damaging. Features not surfaced but provided by spurious logic that the effort for creating them be so less but hope to delight the customer shortens software life. The majority of users are not going to be using these features anyway. It creates complexity costs.

Developers, who understand complexity cost, use data to lessen complexity. Complexity can creep in through well-meaning people on the implementation side as well. It is better to add assumed features later when the user demands them then trying to out think the user.

A simpler designed and built product needs lesser documentation and illustration. It helps everyone – team members, company, customers and users. Look at Japanese, then the Koreans and now the Chinese. They learnt to develop products that did what they promised extremely well. They deliver their products accompanied with bare installation and user manuals. Some companies go to the extent of creating a User Manual on the package itself.

'Elegant Programming' loyalists pushed Ajay to be simple and dramatize it in his product and code. Value of software lies in those functions that are used and not those functions not used and built. Devin referred to Ajay a study that made a compelling case that only 60 % of functionalities provided are used and 40 % available functionalities are never used.

Simplicity is a tough engineering challenge and complexity keeps compounding over time. , Ajay learnt that maintaining simplicity could be a powerful weapon. Especially the best weapon a software company has when competing with bigger competitors. It is all the more important for new entrepreneurial companies. It is a long haul, and the price and the respect the company commands in the market are worth it. It creates its own differentiators and helps the company compete with the best and biggest. He admitted that not all customers would buy these arguments. Those who did would become his customers. The ones who had set on grand computerization plans and fell on their faces would appreciate his logic after failing and lost time. Sadly, there were many such companies.

The seeds of entrepreneurship planted a year ago began to sprout.

Mythili returned spending two months with her parents, which she described as dull and boring. She was physically and mentally fatigued in the sweltering summer heat. She had hardly done anything except laze around the house. People who have lived in the even and moderate weather of Bangalore for some time find the weather in any large metro as unbearable. Summers are too hot and winters too cold. Amongst the big industrial and business cities in the country, no other city spoils you for comfort as this city does.

"Of course in Delhi there was nothing to do. No friends. There was nowhere to go. Sometimes during the day, I would go with mumto the local market or the neighbour aunties would drop by at home. That would be the occasion for mom to show me off. Sometimes I would talk to my former classmates on the phone,Watch tv, read some books and receive instructions and suggestions from parents," explained Mythri in boredom.

"Did you not try to contact your pre university classmates or other friends? At least you would have caught up with their life developments?"Ajay asked.

"Most of my collegemates are married, and I would receive their wedding invitations in Bangalore. I found it a painful to send them greetings or some gifts and thus communications ceased," explained Mythili.

Girls in North India or anywhere in India uncomplainingly sucked into domesticity soon after marriage unless they are working or have supportive in-laws who encourage them to go beyond the domestic hearth. In middle-class families, girls often lose independence after marriage and expected to merge into their new families and follow the new kinship rules.

Mythili had always been a good student and was always in the top 1 % and she took to her MD course, giving equal emphasis to theory and practice. She had a natural love for children and had a way with them. With time, she almost married her profession, becoming inseparable from her work. She was busy and started looking beyond the college and hospital to add to her knowledge.

She was fond of trying new food and restaurants, movies and shopping. She was well informed. She sought what was new, worth patronizing, where and how much discounts were available. She gleaned the city news and kept up to date as young urban Indian professional would. She would be with Ajay and accompany him to these places if he could take some time out of his work.

He had bought a second handcar. He loved taking her around in his car, and known in her college for its uncommon parrot green colour. It had a peculiar horn that sounded like the old pumping horns of a forgotten era. Her classmates envied her.

He had a fixed place for parking and he never forgot to tip the attendant generously. Whenever the attendant had time, he would clean Ajay's car. There was something about Ajay, which was endearing. .

Ajay had been practicing the 'Put your hand on your

heart and know your mood therapy', for the past six years. He had mastered the art of fathoming his mood anytime anywhere under all circumstances.

He must have done it a million times since he began. In the beginning, he was at loss to ascertain his mood even after he tried to figure it. With continued practice, he could distinguish between a positive and a negative mood. Then he came to a point to know precisely what his dominant mood was.

In the beginning, his concern was to turn anything negative or even remotely negative to positive. Later he began to experience the sense of Oneness. It happened by itself without any effort, he explained. Briefly, Oneness is a way of seeing and comprehending nature in all its multifarious interests and behaviors. Nature is wherever sentience is.

Oneness is intuitive. It does need any study or deliberations or even any belief. Oneness needs to be cultivated and is a kind of reverence for life. This principle, when applied, can instantly transform two who disagree into a unity of thought. People who are sensitive to it or in the flow of Oneness can create amazing rapport between themselves without effort. They may come from different backgrounds or be of different nationalities or ages. Ajay's expression of oneness was a simple outpouring from his heart and articulated by his mind:

"Main aasha karta hoon ki sabko aise prerna mile ki woh shakti shali aura atam vishwas pure roop se kar sake.

Main anumanit karta hoon ki jo jan is sansar mein hain prasan rahe, khush rahe tathasafaltapaye.

Mere anumiet he ke charo aur shanti, gyan, satya aur prem har chote se chote se koshika main pragat ho.

Main anumaniti chahta hu ki sachse bhara vastavikta

sarvsadharan is sanasarsthapit ho.

Aman aur sadbhavana sab ko sarvatha ho".

[I wish everyone to actualize his or her fullest potentials and spiritual evolution.

Let all of us gathered here be happy, joyful and successful.

Let peace, knowledge, truth and love permeate every one

And manifest in every cell of their body.

Let a commonwealth of truth be established on earth,

Peace and goodwill to all]

He had many versions from the fuller one to concise ones. He could express concern or wish well silently without anyone being wiser of his willing. He could radiate Oneness with someone known and unknown people. He could outpour his energy at any moment –while shopping, at a bus stop, walking to his office, selling an idea, reviewing a work or a program or simply whenever his heart ordered or felt that it was necessary. His outpouring was guileless and innocent without any premeditation. Since it was that, it affected people.

In business as well as in his personal life he had ceased wishing or desiring outcomes. During his presentations to business prospects or submissions to a client or talking with his team or guiding an engineer he did not force himself onto others. He never held to his ideas vehemently. He trusted the universe as it was. He realized that the urge to control outcomes was a wasteful energy. It was self-defeating.

Did not people see the power of gravity same anywhere on the earth? Water flowed from higher to a lower altitude. The sun rose and set day after day in the same way. The seasons flowed into each other. Vegetation sprouts some to become gigantic trees and others to die quickly. That is how it is and that is how it would continue. We do not have to do anything for these to happen. This was happening before we came into this world and will continue long after we are gone. Trusting the universe and accepting what happens with the belief that it is the best that can happen is for the good of all.

It means that the present moment is the most precious one, much more than the previous one or the one to follow. Valuing the present moment and valuing whatever we are engaged in produces excellence. Ajay found out that honoring the present slice of time gives clarity. It helped understanding the desires of the other and enhanced mutual confidence reducing conflict. A slice of time was a series of moments flowing into the next with singular concentration and intent. . Beyond a point, it could not be broken further and its character did not change. When you reach that point, you have reached the core or the basic property of the thing.

No matter what pressures he was under, Ajay took out a few days to visit his folks in Derapur from time to time. He always carried gifts for his people. Those who did not get a gift would get it the next time. They waited for his next visit. In the past year, he had hosted three of his relatives in Bangalore. However, his greatest joy was when her mother and Chacha came to spend a month with him.

When they were with him, he invited Asha along with her daughter. He also invited the owner of his Company, Dagariya and Sushma. For the meals, his mother took charge of the kitchen. She prepared the best of their community food, all cooked in *desi ghee* The dinner was a success and Ajay's mother and Chacha thanked the Dagariya family for giving Ajay the opportunity to thrive.

Ajay liked Asha's daughter Teja, a modern child with manners and respect for elders. She was 18 and wanted to enter the world of film making. She had tried but could not get admission in the Indian Institute of Digital Art and Animation in Calcutta. Asha was keen that she did a foundation course in India and then persue in the US or UK a professional course connected with film making. She would be better prepared and score well in TOEFL and other entrance exams later. Scoring well in these tests would help in securing free ship or scholarship. Asha did not want her to carry the past. She should go overseas and make her life. Her father still had 4 years to serve in prison before his release but it seemed uncertain if he could survive that long. Asha hoped that she saw him a few times and gave him the news of her success once before she left India.

The Dagariya's wanted to know about Hamirpur. Mahesh Dagariya's birthplace in Rajasthan was about 200 kilometers away. By the time, the party was over they had learnt the changes that had taken place during the last 30 years.

Their purpose was purchasing land around Hamirpur. Nijjer Kamboj could look after these. Sushma conveyed this in a much-disguised manner of speaking. This was not the time for detailed conversation on real estate. Sushma knew that this infact was the time to appreciate Ajay and his mother, which would pay dividends later.

It was at the insistence of Sushma that Ajay purchased a one-year-old Ford Ikon Flair. Sushma had asked his garage owner to arrange a good car for Ajay. When the garage owner approached Ajay with the car, he bought it without asking any questions. He took his mother and Chacha in the car and showed around them the city. He would take them to some spot and leave them and they would return on their own by showing their address written in English and Kannada. A month later happy with the way Ajay was working and living, they both returned to Hamirpur.

~~~

There was bad news for the Company. It was
~~~

unbelievably shocking but it happened. There had been no mail, fax, or phone from Alok for the past fortnight. Earlier whenever Dagariya called Alok, if he could not take the call, he would return his call at the earliest. Dagariya called Samir who after checking informed that Alok was not reachable. His room and the bank account had not been used in three weeks. Hisneighbors or the management staff could not provide any information. His car parked in the basement at its usual place and did not appear driven for many days.

After talking to Dagariya, Samir sought a fax from Venkataraman about loss of contact with Alok. He required that to file a police complaint for missing person. He approached the flat owner, who was worried about the unpaid rent, but opened Alok's apartment. There were no signs of the owner deserting maliciously. Samir filed a missing person report. His photograph and description reported on the local news channels.

A month after his disappearance, his parents came from Bombay to inquire about their son's whereabouts. They had not heard from him for long and worried about his well-being. Venkataraman shared all the information he had and the copy of police complaint. The distraught parents could offer no reason as to why he could have gone missing. He was a brilliant student, caring son and a good worker liked by his colleagues. His supervisor in Bombay called the company on the behest of his parents every few days. When there was no news, he gave up hopelessly. He was full of praise for Alok whom he described as a solid professional.

Alok had simply vanished.

Six months later a badly bruised body, a mile off the New Jersey highway discovered and the police suspected it to be Alok. A year later, his file closed. Ajay was the most distraught and it took over a month for him to get over his grief. His expression was not demonstrative. He sorrowed alone, waking up at night and failing to sleep. Their old conversations would float in his mind. This continued for a month and then he called Agnes Barnes and apprised her of his wretchedness due to Alok's disappearance.

She responded, "There is a segment of the dark underbelly of America which harbors most violent people where drug users and pushers, pimps and prostitutes, areas torn apart by gang violence, abandoned homes and offices which become dumping grounds for all the filth of that areas."

"There are such areas in all the big cities. Only the locals or those born there inhabit it. No decent person enters these areas. Camden is the most dangerous city in New Jersey; where there are nearly 2,000 violent crimes recorded every year."

Ajay was not interested in these statistics. When he kept quiet, Agnes voices over the phone woke him up, "Death is a loss for not only the people who knew the deceased but for everyone because the world becomes lesser. All must die. One never knows when one's call comes. Look at the good times you spent with him. Obviously if you grieve for someone, you received something valuable. Forget the rest. It is best buried with the dead."

If reasoning backwards could unearth the reasons for what are there then there would be fewer problems, reasoned Ajay.

Ajay was on a journey where success and failure mattered little, morality subsumed everything realizing that all the sayings, narrations and descriptions on wisdom were essentially the same, explained in different ways.

Chapter XIII
The Company Begins to Sink

The Total Banking Software had become a renegade child. Spinning out of control the fortnightly reports to the Bank missed and not a single promise made three months ago to the bank, kept. The Company offered the Bank to revoke the Bank Guarantee and released from the project. It agreed to hand over the software data, documents, diaries and test data and everything connected with it. The people working on the project could also be released to the bank if it so desired. It was the best way to come out of a bad deal thought the Company's brain trust. Alternatively, was it? Was it to satisfy the ego of the management and did the proprietor want that?

Dagariya realised it was not as simple as it seemed. He could not realize the impact of transferring employees on Company rolls to a customer's rolls. He had heard about this from Integris, a consulting company in the UK but he had not heard of such a single case in India. If it had happened, it would be common knowledge and added to the flexibility of doing business for large sized projects. Moreover, public sector banks had rigid set of rules for employment. Nothing could make them change or violate these with the trade unions watching. The General Manager showed his annoyance at Dagariya's suggestion.

"Why did the General Manager not tell me that when we met him?" moaned Dagariya. It never occurred to him how could the General Manager tell him that when he was threatening him. He was playing his last card.

From 40 engineers six months ago the team was now down to 19 engineers with a new Project Manager. Engineers had been leaving the firm and those remaining were looking outside for better prospects. It was a colossal waste of work force and energy. For the management it was amonumental distraction. Closing it would be disastrous for the company and carrying on was the sure road to hemorrhaging the establishment.

The biggest jolt came when HP declined to renew the bi annual contract. The Company had forged a special relationship and had 35 engineers on HP's rolls with a billing of Rs. 2,000,000. The Company had been supplying engineers to HP for the last 4 years. This contract was one of the factors for the development and success of the company. From a staffing of four the Company was able to keep increasing their team size every few months to reach 35 engineers. The annual contract for engineer deployed and billings signed and renewed biannually. HP said that it did not want to continue the contract. HP pleaded there were no projects and unlikely to materialize in the next couple of months. Everyone knew it was false.

HP had been utilizing the services of engineers sourced from their quite a few labor contractors on their projects in different parts of the world. As a result, the temporary workers were traveling to HP project sites all over the world. For foreign allocations the Company's billing for the engineer more than doubled. Engineer going overseas would earn a special allowance. It was a good win-win situation. Good, reliable and easy flows of funds in competitive business do not last for long.

The Company when it started this relationship had invested time, effort and management attention. Apart from the few expatriate managers at the top the rest were Indians. The consistent cultivation of HP executives by Sushma through parties, entertainment and gifts helped in creating strong associations. Many senior people in the office were motivated to enlarge the relationship and give a free hand.

It was easy money. As the relationship got stronger and there was a steady flow of receivables,the Company became complacent. Personal relationships got weaker and eventually the company relationship went downhill. Any perceptive manager should have sensed it. "A four year old relationship does not become rotten all of a sudden. It begins with small things and when not corrected the rift, miscommunications, differing perceptions and carrying perceived hurts spoils everything. Somebody senior should have taken charge," rued Ajay.

HP's operation in India in the late nineties was a preferred and top choice for jobs, referrals and association. Being in Bangalore added luster. Bangalore was one of the top ten software cities in the world. Ten years later the press and TV would speak of Bangalore as one of the top 10 entrepreneurial cities in the world.

The Company's engineers at HP soon began to think of themselves as different from the other employees of the company. They wore HP badges and accessed other company facilities like library, canteen and transport. They were present at HP staff get together. Their bonds with the Company started getting weaker and they stumbled in not seeing the deterioration in relationship and felt no need for senior managers to visit the HP office. Few who did, also ceased to come to the company when there was no one from the firm to enquire about their welfare. The earlier fortnightly visits of Company officials to HP were monthly and then later it became a rare occasion. These visits were important for the Company's HP temporary workers could meet their company managers. At the end of the month, the Company invoiced HP and the Company's account credited. The Company's engineers were credited their salaries which were half or less than those of HP staff were.

Hands on experience on HP software development process, and implementing it made these temporary workers valuable. The Company engineers in HP worked in a superior infrastructure with strong failsafe processes and therefore had a high market value. The company realised that a labor business could cut both ways. If contract was not renewed, they could find better jobs with better companies. If they returned to the Company after expiry of contract, the company may have no work for them for months.

HP sourced engineers from other companies as well. On its vendor list, it had 20 suppliers. The Sourcing Manager Srinivasan was an IIT, Madras and IIM Bangalore graduate, both top educational institutes in the country. He had a team of four people to assist him. Venkatraman's guess was that of the 600 HP engineers, 150 to 200 engineers were on contract. Venkatraman's connection with HP was many years old, which began in the US. He went out of the way to traction those contacts that were now holding important positions in HP. His connections in HP and other American companies led Dagariya to make him his partner. Venkataraman initiated the HP relationship and strengthened it. When other managers pressed into the relationship management, he withdrew.

As HP's operations grew and matured, it realised that its pool of temporary staff was valuable. They were loyal, excellent workers, non-complaining, reliable and trustworthy.

The temporary engineers were doing the same work and often more than the HP employees were and underpaid. Yet they coveted temporary HP employment.

In a meeting with the vendors, HP explained that it retained the right to transfer or terminate a labor contractor's staff under certain conditions. The contractor compensated with a one-time fee equivalent to three month's professional fees. It was a brilliant tactic. HP could recruit those temporary workers when they felt like and dangle the option of employment. The lumpsum payment in event of job closure or transfer was a nice parting for the contractor. The temporary worker would be in suspense. These movements and terminations balanced HP's vicissitudes in its global labor requirements. HP could gracefully terminate the contract if it wanted. The irony was that these and many operational procedures conceived implemented by Indians in HP.

There was always pressure on HP India management to cut costs. The professional fees for temporary employees enhanced after they put in 12 months. The fees paid to contractor not fixed but negotiated. HP was averse to keep a temporary worker on its roll for long durations. The temporary workers from Dagariya's Company were the highest paid. Sushma took the job of charming the HP management but like a trader when it looked good and business going on its own steam, she withdrew the attention that given to keep the relationship warm and strong. Neglect and the Indian attribute of everything is fair had taken its toll. A more professional management would have continued its investment in a win-win relationship.

Ajay sensed that HP fiasco would have a big long-term effect on the company. He had no power to do anything. It happened that some of the temporary workers offered jobs with HP and some retained as consultants with better benefits on annual contract. Those who resigned were confident of finding jobs with HP pushing their case. Venkataraman felt the company was slipping. He could with his global experience and insight into the software business could do nothing because it would need Dagariya's approval and he had no fight left. He was losing the zest he had come with.

Asha had spent over two years. She began to sense the unpleasant creepy feeling of unease and disconsolateness. Document preparation did not cheer her any more rather it had become monotonous. Visits of foreign delegations had become a thing of the past and there were no meetings to organize.

They could meet only a few weeks after his return from a long sojourn in Europe. On returning, Ajay requested Dagariya for ten days leave and Dagariya assumed Ajay would be leaving for his village. Dagariya was a bit surprised and when Ajay said his leave was to recoup after an exhausting period. He complained of overwork. He was stale and on the brink of a breakdown. His mind and body pushed to the limit.

Asha called Ajay to her office on Friday evening when most of the employees were thinking of their weekend. "I am scared, Ajay. The company is passing through difficult times. Anything can happen, even the worst. At the start of the year we were creeping towards 1,000 employees and today we have just about 750 engineers left."]

Ajay replied, "I am also scared. Yes Asha, Sharad told me a few days earlier that the attrition rate was likely between 2 % and 2.5 % per month."]

"What will happen to us Ajay? You people are qualified and experienced and can go anywhere. What about me? I will be stuck," Asha cried.

"Do not worry Asha. You have such a strong faith in God. He will take care of you. I think there is some sort of panic in the Company. Separations will continue and reach a peak or they may have already peaked. I expect that within a year the company will be reduced to the strength of 500 men," Ajay explained.

Ajay added, "This is based on the assumption that the Company survives."

Asha was worried and she had only Ajay to depend on and show her the way.

"What will be the result of all these developments, Ajay," demanded Asha.

"The Company will not be able to attract talent. The Company will have to become street smart to survive. Nothing great or extraordinary will happen," explained Ajay.

"It will become an also ran", chimed Ajay and Asha in unison.

"Is there no other possibility? How can we change this scenario?" Asha asked in curiosity.

"Yes it is possible, but I do not think it will happen!" philosophized Ajay.

"Ajay talk straight. Stop puzzling me," Asha spoke in a cold manner.

Ajay said, "Asha, for this to happen we need a change in management. Dagariya must become just an investor and he and her wife must cease managing. And, I don't think he is ready to do that."

Asha opens up placing her hand on her chest for emphasis, ""I am unhappy here. Truly, I am pained being here. My heart is not here."

Ajay nodded his head and looking at her said, "I do not like anything here."

""What should we do? I believe that when one's heart does not agree with a place you should leave it,", confided Asha.

"Come! Ajay let us leave this company. What do you say we go to Ooty for a few days and think clearly?" Asha proposes.

"Let's imagine, think and plan about your new company."

Oblivious to herself, she had hit the nail of entrepreneurship on the head.

"Please! Do not say no. Teja will also be there for a day on the way to her school for reunion. She went with her class to Bombay and will return stopping at Ooty. I would like her to meet you again. Her meeting at the Dagariya's dinner was not the occasion to know her or inspire her. I know Ajay, the way you could inspire her no one can. She has no father to guide her. . Please, fulfill that need of hers," Asha pleaded.

Ajay nodded and agreed to go to Ooty with her. He wanted to unburden himself and share his entrepreneurial dreams with her. She may not know anything about technology or the software business but her instincts were spot on. Her cell rang and Asha stiffened while saying, "Yes Sir I'll be in your office in 5 minutes." Ajay guessed it must be Dagariya and before he could ask her, she whispered, "Dagariya. Don't go I'll be back in 10 minutes at the most." She collected her purse and the cell, shrugged her shoulders and left.

Waiting for her Ajay, looked at the pictures under the glass on her table. She would change them every few weeks but there were permanent ones like of Teja, her hotel, Azure Hotel in South Africa, and a family picture perhaps 10 years old with little Teja in two ponytails. This time he saw the picture of Swami Vivekananda meditating facing the ocean. As Ajay looked at the serene face of the Swami with closed eyes, the image of Agnes Barnes floated in his mind.

Witnessing the energy and debate on 'Greening of America' spawned across the country and the American interest attracted to Eastern thought. To a sensitive person the new sensibility open to eastern thought became palpable. Agnes attracted by spiritual writings became curious about Hinduism and read works of Swami Vivekananda. After reading Paramhansa Yogananda, she became a Yogoda meditation student. She enrolled for 'Self-Realization' retreat at Encinitas, California. She followed a few programs and even met Daya Mata, the spiritual heir of Yogananda and became a practitioner of kriya yoga. She eventually found her own way to meditate and he recalled her insistent appeals to meditate. She instinctively guessed the spirit of Ajay, the first time she met him.

She emphasized on stillness and that she explained was the door to moksha. He leaned back in the chair and closed his eyes. Asha and her room vanished. Closing his eyes he heard in his mind Agnes speaking to him.

Knowing your emotional state is necessary before any meditation. All emotional states create vibrations. They could be subtle and almost barely discernable to violent ones that agitate your mind. Feeling your vibrations is mostly instinctive and partly learnt. Learn to still yourself. Just be quiet and try to be thoughtless which is not that easy.

Hundreds of thoughts are flitting in and out of your restless mind at this moment. These by its nature create more thoughts. What are your thoughts saying? There are many thoughts playing in your mind. They rise and subside. You may or may not be aware of some or all of these slippery thoughts.

To still yourself you do few things. It is not that simple. It comes after lot of patience and practice. You have to stop the twitches in your body by your willpower. You have to overcome the distractions arising in your body. You will have to master the desire to let go, become oblivious to scratch your imaginary itches, to listen to your breath and feel the pumping of your heart and distractions due to discomfort of your postures. You need to master your own body to still yourself. In the beginning, these distractions will make it difficult to be still. However, as you persist and take up the challenge you create stillness in your body and slowly get control over your mind.

After many years or much less of practice, you will achieve stillness for some moments. As you continue, these periods keep increasing. When you achieve stillness during your waking hours and continue doing your daily work you will achieve enlightenment. That is moksha!

I am not talking about that, I am talking about being still for a couple of minutes to be able to know the thoughts in your mind. There are many thoughts intensely battling in your mind. In the cluster of these thoughts, there is one predominant thought for a portion of time that could be for a few seconds to many minutes. I am talking about attaining that stillness when you become conscious of that predominant thought and oblivious to everything else. Listen and control that thought. Agnes emphasized that control means not to be guileful, bewitched, or even fascinated. Let it rise take over you and subside. See the thought. Let them come and pass through your mind.

After you have practiced stillness for some time, one day you will be able to still yourself just by suggestion. Then you will understand and appreciate your vibrations. You will reach your goal when you know your predominant thought and able to control it. This thought creates your mood. When you are able to control it you have no thought, no mood and become the master of your mind. How do you understand your mood? Label it with two words – a volitional part and the material descriptor. Look at the mirror image.

When you consciously label a desire, a thought, feeling, situation, or even a wish you release creative energy. This label sticks in your consciousness that motivates you. I am not talking about outlandish imaginations, which are destructive or unhealthy, but those that create Sattva.

Asha rushed in, opening the door violently and sat down. She had been away for almost an hour and was happy that he had not left. Ajay broke out of his reverie. He saw her sit down but Ajay was asking Agnes, "How do you know that you have achieved enlightenment?" Her simple answer floored him, "When you know whatever there is to know. You have no desire left."

He did not hear what Asha was telling him. When he came to the earth, he nodded. Asha's voice drew him back to reality. In a lighthearted way, she was asking him how tired he was. She broke his silence and gushed, "Come let's go to Ooty and this is the ideal time to go. Bangalore is hot now and Ooty willbe a nice escape from the heat. We will return fully relaxed and refreshed," Ajay suggested.]

"We must go individually and keep it a secret from Dagariya Sir and Sushma."

Ajay nodded. He was seeing her, hearing her but in his mind's eye Agnes was instructing him more by her experience than any bookish explanations. He walked down the steps from Asha's room.

~~~

Joshi ji saw Ajay come out of the PRO's room and walking down the stairs. He walked faster, and caught up with Ajay and hailed him, "Ajay ji, you look sad. What happened? It has been long since we met." It was late in the evening and the office deserted.

"Come to my room and we will chat," And putting his hand on his shoulder steered him to his office.

Ajay replied, "No I am not disturbed. I know the company is going through bad times. I have a job to do."]

"Which work are you talking about, Ajay?" Joshi Ji asked.]

["I am an employee of the company. I have a duty to discharge," Ajay relied in a stern voice.]
~~~

"That everyone has to do. What are you planning to do besides that?"

Somehow, the rumor had started that Ajay was planning a new venture. He had about heard it when one of his old Y2K team members talking about the new wave of entrepreneurs in Bangalore told him about the rumor. Ajay did not say anything except that when he did, he would announce it. He would not withhold it from his friends. That was it. The rumor died as soon as it had sprung.

Ajay replied, "I do not know. It is taking shape in my mind."]

""You want to start your own business?" Joshi Ji asked.]

Ajay quickly became alert. Where was Joshi ji leading to and what did he want to find out? He was Chairman Dagariya's confidant and his right hand. If not disliked, most of the staff and especially senior employees kept away from him. Ajay's interactions with him were rare. He believed that Ajay was a trusted man of Dagariya.

Ajay continued, "Joshi ji you are wise. You have seen the world. What has to happen will happen? No one can stop it. I have no knowledge or the strength to stop it or change the course of things. It is ordained."]

Was Joshi ji trying to test the authenticity of the rumor?

He like others in the company had known Ajay, believed that he was a man of character and not known to lie.

"Joshi ji demanded, "What about the 800 people working here and what will happen to them?"

Ajay, "Who can stop what the Almighty has decided?"

Ajay continued,"No, things just happened that way. Who is responsible? No one is."

"How can you say that Mr. Ajay?", demanded Joshi ji.

Ajay carried on, "You make one error and then to cover it you make another error. Then it becomes a chain of mistakes. Then errors begin to have a life of their own. You can't stop it!"

"It is bizarre. Well, it is like that. Everybody thinks that what he or she does is right. Yes it is right from the personal perspective but in social setting what a person does impacts others. There are moral and ethical dimensions and if you don't factor them then errors go back to the very purpose of a thing's existence."

"You are right. Once you commit an error and if you are caught in the sequence of errors, it is impossible to come out. You become a slave to these errors as an alcoholic becomes of alcohol," Joshi ji concurred.

He was surprised to see Joshi ji's face lose colour and he slumped in the chair.

His hand reached out for the glass of water on his table. After drinking, he seemed to hold his stature again. Then Ajay asked him if he would like tea and without waiting for his answer rang the bell for the office boy and ordered two cups tea. They talked and Joshi ji praised the Dagariya family for setting up the Company and providing employment to so many educated people.

"Mahesh ji had helped many people with projects to get started in business," Joshi Ji referred to Ashutosh Sarkar.

Then he praised Ajay for being a brilliant and hardworking employee. Continuing with his flattery, he added that his contributions to the company were exemplary. He was loyal and the company has rewarded him handsomely. Surely, he must have ideas on stopping the slide of the company.

"Why do you not present your ideas and thoughts to the Chairman? Think and send your views as a note to him. Mark me a copy also so that I can remind him," Joshi Ji's suggestion came.

Ajay had become like an arrow. Once released nothing could bring it back.

Chapter XIV
Happy Days, Butterfly Days

Asha reached Ooty. All that Sushma knew was that she was going to Ooty to meet her daughter.. Teja arrived in the afternoon. As she hugged Teja, Asha felt the pain of being cruelly separated separated from her. Her heart hurt when she felt the loss of seeing Teja grow up. She had to miss the wonder and beauty of her child transform from an awkward, confused teenage girl to a young woman. Teja was puzzled at the changes in her body, in her thoughts and her worldview. She had missed her mother, whose hugs warmed and drove away her sadness, defeats and frustrations of growing up. Now they met more as adults than just mother and daughter. The lost years were lost, lost forever.

Asha too was was the only child of her parents. Asha would see her childhood in Teja. She would wait for her near the bed at times and whatever may have happened during the day she would tiptoe to kiss her before she slept. If she was awake, they would talk for hours before and Asha lulled her to sleep. She felt happy and sometimes felt emotional and moved while she sang Marathi and Hindi lullabies. In the absence of Teja's father, Asha was both for her and she yearned to help her daughter plan her future and share the joys and tribulations of her day. Teja learnt to confide in her as a child does and with a faith that never faltered even as she grew up. How could Asha forget the lullabies she heard from her own mother and then sang them for Teja? It was cruel for Teja to wrench from her suddenly and then separate her. She knew those days would never comeback.

Asha felt guilty of her friendship with Ajay. However, that was how it was. She reasoned both stood to gain and her feelings were honorable. If there ever were an occasion, she would explain to Teja the reasons. With passage of time, she moved from Bombay but her list of friends and well-wishers rarely exceeded beyond Teja and Ajay. There was nothing sly or underhand and she genuinely liked Ajay like very few people she had cared for in her life.

Teja came running and flew in her mother's arms. As Asha hugged her rubbing her shoulders she felt the loss of not sharing her growing up years, and now she could not twirl her around holding her small hands in hers as she did a few years ago. Teja had grown up beautifully; she had remained as loving as before but less demonstrative and a bit distant. Teja was as tall as she was. Mother and daughter talked, snacked, walked around the hotel and witnessed the sunset from the balcony.

Before Teja enrolled as a boarder in the school she along with her mom had been meeting, the Lawyer Ubhayankar had engaged for her father's defense. He would inform her about courses, jobs, institutes and personalities in the world of entertainment. Apart from his law briefs, Bollywood was Ubhyankar's only outlet. He had sowed the seed of a career in films in Teja's mind.

Teja had to go to Bombay a couple of times to sign legal documents of her estate when she traveled alone. Now after two years Teja confided, "Mamma I did not like the last two or three meetings with him. I felt uncomfortable the way uncle looked at me. Then I started to avoid him, and talk to him only on my cell when required."

Instinctively she turned towards her, hugging her she cautioned, "My daughter has grown big. You are beautiful and lovely and wise as well. Are you not my brave son? As I grow old, you have to look after me. How can anybody harm you in any way?"

"My child, girls have to learn to take care of itself. Your school must have taught that. My child, to protect one's honor one never be scared of anyone," Asha explained.

As mother and daughter talked, Asha told her that Ajay was reaching the next day. Asha said she was looking forward to a picnic. Walking to the sideboard, she reached for an apple and asked her, "Teja, my child do you like Ajay?"

"I like him very much," replied Teja.

"Ma, why do you not marry me to him?", Teja suggested shyly.

The apples and the plate fell from her hands as if a knife had pierced her. This was the last thing she expected to hear. As she bent down to pick the apples, she felt the warmth in her cheeks spreading to her neck. Teja was beside her and pulling her up by her shoulders. "What happened mom?"

"Nothing, my hand wavered and everything fell down." As she resumed her seat on the sofa and came back to the reality of the moment, she asked Teja, "Are you serious that you want to marry Ajay"?

"Yes," whispered Teja.

"Don't be foolish. No doubt he would make an excellent husband, but my child,he is much older than you." Teja had shocked her. In the last 4 years, she may have spent 4 or 5 months with her and she had grown in ways difficult to fathom her or her world. She changed the topic and told Teja about her father,"He has become a big drunkard and he gets it even in the jail. His health is deteriorating."

"Yes, uncle told me that papa's liver had begun to get morbid and his hands keep shivering. He will not survive for long."

Tears rolled down Teja's cheeks. Asha sighed and her eyes moistened.

As they turned in to sleep, Asha wistfully thought that Ajay was too old for Teja and too young for her but how could they bring him into their lives. Ajay had entered their lives unobtrusively and made a place for himself. She was ready to join Ajay in any professional situation under any conditions. Ajay was just not any company employee or another software engineer but a leader. He was a champion. He was much above anyone she had seen within or outside the Company.

As they turned away from each other after the heavy conversation, Asha felt guilt rising in her. She was a resolute woman and not the one to be contrite. These rare moments had begun to visit her. They would sadden her and she would feel guilty. When it happened, she would feel the short stab of guilt but slowly it would pass. Sometimes it would take a day or more. She had been trying to ascertain her mood many times a day. She would regain her composure and her love for Ajay would be selfless. Her seduction of Ajay was as much about acquainting him with his sexual identity as it was for her carnal desire. She would be proud of her friendship. Maybe it was a sort of transference where she sought a father figure for Teja.

Coming out of her phoenix moment one day she believed that nobody was to blame for what happened to her husband. Not even him. It was destiny. Even if it was, she was not sure if there was destiny. Ajay had taught her to wait and sense her phoenix moment and trace events to ascertain the reasons for misfortunes. In any case, neither she nor her husband knew of the phoenix phenomena. Why were she and her daughter to be a part of this play? Her mind clouded in confusion and wandered until she finally fell asleep.

Next morning Ajay, Asha and Teja were together at breakfast. They were planning their picnic, when Ajay said, "Teja, don't think too much about small or trivial things. Let them be. Let them unfold by themselves. Enjoy the moment. What can they do or give you? Very little or nothing, for once the moment is over so will be that plan. God has nothing to teach you in these trivialities. Be still, be calm. Feel it and know it. You mark what moves you and reach out to that in gratitude."

"Oh, not like that. Since I came to know that, we are going for a picnic I have been looking forward to it. The thought of going out with mom and you and the picnic has taken hold of me. I am looking forward to the conversations, the drive, and happiness of being together as if there is no tomorrow and no care in the world. I want it to be something that I will not forget," replied Teja.

"Yes, may it be so," replied Ajay as Asha returned from the kitchenette.

"You mean the picnic?" asked Asha.

"Yes. I was talking about the picnic with Ajay. There are days, which are so special, which God gives you, which you can never forget," Teja said innocently.

It was a profound statement coming from an 18-year-old girl.

Asha felt uncomfortable atTeja calling Ajay by name. The times now were different, times had changed.

"Of course, beta that is true. We all want that to happen and make the picnic memorable. Is that not so Ajay?"

"Yes I am so happy to be with you. All I was trying to say was let things happen by themselves. Don't try to force them."

"Do you understand? Are you trying to get the drift of it?"

"Yes] sort of," Teja accepted.

"Yes it is learning, not bookish but real learning," added Asha.

"The challenge for you is to keep learning throughout your life. Create the desire and motivation to see and understand, observe and analyze, read and absorb. Train your mental faculties so that learning becomes as easy to know and feel like thirst, hunger or even like breathing. It is not created in a day or by a particular practice. Once initiated and persisted upon, it becomes automatic like breathing," advised Ajay.

In a short while, Teja changed the subject, and argued whether to attach the sidecar or all three would sit on the single seat and finally decided not to use the sidecar. They drove out into a pleasant cool morning with the wind rushing past them. Asha hummed a ditty and Teja sitting in front of her squeezed her hands.

Driving on the hilly road winding through the coniferous trees, the smell of the mountain air with the sun was playing hide and seek with them. The rays filtering through the canopy of the trees and as the intensity changed so did the green hue of the trees. Then just coming out of a slope Teja exclaimed, "Let's stop here."

Asha stood on her toes spreading her arms screamed, "How strange is life? Sometimes it is beautiful and other times it makes you cry. I am certain there is God and I have full faith in him."

Teja surprised them with wisdom beyond her age, "I have tried to know my own vibes, and sensing my friends and then stranger's vibes. With practice, I am quite good at it. I have also tried at times to impact in a good way and for good purpose mine and other's vibes. I have been successful at times. I know it when I see the other person's response."

"Mummy these emotions in human beings are what you call vibrations. They do not make your body tremble, palpitate, or bring about hot flushes on your skin. It is feeling which if you try to you can feel within you and you can learn from them. They tell you about the nature and purpose of particular vibration of the moment. You can learn to know that of others too," Teja surprised them both with her wisdom.

"There were some girls and nuns whose presence was enlivening and I would love to be with them. Have you ever felt like that for some people?" Teja was talking something Asha had never expected. Hearing Teja, Asha did not know what to say. How she had grown up, musing to her Asha said, "I never realized it."

"It is a useful skill to have. Who taught you this?", Asha asked."There is a young nun from Scotland. One day I was feeling lonely and miserable and started crying. It was evening. All girls were out in the fields playing and I had absented myself. I was crying into my pillow and imploring Jesus as to why this was happening to me. It was games time, the Head Girl of our House was making her round of the dormitory and on hearing me sob, she pulled me up by shoulders."

"She wiped my tears, listened to me, sat with me on my bed, and held my hand and spoke to me sweetly. I told her about the storm in our family, but not about papa going to jail. I blurted out my loneliness and friendlessness. She hugged me and promised to be my friend."

"Later she introduced me to Sister Isobel. Sister Isobel was the youngest and most beautiful nun and only spoke English. I was truthful with her and she heard my story and was kind to me. She told me about her life, her drunkard father who beat her mother, who had to work as a house cleaner in a mansion and her loveless childhood. Her village priest got her into nunnery in France where she grew up and finished her studies. She volunteered; there was no escape, after her ordination she agreed to come here"

"She taught me that God knew what each of his child was up to. He knew the sufferings, the pains and desires of each of his children. He has a plan for each one and sometimes made things difficult for us as he was testing us. If we believed in him and prayed to him, no harm will ever come to us. Jesus wants us to do his command. To know his command we have to train our bodies and mind. We need to conduct ourselves accordingly and not share them with anyone except with those whom God wishes us to."

Asha and Ajay looked at each other. Asha did not like what she had heard. Teja spoke with passion as if it was so easy and the right thing to say. Teja spoke with warmth seeking understanding. The sun overhead warmed them. Teja's confession startled Anita and Ajay when Ajay asked Teja, "Teja your course will finish in a few days. Then how will you meet sister Isobel? Will you not be far away from her? Will you not remember her? You will have to stay away from her. Will you talk to her on your mobile?"

"Yes, I will miss the presence of sister Isobel. When I come for vacations, of course I miss her. When I leave school, I will miss her very much. Sister Isobel taught me that never to call her, unless it was important. We communicate with each other telepathically," replied Teja.

Asha was half reclining with her hand holding her face, with legs stretched out. She got up, kneeling reached out to Teja, and catching hold of her shoulders shook them and cried, "Teja this sort of friendship is neither right nor good."

Teja cut her short and before Asha could say anything silenced her, ""Mom, this is not what you are thinking."

They got up to walk into the woods. As they walked,

Asha asked if they would be able to find their way back. Teja asked half in jest, "I hope nobody will run off with our bed spread and picnic hamper."

Ajay commented, "Trust others and the world will trust you. Minor failures or occasional ones do not count." The sun had begun its descent and they found their way back and hungry by their walk and the mountain air, they ate as if that was only what mattered.

An hour later, they left for the hotel.

∽∽∽

At dinner, Asha confided that when Ajay was in Europe, Texas Instrument had interviewed her and offered her the position of a PRO. Their PRO had married a NRI and she was leaving. A job in TI was a prized job. A job in a multinational company was envied and TI was a great oftware company to work with. Her salary would double, though salary was not a big consideration for her.

Erickson had also shown interest in her. She related how a recruiter contacted her and when she did not respond, Erickson contacted her. She reluctantly agreed and met their Personal Head over lunch. She had no Resume. One thing led to another until a telephonic offer to join made to her. The appointment letter dispatched after she committed to a joining date. The chief of Ericson was a woman who took an instant liking to her.

After she shared her meetings with the recruiter, he was discussing other openings with her.

She had no one she could talk with for advice and Ajay was out of the country. After his return, he was too busy working late into the night. She waited for the opportune moment to tell him and seek his advice. She did not want to make mistakes and she was as genuine and yearning as Ajay wanting to share his venturing Idea. He was deep into his work and she in memories that she wanted to leave behind.

Ajay congratulated her.

The software industry in Bangalore had noticed her. Someone made enquiries, found her talented and a good worker, and recommended her. Employment offer without a Bio Data by top companies was spectacular in 2003. Motivating her, he explained that she could take her time to make up her mind. Yet it was important to keep lines of communication open with them. Honesty was a requirement in these matters as well.

Asha began by explaining that when she saw crisis after crisis in the company, she felt that it might shut down. Maybe it might take a few more months. She explained her debt to Dagariya and that her present arrangement was fine. She was afraid to make such big changes. If by leaving the company Dagariya stopped supporting her hotel, she would not be able to manage it by herself and hold her job. In that case, it would be the end of her and she did not have the confidence to begin anew. Ajay counseled her that life was not black and white but many shades in between. She agreed to rethink and hoped that in the next two days she would be able to help take a position.

Next morning they dropped Teja at the bus stand.

Lunch was still a few hours away. They stretched their legs onto the wooden balcony sill sipping passion fruit juice. Passion fruit is a native of Sri Lanka and Ooty is one of the few places in the India where it grows. Passion fruit is a tranquilizer and removes anxieties. It helps stabilize emotions under stressful conditions. Lovers of the fruit, break the hard woodlike outer layer, scoop the fibrous flesh and seeds, and eat them. The pulpand seeds are more potent than the fruit's juice, which is somewhat like that of an orange in taste more pungent, but warm. Though prized in some parts of the world, it is not popular in India.

Asha was getting bored and she took him to an afternoon movie show. She had shepherded him to the last row and the corner seats As the movie started, they looked around the hall and found few people. Asha took his hand and kissed his palm. He squeezed her hand indicating his comfort and he shifted in his chair and kissed her cheek. As she turned around to find his face, he too turned; their lips met more out of undeliberately. It was an awkward position, Ajay put his arm around her shoulder and she turned towards him, and their lips met. This time they went deeper. She smelt of the lunch and her warm breath of cinnamon and anise.

She whispered in his ear, "Ajay it has been many days."

Their tongues met and she was pulling him closer to her and while their lip locked, she opened the buttons of his shirt and her hands went roaming over his chest. The thrill of a public place heightened their carnal desires. For the rest of the movie they kept kissing and feeling each other. It was warm inside the hall.

She pulled his hands on her breasts. After squeezing her breasts for some moments, he would withdraw his hand. She would pull his hands back onto her chest. He was shy because of the fear of the consequences of others seeing him in a sexually compromising position. It was unconscious and exaggerated notion. He could not throw away his puritan upbringing. When he put his hand under her bra he could feel her perspiration and his hands smelt of her armpits. Before they set out, he had remonstrated but she had shrugged his caution.

She ordered him to come to her suite at eight and she would devour him for dinner. Ajay agreed. He believed that Asha inspite of her tumultuous and sad life was innocent and guileless. He had experienced her winsome spontaneity in her unguarded moments. Like any woman, she sought appreciation, being wanted, desired and loved.

He walked into her room and when she saw him close the latch, she ran into his arms. There was nothing to say. They hugged while still standing. She just about reached his shoulders. As her desire intensified, she stood on her toes and placed her face on his. He tightened his arms around her. In an instinctive moment of homage, he opened her hair clip and her silken hair cascaded down framing her face. Loosening his hold, he kissed her head, then her eyes and licked her ears moving down to her neck. When he came up to breathe she hugged him tightly, opened herself and he started rubbing her back. When he cupped her face in his hands, she bent her neck offering it to his lips and he could feel the blood carousing through the veins in her neck.

As they disengaged, she laughed and said, ""Ajay dear, you suddenly seem to have become experienced."

"Don't interrupt. I will do whatever you ask me. My aim is to make you happy."]

It was not what she expected. She wanted to bedevoured like a woman in heat, and not tell him what she wanted. She wanted to be ravished, possessed by an assertive man who knew how to tame a woman. It was a dark cloud that passed away in the blue sky, like the awkwardness in a gentle bighearted female in her sexual desire.

She led him by the hand to the bedroom. Both knew what would happen. They sat on the bed with their feet dangling and he saw her fair feet rubbed and scrubbed and with a fresh coat of red enamel. They explored each other. She in a pale yellow see through negligee covering her shoulders to her ankles and a matching bra, which he was see through. He was in a red Tee shirt and white shorts.

They turned towards each other and stretched out trying to feel each other. From light delicate touches to hard squeezes that sought possession and feel each other's body. Ajay was responding more by instinct. Ajay's responses were instinctive but his mind sought to make her happy and fulfilled. In his moment of surrender, he felt that this was what she expected. His senses inflamed. They were in a state of dishevel with each trying to drop away the clothes and bring as much skin out in the open.

Dressed only in her underwear, she stood facing him. He caressed her breasts and after removing his Tee, she knealed in front of him licking chest and when she moved for air he bent and kissed her. This was no virginal kiss and his tongue slipped inside her inviting mouth. When she moaned he would breathe long and grunt in response. She turned her back hinting him to take off her bra. He looked at her breasts and then hugged her from behind, his hands cupping her breasts and his mouth on her shoulders. He removed his pants and she was only in her panty.

She swung her legs off the floor and lay down. Standing by her side they looked at each other. She looked at her panty and his hands caught hold of it at the hips. She helped him by raising her buttocks and he pulled it down to her ankles. She swung her legs up lifting her feet and holding its elastic, he pulled it off her. Standing at the edge of her bed, he kissed the arch of her feet and she squealed with joy. He started licking her legs and his lips moving up. She spread her legs wide, inviting him until he reached her crotch.

She luxuriated, spreading her thighs wide open and then brought her feet flat on the bed knees bent, offering herself. He smelt her juices and debated whether to clean her with the paper napkins on the side table or drink her straight. He bent down and licking her inner thighs, he fastened his mouth on her vagina. Her trimmed hair was wet and he drank her juices dripping down her thighs. He shuffled and kissed her clitoris and moving his tongue around her knob that had swelled. As he struggled to pull her knob into his mouth, she moved her hands behind her and clutched the pillow. She rolled on the cheeks of her buttocks exposing more of her secret femininity. She then pushed his head with her palm indicating him to enter her love hole.

Taking a deep breath, he burrowed his head deeper between her thighs. He felt comforted in her warm flesh. She moved and twisted on her buttocks to give him more access. When he pushed his tongue into the top of her vagina, she closed her eyes. Lifting her crotch she levered herself with her bent feet and her raised shoulders. She was nowhere on earth. She was floating like a bubble in a sea of nothingness. She was beyond pleasure and her brain messaging of a wall in front. She knew the journey was beginning. Rarely do people read, let alone acknowledge their instincts.

She was delirious and catching his head tightly between her thighs, she squeezed him and her juices flowing copiously unlike that of a middle-aged-woman. He felt the sticky fluid all over his face. She clutched his hair and ejaculated going through a violent orgasm. The pit of her stomach and her thighs shuddered and moaning, she slumped. Her grip on him loosened. Then once again he felt her juices spurt in his face. He was wet too. Then he pulled himself, lay by her side, and felt the storm pass.

She startled him out of his reverie by asking him that was he not shocked? Did he wonder what sort of woman she was? Old enough to be his mother, seeking sex from a virgin, frank in admitting her desire, inviting him to her to her room at night!

He kept quiet.

Then he turned towards her and said, “In a mature relationship outside marriage, sex is a small part. Their relationship is bigger and deeper to be dictated by sex and subordinate to the meeting of minds.”

She squeezed his hand. She did not know what to say but respected what he said. She may not have understood what he said.

As he came up, over to her face, he whispered that he was fortunate to know from her about life and sex. Ajay's esteem moved up when she confided that after her phoenix moment, he was the only person she had sex with, if you discounted her week with Ubhayankar at Azure. There was another failed attempt forced on her. No man had or could ever measure up to him. She meant it.

His mind whispered that he must fulfill her lust. She knew that her lust was cyclical. It formed every few months and sought to burst. If her hunger was satisfied, it was well and good. If not it would subside in a few days and vanish until it possessed her again. Her need for love for him was what drove her to him. Seeking love, lust was a natural outcome or was it the other way round? His body was willing.

He kissed her moist eyes. She felt as if she had read his feelings and she whispered in that humid warm space between them that they had done nothing wrong. She was grateful to her God to have brought him into her life. He fell back and rising on her elbow, she started kissing him in small pecks as a mother would kiss her child. They were lying and holding each other's naked bodies pressing and squeezing as if to melt into each other. These playful pecks of love and care soon became urgent, wet and more demanding. Her soft hair brushing his chest, were teasing him.

Ajay was soon aroused and could feel the rush of his adrenaline. She was turning wicked, sitting up she started playing with him with her open lips and tongue. She licked his lips and bit his lower lip holding it with her thumb and finger. Then she bit him hard on his shoulder and when he winced, she climbed over him. His penis was hard and strong.

Sitting over him, she eased herself down on his body massaging him with the cheeks of her buttocks. She kept at it until she reached his knees. Squatting on his knees, she took his penis in her hand and grasped it in her fist. It was protruding out of her four fingers to the length of his palm. She started the game of squeeze and let go. She kneeled bringing her face near it and spreading a blob of saliva on it and lapped it around his penis. She did this a few more times and then scooped the wetness from his rock hard penis and bringing it to her face, slurped it. She stood up on her haunches and leaning over him kissed his chest, took his nipple into her mouth, and sucked it..

He could feel his penis touching her navel and then moving like a snake leaving a trail of wetness until she reached his penis. Asha first lip kissed his pink glans and then it was in her mouth and she began a slow dance with her lips slithering over it. Ajay roused and gasping for breath, never imagined there could be something like this. She laid down straight on him. She began biting him, gnashing his cherry and Ajay responded by tying her hair in a knot and holding her cheeks as she bobbed over his penis. She had tasted his precum and when she felt that he might explode, though she was wet herself, she released him and rolling over and lay on her back.

Spellbound, Ajay closed his eyes. He was not aware of his body or its extremities but a globule of air bouncing about light and aimless. He had no desire of his own. He was no longer the master of his mind and body and resigned to let forces do what they would. Waiting for him to catch his breath she opened her legs, wide and nudged him to come on top of her. He kneeled between her thighs and holding his penis in his hand began rubbing the opening of her vagina.

She moaned and calling him by his name asked him to penetrate her. He inserted his penis and slid it in. He was lost in her dampness and putting his weight on the elbows, he brought his hands under her shoulders. Asha stretched her legs out wide and invited him to move inside her. He put all his weight and pushed himself deeper inside her. When he met her, he would pause and rub his groin on hers. There was no particular direction he just rubbed his groin over hers more in gratitude than any pleasure. She pushed her breasts into him and soon she was gasping for breath. Feeling her shortness of breath, he eased and stopped lunging.

He blew on her face, which had hardened, and she gestured and he took her breast in his mouth. He sucked her breast slathering them with his saliva, she later started moving her hips, and he started pumping her again. Slowly and then increasing his movements bringing his body above his crotch in a delightful dance.

She was rocking her face side-to-side, eyes closed. The lines around her eyes were visible as she closed and then re-opened. He started piercing her faster and deeper. When his thighs hit her's it was the only sound in the room. She caught his arms and dug her nails in him commanding him to slow down. She lifted her legs and her thighs inches above and laid her ankles on his shoulders. Resting his weight on her elbows, she lifted and lowered herself on his penis and he started moving in and out as if that was only what mattered. She spread her hands out, clutched at the bed sheet, and started moaning. She closed her eyes, he saw the lines on her eyelids and the skin below the eyes taut, and then she exploded like a volcano. He felt her shudder under him that came with the paroxysm of ejaculation. Her vaginal walls griped his penis and released it a few times until she lay quiet. Her warm fluids swirled around his penis.

They lay like this for maybe fifteen minutes and then he turned landing on the bed. After the storm had passed they talked about his venture and he promising to discuss in detail the next day. Their voices softened and trailed into silence. He waited for some more time and then slipped out of the bed and went to his room.

Ajay becomes the fixed point and realizes there is more meaning and pleasure in giving than receiving, even in sex.

Chapter- XV
The Healer Soars

The next morning, breakfast under the sprawling blue gum tree, the memories of the night, the setting and being the last day of their sojourn was the best that could be for Ajay to describe his venture. She had been waiting to hear and he was eager to get her perspective. Their very purpose for coming here was to tell her about his project. It was serendipity that they could spend a day with Teja also. Teja needed an elder and a wiser male to encourage and sensitize a growing young girl to the ways of the world. Asha pulled back her cane chair as the boy cleaned their table. Ajay leaned forward on his chair and looking at her began.

"Look Asha, I am not interested in setting up some computer operations like Dagariya's or hundreds of others similar to his. To me, becoming an entrepreneur means not just creating an operation that will make me rich. I do not want to set up a business for making money only, though anything well done which meets customer approval will eventually generate profits. I have something special to give to the world that only a few people like me can. Likewise there are few people or organizations that want what I have to give."

"Computer software is a means to achieve given objectives. In real life, objectives change, as they must. In addition, when they change it must be possible to change the software with least pain and cost. Computer software is just that. It makes no different whether for business purpose or scientific or engineering or research. Software is to achieve a set of purposes."

"I believe the way of creating software remains same for whatever its objectives and the nature of the environment in which it must function. However, there are specialists for making each kind. They became specialist because they have the domain and environment knowledge. All developers have programming skills and what coding terminology, they do not know they can learn quickly. But the approach for problem recognition, analysis and design remain unalterably the same."

"This is quite a revolutionary thinking. It makes me different. I am thinking at basic level of creating software code. I understand and with quite good logic; in technical terms understand logical propositions and realize them in code. "Almost 90 % of software for business and industrial uses is made by using software, tools and utilities available off the shelf. This forces the programmer to write code in the way these pieces of software permit and force him. Our company and hundreds of companies like ours write software with these limitations. It is so all over the world. Creating software under these limitations is no doubt a massive business. A programmer like any worker thinks in the way his tools force him to think. I want to get out of this way of thinking and use open source software and not use commercially sold tools and utilities. These are aids and only a means to creating Elegant Software."

"Open Source software is a name given to those

software pieces that anyone can use, change, and share and generally it is free. Many software enthusiasts contribute to the continuous development of Open source software. Made by many people, and distributed under licenses that follow the Open Source Initiative, it provides scope for creative solutions than forced solutions. Programmers are wary because the repository is continually enriched and evolving. Software companies because of market conditions and requirements are afraid of touching Open Source software tools and utilities."

"It is a global non-profit initiative which supports and promotes Open Source movement. I became a member of this organization, during the USPS project. I know many people who subscribe to these principles and ideals and I am in touch with some."

"I want to begin as a one man show. Of course, a solo operation is not an easy operation. It is a rare skill on sale. That is the truth. Hypothetically, I begin my new life as a one-man operation."

Asha listened, hanging onto each word and murmured, "Is this another phoenix moment?"

After a few moments Ajay replied, "No Asha, it's not a new phoenix moment. The last phoenix moment occurred after the passing away of Mythri and that continues, with a change in direction. It's from being an employee to becoming a solo operator to an employer."

"In the beginning, I will make a one-man company. I will get work that is business type of software, and execute it. I will design the work on hand, program it, test it and deliver it myself. At start-up phase, I will not need the services of any other professional. I will also handle money matters," replied Ajay.

Asha interrupting, asked, "What is this solo operator? What does it mean? I am hearing it the first time."

"How long will this one-man company run? Ajay

will you run the company or become an employee of your own company?"

"This will continue for one to one and half years," replied Ajay.

"Maybe at startup, I might take two or three fresher engineer graduates who subscribe to my views. I will decide when I start."

Asha enquired again, "Ajay will you run the company or become an employee of your own company?"

Ignoring her, he continued all fired up. "I have to learn to delineate and create each component in the life cycle of Elegant Software. I must have the rigor and strength to visualize and understand each component. I must see each component in depth to understand its position in the life cycle string. How each component will come and how it fits and takes its situational position. Before I hire anyone, I would have my Development Handbook ready."

"After completing two or three projects, I will know everything about making Elegant Software. My Handbook will be updated at this point in time. I will have two satisfied customers. Then I will expand the company as per requirements."

Asha asked, "How long will you take to complete all this work?"

"*It would take around 18 to 24 months*," answered Ajay.

"Too long!," exclaimed Asha.

"Sushma told me that their company was set up in three months. They started getting regular revenues a month thereafter," helpfully said Asha.

"That's my estimate. I have already laid my pieces on the board. I have two strong prospects in the US. It is initial planning. I do not know what may happen in reality. I am afraid that it may take a couple of weeks to get the government formalities completed. Serve the notice period if Dagariya insists. Asha, I have no problem with time. Being a little earlier or later will not affect me. I have no competitor. Nevertheless, whatever I do it should be solid work. Of course, like any venture in the world I have risks. No matter how hard you might think you never know your risks beforehand though consultants spend good time trying to create risks. If that were so then the word risk would not be in the dictionary. Unpredictability is inherent in risk. Who knows when a risk will strike? Who knows its duration or severity? Its impact makes anything risky including life. Once you start, one's ingenuity lies in moving the pieces on the board to lessen risk."

"Ajay use consultants, they can do everything for you in shorter time. You save time and create revenue streams earlier,", added Asha.

Ajay smiled to himself saying, "Consultants are for running companies and not for entrepreneurs. If that were so, many consultants would have become entrepreneurs."

"When I have that much work at the rate I want, then I will recruit professionals. When I say employees I mean partners," replied Ajay.

"When that will happen and what sort of partnerships will I create I cannot say now."

Ajay was trying to explain his business concept and model to Asha in as simple way as he could. He had gone through his model many times. He had been refining it and now it firmed up in his thoughts, imagination and vision. "As a one man operation, customers are not buying my company, my trademark or my products. They are buying what I promise. They are not even buying the work they have contracted to me. I am I, I am unique and there cannot be any other person who could do what I can and promise to do. Therefore, if someone hires me and I do not give him or her myself in full measure, then I am not fulfilling the promise I gave while contracting work. If I did not do that I would be deceiving them."

"I have 24 hours like you or anybody else of which I can devote 16 hours to working for my customers. A time will come when I will have more customers than I can service and there will be the temptation to hire engineers. That will be another phoenix point diversion, which will open other directions. I will take the direction where I will increase my price and accept work that appeals to me and refuse others."

"How much will you increase your price? When will you do so?" Asha inquired.

"I will increase my price by 30 to 40 %. I will do so after delivering my first contract," replied Ajay.

"After increasing my prices, the cycle will repeat itself. I will increase my price maybe after three, four, or five deliveries. If I have executed the way I dream, then I will increase my price after two deliveries. Over this period I will begin differentiating, meaning I will create my own space in 'Elegant programing'. This space may or may not be narrow but it will be an area that I will know very well and known for that. At the end of year or more there would be few engineers in the world who know as much as I do in that area and I will encircle that and call it my area. I will be making more money in lesser time and also get more business."

"After some time, only after successfully delivering half a dozen projects, I will increase my rates again. This will be a level at which genuine customers in the world can consider and any further increase would drive them away. By the time I reach there, only genuine advocates of 'Elegant programming' will contact me. I would refuse more work than what I take up and can do."

"Each time I raise my price I will have major changes made to my web site. I do not have to market until I move from a one-man company to a company of partners. My prices will be my best marketing statement. With my satisfied customers, willing to pay my prices sends a powerful message to potential clients. I am expensive but worth the price."

"With my references, refused or overlooked customers, and the quality of my work I will be refusing more work than I take up. People in business and professions are always curious why a professional refuses work at his prices. There can only be two reasons for that. Either I am too busy and customers to contract my services have to wait or I am not world class. I could give reasons for refusing work. From not in, my current interests to get work done from others at lesser price to shorter schedules or done immediately. In the beginning,it maybe construed as impudence, but also make them curious, which has immense business benefits for me. They will know me better than from my website and include me in their influence circle. To keep them in my sights I will have an outreach program."

"The worth of a business man lies in his or her chosen field when you have far more work than you can handle. Those whom you refuse will become a part of my outreach program, for which I would be willing to hire a professional PR company. This way my list of potential customers becomes longer and I attract marquee customers. Picking my customers would make me happy and I will do great pieces of work and dominate my space."

"I would, I estimate to reach this position in two to two and half years, knowing my own strengths and my differentiators, maybe I could achieve that, six months earlier. I know my uniqueness and have a few thousand, maybe two or three thousand peers. I would have established myself by that time, built my circle and have strong referrals. That will be the time when I scale up, meaning I begin hiring more engineers. As I told you before, my hires will become my partners. How and in what way, I cannot say now. When that happens, ways and means will suggest themselves."

"When I hire I create an organization which will need

management time. By that time, I will have to translate my concepts for creating software to practical ways of doing so with new joiners. I shared with you my belief that software drives hardware. Today the varieties of hardware are stupendous. Software should be simple, goal oriented, modifiable and yet be long life."

"I propose not to make big issues between different types of software. There are so many different types of software and have their own development models. There are business and commercial software, for manufacturing control, scientific and technology or research purposes. Until I move to this position, I will prefer business and commercial software. I have experience in these; know potential customers, where they are and how to reach them and my peers in this space. By this time I will hire who have experience and insight into the verticals, I propose to enter."

"What they will be I can't say now. People come with their skills and suggest what this one-man operation can become by adding their skills. It will mutate into a fine software engineering company. I do not want to think about that now. The environment will do it, I trust my environment."

"What will be my role?"

"My role will change. From an all-purpose man doing everything, I will now manage only people. Ensure that quality is not compromised; contain costs and overheads with timely deliveries. In short, ensure that new paradigm followed. This software-making paradigm will evolve to becoming unique. To maintain this uniqueness will be a challenge and I will ensure that this evolution is continuous. If it stops my company would be in danger."

Asha was in a tranc.e Sitting before her was an evangelist of new paradigm of software engineering. "Will you realize this?"

"Yes, I was born to do this," replied Ajay with conviction.

"What can I tell you Ajay? What can I give you? I will pray to Lord Ganapati every day to give you that success that you are seeking and even more than that," prayed Asha.

It had been a thorough and emotional performance. Bouncing his venture over Asha was just not that but more. Approval from peers and industry leaders mattered more. A venture fund investor takes a bet on the presumed locked up value and the product's or the service's market strength. Investors develop their own models for investment choices but gut feel remains a favorite metric. Their models updated by their experiences and business climate. In the end, it was the caretaker's conviction and belief in his or her idea that mattered. Simple questions could draw out the fallacies and the strength of assumptions. Runaway successes create new industries, change ways of doing business or revamp existing industries forever. They do not rely on views of others. They would fare poorly on the many evaluation models of the day. It was the belief of the creator.

No doubt, it was a masterly performance.

Ajay must have thought through this many times and she wondered for how long he might have been planning. She had known him for 4 years now but they had rarely talked about his venturing ideas. She asked him as if in fear "Ajay as I understand your project is definitely unique, one of its kind. For how long have you been nurturing it?"

"I myself do not know when the desire for this work was born in me. Like you once told me about your life, 'as time passed my life confronted me with crisis, turned by itself, and deposited me here'. The same thing happened with me. People came into my life and after enlightening me went their ways. Many incidents happened that inspired me. Pieces of a picture began accumulating in my mind. One day a picture formed in my mind. This picture overtook my mind and heart."

Asha wondered there was no thing, no part or anything material. Just an idea in Ajay's mind and he was living with it for God knows, how long. Something he was determined to make it come true. His strength of conviction and confidence was what stirred her. She did not know that a banker or a capitalist would go by that than any report.

~~~

They were sitting in Asha's balcony watching the setting sun. The blue skies begin to get bright red, crimson and golden yellow and shortly fade to grey and black with millions of white glimmering specks. The trees whisper and strange winds blows through them, and the insects and birds begin returning to their places of rest. They were silent perhaps dreaming of days gone by or yesterday.

The lines on Ajay's forehead disappeared and he had no care or concern in the world. Even if fortune forsook him, he would not be sorry. Tomorrow evening he would take the bus to Bangalore. Then suddenly Asha began rocking on her chair and disturbing his serenity.

"Asha how strongly do you want to get out of the clutches of Dagariya's? How important is it? Do you think your hotel is running on his goodwill?" Ajay questioned.

"My hotel is running well. Dagariya and I have earned quite a lot of money out of this deal. Did I not tell you I pay 12 % of my monthly collections to Dagariya," answered Asha.

"Since when?" Ajay inquired.

"I started paying Dagariya two or three months after he took over the management. Sushma hinted 15% and after a year, reduced it to 12 %. The accountant, Joshi ji was present for all conversations and transactions. I also pay Joshi ji fifteen thousand rupees per month. Nobody knows about this", replied Asha.

"Does Dagariya not know this?"

"I don't know," Asha answered.
~~~

"I pay him separately. He does not give me a receipt. I could not pay him two or three times. It was not shortage of money but due to circumstances. The matter ended there. He never asked me for it. If it were for Dagariya, he would have definitely asked for the arrears."

Ajay advised her not to precipitate matters. Maybe after a few months matters would change and it would be easier to move out.

Asha described Dagariya as a person who cared only about his own good. He was one who believed that he thought at many levels simultaneously. He has so many thoughts flitting in his mind and unlike most people; he tracks all of them and is conscious of them. He always had a reason to give you that appealed to you no matter what he was up to or what brought you together. He could be ruthless but he can be ruthlessly accommodating as well. He may even believe he was being good, moral and helpful but it was only to serve his interest.

"Yes," said Ajay, "He believes he thinks strategically. Maybe he does. He is not straight forward and it takes long time to find out."

Then Asha pounced on him asking him that when he was starting his business and she wanted to be a part of it. Ajay nodded and said yes. And then there was silence.

Ajay's mind was not in the sunset or on Asha's conversation but on Teja. What a terrific and precocious girl, he mused. She had become an intense young woman who was curious but cautious. She was high strung and liked being on the edge of situations. No doubt, she was energetic but to live life on your terms one had to be durable like a marathon runner. It was not just being positive, which is necessary, but also the ability to know your environment and create your future in it.

"I am very happy about her attitude to life. I wish

her happiness and joy in her life," said Ajay. He reasoned that Teja was an adult and had the right to take her own decisions. However, if she shared and consulted them she would benefit. They could add more information or enlarge her context leading to a richer sensibility.

Asha reached out and squeezed Ajay's hand and her eyes glowed under the darkening skies. All lights, as far as they could see up to the heavens had become glowing points. Asha gushed, "Ajay she wants to marry you!" Ajay laughed and as Asha saw his laugh spread to his eyes in the falling light, she joined in his laughter, saying, "Isn't she such a sweet girl? Yes, this is the time and her delicate age is on her side. Taking correct decisions, her life will take the right turns and she would be able to realize her full potential."]

"Teja, my daughter perhaps does not know how much we care for her. We pray for her success. In a way she has grown without a father and yet how understanding and loving she is," added Asha.

Now it was completely dark. The skies had no colour except inky blue black with thousands of stars looking down on them. It had become cooler. Asha demanded that Ajay make her his partner. When and how did he propose to venture?

Ajay was waiting for her to ask this.

Ajay began, "At the moment and even before start up I don't want anyone to risk their money, time and energy. Few people will understand my project. Evaluation by usual standards and yardsticks will not do or be fair to my judgment. Neither do I want anyone to tell me what to do. Moreover, neither do I want anyone to tell me how to do it. If the venture fails, let me fail. I do not want to drag anyone down with me. In the final analysis, I do not intend to have any partner for the first three years."

Asha got up surprising him, walked into the room, and returned switching the balcony light. Bathed in the harsh tube light they continued with their conversation.

Surprised, Asha asked, "Not even me?"

Ajay saw the dejection in her wide-open eyes as if in fear or hearing the unacceptable or the inconceivable. She had never imagined this possibility. Breathing deep and easy she looked at him imploringly.

"No, nobody . Let me explain," he answered.

"Did you ever imagine I would let you down?" continued Ajay.

She felt assured. Her smile was genuine and trusting and Ajay reassuring her, said, "Asha, you have played an important role in my life. I have received so much from you. I am indebted to you."

Then he launched into his venture, "Of course, I need money to start. I have some but not enough. You know well the day a business is set up the money meter begins ticking. The business will need money until customers start paying. At the beginning, I do not need a swanky office. Maybe I do not even need an office. I could work from my home itself. For the first few months, I do not even need anyone to take my telephone calls. The first thing I need is to create a web presence. I have ideas and some statements and narratives I created in the last 6 months which I hope to use. I have a good friend in the US, an Elegant Software evangelist who will create my web presence."

"I will have assurance from customers; I would like to call them that though they are friends. I also have a contact list of prospects with their details. This has been in the making for the last many months. I have references whom I will dialog with. They are aware of Elegant Software and its immense power. At the other end there will be various approvals and government sanctions that I would need. I will outsource this work. There will be banking work that is a must, which I will do myself or do it with an outsourcer."

"How many days you need to do this?" Asked Asha.

" I would need 4 to 6 weeks," replied Ajay.

"I may borrow money from some people." Looking at her, he smiled and continued, "The first person I will ask is, you. Maybe I will ask one or two more people. This money will be a loan on which I will pay interest and return the money in 3 years. If my company fails or closes for any reason, I have a strategy to return the same in 3 years or earlier, if so required. I do not think that my company would close down. The chances are remote. After 3 years I would love to convert loans into equity."

"Ajay, why do you want to borrow money from anyone else? I will give you all the money you need. No matter how much you may want. I know it is not too big a sum." Her sincerity touched him.

He did not say but believed that personal affections and business was never a good mix.

"Which other people have you thought of taking a loan from?", Asha asked.

"He tried to reason and explained to her, "I may invite Dagariya to invest. It is not that there are no other people but asking Dagariya would be strategic. I will be straight and honest with him that any stake considered after three years and his involvement was his being a loaner. He has his hands full to save his company."

"If he does not let professionals like Venkataraman run the company, the company won't survive for the next one year. The company every few months takes overdraft to pay salaries. Half the management staffs are family or political appointees. Many of them employed to please his friends and accommodate relatives. Venkataraman could run the show alone when the company size was 300 engineers. He can't do it with 750 people."

"What strategy will it serve taking money from

Dagariya? He will interfere and force things on you. I do not like your idea of taking a loan from him," pleaded Asha.

"Ajay you will not take a single penny from Dagariya! That is final. What do you know about him," said a stung Asha.

Rarely did she speak like that. Ajay conceded he did not know much about Dagariya. If she felt it that way, he could revise his loaners list.

"By getting him to be one of the loaners, we will ease any pressure he might bring on you. For the next few months, he will not have the time or the inclination to interfere. He has a lot of firefighting to do. Losing the HP account means losing 10 percent of his cash flow with 50 % margin. He is losing proposals and his hit rate has slipped from 1 out of 2.5/3.0 to maybe 1 out of 4.0/4.5. This makes his cost of marketing high and his SGA is way above the industry average."

"If there are few projects and a paltry pipeline, engineers are idling. This is a frightening situation for engineers. This is hurting their aspirations. I bet more than half are looking outside. If he does not rectify and control his operations then the company will have to close. I mean he will have to sell out. Bankers may not like to come in. The bankers may like to bring in a new set of investors, most likely professional engineers and managers. To avoid this he has to induct at least half a dozen experienced professionals and give them a free hand."

"If you say so I will not ask Dagariya to loan money," affirmed Ajay.

"Sushma will not allow this. It is impossible to imagine Dagariya to stop interfering in the Company," replied Asha.

"I don't think it will be Sushma's call. As you imply Mahesh and Sushma are a devoted couple. Sushma will do anything for his happiness and Mahesh will indulge in any of her idiosyncrasies. You think Sushma does not know about Mahesh making a pass at you?"

"Sushma with her instinct of preservation when confronted with survival issues will see light. In his personal matters and especially in money matters Mahesh is instinctive. His instincts are always aroused when he fears loss, injury or other negative changes to his net worth," said Ajay.

Asha responded, "Ajay if you do not invite Dagariya ji to invest he will know one day that I have invested. When he knows that what will he do? He may try to hurt both of us."

"Such a day will not come. Do not be afraid."

"Ajay, I have lots of money. How much ever you want I will give you."

Ajay laughed and said, "Asha by now you know Dagariya. He thinks he is too smart and proud to call himself strategic thinker. He gets others to do his dirty work but keeps seeking advice from many and chooses his response from these. He may pass it as a position taken after great internal debate. Maybe he does or Sushma decides on his behalf. Sushma definitely sets the line on some company's matters. Dagariya is not my antagonist and I have nothing to prove to him or compete with him or anything like that."

Ajay continued, "Of course, he will know that you are an investor in my business. Getting him to become an investor will bind us together with shared interests. His pressure and hold on you will become lesser and manageable. I think you should continue with Dagariya for another year. By that time, Teja would have found some calling and settled for the next 3 or 4 years."

"Look Asha, you already have other options, which you can fall upon. There is nothing to worry. Your fears about running Pine Woods are also misplaced. We can make better arrangements to run your hotel than the present one."

She found sense and comfort in his reasoning. He stood up and looked at the door indicating his desire to leave. She stood up and spread her arms pulling him. There was nothing sexual. She wanted to be hugged. She found strength and reassurance in his strong arms. This was her feminine sensibility speaking which very few males understand. Secure in his arms she blurted, "Ajay, I must have done something good in my previous life to have met you. I look upon you as a wall around me. I find myself safe and secure within it."

Changing the subject, Asha said that at times she would function as Dagariya's personal secretary without any official position or designation. Fill in when her secretary is on leave. I also get to listen tosome of his communications and the people who come to see him or fix his appointments. This is generally between lunch and close of the day, when Dagariya attends office. Many of his visitors are builders and some from the local film industry.

"I feel he knows many builders and has good friendship with them," continued Asha.

"Yes it is the builders today who have lots of money. And, black money."

Asha responded, My heart says that Dagariya ji does illegal transactions with the builders' black money. We know very little about builders and the construction industry. Nevertheless, we know that the builders are the emperors of black money."

Yes, we will investigate after returning to Bangalore.

Asha suggested that he talk to a high placed executive she knew in the construction industry in Bombay. He would provide the information on the economics of the house building industry. It must be of great interest to both the builders and Dagariya to meet surreptitiously and away from Bangalore. Her acquaintance, Mr. Abdul Dalwai in Bombay was knowledgeable, helpful and a good man. Knowing her problems and the notoriety her case acquired, he understood Asha's trauma. Dalwai went out of the way to help get her papers of her flat. They continue to exchange New Year greetings and sometimes talk on the phone. Yes, she had met his family and they had spent a few days at her hotel. She would introduce him on the phone.

People love all that is bizarre and outside the conventions and humdrum routine of everyday life. Ajay had heard of Lao Tzu, the Chinese philosopher and military strategist. He intuitively understood what Lao Tzu meant when he said, "Being deeply loved by someone gives you strength, while loving someone deeply gives you courage".

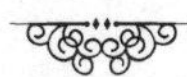

Chapter- XVI
Silent and Furtive

Ajay was up at four in the morning, fresh and ready for a jog. Though summer, it was cool in Ooty at this time. When he stepped out, he felt the moisture in the morning mountain air and darkness engulfed him. He could not see the road three yards ahead of him. Such a combination of elements was excellent for a fecund mind.

As he ran with careful measured strides, he thought it was time Sarkar and Mythili knew his venturing plans. He had given hints to Mythili and though she had not shown much interest except listen, she had a sharp memory and she would remember whatever he told her. Ajay felt guilty for not giving Sarkar an indication.

Sarkar should have been the first person with whom he should have been sharing his plans. When he admitted it to himself, filled with guilt and remorse because Sarkar had been encouraging him to venture. It was not for the sake of trying but Sarkar considered Ajay could be the man for runaway entrepreneurial success because he was a solid person. An expression which included trustworthiness, honest, fair, hardworking with a never give up spirit. Ajay was a man who would not admit defeat when he put his shoulder to something he believed in, no matter how improbable it might look. He was also one who loved technology and his felicity to learn fast and go deep into it. Blessed with the adventuring spirit, applying technology came easily to him. When he was engrossed with technology, he became impersonal.

He was back in an hour. As he climbed the stairs, a waiter stood at the foot. Giving him a smile, Ajay ran up the stairs. It was beginning to get lighter. As he sat resting, there was a knock on the door and there stood the waiter asking him if he would like to drink coffee or tea. No, he did not want tea or coffee but started conversing with him learning about the sort of guests who patronized the hotel. The waiter's name was Kashung Kengoo, a Manipuri young man of about30 years old. He had been with the hotel for the past 5 years and along with the cook, was one of the oldest employees. Yes, he remembered Ajay's last visit. Ajay asked him to come inside and had him sit on the sofa facing him while he sat on the bed.

He wondered why Dagariya came once every few weeks and would spend a day or two. Sometimes Dagariya came with Sushma sometimes with his accountant, Joshi ji. Kashung further told him there were other people who came to the hotel and met Dagariya as if by appointment. Kashung did not know who booked for these guests but they had reservations. Ajay surmised that hotel bookings could be from Dagariya's office in Bangalore.

Listening to Kashung, Ajay concluded that the people whom Dagariya met were rich and often arrived in big chauffeur driven cars. Kashung knew this because he often interacted with the drivers. He could not say about the number plates, about which he knew little. He assumed they were from within the state and maybe from the neighboring states. Kashung was quite sure that they were arranged meetings. They met as per agreement. He believed so because they ate with Dagariya and Dagariya paid bills or debited to Dagariya's account. Sometimes they had soda and snacks sent to their room, which had a party like setting. They brought their own alcohol and rarely asked a hotel staff to buy from the market.

Did Asha know about his visits? "Definitely sir," said Kashung. It has been going on for over three years. Her manager or someone would have told her. Maybe she concluded that whatever it was it was. Nothing unusual, it was just that.

Kashung was asking loaded questions, which he should not as an employee. Ajay was uncomfortable, but did not try to evade choosing silence as a reply. Kashung Kengoo was in a roundabout way inquiring about Ajay's relationship with Madam. It could also be harmless seeking to know about the owner of the hotel. Kashung would have some idea about Asha's age whereas he could guess his age.

With the silence hanging at a cliff, Kashung continued, "Yes, Madam Visits at least once a month. She is alone or with Joshi ji, does so on a weekend to check up on the hotel, and leaves the next day. Madam gifted with a good memory and her questions were sharp when she questioned an employee. It was also certain that he not only knew what went on in the hotel but also could be Asha's informer."

Given her momentous life of the past Asha became cautious and necessity had made her to be on guard at the slightest doubt of anyone or any situation. Therefore, it was reasonable to expect to grow a confidant who could report on the hotel.

Of the three suites on the third floor one was permanently reserved for Asha when she visited, and one was for Dagariya whenever he visited and the last, for the person she chose to accommodate there. She would inform the Manager if she wanted someone accommodated in this suite or the other when Dagariya was not using it. That was rare. Kashung was under her orders to maintain these suites and no one was given these except those she authorized. He had to be sharp on what transpired here so that when called, he had to report and answer any query Madam might have. Having seen him come with Asha, he might have been curious. She always came to the hotel alone and the only person that ever accompanied her except her daughter was Ajay. Others came and met her here but they came separately. Therein lay his curiosity.

Then Kashung surprised Ajay saying that he had a few papers, which were left behind by Dagariya ji, and would he like to see them? Ajay remained non-committal. He wondered. Rather than arouse suspicion at his simulated attention he asked him if Asha Madam had seen these papers. She had seen them. She had asked him to keep it safe and he wondered if he was being more than protective and cautious. He could not read, and due to his respect for and commitment to Asha, he would like Ajay Sahib to see them.

Ajay nodded his head and asked him to fetch those papers.

Kashung returned with two sheets of paper on which were a table with many entries. Ajay asked him, "Do you have any idea who could have left it?"

Kashung replied, "Sir, Dagariya sir or Joshi ji might have left it in a hurry. I found it under the bed."

He took the paper from Kashung and said he would see it and return it to him later. Ajay thanked him and suggested him that he should be loyal and honest to Asha Madam. She was a good woman. After some casual talk, he left.

Ajay scanned the two sheets; the first thing that struck him was the names of companies on the papers. What made companies with strange names like Evergreen Investments, Shining Coal India Limited, India Green Dollar Inc., Nilgiris Tea investments Ltd., Coffee Warrior; Kashinath, Banerjee and Taparia Chartered Accountants; Nagappan, Shanmugham & Sia Tech Civil Engineers, Great Bombay Builders and Architects etc. to be of interest to Dagariya or Joshi ji. He counted 21 companies and their names appeared to be old names favored by companies sixty or seventy years ago. Against each company was a name of a person with what appeared to be a telephone number and city, which was Bombay, Calcutta or Madras. There was another column, which looked like year and ranged from 1940 to 1995 though most were between 1960 and 1980. The last column was of a few alphabets, 3 to 6 in capitals. The writing was in small neat characters in pencil.

It seemed like a repository of secrets. Ajay was intrigued.

His brain mapped the table and he set about thinking if it was important. If so what did it represent? Who could have made it and for what purpose? If only he could connect the small bits of information, he would be able to create the big picture. As he mulled over, his software engineer mind began drawing who would likely need these bits of information. Ajay worked it out that it was a list containing names of companies along with a name. Perhaps he was the representative of the company with his contact number and landlines with the three city code digits. From the landline code, it was possible to figure out the city. The extensions of the city code were six, seven or eight digits. This suggested that these representatives were across the country from small towns to big metros. After imagining possibilities, he wondered if these companies listed on the stock exchange.

It was early in the morning and he looked at his watch that showed seven. He did not hesitate to call Bhuvan, who was now involved full time in his business, and seek his inputs and check up on his business. Giving him the names of the companies, Ajay asked him if he could check whether these companies were on the stock exchanges. Bhuvan should know or be able to find out. He had been dabbling in the share market from the first day he came to know him. As he read each name and came to the last Bhuvan responded, "These names look like names used 30 to40 years ago. Yes, some maybe listed long ago. Checking is the only way of being sure."

Ajay was convinced they were companies on the stock exchanges.

Ajay was eager to know about Bhuvan's business and expressed his happiness that it was doing well. Listening to his business development activities Ajay congratulated him. Ajay explained in brief his business plans. Returning to the purpose of Ajay's call Bhuvan advised, "In each state there is a Registrar of Companies who could help him. In addition, he could look for these names in a large 21-volume encyclopedia of listed companies published from Calcutta. It contains details of listed companies.

"Ajay you can find this encyclopedia in big libraries and business schools. I can find a 10 or 20-year-old volumes. They would give you definitive answers."

"Which could be the best place to go," asked Ajay.

"They will be at the Registrar of Companies' Office in Bangalore," replied Bhuvan.

Ajay spent 10 minutes and texted a few names to Bhuvan.

As he scanned the paper for the umpteenth time, he guessed that the alphabets in the last column had to be banks. SBI was state Bank of India, UCOB was the United Commercial Bank of India and BOFMAH was the Bank of Maharashtra and so on. Yes, it had to be that!

Under the shower, Ajay pondered over the possible importance of this information. Could it lead to something important that he could not figure out now. Why should Dagariya or his confidant need to maintain information in a secretive way? If so, what was this information about? Additionally why did he hide it? Did it have anything to do with the company? If so, then he felt he was entitled to know.

Many hotel guests leave papers that were useless or outdated. Why did Kashung pick this one many months ago and keep it with him. He did not go about picking papers left by other guests. Nor did he keep them for so long. What made these papers so fascinating and important unlike papers left by other guests? Hotels have a rule to throw leftovers of guests and if perceived of value stored for a year. Someone would inspect and authorize retention and like in this case shown to the manager or Asha. Why did he not return them to Dagariya or Joshi ji when they visited next time? Was Kashung trustworthy? Could his explanations be reliable? Did someone set up Kashung?

What was intriguing that he claimed it to have found them in the room, which most likely used by Dagariya's or Joshi ji? He never returned the papers to them when they visited next. Did Asha tell him not to do this? Ajay pondered over the quandary he had created for himself. Maybe ye,s maybe not. He felt the vibrations in his body, which seemed to say, Asha was connected. Kashung was perhaps acting on behalf of Asha.

Kashung had retained these papers for six months or more and was now showing it him. He admitted he had not visited the hotel in the last many months.

His curiosity piqued he wanted to find the answers to these questions stirring in his mind. Asha had to tell her side of the story for finding answers to these questions.

Bhuvan called as he was changing. What was Ajay up to? Ajay most likely connected with the information, because he would not want clarifications without a purpose.

What was he trying to put together and for what purpose? Ajay had no answers. When he espied the list, it was mere curiosity but now he felt it might have something to do with the proprietor of the company he worked with.

Bhuvan felt that these could be shell companies. Then Bhuvan let loose facts which seemed to be strange, but nonetheless giving life to the papers he held in his hands. Bhuvan continued. Shell companies he repeated again.

"A shell company is a company that exists but does not do any business or have any assets. The most valuable thing about a shell company is its listing on the stock exchange. Once listed gives it a legal entity and by law permitted to conduct a variety of businesses. Yet, it may choose not to do any business. It remained listed as long as it complies with the rules of the stock exchange. There are people willing to buy such companies. Often these companies set up with illegalities for now or later. However, at times shell companies could be doing legitimate businesses too. When a single entity owns many shell companies than the underlying purpose is for illegal purposes."

"A listed shell company must have had an active business in the past otherwise it could not have met listing requirements. Given that, it takes time and money to get a listing. If it did not satisfy listing requirements, a bribe indicated. A listed shell has significant value even if it does not have any assets."

"It is possible that some shell companies were set up years ago. They at that time had operations, but those operations shrank due to any of the many reasons. Sometimes shell companies willfully made sick. Sometimes legitimate shell companies created for owning intangible assets such as royalties or copyrights. They could also receive income from them. Sometimes tracts of land become shell companies, for protection against litigation or tax benefits."

"Sometimes a shell company can also mean a company that has never had a business but somehow deceitfully listed. The businessman - bureaucratic nexus enables this. Can the politician be far away? Sometimes, fraudulent companies become private limited companies that not listed, but could be converted to a public limited company and listed quickly and easily. This is set up to sell the company or offer illegitimate services."

"Tax havens like in Switzerland, Cayman Islands, Isle of Man, Bahamas and Guernsey etc. offer these services. Ready made shell companies are available in those countries at a price. This is a convenient alternative to setting up a company from scratch and laws of these countries are lax and permitting. The name of the company altered, changed, new directors appointed and shares issued. In India, if a shell company has no active business, and not been functioning for some time, it becomes a dormant company. A dormant company may be exempt from many reporting requirements. They are valuable to certain class of people."

"Ajay, it will surprise you to know many respected public figures use shell companies," continued Bhuvan. "They are business men, entrepreneurs, politicians, trading houses, drug dealers, flesh traders, film personalities. Terrorist organizations look for such companies and they become more valuable if they are old. It serves them for stock trading, consigning and delivery purposes. By stock trading, I mean in spurious or banned goods. There are many high profile and respectable businessmen and women who own shell companies. Many set up these shell companies to avoid tax, conceal black or untaxed money, and even launder money. They are vehicles for political payoffs and such illegal activities. Your company's proprietor could for all his respectability be loaning shell companies. He may not be doing anything illegal himself but enable others to do so and charge commission or his rightful cut."

"How large can these commissions be?"

Bhuvan explained further, "Transactions run in hundreds of thousands of Rupees. Depending on nature of transaction, the commissions could be 2 % to as high as 6%. Illegal transactions are not just one debit and credit, but many. They could be 5, 6 or even 7. Complex transactions, where the stated purpose of each transaction is different can be with one bank or many banks. There could be many transactions to hide the trail of where the transaction began or finally ended. They could be through banks in Tax Havens or domestic banks. Transactions could be from banks within the country to banks outside for parking money. Sometimes shells facilitate money to be spirited back to another account in the same or a different country. At each transaction the fee may be one to one and a half percentage point, adding up to neat figure."

"Are you going to do detective work now?"

"No Bhuvan, I don't have the foggiest idea what I can or should or should not do. Your information overload has rather clogged my mind. No, not clogged, but I feel bombarded by too much information in too short a time. I mean, there could be damning possibilities or I am just imagining or it might not be my business."

"You asked for it. Mull it over I am always available for more or clarifications," added Bhuvan.

As he was about to cut the call Bhuvan interrupted him. "Ajay look for that one bank account in his or his wife's name or both or even a shell company where monies finally land. That branch would be beholden to him ifit handles many transactions in many currencies and together they are large. This bank account will have a healthy credit. Many a time, a transaction chain begins from this company and through this bank. Most chains must end here. "

"Knowing this bank or account holder makes it easier to investigate. Enforcement agencies know how to make the bank people show them transactions of such an account."

Was it a new angle for Ajay to investigate? Was he to mull over the information and extract that that would help him?

Ajay hissed, "Yes I get the drift, there has to be a bank account where his commissions finally land."

Five hours later on a breakfast spread under a shady tree in the courtyard of the hotel, Ajay appraised Asha. He began with the list Kashung had shown him and his conversation with Bhuvan. Had she seen the list? When was this? Had she examined the matter? Did she ever felt suspicious? Had she tried to investigate? Did she advise Kashung not to return the papers to Dagariya or Joshi ji?

Ajay wondered that if she thought there was something in it, she could have mentioned it to him in Bangalore. Quickly he erased the question out of his mind.

Yes, Kashung had shown her the list and it was many months ago. She did nothing about it because she could not make anything of it. Perhaps she may have told him to keep it and show it to you when you came next. That is a strong possibility. No, she would not tell Kashung to return the list to Dagariya. If he was to show him,then how could it be returned to Dagariya?

Yes, she trusted Kashung. He reported on the goings on in the hotel. He was her informer.

Ajay asked, "Suppose you did tell Kashung, why?"

Asha thinking hard said, "I do not know.. Perhaps Kashung said it in a way that made it seem important. After all what you have found about this list, it gives an idea of the nefarious activities of the person who made it. They might be vile people."

Asha then blurted out, "Ajay, Mahesh and Sushma care too much for me. I am also scared of them. Do not ask me why, because I myself do not know. I used to have a fear of some kind of them. With time I have learnt to ignore it but not forget it."

Asha called Kashung, who came running and stood in front of them looking down with hands folded in front. He could only recall that he found the list 6 or 7 months ago. No, he did not know the person who occupied the room that day. He found the list under the bed the same day, the next, or still the next day. There could be few days between two occupants when the suite is vacant. Was it important? It was his sixth sense.

Asha dismissed him and observed, "I feel Kashung found this paper in April." After confirming, that he appraised her that she had visited the hotel in April. After a quick calculation, he said that she was here on April 26, 2003 that was a Saturday. Somebody left this paper without knowing or by mistake after her visit in April and before the next visit. It could not be a deliberate act.

They ordered for the room-booking ledger and pored at the arrivals in the three suites during this period. What they found was astonishing. Dagariya visited the hotel twice during this period. During both his visits, prominent Bangalore builders had booked suites. The conclusion was stark and damaging.

Was Dagariya involved with the Builders?

Most likely Dagariya left the list without knowing. Joshi ji could not. Asha who had dealt with Joshi ji and knew him too well said he is too careful and painstaking. He would never commit an indiscretion like this.

He left for Bangalore on Sunday night and Asha left the next evening. Bhuvan called him at night the next day to find out what Ajay planned to do. Talking with Ajay, Bhuvan drawn in wanting to keep abreast of investigations Ajay was making. Before they concluded Bhuvan said, check the builder and your proprietor link. "Why builder?" asked Ajay. Bhuvan explained that the rate at which flats added to inventory was the highest in Bangalore than anywhere else and absorbed without resistance at asking prices and he signed off.

He did what he had never done before. Call Asha at midnight. She picked up the phone on the first ring. Yes, this was another instance of bonds of delicacy. He impressed upon her that for the wellbeing and justice to the many, they should investigate to confirm their suspicions. Asha shocked him by saying that the suspicious were his and she did not care too much about them. She continued and warned him about the dangers of becoming Dagariya's adversary. When he reminded her about the builder in Bombay she had talked about, she promised to introduce him to the builder's manager, Abdul Dalwai in Bombay.

Abdul Dalwai was from Mangalore and there was a rare chance he and Dagariya might know each other. If so, it would be a sticky situation. She warned Ajay that discretion was essential and it would be appropriate to pose as a journalist.

"Yes, what you are saying is true. I'll tell him this information is for some economic research," said Ajay.

It would pain him to pretend what he was not, but that was the price to continue with his investigations.

The next day he was talking to Abdul Dalwai from a public booth. As they made the first conversation after Asha introduced him to Ajay telling him that he was looking for basic facts for a story for his newspaper. Ajay continued that his story needed some undeniable truths about how the building industry generated black money. He knew that if they ever talked again he would not be able to change his story. However, the hidden facts of the building industry dug out for continuing with the investigation. What would he do after knowing if Dagariya was involved? How the building industry generated black money and the sort of people who handled it would give clues between Dagariya and his builder friends and their assignees. It was easy to ascertain what sort of people from the building industry called upon him and their reputation in the builder's lobby. Karnataka had a strong builder lobby with deep political roots. After knowing this, then what?

Dalwai began with the assumption that he was talking to a knowledgeable journalist, "You know well that the building industry cannot function without black money. It generates 8 to 10 % of the country's black money. Virtually in all major cities, there is the politician, gangster and builder network in an unholy coalition. Had it not been for the politician the builders would not be able to operate in the cavalier fashion they do? If the builders were honest and did not worship money, why would they need gangsters? They use gangsters to blackmail and extort."

"There are many sanctions and permissions which builders have to obtain from the local government – the City Development Authority or the Regional Development Authority, Land Titles, Approvals for Layout, Building Plans, No Objection Certificates from the cities' Electric Supply Company, Water Sewage Board, Pollution Control Board, Certificates for Completion and so on. These are government bodies controlled directly or indirectly by the politician civil servants nexus. For every clearance, a builder has to make a payment. Often this paid in cash or through benami bank transaction (when property or a payment transferred or paid to a person not directly but in another person's name). This generates huge black money, as there are thousands of such transactions daily. The benami money needs to be transferred into the ultimate beneficiaries' account in white so that it can be enjoyed and easiest way is to spirit away to tax havens."

Ajay remembered attending a public lecture by a public spirited accountant who spoke of this benami money who had computed the building industry contributed 15 % of this unaccounted money or black economy and was impoverishing the exchequer at the expense of builders.

"The other set of transactions where black money is generated is by the builder himself who is happy to collect a part of the cost of the house in cash without receipts and happy to give a discount. A part of this unaccounted money lands up with the politicians for protection purposes."

Dalwai continued, "It is simple and straightforward. You get the drift Sir?" Ajay who was experienced to hear bits of a business process and construct the total process end to end, "Yes, Mr. Dalwai."

Dalwai, continued, "Apart from the basic cost of the apartment, other parts of the building like the car park, extra amenities and sometimes the interiors a good percentage may be settled in cash. Costs for interior decoration, furniture and fixtures accepted in cash and the builder willing to accept a lower price in cash and buyer happy to meet the builder's munificence. The higher the cash component, the better is the negotiated price of the building. The cost of a flat can vary as much as 10 to 15 % depending on the percentage paid in cash. There are unethical home loan companies who encourage the system and the builder is happy to recommend the buyer to these loan companies. There are many house buyers who patronize these home loan companies because they are not in position to approach big banks."

"The black component ends up being the cushion for home loan companies, who have to extend a loan only on the lower agreement value, though the flat mortgaged with them has a much higher market value. The home loan companies even facilitate the black component by inflating the loan amount."

"Black money generated by the housing sector does not end with getting clearances and build houses and apartments to sell but even at the time of sale you invariably get a buyer who insists on a higher agreement value to qualify for a bigger home loan. And the seller is saddled with capital gains tax even if he/she had not earned any real appreciation."

Thanking Abdul profusely, Ajay disconnected before he could ask him for other details. It was a wayside phone booth and he would notice no number on his cell. He felt guilty at his furtive behavior, a constriction in his heart reminded him of his guilt, the heat spread over his face, and his ears felt hot. He would ask Asha to call him before he did and have Asha handle that.

Asha followed up with Abdul Dalwai in the evening on the pretext of buying a flat in Bangalore. She had to make an effort to convince him that she had given up on the idea of returning to Bombay and if she ever decided, his would be the first stop. Yes, it was possible that Teja might think of setting in Bombay as she planned to do a film related course in which case Bombay would be the ideal location.

Dalwai assumed she was wealthy but had no idea of her wealth. She had all her money in bank where her salary and earnings from her hotel deposited. However, she could arrange to pay in cash. Yes, she would be glad if he could suggest a builder in Bangalore. He promised to call her the next day during lunchtime and get her started.

They had no way of knowing how a reference to a Bangalore builder would help. There was nothing to do but hope that something emerged out of the conversation, which might take them a step nearer to the truth.

After her lunch, she walked up and down the stairs adjoining her office and the usually packed floor below. Engineers kept quitting but the first floor always kept full and now with the lunch hour, it was deserted. She felt her stomach tightening. They mostly talked in Marathi and nobody could make out their conversation. Then her cell buzzed. She knew it was Dalwai and picking her phone, she backed into the rear wall farthest from the closed door.

Dalwai told her that there must be at least a thousand developers in Bangalore. Fifty percent were small timers who could handle one or two complexes at one time. There was about 50 labelled as big and of them a dozen who were reliable and ethical. "I would suggest you select from them. They do not entertain black money transactions. Yes, these builders insist on all payments by cheque but their prices are at least 10 to 15 % higher than the prevailing rate in the area. Smaller and medium sized builders do and do not deny taking payments in cash. They would be cheaper but cut corners on quality."

"Asha ji it is your call," ended Dalwai. She kept the cell on and he could hear her breathing.

Asha absorbed what Dalwai told her and quietly asked if he could recommend a small or an upcoming builder. She sought an open, well lit, airy, 2,000 to 2,500 square feet spacious flat in the city. Her money was in the bank but Mr. Dalwai advises her how to pay a part in cash. A bare shell meeting her requirement would not be less than 80 to 90 lakhs calculated Dalwai. The other amenities like car park, sewage and electricity connections, registration etc. will be over the basic cost and would be another 20 %. If she paid the amenities in cash and her early instalments partly in cash, she could save 15 Lakhs.

Asha led him on and Dalwai confided that there were companies wichh arranged for cash payments. She pleaded helplessness and sought his help and he promised to put her in touch with the right people promising to find such a company in Bangalore. Then a thought formed in her mind that if he expected anything from her in return, and the next moment it vanished.

She still had not detached herself mentally from Dagariya. It was against her instinct to entangle herself in such deals but her feelings for Mahesh and Sushma were a mixture of gratitude, fear, hatred and appreciation. The die cast.

The next day she called Dalwai who told her to contact one Mr. Joshi of Lakshman Investments and Financial Consultancy located on Ali Asker Road off Cunningham Road. When this registered, her knees shook and she was certain that Lakshman Investments and Financial Consultancy connected to Dagariya. Did he know Mr. Joshi? There was silence.

Thanking him, she disconnected and hired an auto rickshaw and had him cruise that area. Stopping the auto rickshaw, she asked him to wait and walked Ali Asker Street and then she espied a double storied house with a small nameplate saying Lakshman Investments and Financial Consultancy. She hurried to the waiting auto rickshaw and sped back to her office.

Lakshman Investments and Financial Consultancy were at a walking distance from Dagariya's flat and Mr. Joshi had to be Joshi ji. Dagariya traced his roots from Lakshman Nagar an outpost of the Mewar region in Rajasthan that gave the name to his fallacious company. Now she was convinced he was a crook. Like many high profile and wealthy people she had known powerful, paragon of virtues and generous and when they were unmasked their knavery and false bravado withered like a violet under a blazing sun.

Shaken, her feminine instincts of being cautious saved her from the blushes. Did Dalwai know Dagariya and Lakshman Investments and Financial Consultancy? Did he obtain this contact through his professional circle? There were possibilities. She could not ask him.

Sitting in the auto rickshaw, she felt cold, a shiver running through her body in a bright sunny afternoon. She knew she was weak and that made her vulnerable. She blamed her conditions and at times, she doubted if any other woman in her place could have done what she had created. Like people who fear, to go back in time she was forgetting that it was more because of others than her own efforts where she was. She lacked that toughness and the power to hold fast to moral virtues, which she believed and held them to be right, in face of threats. She explained her frailty emerging from being a single woman with a teenaged daughter and a convicted husband, disowned by relatives. That was one part; the other that made her guilty was being beholden to her benefactor. This was a heady mixture, and she had to live with. It was a sort of consolation explaining her weakness but not completely.

If she lost her job in Dagariya's company and he withdrew his support to her hotel, everything would crash. That had become a constant fear in the last few weeks. Ajay was quite the opposite. He was a self-made man, with high ideals ready to stake anything even his life to live by them. Religiously honest and trustworthy he believed in his personal spiritual development and goodwill of all. He had been a pillar of strength to her and that was what attracted him to her.

Her mind was in turmoil. She was afraid also.

Talking with Ajay would help. She longed for his strong arms around her. She messaged Ajay and he soundlessly slipped into her room as others were leaving. She went through her day with him and shuddered, "Your suspicion turned out to be right. If not 100 %, correct then at least 99 %. I feel somewhat scared."

"Ajay let us not do anything in a hurry. You are intelligent and lets think and then do anything," pleaded Asha.

""Asha,why are you being scared. Whatever we have

to do we need to do in the next 24 hours," replied Ajay rising to the challenge.

"Do like this, strike such that you kill the snake and save the stick," suggested Asha.

"Yes," grunted Ajay.

~~~

Ajay explained that they could inform the Enforcement Directorate; or set the newspaper on the trail of Lakshman Investments and Financial Consultancy; or share this information with a builder with impeccable honesty; or write to highest in the political hierarchy of a party that stood for clean politics; or send details to a TV channel like NDTV. He had met NDTV's star investigative reporter in a flight. They had exchanged cards and talked once on the phone. He could call him if need be.

He added that the government rewards informers in cases where the information led to conviction. Of course, they were not for that. Unless they revealed what they do no one would ever know. It would continue to remain hidden.

They finally decided to warn the Enforcement Directorate and contact NDTV later. It was now necessary to search the Lakshman Investments and Financial Consultancy office on Ali Asker Road. They agreed to take final call next day that happened to be a Friday before 10:00. This according to Asha was an auspicious time.

Ajay remembered Alok Marathe giving the contact details of Bahula. He was a colleague of his from IIM, Ahmedabad and joined the Income Tax Department. Last Alok knew that this man was in Bangalore and in charge of raids. Bahula was an idealistic young man, liked by his seniors, feared by his staff, and had contempt for the crooked businessperson. He rang Bahula who asked him to come.

After explaining his relationship with Alok Marathe, he asked to see him. It was urgent, the matter of great importance
~~~

and secrecy was necessary. Bahula invited him straight away. After commiserating Alok Marathe, Ajay told him what all he knew. Ajay suggested that the office of Lakshman Investments and Financial Consultancy checked. He could collect evidence without anyone getting wiser.

Bahula added, "Checking was necessary. It is not checking but raiding. We raid clandestinely and sometimes in presence of limited people or before everyone. We do it with the purpose of collecting evidence of wrongdoing. To make a case you need hard facts like copies of their account books and records of money transactions etc. You need hard nosed professionals to do such raids. Professionals know by experience and by just a look and isolate documents that may point to illegality."

"We can have the office broken in the night and two smart investigators go through the office with a comb in 2 or 3 hours." Bahula explained there are people with such skills and the IT Department hires them sometimes for cases before they make their raids. If I do so, it will come on our records and I will have to get the Department pay the raiders. It works like this – the Department gives the raiders cash for such jobs and even have they subpoenaed as witnesses in the court of law. In successful convictions, they stand to get a small percentage of money seized or fined. For that to happen I have to make a case and it will go through my superiors till the Commissioner orders such a break in. It may take a few days to a few weeks. That's how we work."

Ajay's face fell with disappointment. Bahula read it. Bahula asked, "Would he like to hire these housebreakers?"

"How much would it cost?" inquired Ajay.

"You should be ready to shell out 50 thousand on private basis. They charge less than half, working for the Department," answered Bahula.

He had to decide and that too fast. There were phone

calls which Bahula did not take in the fifteen minutes they spent together. There was no time to think. Ajay then requested Bahula, "Sir please go ahead and if possible do it this night itself. You know these people and could negotiate their fees."

Bahula smiled. He had taken an instant liking to Ajay on the phone.

Bahula replied, "No Mr. Ajay Khanavkar, it is not possible in the night. Investigation is not done that way. You have to do recce one day and after knowing the neighborhood and the people who work in the office, the habits of important people and so on. You don't go checking all people and look for evidence. You need to have an idea where to look. After collecting all this information the search is undertaken. I know that area and we have broken there before."

Ajay conceded, "Ok sir, if those are your requirements. Just for the curiosity sake you must be doing many break-ins' in a big city like Bangalore. As you said you have to hire outside staff because you do not have enough staff."

Bahula laughed and answered, "Of course we don't encourage industrial espionage. We do such operations in entire state, of course most are in Bangalore. We do raids also when we are sure. Maybe we do 15 to 20 in a year."

Ajay could not make out whether in Bangalore or the entire state and whether breakins' or raids or both. Bahula was encouraging him, being law abiding and being vague at the same time.

"Ok. I take your word; you'll pay them in a week or so. I will try to schedule it on Sunday," assured Bahula. They shook hands and Ajay left.

He met Asha just as she was getting ready to leave. He told her about the meeting with Bahula. Asha wondered why he was in such a hurry. But she reasoned that he wanted to get this off and then start his venture. She finally added, "Ajay if you feel the need for money ask me."

Saying this Asha left and Ajay walked to his table.

Ajay was clearing his table when a mail from Devin popped on his screen.

from: Devin Hayden<devin5_in@gmail.com>
to: Ajay<ramaurshyam204@gmail.com>
date: Fri, July 30, 2004 at 3:59 PM
subject: New Paradigm for Software Development
mailed-by: gmail.com

Here is 1 of the 5 the most important messages in Website I intend to give prominence to.

I set below the model for Elegant Automation Software:

1. **Purpose** (understanding of what is to done, why, purpose of software, list of problems to be solved)

2. **Environment** (understanding the bigger environment in which the solution will fit in)

3. **Incubate** (generate solutions relaxing constraints, seek similar solution ideas from other knowledge areas)

4. **Illuminate** (Select most elegant solution – simple, effective, changeable, straightforward, implementable and long life)

5. **Solve** (design, code, test and install)

These are not stand alone discrete phases. They can be as parallel as the situation demands. The workload and labor will have a bearing. The heart of 'Elegant programming' is documentation. Documentation will be the next important message on the web site.

My friend Stephanie knows about your project and is keen to develop your web site. She is an Italian and you could expect a stunning website. Once you give me the clearance, I will coordinate with her to get the website up with you in the loop.

Link of her websites sent separately by SMS.

Devin Hayden

Ajay was overjoyed. He could see the finishing line.

Ajay learnt in his short life that nothing ends. An end presages the beginning of something new.

Chapter VII
Ajay the Bloodhound Picks the Scent

This day would change the lives of some people.

As soon as he reached the office, Dagariya called him. It was unusual, for he rarely arrived before lunch and now it was only 9:30 am. Dagariya seemed worried. He came straight to the point. The company had been losing money every month for the last 6 months and its utilization factor was a dismal 50 %. These sorts of affairs could not continue. If it did, the Company would not survive. Did not Ajay already realize that the survival of the Company was at stake? If the company had no future, where could the future be of its employees? What future could such a Company give to its stakeholders?

Ajay had to answer. He wondered what a Head of the smallest division could do to stop the slide. It had begun a year earlier. The division had little scope to expand. It was under the threat of being closed or merged with a bigger division immediately. Dagariya should have been the first to take action. What action could he have taken? He had shared his views with Joshi ji and Venkataraman. He admitted he was not strident enough. Sure, the company was bleeding and if were not stemmed, then itwould hemorrhage to death. Time for action was ebbing away. If not controlled now, surgery would be the only option. Surgery had many faces and shapes. Whatever the surgery be, Dagariya would lose control and his day-to-day interference would stop.

"Yes sir, the situation is bad. The attrition has increased over the last six months. It was alarming and above industry average. The signals were there but nobody took action. Attrition in services business is life threatening. It signals serious problems ahead. Unless solved it could get worse. When stalwarts leave any company it lowers morale, there is panic that saps the strength of organization. The industry picks up signals and competitors lure the brightest. Project staffing gets unbalanced and scheduling throws up new challenges. Deliveries slip. That affects receipts and aggravates morale. Employees lose confidence. Their feeling of their usefulness and purpose in their efforts begins to erode."

Dagariya nodded and added that it was so and demanded what were the senior managers with big degrees and experiences doing? The drift was not of a few days creation. It had been going on for some time. It was a creeping failure but high paid managers should have been alert. He kept raving like this for a few minutes speaking to his unseen enemies.

"Our hit rate for bids submitted has fallen by half. We are losing more projects than we win. Losing the services of Alok Marathe and Samir has hit us hard. They had little to do with what goes on in our campus. Their leaving has not added to the pipeline of foreign projects. I hope Andrew does not give us the shock by leaving all of a sudden. Perhaps you should go and meet him. He told me that he thinks highly of you."

"Yes sir. If you want me, I will call Andrew Barnaby,

fix a day, and meet him. I hope you have been talking to him once in a while," cautioned Ajay.

"So you think we have failed on customer acquisition front?"

Ajay bowed his head. There was nothing to answer.

The silence was killing. The stillness was heavy and their patience was on the edge. "The company needs mentors who can talk to restless people across the office. Before we do this now we should have encouraged informal ways of identifying engineers who were looking outside. Mentoring unsatisfied people helps to maintain vitality and the achieving culture in the company."

Dagariya sniggered under his breath. His informers had told him that most engineers with 5 years of experience and less were trying to quit. It was difficult to know about senior people because they changed jobs using their own networks and rarely through man power companies.

"Further, we do not have a robust operational model. A robust model prompts examination of unusual changes and seeks course correction."

"What are you blabbering? You want me to start a mentoring project?"

Dagariya continued, "You are talking like those fancy consultants. A robust model cramps our style of working. Have we not put in place elaborate processes, insisted on strict compliance to the Development Handbook? Everyone including me is proud of our second attempt for ISO certification. All these are company wide and done at the behest of consultants. If they do not foster and encourage our engineers and managers to be innovative and entrepreneurial, then of what use are they? Companies become great only by increasing revenue and improved margins year to year. Nothing else matters."

The reality is that neither ISO certification nor comprehensive Development Handbook or elaborates processes guarantee bug free, robust long life software. Both knew that the application of the Development Handbook was more in breach than followed.

"Having a lean workforce should be good with fewer projects. You need anachieving work force."

"Sir, we are in a manpower driven business, no matter what name you may like to give. Taking 60 to65% utilization is what we should be aiming at. We have not been able to achieve that. The top IT companies have utilization over 80 % and more."

"Hiring good people takes much more effort and time than seeing people leave. People who leave may or may not spread a good word about us. We lack a system to understand why people are leaving. A feedback form we use is of no value. It does not tell us anything."

"Manpower business is like that sir. Once we scale up, we need to keep finding business for our engineers. India pioneered software offshoring services business. The better companies have had an increasing foreign business year on year. Between 2000 and 2003 the industry's foreign business has more than doubled," replied Ajay.

Actually,the big companies grew their exports over the last 3 years by 30 to 40 % year on year.

Dagariya more assertive than sensitive was not mentally prepared to be patient and think through. He had answer for anything. "I think all companies have their ups and downs. In years of success, and we have had good successes, a bad year is nothing much to worry about. In our case, one bad year has hit us hard. I did not think much about it as the industry was going great guns. But I am afraid our bad year has been disastrous," added Dagariya.

"I have been auditing all kinds of businesses for the past 20 years and understand the anatomy of sickness. Companies do not become sick so easily and not by themselves and often made sick. Of course, we are not talking about sickness of our Company. We need to solve our problem ourselves. If we are not quick we will have to close our doors and you people will be on the road."

"Maybe other internal matters combined making the situation bad. I don't believe they are not solvable and we need to get back to our old ways of winning," concluded Dagariya.

"Sir, the impact of a poor pipeline means fewer projects and more people idling. The cost of projects goes up, because requests for additional labor are happily accepted. There is pressure to find work for idling engineers. Unless the Project Manager refuses, labor dumped on him. Not only cost of projects go up our overheads also rise."

"What do you think we should do?"

"We need to revamp our HR Department. We need to induct managers that are more professional and give them freedom. We have to write a statement about our culture and way of working beyond the Development Handbook, followed rigorously by engineers and managers after a MC buy in. This needs supervision by senior managers. This needs their time. Unfortunately, our managers do that what is just enough to complete work on hand. They have never stretched. Neither there was any incentive nor was it ever demanded."

"An exercise needs to done to match businesses we are running after and its possibilities, and the skill sets required. Our existing labor and future requirements worked out and then recruitment plans devised. This will help us charting technical training requirements and cultural sensitivity trainings," replied Ajay.

Dagariya showed his annoyance again. Unable to hide the scowl on his face he was silently saying he was at his wits ends. In the ensuing struggle of wills, Ajay marveled how complex a person Dagariya was with his fingers in many businesses. Ajay's suspicion of the weak intensity of Dagariya's care for the company became stronger. The firm was for his vanity. Whatever he wanted from it, he had received in ample measure. Recognition, power, position, foreign travel, money, government invitations and all these opened doors.

He had entry into many influential business and software circles. His friends included builders, politicians, civil servants and film personalities. In spite of all this, was the company a front for illegal business? After enjoying this, why did he have illegal business? The company was a talking point for him and it stoked his vanity. It was 8 years old and no one knew how many other businesses he had. His accountancy and auditing business was 20 years old.

It was quiet. In the silence, the only sound was that of the air conditioner. Ajay ventured, "Sir, my Chacha told me that you had someone contact him and he took him around Hamirpur. Anything finalized?"

"No, we have not finalized anything yet. My purpose is to buy over 100 acres anything up to 50 kilometers from Hamirpur and if it is agricultural land all the better. Your Chacha knows everything. He is a resourceful man. I have no idea of what I will do over there immediately. Nevertheless, with time, some visits and knowing people possibilities suggest themselves. It will appreciate no doubt."

Ajay became bolder and asked, "Sir you must be having land at other places too. How did you get interested in Hamirpur?"

"Hamirpur is not far from my ancestral place Lakshman Nagar in the District of Jodhpur." Hearing Lakshman Nagar, Ajay's ears pricked up. "My father left Lakshman Nagar in 1922 and moved to Jodhpur. However, we maintained a fair sized house in Lakshman Nagar. We would visit our house once a year and spent a month or so. I had been going to Lakshman Nagar until the last 4 years. When we did, we went for a few days every year. One cannot forget one's ancestral place. "

"Yes sir, what you say is the essence of culture and belongingness. I agree with you fully. I go to my hometown every few months, no matter how busy I might be. I take out time and organize my works to spend a week at home," replied Ajay.

"I never got to know you and your real life. All I know about you are the stories I hear in the office," Ajay requested.

"I finished my accountancy in 1964 in Jodhpur. My father got me employed with an auditing firm in Bangalore. He knew the partners. Bangalore was a small town then maybe as big as Jodhpur. Jodhpur was a concentrated urban entity but Bangalore spread out. It had a large military presence followed by public sectors occupying huge spaces."

"I worked for 15 years here. I found lodging in Richards Town, an Anglo Indian neighborhood. Getting accommodation was difficult for an unmarried male. Richards Town was famous for non-vegetarian eatinghouses. I am a strict vegetarian but managed for 4 years and after marriage moved to Malleshwaram, a strict vegetarian area. It was then and still is a South Indian elitist neighborhood."

"In 1980 I partnered with two elder Anglo Indian Chartered Accountants whom I had known from my Richards Town days. It was not doing well. My Anglo Indian partners because of their children's plodding immigrated to Australia and left the firm to me in 1984. I got new partners, changed the name and we put our heart and soul and soon had 5 branches. I was earning much more than our needs. I began investing in other businesses. They were my clients. I wanted to increase my wealth without dirtying my hands," continued Dagariya sharing his life story.

"Sir, you must have been busy with little spare time. What made your attachment to Lakshman Nagar? There must have been memories that brought you to Lakshman Nagar so often," responded Ajay.

"My childhood memories of Lakshman Nagar and my family are strong and will never leave me," whispered Dagariya.

"Yes Sir, some of our childhood memories and desires take such a strong hold on us that we connect many of our activities to them. Wise people say that personal growth requires to routinely shedding the weight of our old remembrances. I think it is not easy to do that. You have had a rich life full of adventures, seen and learnt much and so successful," replied Ajay.

It touched and moved Dagariya.

"I was ten when my grandfather told me about Mohar Singh. This was at the end of eighteenth century. Mohar Singh had become a legend. His abode called Mohar Palace. It was a large mud house. The Mohar Palace had many rooms, verandahs, kitchens, bathing rooms and tanks for storing water. There were covered and open gymnastic areas with instruments for building physical strength peculiar to its time and a wrestling pit out in the open. There were gardens and agricultural land spreading outside the palace. After his death people recalled Mohar Singh as a dacoit, a thug, a soldier, a pious spiritual person, a religious reformer, a wrestler, a lawgiver, a rogue and even a raja."

"What he meant to you depends on who you were and your sentiments. For me Mohar Singh was a childhood hero. Mothers invoked him to inspire fear in unruly children. Physical culturists spoke of his strength and the shape of his body. The public for miles around spoke of his munificence. In his palace, the kitchen fires lit at six in the morning. They continued to burn until midnight. Those who came to his palace seeking food or shelter never turned away. He settled disputes of people for miles around once every month. Many men and women were in his service some lived in his palace while others scattered in villages around."

"There were rumors that childless women came to him for a child. There were stories that their husbands and keepers could not satisfy a woman who had slept with him. He never looked at or touched a woman in his palace. Women begged him and if he felt, he visited them at their places. His visits to other houses was considered good and worthy of respect. It was never talked about."

"I am talking of 1820, give or take 5 years."

"Nobody knew from where he came. There were many stories. Of these, the most plausible one was that he was a *baghi* [outlaw]. People who committed robberies with assault were thugs and dacoits. Committing crimes against the English rulers and rebelling against the British government called *baghis*. When he arrived in Lakshman Nagar, he was probably 25 years old or so. A big made man, he commanded respect by his mere appearance. He used to sleep in the open and eat what the poor folks could give him. He never asked, he never talked to anyone. After some years he became a fixture in the village, children ventured to come out and look at him from a distance. Then one day he called them and after a few attempts, they came and stood before him. They were afraid as well as curious. He began telling them stories. Then the village head gave him a piece of land and he built a hut and lived there and never mixed with anyone and kept to himself."

"One day he left his hut and returned after a couple of months later with half a dozen people. During this period, something drastic had happened. When he returned, his head and mustache had become snow white in color. After that, he rarely shaved and once a while, he had his beard and mustache trimmed. People from miles around referred to him as Mohar. Most often people would attach *Chacha* [father's brother] or *Mama* [sister's brother] to his name. He and his men had strong horses and they would go out on them, traveling for miles."

"What transpired after he returned with other men was astonishing. Mohar and his gang started acquiring pieces of land around. In many cases, people sold their land to him and became sharecroppers on the same land. How he was able to acquire these lands, we do not know but only conjecture after knowing the social scene of those times. He treated his sharecroppers as of his own family. Woe beto the man who crossed him. Over the years, his lands ran into many hundreds of acres. As years passed, he would pray and undertake penance, exercise and wrestle, listen to people and help them out and dispense justice. Whoever came to his door never returned unsatisfied."

"How did this saga end? In what ways did Mohar fascinate you?"

"Leadership! His leadership extended over everyone and in all things that mattered during those days. His traits, morals, awareness and sensibility together habbits He achieved much and without shouting or coercing people. He extracted loyalty, which came from the power of his personality. Being a Marwari, we are by instinct merchants. To build an empire running to thousands of acres of land and without any rebellion was remarkable. He made the law, which may not have been in conformance with the law of the land, but people accepted it. His strength was extraordinary and there were many stories about his feats. I admired his restlessness which drove him to colossal achievements," admitted Dagariya.

What began as an attempt to break the stillness of silence or to divert his mind became a new level of intimacy. That went beyond an owner and an employee. Was it that important? Did it evoke an added loyalty? Then the brief discomfort between them righted and it was as usual.

Ajay told him about his venture. He briefly outlined Elegant Automation Software.

Sharing his plans, he concluded that every person carried responsibilities. He had a responsibility to himself and his maker to test the limits of his potentials and give the world the best he could. After he got it off his chest, he felt better. There was no guilt. No sense of betrayal. Nothing!

Dagariya let loose a torrent of questions, "When will you open the doors of your firm? Do you need money? Would you like me to invest in your firm? Is there anything you want from me?" Then finally came, the words, "I hate to see you go!"

Ajay promised Dagariya his availability and explained that his venture did not require a big amount to start with. However, if he fell short he would come to him. Giving the same reasons he gave to Asha. He had worked out the terms and conditions for loans. Ajay concluded, "Sir, it is not business in the normal way but a passion that I am pursuing."

Dagariya asked Ajay to explain the money angle of his venture to Joshi ji. Joshi ji would make meticulous notes of what he told him and send it to the Chairman.

Wishing him success, they parted.

Ajay returned to his seat, reviewing his life in the company and his relationship with Dagariya concluded. Mahesh and Sushma Dagariya would always harbor a grudge against him. They would think that after picking him up from the street, they had given him the opportunity and he betrayed their trust. They went out of their way to help him create a new personality. In addition, they kept creating opportunities and earning situations for him. Yes, that was true. He had brought success for the company and for himself entirely on his own. This was equally true. They would think he had been ungrateful. If they knew, what he was up to they would be livid with rage.

Value for life in India has always been little unless you are part of the elite. Elite are those who have power to get their way. Life has little value if you are powerless. The elite could do no wrong and get away with murder. Being poor, helpless, friendless, or ignorant were all components of weakness. For a moment, he felt afraid for Asha and then it passed. He would like to believe the masthead of the popular newspaper "Truth alone Triumphs" knowing inside it was a lie told day after beguiling its readers. Was he being too idealistic?

When the powerful decide to oppress the defenseless there is nothing that the powerful would not do. He had seen it often and Indians at rare times become most cruel. A country's cultural roots lie in their mythological works. Did not some incidents in our mythologies speak of abominable cruelty?

What level could the Dagariya's stoop to? Sushma could be vindictive by her upbringing. Could she be graceful in her vindictiveness? When the truth of Lakshman Investments and Financial Consultancy comes out everything would change. Ajay was not fixated on changing Dagariya and their business empire but bound on establishing justice or dharma as he said.

There was a message from Vijay Bahula to see him. He drove to the Income Tax department on the Queens Road. Bahula handed him a light green cloth backed envelope. The envelope sealed all round with cellophane tape making it look secret and secure.

Bahula gave him a rundown of what had emerged from the break in. Another company name board found inside similar to the one fixed outside. Both were small and inconspicuous in design that Asha had discovered. A picture of it printed on a white paper that Bahula said was in the sealed envelope. Letter heads, seals, balance sheets of some companies from the list and a daybook perhaps in code. The day book was a ledger recording incoming and outgoing transactions for the day in coded letters. This began from fiscal 1999, indicating that the racket was at least that old if not more. There were a few reams of green colored legal papers. A boxful of visiting cards with different names some with addresses. The rest were without addresses. There was a bunch of non-judicial stamp papers and a strong envelope containing revenue stamps.

"The cabin furnished like that of a big official's with a trick lock on the door and a safe behind a large painting of a rural setting in a desert. The people who broke in are experts and on a glance make out what is or could be. Breaking the safe without a proper search warrant would be illegal and would have created problems so not touched," said Bahula.

"There were two PC's, one printer, a UPS, filing cabinet and all the paraphernalia of an office. From the inspection of the pantry, they could conclude there were no women in the office. A shredding and two xerox machines were in the pantry hidden behind the door. There was a register where each day's office opening and closing recorded with a statement of anything unusual. The statement was in pencil and written in Hindi."

"Most likely written by Joshi ji," exclaimed Ajay. Bahula heard Ajay and kept his counsel. He nodded his head to convey that he had heard Ajay.

"There were black plastic carry bags with a closing plastic strip with an in built lock. Once the bag was sealed, it was not possible to open without tearing it."

"The cleaner who cleaned the office was well paid and they made no effort to ask her anything. The neighbors spoke of a quiet office where the workers kept to themselves. No one had any complaint or could remember anything unusual had ever happened."

There were two motorcycles parked in the garage.

"After talking to the men who did the job, I feel there had to be a few people who would have worked throughout the day to complete daily tasks. The number of daily entries in the day book indicates that there had to be three or four people. Each entry entered into the computer. It was printed and coded by hand and then entered into the day book. The original destroyed. Only trained people could do this job. They had to be loyal and discreet. They may be his relatives or carefully selected," explained Bahula.

Bahula pushed the envelope on the table towards Ajay. He explained, "In this are specimens, xerox copies and photographs. You will find a list containing or describing what I am telling you. It is quite comprehensive to make a case if you care to."

There was complete silence. The noise of the traffic outside and the fan were the only witness to their conversation.

Bahula then surprised him, "I have a letter made as if from you. Just sign it and we will take up the case and you do not have to pay anything. If it leads to conviction you would be rewarded."

He did not know what to say. Being overwhelmed would be an understatement. "Will it be your Department that will carry out the investigations?" asked Ajay.

"If there is any foreign exchange violation we involve the Enforcement Directorate," replied Bahula.

Ajay, "I would be to glad that you take it up. However, Sir, do not force me to sign any paper. In 5 minutes, I will walk out of your chambers having forgotten we ever met. I don't want any reward."

Driving back to the office he decided to update Asha. He realized that Asha's life had been one of great challenge and she was far stronger than she cared to admit.

The rapidness and her misgivings, she had tried to bottle, stunned her. She quickly recovered her composure and said, "I am sure that Abdul Dalwai said meet Mr. Joshi at Lakshman Investments and Financial Consultancy on Ali

Asker Road. Does he sit there? I do not think he spends much time there. He does not have the sophistication required of such dealings. He is too greedy. Does Dagariya not pay him enough?"

"Joshi ji must be visiting Lakshman Investments and Financial Consultancy offices sometimes perhaps a few times a week. If he notates out of the ordinary happenings he must be in the office or ask a trusted and trained staff for details. He may have one who had the instinct to identify the exceptional of the ordinary. Three sigma spread would mean out of a thousand transactions only one or two needed to investigated. Those he put down Joshi ji would investigate therefore he need to spend an hour or two weekly, "whispered Ajay.

"The staff that he trusted had to sift these happenings. These are notes cannot be delayed by more than 48 hours. It had to be written as near to the time of occurrence and investigated immediately," reasoned Ajay.

"Ajay, this trusted man will also fall sick, take leave therefore there must have been a backup," insisted Asha.

Answering, "In which case Joshi ji attended the office on those days," completed Asha.

Concurring Ajay added, "If this gang took such extraordinary precautions and after Joshi ji's investigation anything suspicious dealt so that no trace was left."

"Yes these notes and Joshi ji's investigation must have been recorded and not casually destroyed?" questioned Asha.

"Exactly! You think Dagariya read them?" countered Ajay.

"Sure he must be seeing them occasionally if not regularly," explained Asha.

"Which means he must be visiting Lakshman Investments and Financial Consultancy on Ali Asker Road? I am sure he does go there even if rarely," added Asha.

Ajay cautioned, "He will be going there rarely. If this is hidden place why should he risk himself being seen there?"

"True! Joshi ji made notes to keep Dagariya informed."

Before Asha could complete, Ajay added, "This way Dagariya could also keep an eye on Joshi ji."

Knowing Dagariya, they reasoned that he would not do any dirty work himself and he would have it done. Since he had implicit faith and trust in Joshi ji, Joshi ji was the ideal person. Here was an instance when brief entries assumed importance and became a proof of their complicity. Dalwai had specifically mentioned meeting Joshi. Therefore, it tied up.

They wondered if Joshi and Dagariya promoted some builders. Dagariya may not be promoting any builder but he could in league with a builder or builders. He could have parked his money with the builder. If a buyer of a flat advised to contact, Lakshman Investments and Financial Consultancy who would identify a builder willing to sell a flat at a discount if part of the payment made in cash. Thus, 90 % of visitors must have been buyers of flats or anything Dagariya did to help people convert black into white money.

Chimed Asha, "Both the builder and buyer gained. Surely, the Lakshman Investments and Financial Consultancy too would benefit. Maybe the Consultancy got a percentage of the flat value. Realtors get a commission. Here it was a bigger and more comprehensive deal."

Ajay's sense of rightness awoke, "All gain but the government losses!"

Asha said, "I strongly feel that Dalwai doesn't know Dagariya Sir. Surely, since the time I have known him, he would have mentioned something or hinted indirectly about it. He and Sushma have been advising me to buy a flat for long. We have talked many times about it. Neither did I sense any connection from Dalwai's conversation."

"Remember me telling you Dalwai visiting Bangalore

and staying at my hotel in Ooty?" Asha reminded Ajay. As Ajay nodded Asha continued, "He never met Dagariya, though I asked him if I could set up a meeting for him."

"Which means Dalwai knows Dagariya's benami company converting black money to white for flat buyers and maybe others, but does not know Dagariya, "summed up Ajay.

"Yes he knows the company as a professional in the field. There may be many more such operations in the country," swore Asha.

"Yes what you say looks right. Maybe Dalwai does not know Dagariya. He got this information for you. Amongst builders, this information would be an open secret. Passed on discretely to known people. "

"Is that so? All right, I will call Dalwai Sahib. Have I not to thank him?"Asha said.

The suspicions of illegalities leading to Dagariya were worrying. Schemes hatched in Asha's hotel between Dagariya and unknown people were intriguing. Only illegal reasons must be there for these clandestine meetings but could embroil the hotel and mar its reputation. The Company would lose its goodwill that it had acquired in 8 years of its existence. The sadness of a sinking company to which the employees had given so much and their uncertain future worried Ajay no end. Dagariya had been kind and helpful to both Ajay and Asha that made them feel guilty. His strong sense of moral and ethical behavior wracked his mind and gave him no peace. These were troubling matters and not to be trifled. Ajay tormented with a sense of betrayal and tortured with uncertainty, however he must carry his investigations to conclusion and find the root from where evil sprouted.

If Mahesh Dagariya helped, people convert black into white or launder money it was criminal. Moving unaccounted money in and out of the country through his shell companies was worst. It was treason. He was angry that he had worked for him for five years without the remotest of suspicion. Now these were fears and he wished they were false but they added to his confusion and to maintain peace of mind he must find out.

Exorcising the evil had become important, as important as his venture. He prepared himself to handle both together.

Ajay knew the problems the Company was facing. He believed he knew how and why they had started. He believed they were resolvable. Nevertheless, if his suspicions came out to be true there were would be only one way to salvage the company.

The Company had to pull through not for Dagariya but for the interests of hundreds of employees' wellbeing.

He could walk away but that would question his integrity and akin to forgetting the last five years of his life. It might be easy to think that way but it would leave him with a gaping hole in his heart. A load that he would carry for the rest of his life knowing he did nothing.

The world would forget the closure of the company as another incident, but his soul would not. He would carry the guilt knowing he let the forces of evil triumph and did nothing to let the forces of good salvage what could be. No, he would not let evil triumph.

Ajay understood what Agnes meant when she quoted Calvin Coolidge's Presidential Inaugural Address, "If we expect others to rely on our fairness and justice we must show that we rely on their fairness and justice."

That settled his turmoil. He learnt to never leave conflicts open. Resolve them as soon as possible.

Chapter XVIII
Beginning of the End

The news spread like a wild fire. Venkataraman had left. Venkataraman had not reported for a week. He was officially on leave. Old timers in the company could not recall when was the late time he was on leave for more than 3 days. There must be more reasons than what met the eye. The rumor mill attributed his absence to differences with Dagariya. It had been simmering underneath for some time but no one had a whiff of it. Even Asha who had many sources in the company could not conclusively say what was true.

The old timers swore that if he left, the company would be in a big mess. Venkataraman had a dignified demeanor and professor like mannerisms. He had a total grip on the company's operations even if he was unable to change things he would have liked to. Dagariya, his senior partner had brought him in with unwritten rules and with time defanged him. Venkataraman was happy running the operations and had a free hand barring situations that had accounting implications. These were minor pinpricks.

Not that Dagariya knew much about situations Venkataraman handled. Dagariya goaded by some of his embedded employees and favorites to financial powers rest with Joshi ji. If they could not get his ear, they could bring pressure on him through Sushma. These cronies imagined they were exercising power. Venkataraman knew these shenanigans of the dirty dozen as he called them. He knew more engineers than anyone in the company. He was up to date with who was up to what with whom and since when.

In the evening Ajay met Sarkar who shared his apprehensions the way the company was going. It was perhaps not the right time. Ajay was adamant to tell him but not let him in into his venture. It could not wait. It was already late. Sarkar had been hearing bits and pieces and he had taken them to be an outpouring of an idealistic person but here he was ready to take off. Sarkar reflected on the change he had seen over the now determined young man he first met 5 years ago as a shy, awkward, unsure and gawky lad. It rankled that it was his effort,that got him into the company. He failed to acknowledge that he had received a lot from Ajay in return. He could and gave Sarkar a lot - whenever and whatever he asked. Yes, Ajay had learned fast. He had been lucky but hard working as well, admitted Sarkar.

He could not help comparing himself with Ajay. Of course, he grabbed every opportunity that came his way. Opportunities are always there big, small and the one in a lifetime. It was very different from what he had expounded earlier. Putting your finger on the right one is what matters. What is right for you may not be right for someone else. Sarkar wanted and pursued business ideas for a piece for himself. To all he was a votary of entrepreneurship who took pains to inspire others. He imagined opportunities where there was none.

In his innocence, Sarkar advocated and thrust these

opportunities on people he cared for. He was scheming, deliberate and counting his gains all the time. Ajay was trusting to a point of being naïve. Ajay gave, helped and sympathized without ever thinking of anything in return. For Sarkar any contribution was an investment. Sarkar thought the way Ajay's career had developed he could be as big a businessperson as Dagariya in a few years' time. Sarkar admitted that he was successful too, but detesting to admit in an insignificant way. He was confident that if he ever asked for a favor or a request, Ajay would oblige.

Ajay's refusal to take any business partner made sense, as his venture was a personal passion. He was unwilling to share risk until proven. His was an untried business model. Nothing in business is right unless it delivers results and this was what Ajay wanted to prove with his model. Sarkar admitted that Ajay had a right to do so.

People when confronted with new thinking other than conventional wisdom are willing to look at it academically but when it comes to making investments many find flaws to back out. Sarkar was on the fence as he generally was in situations that had yet to turn around. How in his estimate the cookies would crumble decided his position. No one knows that. A good entrepreneur believes that he will succeed. Ajay knew Sarkar well but did not like to make his story that would force him to take the position Sarkar wanted. He would be objectively fair.

When Sarkar said that all start-ups were a passion, Ajay choose not to answer knowing that his answer would not find agreement. However, both knew that business was people. People skills counted more in some businesses than technical brilliance. Executive success came more from inter-personal skills than managerial or technical abilities. They were important but without people skills, they are ineffective. Ajay's was a skill-based project where he was the company, which Sarkar would not understand.

For Ajay educating the customer was a part of his business. He believed the customer should feel his passion and if he did not, he was willing to forgo business. His promise on his website articulated it and found its way into the product. It was his duty to do the right things and from there it would be a work of art and delight the customer. Was he being naïve?

He felt unpleasantness creep into the conversation. Sattva obstructed. It was not flowing. Ashutosh could not appreciate his beliefs. In his search for excellence, his tireless efforts to create Sattva that had led him to his venture. His success was certain, he believed. His modesty constrained him and refused to say it vigorously. Sarkar was blocking Sattva.

He first heard Sattva from his tutor Pandit Badri Dutt Pandey. He was 12 and his tutor told him that when you helped someone you generated Sattva. It was as simple as that. This also happened whenever you were altruistic. The learned Pandit explained that Sattva was something like sap that flowed in the tree from the roots upwards. It nourished the tree and kept it healthy and alive. Belief in this notion enabled the believer to discover possibilities in forms, creation, dispersal and its impact. It was health, vitality, happiness and joyfulness. Nature in the form of rain or sunshine or gravity had no favorites. They were the same and equal for all. When you were in harmony with yourself, people and things around you created Sattva.

When you encounter Sattva, its presence resonates in the envelope around you. It calms and reconciles the contradictions in your mind. Sattva helps us understand the impermanence of everything. It helps us coming to terms with the inevitability of ending or dying. Without Sattva life could get unbearable and full of contradictions and inabilities. This leads to stress and tensions. Knowing and acknowledging the temporariness of everything influences, touches and moves us.

Sattva is in 'Elegant Programming' that is complex and simultaneously simple. Sattva is in a great piece of music or a film and in beauty. Any of these could be simple or painfully created. Its strength lies in minimalism, loneliness, simplicity and it is universality.

Sattva moves and inspires us because it is pure, innocent and elegant. It is also beauty, which our minds and hearts are forever searching. Our sensibilities are constantly reaching out for it.

It was confusing for Sarkar. Ajay was an unfortunate person, thought Sarkar for here was a man oblivious to the oncoming collapse of the company he worked in. He had the gumption of starting a venture with a business and a development model nobody had heard of. God knows how long he would have to wait to see money and by the time it came, he might not be solvent. Here, was Ajay sitting without a care in the world. No sir, he would not join him rather keep away.

Sarkar, "Ajay, I admire you and wish you the best. If there is anything I could do for you, never hesitate to ask."

"Yes, I know I can count on you. Someday you will be connected with this venture in some form."

Sarkar's low spirits warmed and they parted.

At night, he was surprised to receive a call from Venkataraman. They had never been overtly friendly. They had respect for each other, which comes from professionally knowing each other's work even after not having worked together. When Venkataraman first met Ajay, he thought he was Dagariya's man. When he realized Ajay was an independent person, they warmed up to each other. "You may have heard the rumors that I have left or resigned. I am unhappy with developments here and find no reason to stay here. You are the only person in the company I have spoken to on the subject."

Ajay said, "Sir, I have always admired you. If there is any person who can save this company then it is you". After a pause he added, "Are you leaving?"

"Accounts have been falsified. The company has potential. Mr. Dagariya maintains accounts audited. There is nothing I can do about the accounts in spite that they do not represent the correct picture of the Company's working. If I stay, I become an accomplice, and subject to blackmail. I am first a 20 % partner and then an employee. What would you have done if you were me?" asked Venkataraman in anguish.

"Sir you have a standing in the industry. You can go wherever you want and whenever you want. You can also create a new company and get the right people and finances."

"With your experience and knowledge you could set up a consulting outfit. I am also leaving to start a business of mine," added Ajay.

Rumors of his venture had begun circulating in the company. Venkataraman had probably heard it. "That's good news. Let's meet today or tomorrow,"echoed Venkataraman and signed off.

Those were shattering news. Too much was happening at a bewildering pace.

As he switched off the lights, he reminded himself of meeting Mythili early morning when she finished her night shift.

He dreamt of flock of peacocks strutting and dancing and their plumage a riot of colours. They were dancing now and the next moment they walked past him in a single file. The breeze wafted across the fields of wheat and the stalks bent as the wind rustled over them. This was a recurring dream of 6 to 8 peacock in a row marching in a military fashion. His mother and Chacha believed that when you have this dream it presages something momentous. Some amazing things are to happen and promise to affect people close to you. In the village folklore, peacocks represent confidence and success. He woke up thinking as if he had just slept and when he saw the time, he rushed driving to Mythili's college.

As they ate their breakfast in Mythili's canteen, she perked up hearing the details of his venture.

Mythili's professional experience was limited to being a house surgeon. She spent 18 hours a week in the pediatrician clinic of the hospital. She had the making of a successful hospital staff. She was friendly with the senior doctors. They taught her about their profession and professional success. She knew that professional growth required adventuring outside your comfort zone. She had noticed this streak in Ajay from their first meeting. Both were curious and grateful for professional ideas no matter where they came from. They were ever ready to help others and made them their good friends. While she had little opportunities for seeking those professional experiences, Ajay mentioned in having traveled far in professional friendships. In the medical profession unlike software, they came with age and regurgitating one's experiences.

One learnt easily and quickly what was within 3 sigma limits. Confronting novel or complicated medical situations was real experience. Cases when outcomes were likely to be beyond the normal distribution, percentages were the challenges and learning. Learning experiences take time to come in any profession. This was priceless. Mythili knew she was a good student and could cram huge volumes of information. Extrapolating them with new insights, she knew it would make her a good practitioner.

Listening toAjay who was stretching his neck and trying out things, which inspired a few, and stake a claim for his belief was inspiring. She had seen it happening before her eyes and if he achieved the success he was aiming,there would be stories written on his life.. Software engineers were forever in competition and conflict, while the physician fraternity was closer and helping.

She recalled when she enrolled for her MD; she had demanded to be his best friend and wanted his support. When she encountered difficulties she reached for him and he responded by being at her side. He would hear her and ask pointed questions and solutions emerged by itself. Whenever she had been remarkably successful, she would celebrate with him.

When he took the stand of being one of the best 'Elegant programmers' in the world he found a purpose in life. There was no risk, no hardship he would not take, no sacrifices he was not ready to make to achieve what he set out to. Most people would call Ajay idealistic and unaware of the practical side of business. She knew in her heart that he would sail through safely. Her eyes moist, she realized that professional excellence could make one as happy as anything else could. She squeezed his hand saying that she would always be there for him. Promising to call her father, he left.

It seemed to be a long day. Driving towards the office, he called Venkataraman and suggested they meet, as no one was sure of their time. He asked him to come to meet him in the lobby of the Oberoi hotel. There was Venkataraman waiting for him and they decided to sit in the small garden that provided privacy. They sipped coffee and Venkataraman replied, "I am in a bit of a spot," reverting to his Americanism. "I lose if I quit and I also lose if I stay. I know the company is under challenge and I doubt if Mr. Dagariya can turn it around. We have had 150 people leave in 5 months and our reputation in the IT industry does not help."

Ajay responded, "Sir, have you not thought of starting your business?"

"It needs lots of thinking, planning and contacting people. I am sure you would not have decided to launch, if you had not planned to great detail, without at least 2 or 3 commitments."

"Yes. I have two customers who agreed to give me jobs the day I start within 6 weeks of request. I have another party who is ready to offload many small jobs after my initial success. I worked for long time for these commitments," replied Ajay.

"I am damn sure these must be American customers. No other country support companies the way the Americans support the new business models or new ways of doing things. It is the sense of adventure and if you know what Americans mean by being a frontiersman you will appreciate what I am saying. No matter how strong perceived and promised values and benefits the notion of doing it the first time and newness applauded. The Americans have been responsible for the most breakthroughs in technology and application engineering. They are open and patient with new ways of doing a business including funding."

Both forgot for a moment that America was commerce, commerce and more commerce.

Ajay nodded and added, "I have two strong prospects. One has promised to release an order within a week of my website coming up and to clinch the other I may have to go and see them."

Venkataraman added, "That's great. You know, companies in US with new offerings can have a long life though the initial year or six months set the tone. Respectable first year, good happy customers, proven ability will keep you solvent. You survive and fulfill your dream but at a big cost. That is all. Only in exceptional cases think of big money, big company and marquee customers. Did I disappoint you?"

"India is no place for ventures of your kind. All

ventures are set up to make money and if it does not then the venture will suffocate and die. Of these, few built on idealism. It may range from getting together like-minded people to try out an idea or go deep in your urge to be different, reorder industry, create a new market to personal idiosyncrasies etc. Of course you can establish them anywhere in the world but the American environment is the best for them to sprout. The American civilization is built on innovation," continued Venkataraman.

Venkataraman added, "I wish you success and think you will survive. Growing it will take luck and the good will of your stakeholders like all new businesses. In your case, they will be more than what goes for new businesses. I think you are on the threshold of finding the meaning of your life. It is an asymptotic point in life's journey. The curve of your ambitions and that of death meet only when you are enlightened. One-day one curve will explode. That is the motivation for adventurers."

"India has too many problems which it must solve in its quest to become an achieving society and innovators here need to tackle these problems. Global problems invite a different breed of people, "concluded Venkataraman.

"Thank you for your encouragement. Being honest creates opportunities. When you create Sattva, people will come to your aid, be it customers, employees, advocacy groups and so on. I am never afraid," replied Ajay.

Venkataraman had no answer. Not only was it naïve but against the grain of business he surmised. Privately he was willing to accept hair brained projects and way out ideas. Sensational schemes succeed sometimes. Failing to acknowledge that many schemes like these had been the source that inspired progress in the world was one's limitation of thought and vision. The meeting was more about explaining positions than anything explosive, the purpose they thought of the meeting. Venkataraman asked himse lf that is why they had met.

Ajay intruding broke into his thoughts rudely, “Sir, what have you decided to do? Is there anything you would like me to do for you?”

“I have a job offer as the Chief of TCS, Hyderabad branch. Anything else I will have to generate. Please keep this conversation to yourself.”

Ajay did not want to hurt Venkataraman by saying it was going down career-wise. TCS, Hyderabad was just a 150-engineer stop. They talked about the company when Ajay asked, “Sir what sort of falsification did you find?”

“Payment terms of overseas projects were not in favor of the company. There were two contracts, which were due to Samir Arora. I am sure of that because our engineers provided all the technical support including support for price negotiations. Abruptly, there was silence. I was certain of winning because I had a long conversation with the prospect’s CEO. Won and sold to another Indian company. I suspect some domestic and overseas projects sold on a percentage. That percentage never entered the book of accounts. Some non-existent expenses, commissions to unauthorized persons were also there. I think they were his household and entertainment expenses. It will be difficult to find proof or have them checked. Asking Mr. Dagariya for a check will make things ugly,” answered Venkataraman.

“I did not want to create ugly scenes, but I know that Dagariya should be confronted. He has all the jokers in his hand and I am not that kind of a person to pick fights.”

Ajay was not surprised after all he had unearthed about Dagariya and happy that there were people like Venkataraman who were principled in their professional and personal lives.

Ajay thought that this information should beconveyed to Bahula. Summoning courage Ajay asked, “How did you come to this conclusion, Sir? Who told you?"

Venkataraman blurted out that he had suspicions about falsification of accounts for more than a year. "Mr. Dagariya had such a grip on billing, collections and purchases with his handpicked people. No one could get information including me. Joshi ji's department supplied information but it was something I did not need or could not decipher it. Then I stopped querying until a smart trainee FCA of the company's external auditor let me on. She happened to be the daughter of a good friend of mine."

More information for Bahula, thought Ajay. Ajay put a proposition, "Sir, if you like you could become a consultant to my company. You are welcome, but I will pay your professional fees when I can."

They had hearty laugh and agreed to keep in touch, and parted. Venkataraman volunteered that he would be pleased to steer his contacts in USA and Canada towards Ajay. He could traction them as he thought best.

It was the beginning of the day. Bahula's SMS reached Ajay when he was pulling out of the parking lot. In the fitness of things, it was wiser to use cell sparingly with Bahula. Ajay was with him in half an hour. Bahula pressed the bell for the peon and asked him to get coffee. Bahula attended to a phone call and the peon returned with coffee.

As they sipped coffee, Bahula told him that the Commissioner was in Bangalore and he would like to see him. He was stunned. Within a week Bahula had done so much and subtly. His opinion about government changed. There were islands of excellence amidst drab and dreary government organizations. Then he explained, "The Commissioner likes to meet upright citizens. He conveys the government's gratitude. If he wants he could order a formal raid within hours."

Finishing the call Bahula told that they could meet

the Commissioner half an hour later. "You must be wondering why after my diploma from IIM, I chose to take up government services. I am not the only one there have been others. Their numbers are insignificant."

"I come from a moneyed family with deep roots in land. My father had great respect for the government and desired me to join the government for public service. Convinced that the government had gone wayward it needed honest people more than ever before to set it right. He passionately believed so and hence I joined the Department. My father was a Gandhian and a staunch nationalist who believed in public service. With independence he believed that good and humane government officials could make the country modern and prosperous like the European countries he had visited."

Waiting for it to take effect Bahula said, "I believe poverty is our biggest problem as well as challenge."

"I learnt from my father and his brother that money could do many things but not all things. Many things happen quickly enough and then what do you do. Many of them rarely bring happiness and fulfilment. It takes you near to it. There is a fork there. It could make you terribly unhappy or make you greedy and acquisitive. Neither is good for the soul."

"Learn to be happy with whatever you have and wherever you are," my father exhorted. "Happiness is condition less. You do not go looking for happiness. It is within you. Still your mind and you will find it. An agitated mind is restless. Unrest comes from a feeling of inadequacy and unfilled desires."

"Instead of wanting and wishing for money and power, be satisfied with what you have. Be grateful for what you have. If you do not, you run the risk of becoming selfish. From selfishness arises covetousness and that is the road to ruination. Public service is God's service, he believed with Gandhi ji," said Bahula.

Bahula then took Ajay to see the Commissioner.

The Commissioner was a big built genial sort of a man in old classical attire. He wore a sweater under a brown suit with the old type tie with encouraging manners. He pushed his big puffy hand and shaking it, Ajay could not help notice the watch hanging from his lapel like in old period movies. Magnetically drawn by the Commissioner's piercing eyes, they bore through him.

After Ajay gave him more information, the Commissioner expressed his pleasure. He ordered Bahula to make a case file by evening and he would order investigation. They chatted for a few minutes and then the Commissioner closed the meeting.

Bahula took Ajay to his room requesting him to share any information he make come across which would be helpful. Once the investigation began, Bahula would not be sharing any information on the case.

Ajay related what Venkataraman had told him about selling foreign projects after winning to other Indian companies. He thought these were foreign exchange violations if not shown in the company's book of accounts it was criminal action inviting censure and relevant action.

He took it as his duty to get to the truth. Yes, he would do anything to unearth proofs that would lead to conviction. He believed this to be his moral duty.

Whatever happened later was not for him to bother about. Having done his bit as an upright citizen he would be able to concentrate on his venture fully. As he moved out of the IT Department he felt a load lift of his back. There was no one who could feel his relief. A demon born 3 weeks ago, had now been exorcised.

Ajay realized he had become a bloodhound.

Chapter - XIX
There is no Ending

Nothing ends. Even death does not mean the end. Transformation is a reality. It continues relentlessly. A massive transformation brought us into the world. As with our birth, the next greatest transformation will be when we die. Ajay's upbringing was about rebirth after death. This belief easily translated into his Phoenix moments. He believed strongly in continuity and conservation. The week would make and break fortunes of some.

The die cast. Nothing could hold him back. He was on the verge of his momentous moment. Ajay wanted success. His venture was all that mattered to him. He had broken and assembled, many times in his mind. It had to succeed. Success had become as vital as his own life. It was almost like 'bet everything on it' and even if it failed, he was ready to pick up the pieces of his life and begin anew. In the depths of his heart, he knew he would not fail. What made him so confident? He had staked his life on it.

He, when the need arose, could cut the Gordian knot neat and quick. He had done that many times in his life.

During these decisive moments, he did not consult or seek advice from anyone but followed his inner voice. He had let his venture germinate for long and now he was connecting all the dots and more.

It began with the belief that development of software as practiced was about money making first. Application software contracts drawn up in such a way that before a contract executed a part collected before start and in parts along the life cycle at various points until the end. Each collection ensured money collected was sufficient to complete the work of that phase until an invoice for the next part. This had become a worldwide practice. The supplier worked on the client's money. Everything else followed.

The implied rule was that problem solving followed moneymaking. Long life, maintainability and design that were adaptable to new situations were all secondary considerations and though all promised few delivered in breach. Rework could kill projects, teams and even companies. Prescient CEO's avoid rework like the plague. Ajay believed that software once deployed should be long-life, which meant being capable of accommodating changes. Changes were a reflection of the new realities and understanding. Such interventions should be quick, painless and inexpensive.

Not the one to wait for auspicious signs, he girded himself and moved with speed, eyes firm on the ground. He knew deep within what all had to be done to succeed. It was like a game now, and the pieces had been set on the board.

He was careful not to leave anything connected with his venture in the office. Next morning, Ajay rummaged through his papers and discovered the visiting card of Lalit Jaiswal. Lalit Jaiswal was the Marwari founder and senior partner of Jaiswal & Associates, an auditing and a consulting firm. He had met him when he had come to see Dagariya on a marketing call, seeking business.

As Ajay stood up to leave them to talk privately, Dagariya gestured Ajay to sit and introduced him to Lalit. It suited Dagariya to keep the meeting with Lalit Jaiswal short. He praised Ajay's work while Jaiswal informed them about his company. The consultancy apart from accounting and legal services provided 360-degree services for new companies in the software sector. His consulting outfit offered services from opening to accounting, auditing, legal to support to teaming arrangements. His son, who returned from UK after completing his management accounting degree, set up a consulting unit within which he catered to all needs of a startup.

That was two years ago and at that time the company could do no wrong. Chairman Dagariya considered his company to be another INFOSYS in the making. Jaiswal was a thorough professional with no sympathies for regional or linguistic identities. He left a strong impression on Ajay and he had made a mental note of his feelings for Jaiswal. He was in an ordinary business of consulting but what set him apart was the way he went out to extraordinary limits for a start from day one. That was extraordinary about Jaiswal. As they parted, Jaiswal shook Ajay's hand he said, "Our paths will cross again."

Getting him on the phone, he refreshed Lalit's memory of their meeting and asked him to handle the setting up of his company. Lalit invited him to his office on Sampige Road in Malleshwaram. Malleshwaram is an old part of the city with Nobel Prize winners, writers, sports persons, film and other celebrities living there. It is a cultural and religious hub and with growing wealth in the city spoke of knowledge, enterprise, wealth and hard work. Malleswaram's public spaces were under renovation. The locals were proud of the heritage that was visible every few yards.

Ajay pushed a three quarter sheet of paper describing his project, which pleased Lalit. Rarely a new client engaged, thus he mentioned, "Let me tell you what you have to do. My colleague will give you a more detailed printed statement and take your case. I think your timing is perfect. There could not be a more auspicious start with two clients. So many youngsters set up software companies without clients and half of them fail."

"You will have to register your company first. Without this, you cannot open a bank account for your business. Have you met any banker? Have you any preferred bank? After these work finish, we will go for acquiring statutory compliances," went Lalit in a machine gun like staccato.

Ajay softly replied, "No sir, I have not talked with any bank. Whatever you say I will do,"

Lalit buzzed the intercom and a young woman with a notebook and pencil entered the meeting room. After introducing Rekha, he quickly took leave saying that he had an out-of-office meeting. He was running late and that Rekha would prepare the Case Sheet for his assignment. He would catch up with him later. Perhaps that was the reason for his abruptness.

Rekha took over and asked him if he had selected a place for his company, "Have you leased it? Do you have property owner's permission to run your company from this location?"

Ajay explained that he had seen a cubicle in a business centre from where he planned to start. He wanted to start as a proprietorship concern and would be working alone for some time.

"I don't mind starting from my house itself," added Ajay.

Rekha had heard such requests but they came from unprepared entrepreneurs. Taken aback, she politely told him that he did not need consultancy to start a proprietorship concern. Nobody came there for that.

Ajay had to think fast. If he sought another accounting and legal consulting company, its advice may not be different. He could not seek Dagariya's counsel for he did not know where it might lead him. Time was the essence at this time. Finally, he realized there was no one else he could consult.

Rekha trying to be helpful said, "Proprietorship is a sole business and governed by the Karnataka State Shops and Establishment Act. Company registration under proprietorship will cost about Rs. 1,500 and you can do it yourself. Forming and registering a private company with a capital of Rs 3 to 5 lakhs may cost Rs. 20,000 to Rs. 25,000 inclusive of connected paperwork, sorting out landlord's consent and opening a bank account. If you are short of this amount you could bring it within 2 years."

Ajay was now ready for any form of company. Returning to get more information or wait to take a position would not be the right start. He wanted to leave, reassured that consultancy and company formation be started at once. Once done, timelines for other formalities would emerge, as Rekha would know from her experience what was practical and feasible.

"Sir, you already have a foreign client and most of your business will come from overseas. Your work will create intellectual property that you need to safeguard. Later you may decide to have foreign directors, you may have to offer bank guarantees in pursuance of foreign business. Not that you cannot get these through a proprietary concern, best achieved through a private limited company, which gives comfort to foreigners. I suggest you to form a private limited company not because we offer these services but it is good for you and your business," Rekha suggested.

It made no sense to seek time to think, these people had handled many start-ups, and he had to take a position now. When he thought of partners, he could only think of

Asha, Bhuvan, Mythili or her father, his mother and Chacha and the listended right at that. He turned to Rekha and asked, "Rekha, I have no partner and where will I get one?"

"Not to worry. Request Mr. Lalit. He may become your nominal partner. You can have a relative or anyone you trust as a nominal partner or partners. You can have hold of the 90 % and the rest by a nominal partner or partners. You can invest for them. If you ask Mr. Lalit, he may be able to help you lease a place as well."

"After completing this, what else will I have to do?" asked Ajay.

Rekha reading from a typed statement in front of her explained, "You will need to get a Certificate of Incorporation from the Registrar of Companies, Ministry of Corporate Affairs. Further, you need to register with a couple of government institutions like Value Added Tax (VAT) at the Commercial Tax Office, Professional Tax at the Profession Tax Office and a Professional Tax Account Number for Professional taxes deducted at source from employee's salary. These are necessary and we can get these registration and certificates within 4 weeks. You continue with your business. Their absence does not stop you from doing anything you want to in the name of your company."[13]

"There are other statutory compliances some of which would not apply to your business. Like registration for medical insurance at the regional office of the Employees' State Insurance Corporation; registration with the Office of Inspector, Shops, and Establishment Act with BBMP (Bangalore Bruhat Mahanagara Palike); receive Director Identification Number (DIN) online from the Ministry of Corporate Affairs; get digital signature certificate from the Ministry of Corporate Affairs. We can forget these."

"There is some other compliance which is necessary for you. These you could get later. You will need to get a

[13] *As they pertained in 2004*

Permanent Account Number (PAN) from the IT Department; get the company entered in the database maintained by the Registrar of Companies (ROC); stamp partnership deed at the State Treasury or bank authorized by the treasury. You can complete these within a year of start-up but we will do it for you over the next 6 to 8 weeks."

"No doubt, India is a difficult place to do business." They both laughed and Ajay asked her to get the place finalized and begin at earliest. How much would it take and what would be the total cost?"

"After incorporating your company we will get all these completed within 30 to 45 days and definitely within 8 weeks. Obtaining these approvals and compliances will cost you Rs 20,000 plus the fees incurred."

"Within Rs. 45,000," concluded Rekha.

"For some of this paper work, the payment under the table would be more than the prescribed cost."

As he was leaving, she asked him that what the name of his company was and if he preferred any bank. When he said 'Elegant Automation Software' pausing after each word, he realized the beauty of the words flowing into each other. He remembered that he had discussed his project with David Hayden and some other Americans for many hours on the cell, on chats and emails. The name Elegant Automation Software came so easily and so effortlessly. The name said everything. Each word emphasized what the company offered.

No, he had no fancy for any particular bank. She suggested Citibank. Citibank offered personalized service, was accessible and easy to park or withdraw surplus funds. These were or from short term funds, which are risk free and earn a good interest rate of 6% p.a. You will have to open a current account and that gives no interest by law.

In the evening, Lalit Jaiswal called him up on his phone, assuring him that applying for a partnership or private firm was the right thing. Ajay need not worry about anything including the fees and he would be happy to accommodate him in every way. Ajay agreed and Lalit Jaiswal wrapped up the assignment. Lalit informed Ajay that he had thought of premises, which were fit for Elegant Automation Software.

He would arrange for him to see and inspect it and if it were agreeable, he would get minor works done as required. He asked him to come within 2 or 3 days at his convenience. After that, all matters connected with opening of his office would complete in 2 to 3 weeks.

Ajay was in a dilemma. "Who should I Invite to be my partner? Would they accept?"

His possible partners were few. What seemed straightforward ealier now required hard decisions? He had created a two page Project Description, a description of his hopes and dreams, the necessity for the project and his expectations to which he added a paragraph. The para listed the roles, expectation and investment options for the partner. He mailed to Asha Ketkar, Mythili Ramachandran and Bhuvan requesting discretion.

Taking up with Asha, he explained the change and invited her to become his partner. They discussed the pros and cons of partnership as Asha or her daughter Teja. The question of Asha continuing employment with the Company cropped up. She was afraid about Dagariya's reaction after he knew of her investment. Ajay closed the conversation saying that by the time Dagariya came to know about her partnership a lot would have happened.

There was the impending fall out of their investigations. Asha agreed to become a partner on her own. Mythili called him to say how honored she felt. She suggested he invite her father who would be able to contribute to the venture. Bhuvan had no second thoughts, and would be send a cheque whenever he desired. They discussed the importance of Lalit

Jaiswal as a partner.

Two days later, he went to see the place Lalit had found for him. They drove to Wilson Gardens, a quiet residential area with a few small commercial establishments. Lalit took him to the first floor above a big Korean motorcycles showroom. It was a two thousand sq. feet, three bedroom house and climbing the stairs they stood on the roof from where could see the lay of the land. It was green with gardens and the roadside coconut and Asoka trees spoke of quiet and peace. They returned to the apartment and Lalit took him in once again. The bedrooms were large, airy with small bathrooms. It was in good order but spoke its age. Barring some repairs and sprucing up, Ajay felt that the premises were ideal.

As they walked down the staircase, Lalit advised him that he could organize new or used furniture to start up immediately. In case Ajay wanted to hire instead of buying, he could have that arranged too. His 360-degree services for startups included acquisition of computer systems, data storage units, backup drives, internet connections etc. Ajay agreed to the hiring of the place and he would supply a list of his requirements shortly.

Expressing his satisfaction, Ajay asked Lalit about his add-on services. This was his son's ideas. He saw these infrastructure services offered by consulting businesses in UK and he was keen to offer them here. The British Government was promising complete infrastructure where the entrepreneur after signing a few papers, take up site, equipment etc. in a day's time. The entrepreneur could start his venture within 24 hours. He built a network of suppliers who can arrange for these supplies on cost effective way and in quick time. "Entrepreneurs waste a lot of their valuable time in provisioning," emphasized Lalit.

In Lalit's car, Ajay thanked him and Lalit replied, "Yes Ajay this is a small piece of work. Our company's reach is everywhere. I am your partner, also. For your success, we will do anything that is lawful."

Lalit dropped Ajay, informing him that the partnership deed would be ready by the next day. More partners could be added as and when he wanted to. He could do that before or after filing the Partnership Deed with the Registrar of Companies. Including them before, is always better. Ajay promised to mail him the aims and objectives of Elegant Automation Software.

He was keen to invite Devin Hayden as a partner. Being an American meant the invitation had to be formal. They had talked many times about Elegant Software and things germane to it but never touched about ownership matters and becoming patterns. Was it agreed, or expected,assumed or that he was to invite him, began to trouble him. The only flaw was the distance and time zones. He was familiar working with customers at once in different time zones. He sent the invite, which Devin accepted immediately.

Mythili's father also accepted his invitation. In his humility, he wondered what he could contribute sitting far away, from Delhi. He was up for retirement in a few months. There was a possibility of post retirement sinecure with the government. Government offer assignments to loyal and efficient burcaucrats after their retirement. The Ramachandran's would decide their retirement city after government's offer of possible extension. To relocate from the extreme climate of Delhi with their large friend circle to the comfortable and pleasant climate of Bangalore, an unfamiliar city would be a tough decision for them.. They were well set in Delhi with an active social circle and the familiarity of places they frequented. While in Bangalore, they knew no one except their daughter.

With changed nature of start-up, he had to look for the first few employees. Within a week from filing with the government, Ajay had a list of four potential employees. All referred by people whom he valued. There was a widowed retired state government employee and a relative of Venkataraman. He would function as an accountant; handle receptionist functions, which would not be required for some time. He would be a multipurpose employee handling outside work and liaising with the government.

The other employee was a postgraduate student pursuing Engineering Management postgraduate studies. He was studying at the Indian Institute of Science, the country's premier technology college in the city. His experience and strengths were in data management and promised to spend a year on part-time basis. The third was an unemployed engineer recommended by Lalit Jaiswal. He was down to earth with a passion for developing applications on very large databases. After talking to him, Ajay realized that instead of zero experience, he was an unusual thinker. The younger brother of Bhuvan completed the Elegant Automation Software team.

He issued their appointment letters and they agreed to join within a month. Ajay offered them to stay and sleep in the company premises, in case they were looking for accommodation. He had decided to pitch his tent in the premises itself for the time being.

On 25 August2004, there was a news item in the papers mentioning a raid on Mahesh Dagariya's house and office. The details spoke of the raid by the Enforcement Directorate (ED) on suspicion of money laundering. The operation had been swift and thorough. Apart from a few employees who witnessed it in person, others read the raid in the papers.

ED officials inspected Dagariya, Joshi ji and Venkataraman's offices. They were after incriminating and suspicious papers, files, items, Indian or foreign cash etc. After they had searched with a fine tooth and a nail, they made a pile of those they felt needed further investigation. The ED officials put the heap outside the room. Another official made a handwritten list of each item in the heap. The searches went parallel.

Summoning the person whose rooms they had searched or their assignees, they put them in gunny bags in their presence and sealed the bags. The ED raiding leader went through the material list and after being satisfied, signed it. Then he obtained the signature of the recipient and a xerox copy handed over to him.

Cupboards sealed with the red seal made of lac embossed with the Directorate's inscription.

After the raid, they put their locks and affixed their seal on them. They gave strict instructions on not to touch the sealed cupboards and any attempt would attract stiff penalties.

Venkataraman was absent on that day.

There was a raid on Lakshman Investments and Financial Consultancy offices the next day. Dagariya knew it was imminent and ordered Joshi ji to remove incriminating documents. When he reached in the morning at 5:00 am, the ED officials in civil clothes confronted him. They had been keeping around the clock vigil on the office for the past two days. They allowed Joshi ji to enter and keep working with an IT official keeping an eye on him.

Lakshman Investments and Financial Consultancy staff had tried to displace the material, the previous night. These were in two suitcases that contained what could be the most incriminating documents. Every day before closing Lakshman Investments and Financial Consultancy offices, the two suitcases examined and new material, if any put in these and locked. Everything kept in a state of readiness so that during emergency suitcases taken out at a moment's notice when required.

An earlier raid had given the sleuths the layout of

the office and when they arrived, they knew where to search.

The previous night, the two Consultancy staff members trying to remove the suitcases, were caught red handed. The car they were to use confiscated. The employees made incommunicado. All phone calls made from the office over the last week monitored. The office sealed and a lock put on the entrance. The ED sleuths were waiting for Joshi ji at the financial consultancy and as soon as he reached, they arrested him. He was taken to the magistrate's chamber and at 10:30. When the magistrate arrived, he was immediately sent to prison.

Dagariya resigned as MD and Chairman. Sushma and Dagariya made repeated pleas and subtle blackmail to Venkataraman to become the next MD. Venkataraman could do little but agreed until a suitable replacement. Venkataraman knew little of what had happened. In the fast moving environment, few knew who had been raided and why and what the next couple of hours bring about.

Venkataraman knew he was clean and the argument that he was the only person who could save the company and salvage what could be. Arrest of Joshi ji spread through the company like a wildfire setting tongues wagging. It would be a tough job going ahead.

Maybe he could get to run the company the way he wanted. In any case, he would be on the disposal of the ED and IT until they filed the Charge Sheets. No one knew when the ED would file the Charge Sheets.

Dagariya's questioning began immediately. Grilled nonstop for the first three days from 11:00 am to 4:00 pm, he began to tire. On the third day,he had to answer questions in quick session for 2 hours at a stretch. After pointed questioning, left alone for half an hour, and then it would begin again. During the recess, his answers studied. The purpose was to fatigue him physically and psychologically. The same question asked many times, each time framed in different words. Inconsistent answers revealed areas and actions that were suspect and marked for further probing.

This would continue for 8 to 10 hours everyday. It was taking a toll on him and draining his energy. He was getting edgy and sometimes failed to remember what he had answered to the same question earlier. His questioners were to exhaust him. Exhausted, he might err and become honest to come out of the intense scrutiny that was damaging his emotional wellbeing. They attacked at mental, intellectual and emotional levels. During questioning if he relaxed and went slow, he would be facing jeering accusations.

On the third day, he was exhausted. After three days, his judicial custody was over, his lawyers moved for bail which ED contested seeking additional custody for three days. His lawyers produced medical reports of his deteriorating health, and the judge forbade further custody and he was released on bail.

From his answers the ED officials were able to put together what he was doing and how and what he may have done. They had searched and found little evidence. ED prosecuting officials provided evidence of wrongdoing based on letters, phone numbers, names of people and their contact addresses. His lawyers brushed them as ingenious proof meant to make their clients a scapegoat. The prosecution team knew if they satisfied the court of his direct involvement, they could force him to turn approver. They could apply third degree methods. If they could not get Dagariya to part with any information wittingly or otherwise their case would become weak. Failing which, they would try to nail him on circumstantial evidence. A case built on circumstantial evidence was never a strong case.

A lot depended on the judges and the political climate. Some session court judges are easy to influence and just like bureaucrats who had strong lobby so did the judges. Unless the Chief Justice of the High Court took a position, most judges in a lower court was approachable. Many could be purchased. Few had the backbone to stand upright in face of inducements or coercion from higher ups or even blandishments. That maybe the case but it was not that bad.

If the Session Court judge demurred, ED would splash the case on the important newspapers and force regular updates and outcomes in these newspapers. Once a case became notorious, wriggling would be difficult. Adjournments are a part of Indian judicial system and used to make life hell for the plaintiff or the defendant depending with whom the judge colludes. That is how it is. In the allotted time, his questioners would have to dig that information out of him.

Over the next fortnight, they examined the papers they had collected. His expensive lawyers were smart and showed his name figured rarely, as did the letters behind the crime. Perusal of these documents revealed that Joshi ji's footprints were large and everywhere. It was as if Dagariya had no connections with the fraudulent operations and as a good employer believed his managers, he let his managers do what they did in good faith and belief.

ED could not provide proof of bank accounts where the money finally landed belonging to him or his family members. He could not produce letters or agreements he had signed. The investigators believed that there had to be such records that incriminated him. Unable to find them, Dagariya had to have a final destination where the money trail finally ended. They figured that it has to be outside the country.

An important partner and director of the Company was his naturalized professor brother in New York. ED reasoned that he was the final destination of the money and the Indian government could do little with him. Without a motivated bureaucrat pushed by a powerful moralistic politician, things are difficult. He had powerful connections and it looked like nothing much could be done to him. There were many such cases lying in the soft underbelly of Indian politics. The perpetrators knew that American citizenship of his brother gave him security. This was the point where money finally landed. Without dragging, that into the case ED's case, it was weak.

The other director was Satya Narayan Agarwal, a local steel manufacturer indicted for evading excise duties. Mahindra Agarwal another director. Aggarwal was an industrialist owning a variety of manufacturing companies. He had interests in industrial gases, aluminum fabrications, transport etc. but no connection with Information Technology. Govardhan Rai listed as a director as well as Dr. C. Shivalingaiah, a management consultant.

Venkataraman listed as an alternate director to Dagariya. Taking the position of an alternate director, he attended board meetings on behalf of Dagariya when he was not available. He had the same powers to attend, speak and vote as Dagariya. Over the time span of three years, he had attended just five meetings. Sharad Zende, not named director in spite of his 20% investment, as he was an employee of another company that forbade him to hold such posts. Therefore, his directorship was benami. Joshi ji was the secretary to the board. Dagariya had a packed board and could get away with anything.

The ED was finding it difficult to prove that the fraud had been going on for a few years in an ad hoc manner. After the formation of his company, it had become a smooth well-organized operation. It was a company within a company, which Venkataraman could not fathom.

Dagariya's lawyers tried to prove that Joshi ji was the mastermind and their client implicated by default. Dagariya had innocently acquiesced. Dagariya had himsuspended and a committee formed to investigate further into it.

Joshi ji's plea was that it began with a small one of a type project and with time it became bigger and he could not get off the tiger's back. Even though he knew the operations of Lakshman Investment and Financial Consultancy were involved in illegality he was stuck, and could not come out. The court sent him to jail, pending the completion of investigation.

Joshi ji finally took up the role of the approver. There was political pressure on ED of not allowing Joshi ji to become an approver. There was pressure brought on his family too to dissuade him from siding with the prosecution. The reason was to stop Joshi ji to tattle. He may cooperate only to an extent to save his skin. If he refused to cooperate and provide information that would nail Dagariya there was little the ED could do. There was always the possibility of an understanding between them where he could take the rap, and bail Dagariya off the hook? He could be a plant and weaken ED's case.

It had all the making of a secret arrangement and scandal that is part of the Indian politician-bureaucrat nexus. The powerful were those who had connections and could leverage them to suit their purposes. If not, you should have deep pockets. Almost anything is purchasable in India. Finally, it reached the boss of ED who had ED accept Joshi ji as approver.

That is the reality of white-collar crimes by the big and mighty. The ED Chief knew that they could get any jailbird to sing if they had a free hand. The law was ambiguous and the newspapers generally sided with the businessperson.

Therefore, they did accept Joshi ji's bargain plea. They knew there would be another occasion.

It was during his imprisonment that he decided to come clean and take the blame for his involvement, thrust onto him.

~~~

The court, on the plea of the bankers gave Venkataraman a free hand in the running of the company and he immediately called for an out of campus meeting with the entire staff. He placed before them the bare details of the fiasco and even exonerated Dagariya. He unabashedly said that Dagariya was forced in some matters and he did all to help the company. He urged the staff to help him restore the company to its original heights. He shared his plans and spoke about revised roles and responsibilities that were on the anvil.

Resignations continued. Venkataraman over the next two months visited major clients within and outside the country. He was candid and explained the upheaval in the company that he promised to clean up. He assured them of the Company's continued services. In the Indian business world, such fraudulences were nothing exceptional and carried little stigma. Venkataraman carried his task exceptionally well.

The first major organizational change he bought in was a new billing system. He got one of the foremost management-consulting firms in the country to take up the job. He had the entire accounting department revamped and brought in fresh staff. He tried to resist as much he could the veiled pressure and suggestions of Sushma.

Next, he augmented his office and hired new staff. Their only job was to track all ingoing and outgoing communications before routing to concerned people. Venkataraman immediately attended to any suspected communication.

~~~

Asha based on her sensibilities and aesthetics made a list of required furniture and passed onto Lalit. The premises were repainted with colorful vibrant hues. Minor alterations made from functional and aesthetics considerations. The name board with glow signs hoisted one on the frontage. Another name board with glow signs strung parallel to the road and inscribed on both sides. Elegant Automation Software offices not missed. The credo suggested by Devin Hayden said, “Software for Solving Your Problems”.

Elegant Automation Software had opened its doors for business.

Postscript:

Joshi ji let off with a year of imprisonment for turning approver. Two years later after a bitter court battle Mahesh Dagariya awarded a one-year jail sentence after a bitter two-year legal battle. He gave up as ED decided to implead Sushma as an accomplice. Asha joined Elegant Automation Software as a woman for all seasons. Ajay thrived, as did his company. Two years later Teja joined Los Angeles Film School where her program cost her USD 80,000. Venkataraman pulled the company out of its morass, selling his stake joins Ramakrishna Mission in Madras.

The eagle had landed.

May I Ask You for a Book Review?

The success of any writer is in the reading pleasure of the reader. Word of mouth or refereeing is crucial for any writer to succeed. If you enjoyed Ajay's Restlessness please consider writing your review and sending to me or my publishers, even a line or two. It would make all the difference and I will very much appreciate. If you have suggestions for improvement, I would consider them for my next book.

Thank you.

Devinder Sharma
Shyamdave41@gmail.com
Bangalore